COME HOME, KATIE

DEAR CELESTE

J.R. ERICKSON

DEDICATION

For Avery.

PROLOGUE

Dear Celeste,

It started with a single drop of blood. One startling red drop on the gaudy marble coffee table Katie and I bought at a yard sale. I didn't know yet that Katie was gone, but something in me saw that single drop of blood and started to fall. I still haven't hit the ground.

In a week, it will have been one year since Katie disappeared. Three hundred and sixty-five days and nights since my seventeen-year-old sister walked out of the schoolhouse museum where she worked and vanished into the night.

It's hard to breathe when I look at that number and yet it hardly captures the weight of the year soon to be behind me. The days I've stared at her empty chair at the breakfast table, passed by her closed bedroom door—I rarely open it anymore. The endless nights I've climbed into bed and lain awake for hours, wondering what happened to my beautiful, brilliant little sister who dreamed of designing clothes, who loved to roller-skate and who idolized the sixties and seventies. Countless nights where I've whispered again and again into the darkness, "Come home, Katie."

As I type this, I'm gazing through a window at the deserted, snowy street outside. The light poles are wound with red and white ribbon. There are Christmas lights in the windows of the surrounding apartments, but I didn't decorate a tree this year. I get a knot in my stomach just looking at them. I spent this Christmas alone, the first Christmas in seventeen years I didn't see my sister's face light up as she opened presents.

I realize I'm baring my soul to an online advice columnist. I don't even know if such a person as Celeste exists. Perhaps you will never open this email and this late-night plea will disappear into the wind, like my beloved little sister.

The police have investigated, or so they tell me. They've questioned people, attempted to trace her phone, performed searches. Not a shred of Katie has surfaced.

Can you help me find Katie? Or, if that is beyond the scope of your reach, can you help me learn to live with the not knowing? I want to get out of bed, walk barefoot from my apartment building into the icy street and disappear into the darkness. Maybe that's the only way I'll ever find her.

Desperately searching,

Joanna Ellis

1

Celeste took a sip of her Scotch and finished reading the letter. At the bottom of the email Joanna had added facts about her sister: *Katie Ellis, seventeen, disappeared from Graves, Michigan, on January sixteenth.* Celeste minimized the web page, opened a new browser window, and searched for Katie.

Only two articles highlighted the seventeen-year-old's disappearance. Both displayed little urgency.

In the single photograph that accompanied the second article, Katie stood in front of an old stone building. Her long dark brown hair, parted in the middle, hung over each shoulder. She wore vintage clothes—a corduroy coat, the collar flipped up, and white bell-bottom jeans. Instead of a millennial, she looked like a child of the sixties.

"Katie," Celeste murmured, closing her eyes, letting her thoughts run. She searched through the stream but came up empty. Sometimes it was that easy—a name, a face and some shred of her whereabouts became known. Not this time.

Celeste started when something brushed across her legs.

"Cash," she grumbled leaning down to run her fingers across the cat's silky black fur.

The cat purred and snaked between her legs then readied to jump in her lap. Celeste leaned back to make space and grunted when the heavy cat-who still fancied himself a kitten-landed on her thighs, turned twice, and formed into a black nest with two yellow eyes watching her expectantly. She scratched behind his ears and returned her attention to the computer screen.

A shadow passed in the hall, paused, and the door cracked open. Her husband, Jonathan, said nothing.

"Yes?" Celeste asked.

"Still at it?"

"I'm coming to bed soon."

"Sure," he murmured, not closing the door.

She listened to his footsteps down the hall, heard their bedroom door creak open, the bang as he shut it harder than was necessary.

CELESTE WOKE and blinked at the slowly whirring ceiling fan, useless in the stifling heat. In winter, Jonathan, thin-skinned and prone to chills, cranked the thermostat before bed despite Celeste imploring him to add another blanket instead.

She sat up, swung her legs over the bed, and searched the nightstand for her cell phone. After she found it, she gritted her teeth against the ache in her left leg and hip and stood. At the door, she tugged her robe from its metal hook and eased into the hall. She wore only a t-shirt and underwear and didn't want the robe for warmth, but to slip her cell into the pocket so her hands were free to grab a wall or chair if she went sideways.

In the kitchen, she filled a glass of water, then, eyeing the Scotch she'd forgotten to put away the night before, poured a glass of the pungent liquor. She sipped it, walking to the sliding glass doors that displayed the swirling snow in the backyard.

A layer of frothy white covered the porch railing. The falling snow caught by the deck light sparkled and cast prisms of color on the white mounds. Mesmerized by the crystals of snow, Celeste hadn't immediately noticed the footprints, but her eye caught them now and she leaned closer to the glass, wiping away the halo from her breath.

The trail of footprints led from the back of the house into the forest. Prints weren't unusual. Despite living in Grand Rapids, one of Michigan's larger cities, they had their share of forest creatures—mostly raccoons, the little scavengers who survived on garbage—but as she pressed against the glass, the icy pane a relief against her hot forehead, Celeste realized the prints were unmistakably human.

She finished her Scotch and slid her feet into her rubber-soled slippers. Her cane rested against the wall, but she ignored it and opened the sliding door, closing her eyes as the wind, refreshingly cold, whooshed back her robe and hair.

Gingerly, she stepped onto the porch, closed the door and hobbled down the deck stairs, holding the rail to avoid slipping. The footprints—fresh, or they'd have been buried by the falling snow—were smaller than hers, definitely not Jonathan's. Too large to be a child's, but not by much.

Pulling her robe tighter, ignoring the grating sensation in her left leg and hip, Celeste followed the prints. Snow piled around her ankles and into her slippers. It was cold, cutting, but she savored the discomfort. Since her accident, her left leg and foot migrated between numb and throbbing—anything else was a welcome reprieve.

Eight months ago, Celeste wouldn't have dreamed of following strange footprints into the frigid black night. She'd have shaken Jonathan awake, scared, insisted they phone the police. But that had been before the accident, before she'd died and been brought back as a different Celeste.

She moved into the canopy of trees, no longer skeletal thanks to the storm. Their branches were heavy, bending beneath the white quilt nature had tossed over them. They largely obscured the three-quarters moon, but she could see well enough, the snow-laden ground reflecting the cold, pale light.

The footsteps stretched into the forest, growing erratic, as if the person who'd made them had begun to take giant lunging steps.

And then abruptly they stopped.

Celeste lifted her gaze, half expected to see the owner of the footsteps staring back at her, but only a stretch of black trees and unmarred white ground greeted her.

And then behind her a noise, a puff of breath.

Celeste turned slowly.

The girl stood on the path, as still as the frozen landscape. Brown hair parted in the middle, the sleeves of her Jim Morrison t-shirt so long they concealed her hands.

Celeste gazed at Katie Ellis, unmistakable despite her milky sightless eyes.

"You want me to answer the letter..." Celeste murmured. "To help your sister." It wasn't a question. She knew what the girl wanted.

"Celeste!" Jonathan's voice split the quiet, and the girl was gone.

For a moment, Celeste stared at the place she'd been.

By the time Celeste made it back to her house, her feet had grown prickly and sore. She dreaded the look on Jonathan's face and, when she ascended the steps to the back porch, he gave it to her—alarm laced with annoyance.

"My God, Celeste! What were you doing?" He grabbed her arm and steered her into the house, his eyes roving over her, bulging at her red feet as she stepped out of her slippers. "Jesus. It's ten degrees. You could have frozen to death. Why were you out there? You didn't even put on boots?"

He wanted answers, but not really. He didn't leave an inch of space within which she might have offered one. He rattled on as he led her to the bathroom upstairs and started the bath, insisted she drop into the scalding water, which she did. Again, any sensation beyond the numb or the ache felt good in her hip and leg. The pinpricks were sharp and jolting. She released a laugh—it almost tickled, felt as though her foot had been punctured by a thousand tiny needles.

"What's funny?" he demanded. "Are you okay? Why were you out there?"

Celeste leaned back, sighed. "I'm fine, Jonathan. I saw a raccoon, followed it into the woods."

"Are you out of your mind? What if it had rabies? Turned around and bit you?"

"Then I'd have died or gone mad. What difference does it make?"

He stared at her, face ashen, and she felt bad for her words, for her indifference. She patted his hand on the edge of the tub. "I'm sorry. That was a cruel thing to say. I didn't mean it." Though she did mean it, and she suspected both of them knew as much.

"Do you need a pain pill? Is that what woke you?"

No, it was the heat, the suffocating heat of our bedroom, our house, our life. "I'm fine. Maybe some Scotch?"

His brow knitted. He didn't want to give her any, hated this new habit of hers, but after a moment, he nodded. "Okay. Anything else? Maybe you should go see the doctor tomorrow."

Which one? She didn't ask the question. She knew he meant Dr. Stahl, her psychiatrist. Anytime Celeste did anything unusual, Jonathan needled her about seeing Stahl, who did little more than update her latest prescription of mood-damp-ening drugs.

"I'm okay, really. Just the Scotch."

Jonathan frowned, stood and departed the room. He didn't close the door, but left it wide open as if she were a child taking a bath and he needed to be alert for the slightest sound of crisis.

Several minutes later, he returned with her drink, barely a shot, heavy with ice, and Celeste thanked him, balanced the glass on the lip of the tub and closed her eyes.

She waited for the sound of his departure, didn't hear it and opened her eyes to see him watching her.

"What?" she asked.

He gestured at her. "The red hair. I'm still getting used to it."

Celeste touched the tips of her new red hair—rock 'n' roll red, according to the stylist who'd dyed it several days before. For the entirety of their marriage, Celeste had mid-length blonde hair and, she suspected Jonathan did not approve of her new look.

"So many changes lately," he said. "I can hardly keep up."

"Me too," she murmured, leaning her head back and closing her eyes. After a moment, she heard him leave.

Celeste lay in the steaming water and thought about her Dear Celeste column. She'd started it eight years before on the eve of her wedding to Jonathan. She'd been having second thoughts, had woken in the night with a terrible premonition that she was making a mistake, that she and Jonathan were not meant to be together. In her desperation and insomnia, Celeste had gone on an online forum and put questions into the void about marriage and 'the one,' and 'what if you choose the wrong man?'

There'd been no responses. None. In retrospect, it was unsurprising. She'd been posting the questions feverishly at two in the morning. But as the emptiness folded around her, she'd made an offer to the forum. *Ask me anything. I promise you'll get an answer.* And Dear Celeste had been born.

For nearly a decade she'd been offering advice to strangers, answering questions ranging from 'should I quit my job?' to 'should I search for my birth family?' She didn't claim to have some fountain of wisdom. She merely offered a listening ear, a response. That was enough, she'd realized. For so many people, what they needed most of all was someone to listen, to say *I hear you. It's okay.*

In the weeks after the accident, the Dear Celeste column had taken on a new life. Before, her job as a researcher alongside Jonathan at Dynamic Laboratories had prevented her from focusing too deeply on the column. It was a secret, after all. But, trapped in a broken body for more than a month in the hospital, she'd grown obsessive about the column—answered two dozen or more questions a night.

She'd seen the first spirit hours after waking from the coma she'd been in for nearly ten days. An old man, hollow-eyed, whispering to himself in the corner of her room. Even in her disorientation, having been unconscious for days, brain heavy with medication, she'd known he was dead.

2

Calmly, Celeste had told Jonathan she'd died and crossed over.

'The death of the body is not the death of the soul,' she'd announced, the memories of her near-death experience exploding like fireworks in her brain.

Jonathan had not taken the news well and, though she'd already been subjected to a battery of tests due to her closed head injury, Jonathan had insisted the doctors perform more.

Now seven months had passed, and Celeste had gradually realized her former self was gone—the Celeste who'd married Jonathan, who'd devoted her life to scientific research into pharmaceuticals, who'd happily passed her days in the lab, her nights discussing work over dinner with her husband or watching *Jeopardy!*. This new Celeste felt constantly uncomfortable with the whole charade. That was what it seemed to be. Not a life so much as a play, a series of roles they acted out.

Celeste drained the last of her Scotch, wiggled her left toes and ankle. Comfortably numb. A better sensation than the other numb, the feelingless numb.

She thought of Katie, who'd led her into the snowy woods,

who wanted her to help. But how? Celeste was a smart woman. She'd answered hundreds, maybe thousands of readers on her advice column. She'd leaned on one of her most valuable skills: research. She didn't have all the answers, but she knew somewhere in the world they existed and she could find them.

But a missing teenage girl…

"Not missing," she murmured. "Dead."

Because Katie had to be dead. It hadn't been a living spirit that had drawn Celeste out of her house that night.

"How do I know that?" Celeste asked, clinking her ice cubes around her glass, staring at her knees poking out of the bathwater.

In any experiment, it was important to question the premise, not fall back on assumption. She knew almost nothing about the world of ghosts. Before her accident, she'd rested in the belief that people who made such claims were either frauds or mentally ill.

Celeste had pondered the origin of her new perceptions ad nauseam and had come to the simple conclusion her accident had damaged some part of her brain that filtered out an ethereal layer of reality. The physical body was full of filters—organs to digest and detox, mechanisms to sift through the constant barrage of data flooding into the system. Somewhere in her brain, there'd been a bit of gray matter that prevented Celeste from perceiving spirits. Her head injury had damaged the mechanism and given her access to a previously unavailable level of discernment.

But just as she didn't have a complete explanation for her ability to perceive spirits, Celeste also didn't know irrefutably that they were all dead. She'd heard of other types of psychic phenomena, astral projection and the like. Perhaps some of the spirits she encountered were living beings out of their body making remote contact. Before the accident, she'd have dismissed such an idea with little thought. But now... anything seemed possible.

Celeste stood from the tub and stepped out, bit her cheek against the jolt of pain through her left leg when she planted her foot on the bath mat. She could have easily leaned on her right leg, but she needed to challenge the left leg to bear weight, to do the hard work. It would never heal otherwise.

In the hall, she could see the light from Jonathan's bedside lamp. He'd likely be flipping through a copy of *Scientific American*, the magazine he kept on his nightstand. He was waiting for her to come to bed, would likely not sleep until she did, but Celeste was wide awake and the thought of lying down staring at the ceiling for the hours ahead made her want to scream.

Celeste paused at the bedroom door. "I'm going to sleep on the couch, watch some TV."

Jonathan frowned and set his magazine aside. "You are? Why?"

"A little restless tonight."

"Are you sure I can't get you a pain pill?"

"No. I'd rather not. I'm going to doze off to some old episodes of *Dexter*."

His lips were pressed in a line. "Television is extremely disruptive for sleep. The blue light alone is going to ensure—"

"I know the studies, Jonathan, but I assure you my sleep is already disrupted tonight. I won't fall asleep up here and my tossing and turning will prevent you from sleeping too. I'll see you in the morning." She blew him a kiss and turned before he could say more. She heard his sigh as she walked away.

Celeste grabbed her laptop from the office and carried it to the couch. She opened her email and clicked to reply to the message from Joanna.

Dear Joanna,

I thought about your letter for some time tonight. I thought about the words of advice or encouragement I might offer—"hang in there, I'm sorry for your pain, in time the truth will emerge." And don't get me wrong, I want to convey all those sentiments, but I want to do more than that.

I'm not publicly answering your question on the column for one simple reason. I'd like to come help you in person. I have no experience with law enforcement. I've never found a missing person. Perhaps I will get no further than any of them, but if you want it, I'm offering. I have some time off. Say the word and I'll be there.

Thank you for writing.

Celeste

Celeste stared at the unsent message for the longest time. She was offering to help a random person on the internet search for a missing teenager. If Jonathan knew, he'd have her committed.

She hovered over the mouse and then clicked send.

3

———

Joanna slid into a booth at the diner. She'd wiped down tables and rolled the silverware. Her feet ached, and she slipped her tennis shoes and socks off beneath the table, felt the pocked linoleum against her bare feet. It was slightly sticky, but she didn't care. It felt good to wiggle her toes, let her feet float weightless without her body pressing down as she pounded from table to kitchen to table to cash register.

She tugged her tips out of her apron. A birthday candle, pink and white striped, fell from the folded-up bills.

Joanna picked it up and shook her head. "Where did you come from?"

Her shift hadn't been exceptional. Seventy dollars in tips, one regular who'd also left a five-dollar gift card to Espresso Mike's—a treat she'd savor some morning when she didn't have to clock in, when she could sip a latte in the window and watch the snow blanket the world in white.

Beyond the plate-glass windows the snow fell in droves. There'd been blizzard warnings all day, and by nine, when Floyd had locked the diner door, Main Street had gone dead—

locals fleeing from downtown for the safety of their homes, cars abandoning the slick roads.

The diner, named the Sidewinder after a Lee Morgan song of the same name, thanks to the owner Floyd's love of jazz, was practically Joanna's second home. *Almost Blue* by Chet Baker drifted from the speakers in the ceiling.

Joanna released her hair from its ponytail, winced as she rubbed her aching scalp. Nearly every bit of her hurt and yet there'd been a few hours before the snow really started falling when she'd been blissfully entranced in her work, too busy to think of her cold little apartment and the closed door to Katie's empty bedroom.

"Give ya a ride, Jo?" Floyd asked as he untied his grease-stained apron and slipped it over his head. He turned a dial on the stereo and Chet faded away.

Joanna yawned, shoved her cash into her apron and nodded. "Yeah. Thanks. I wore my boots and heavy coat, but I suspect I won't be able to see my hand in front of my face out there."

"You're right about that. I stepped out for a smoke twenty minutes ago and couldn't see my red truck. Doesn't get any nastier than it is right now."

"Better not let Camile smell the cigarette smoke on you or you'll be in the doghouse tonight," Joanna said. "I thought you quit."

Floyd rubbed his face. White stubble that matched his hair dotted his chin. "I did. At least I'm working on it, but something about these long winter nights makes a cigarette sound almost as sweet as being home by the fire. One of these days, I'm gonna retire and then I'll kick the habit for good."

"Retire! What about me?" Joanna demanded.

"You can take over, Jo. You practically run this place as it is."

"Hardly," Joanna said. "I think we both know Camile runs this place."

Together, Joanna and Floyd turned off the lights, double-checked the doors were locked and stepped into the frigid night. The snow blew in gusts, heavy and wet against Joanna's face. She blinked as the flakes landed thick on her eyelashes.

"Shoulda come out and fired her up," Floyd said, as he unlocked the truck and opened the passenger door for Joanna. "Gonna be colder than an Eskimo's outhouse in here."

She hoisted herself inside and rubbed her gloved hands together. Floyd climbed behind the wheel and started the engine.

"I'm gettin' too old for this kind of cold," he said, reaching through his driver's side window to push snow off the windshield. "I need to move to Arizona."

"You once told me Arizona is so hot the potatoes come out of the ground cooked," Joanna reminded him.

Floyd laughed. "And I was tellin' it to ya straight, but gosh if that miserable sweltering heat doesn't sound nice right about now." The truck slid and nearly went sideways as they drove from the parking lot behind the restaurant.

Joanna lived only two blocks away, and Floyd stopped the truck in the middle of the road. There were no other cars in sight and a snow plow had buried the curbside parking in a mound of snow several feet high.

"Thanks, Floyd," Joanna told him, opening the passenger door.

"Hey, next weekend is my sister's birthday and we're having a little party. Camile's making a prime rib, and I'm whipping up some garlic mashed, and my niece is gonna bring over a fancy chocolate cake. You're welcome to join us."

Joanna smiled, swallowed the lump in her throat, and nodded. "I'll think about it. Thanks for the offer."

"You're always welcome at our place. Camile's been going on and on about those cocktails you made at the Sidewinder

New Year's party a couple of years back. What were those things called?"

A rush of wind stole Joanna's voice and snatched the door from her hand. She grabbed it before it slammed shut. "Jesus," she gasped.

"A fitting name." He grinned. "Tell me later. Go on, git. Maybe you'll make 'em on New Year's."

Joanna nodded, closed the door, and trudged through the snow to the apartment building.

Her apartment was also as cold as an Eskimo's outhouse. Her breath formed a white plume as she locked her door behind her, then hurried to the thermostat and turned up the heat. She used to leave it at seventy-two all the time, otherwise Katie walked around in wool socks and earmuffs. But Katie was gone and there was no point heating an empty apartment.

Not stripping out of her coat, Joanna moved to one of the antique radiators and waited for it to kick on. She leaned close when it did, allowing the moist heat to thaw her chapped face.

Behind her, a door slammed, and she jumped. She spun around, scanned the dark hallway, and took a step.

"Katie?" she called, a mingling of hope and fear pumping through her blood.

Of course it wasn't Katie. Katie had vanished nearly a year before, but still...

Joanna walked into the hall that led to the bedrooms. Her door, which she usually left open, was closed. She walked over, took a breath, and turned the knob.

Her bed was made, the dark bedspread tucked in place. Nothing moved in the room, but she walked inside, peered in the closet, crouched and looked beneath the bed. She checked the bathroom and the hall closet even though it was too packed with stuff to hide anyone.

Finally, she paused at Katie's door, which she hadn't opened in weeks, maybe months. Fighting back her nerves, she twisted the knob and thrust the door open.

Empty.

In the dark, she saw the shape of Katie's twin bed, her bookshelf arranged with vintage lunch pails and books, her walls adorned with posters. Joanna closed the door and rested her forehead against it.

There was no one in the apartment.

Joanna was alone.

She made her way to her room and sat heavily on the edge of her bed. Joanna had not slept well the night before. She'd woken repeatedly, sure she'd heard a sound in the apartment only to search and find nothing. Finally, she'd closed her bedroom door, wedged a chair beneath the knob and drifted off.

Now the lack of sleep, combined with her busy day at the diner, had caught up with her. Not bothering to brush her teeth or change into pajamas, she curled on her side and closed her eyes.

Another sound came from the hallway and her eyes shot open. She went quiet, breath held, straining to hear. She wasn't even sure what it had been.

When no additional noises followed, she stood and returned to the shadowy hallway. Katie's door stood cracked open.

Joanna walked to the sliver of opening between the door and frame and peered into the black room. She could discern nothing in the dark and staring into it transformed her unease into fear. A person could be standing feet away staring back at her and she wouldn't know. Maybe she'd missed them moments before—they'd been deep in the closet hunched behind Katie's clothes.

Feigning courage she didn't feel, Joanna pushed the door open hard, strode into the room and turned on the lamp. The light chased the shadows to the corners. No one stood in the bedroom.

Katie's patchwork vinyl purse—a vintage bag she used only on special occasions—sat on the floor in front of the closet door. Joanna stared at the bag, which had been hanging from the doorknob moments before.

The closet door, half open, could easily hide a person. Very still, Joanna strained to hear any sound within the space—the clack of hangers, a whisper of breath.

Nothing.

Joanna reached a shaky hand to the door and pulled it open and then stepped back quickly, prepared for someone to leap out. No one did. Not a single one of Katie's signature classic t-shirts shuddered. Still, Joanna pushed the clothing apart and peered into the darkest corners of the closet.

Satisfied the room was empty, Joanna picked up the purse, carried it to Katie's desk and left it there. When she exited the room, she pulled the door closed hard and then pushed it to see if it'd swing open. It didn't.

Back in bed, Joanna stared at the ceiling and willed sleep to take her, but her mind stayed fixed on Katie's partially open door. Her brain seemed intent on offering a litany of possibilities—a faulty lock system, a door that had become misshapen with the cold, a breeze from a heat vent.

Obsessing about the open door was easier than the alternative, her nightly ruminations on what had happened to her little sister.

Joanna thought of the email she'd sent to Dear Celeste. She didn't really expect an answer, but now she'd not sleep until she checked. Groaning, she sat up, fumbled her phone from the nightstand and opened her email.

4

———

"Have you become a birder?" Megan asked Celeste, tapping the notebook scrawled with dozens of ravens and plumes of black feathers.

They sat at Celeste's kitchen table. Morning light streamed through the sliding glass doors that overlooked the snow-laden backyard,

Celeste eyed the drawings—an attempted reproduction of the vision of the black wings spreading, growing immense and beautiful and so achingly familiar, that had happened during her near-death experience and now flooded her psyche daily.

"That's funny," Celeste said. "Jonathan asked me the same thing. Maybe I have. I have a lot more time on my hands."

Megan, her closest friend for more than a decade, watched her across the kitchen table with curious, slightly worried eyes.

Celeste flipped the notebook closed and stood—doing her best to conceal the cattle prod to her brain when she bore weight on her left leg—and moved to the counter. "More coffee?"

"If I drink any more coffee, my head's going to pop off and roll down the hallway."

Celeste walked the pot to her own mug, filled it, added cream and sugar and eased back into her chair.

"Cream and sugar? You've been drinking black coffee since college. It was practically a hill you'd die on. Bright red hair, milky coffee, pages of black feathered birds... Are you having a midlife crisis?"

Celeste raised an eyebrow. "It's not a crisis. It's an evolution. Plus, who's middle-aged? I'm thirty-five. Have you foreseen my death at seventy?"

Megan smiled sadly. "I was afraid you wouldn't see thirty-six, but you're right. You won't be middle-aged until you're fifty. I, on the contrary, am turning forty this year and feel quite over the hill."

"Spare me. You came here from spin class. You're still in your spandex, for God's sakes."

"We miss you around there, by the way. Tony has asked about you more than once." Megan grinned.

"Tony is twenty years old and looks eighteen. Not to mention I'm married. He's worried about keeping his class full, so he gets paid."

"Hardly. How's the physical therapy going?" Megan glanced at Celeste's cane.

"Excruciating, but maybe helpful. Lorenzo insists I'm improving, and on my good days I'm sure he's right, but other days..." Celeste shrugged. "I feel pretty confident I'll be dragging that thing around forever." Celeste gestured at the cane.

"No way." Megan picked up the aluminum cane and examined it. "You'll have upgraded to something sexier than this."

"Sexy? I'm not sure such a thing exists."

"Then I better get you stickers for this hideous thing."

"Are you going to sign it too like we're fourteen and I broke my arm?"

Megan returned the cane to the floor. "How's Jonathan doing? He seems..."

"Pissed?"

"Sad."

Celeste frowned. "Maybe he's a little of both. He wants everything to return to the way it was."

"And you don't?"

"It can't. I'm not that person anymore."

Megan looked troubled. "I understand it was traumatic and that... the healing may take a very long time, but... you've always had such a great life. You and Jonathan were happy. At least, you seemed happy."

"We were, but... we were also so immersed in our work that there wasn't a lot else."

"So, what then? The spark's gone? You guys are fighting? I don't get it."

Celeste considered the question, searched for the spark. Had it ever been there? "I don't have a satisfactory answer. Dr. Stahl, the psychiatrist Jonathan insists I see, believes I have PTSD. He says it's normal after a major event to feel... different. To avoid things, even people, that were once familiar. 'All in good time,' he's a fan of saying when I ask how long before I'll return to normal."

Megan sighed, and fanned the pages of Celeste's notebook, each page a menagerie of dark feathers. "I support you. You know that, right? In whatever you do. I just don't want you to blow up your life and regret it later."

"I dyed my hair, Megan. I'm taking cream in my coffee. I'd hardly call that blowing up my life."

"That's not what I'm talking about."

"I appreciate your concern. I'm good. Really. And I have to go. Don't worry about me, please."

Megan looked like she wanted to argue, but she stood and plucked at her spandex shirt. "I'm going to pretend you're not blowing me off, because I need to get home and take a shower.

This spandex is like a second skin. Where are you off to, anyway? Doctor appointment?"

"I'm not blowing you off," Celeste insisted, avoiding answering Megan's question.

She hated lying to her friend, but didn't have the energy or frankly the words to explain her plan to drive over two hours north to Graves, Michigan, to meet a woman whose little sister had vanished—a woman who'd reached out to her via an anonymous advice column mere days before.

Megan squeezed her shoulder. "I'd hug you, but you'll stink like me," she said. "Call me?"

"I will."

THE DRIVE to Graves took over two hours. It was the longest drive Celeste had taken since before the accident, and the more distance she put between herself and home, the easier it seemed to breathe. For whole stretches she got lost in the scenery, the trees rushing by, billboards advertising fishing stores and boat marinas.

When she turned onto Main Street in downtown Graves, the ache in her leg murmured as if aware it soon would have to work again. The town was quaint, light poles hung with candy cane-striped ribbon and a Christmas tree in nearly every shop window.

Celeste parked on the street in front of the Sidewinder, where an email from Katie's sister, Joanna, had said she'd be working.

Celeste stared at the glass windows into the diner and wondered yet again what she was doing. The ever-present niggling voice was as frustrated as Jonathan and as surprised as Megan about the shifts in Celeste's personality. *This will end badly*, it told her. *You'll get this woman's hopes up, for what? You can barely walk, let alone find a teenage girl who's vanished.*

As the thoughts marched through her head, ticking off the list of reasons she should turn the car around and drive back to Grand Rapids, she caught sight of a young woman standing a block away watching her.

She wasn't clear, but Celeste saw long brown hair and a camel-colored jacket like the corduroy one Katie Ellis had been wearing in her photos online. As Celeste watched, two older women clutching shopping bags walked right through the girl, scattering her like the flurry of snow on the sidewalk.

Celeste popped two painkillers into her mouth, took a drink from her water bottle and swung open her car door. She took her cane, though sometimes the mere sensation of it in her hand made her furious that she still needed it. More than once, she'd imagined throwing it from her window as she sped down the highway.

She pushed open the door to the diner and stepped inside to the smell of coffee and the sounds of chatter and clinking silverware. Black and white floor tiles shone beneath the warm yellow lights. Red leather booths lined the walls, several of them occupied. Black and white posters of musicians holding saxophones or trumpets hung above each table.

A young woman wearing jeans and a white button-down shirt, a black apron cinched at her waist, started over and then slowed. She brushed a lock of dirty blonde hair that had fallen across her forehead behind one ear. Puffy shadows beneath her eyes betrayed she'd likely not had a good night's sleep in some time.

"Joanna?" Celeste asked.

The woman searched her face as if trying to place it, then realization dawned. "Celeste?"

Celeste nodded and smiled, extended her hand. "Good to meet you."

"And you. Again, thank you so much for coming here. What can I get you? Coffee, soda? Slice of pie?" She gestured at a glass cake display with a cream pie inside.

"Nothing for me. Thank you."

"Here, let me put your coat on the rack. We're pretty slow, but I'm going to run in the back and ask Camile to cover for me."

Celeste slipped out of her suede coat and handed it to Joanna. She crossed the restaurant and eased onto the bench in a booth.

When Joanna returned to the booth, she looked nervously excited. "I can't thank you enough for answering my letter."

Celeste threaded her fingers in her lap and wished the damn painkillers would hurry up and kick in. When her leg and hip ached, her brain fixated on the throbbing, which made concentrating on anything else a struggle. "I want to be really clear up front, Joanna."

"Call me Jo."

"Okay, Jo. I started the Dear Celeste thing on a lark years ago. I'm not an investigator. I don't know the first thing about missing persons cases. For the last eight years, I've been offering little more than advice, also something I'm not technically qualified to do. I never studied psychology. I have a degree in biochemistry and work in a pharmaceutical lab. I've never met any of the people who write to me."

Joanna nodded. "I've been reading your column for several years. You might not have a degree in therapy or whatever, but you really help people. That night I emailed you I was at the end of my rope. I felt so lost. I needed to reach out to someone, anyone. I never imagined you might not only answer, but..." Joanna gestured at her.

"Come here?"

"Yeah. Why did you?"

Celeste shifted in the booth, winced at the tremor of pain in her hip. "Last summer, I got hit and nearly killed during my morning walk. Everything changed for me. I was in the hospital for a month. I'm still in physical therapy. Before the accident, I was a researcher at Dynamic Laboratories in Grand Rapids. I've gone back one time and I..." She shook her head. "I couldn't do it. Couldn't tolerate the lights, the sounds. My work was my life before. After the accident, it's like my life didn't fit anymore. Like I'd put on weight and the pants were skintight." She frowned. "That's a weird analogy, right? I'm not sure why I keep thinking of it like that, like my former life is this too-small itchy pair of trousers I can't fit into anymore."

"That sounds so horrible," Joanna murmured. "Did they arrest whoever hit you?"

Celeste shook her head. "No. They never found them. It's an active case, but for whatever reason, I don't really care. I don't have some burning desire to find out. Honestly, I figure it was some distracted driver rushing into work, texting, and bam, didn't see me walking down the side of the road. I lived. It changed me profoundly. I haven't even grasped all the ways yet. But my coming here? That's part of it. I read your letter and something in me needed to come here." She thought again of her snowy walk in the woods, of Katie's wordless plea for help.

"I'm so grateful," Joanna told her. "From the bottom of my heart."

"But like I said, zero experience. I need you to have low expectations. Rock bottom."

"I can do that."

"And here's what I can do. As I mentioned, I was a researcher. I am a researcher. Maybe I can help, maybe I can't."

"Anything you can do would be so great. I've been spinning my wheels for months. The police in Graves are doing nothing. I have support in town—Floyd, who owns this diner, and his wife, Camile—but we're all totally lost in what to do next."

"Let's start with Katie." Celeste took out her phone and

opened the recording app. "Do you mind if I record our conversation? I'm having some pain today in my leg and hip and sometimes that does a number on my short-term memory."

"Oh, yeah, of course."

"Great. Tell me about Katie."

5
———

Joanna took a cell phone from her apron, scrolled for a moment, and then slid it in front of Celeste. A photo of Katie stared back at her. She sat in one of the red vinyl booths they now occupied, wearing jeans with flowery patches sewed on the knees, paired with a yellow peasant-style blouse.

"Katie was a retrophile. Is that even a word?" A pained smile curved Joanna's lips. "She called herself that anyway, and I didn't have any better term. She was obsessed with the past, and not like her own past, but the 'fifty years ago' past—the sixties and seventies. Wore the clothes, listened to the music. Bell-bottom jeans and band t-shirts and long, stick-straight brown hair parted in the middle. She wore those round, yellow-tinted spectacles. My boss here at the Sidewinder called her Fonzie."

"She's very pretty," Celeste murmured, studying her eyes. When Katie had appeared to Celeste in the forest, they'd been cloudy, colorless.

"Yeah. She has our mother's eyes. I'm not sure about the nose. It's so little and perfect."

"Are your parents in the picture?"

"No. We didn't share a dad. My dad moved to Texas when I was a year old. He sends me a Christmas card about once every three years." Joanna rolled her eyes. "Katie's dad Travis isn't much better. Our mom didn't have great taste in men. He has issues with drugs, been in and out of rehab. I was nine when he and my mom had Katie. He lived with us for about two years after Katie was born, then he got into heroin. Went into rehab, relapsed. On and on it went."

"Is he around at all?"

Joanna darkened her phone. "I see him in Graves sometimes and other times he's gone. His brother, Randy, has been sort of a faux dad for Katie, or at least a really supportive uncle. Once my mom died, Travis really spiraled. He and Katie barely spoke."

"How did your mom die?"

"Cervical cancer. It was terrible. The doctors gave her two years when they found it and she lasted two years and two weeks. I moved into the house for the last six months. She needed constant care. It was so hard on Katie. I could see it in her eyes, this haunted, terrified look. I promised Mom I'd take care of Katie and that's what I did. Katie was fourteen when our mom died. I was twenty-three. She moved with me into my apartment and was here until she disappeared." As Joanna talked, she shredded a napkin on the table.

"We sold Mom's house, but the market was upside down. We barely got out from under it. Randy helped us. He still does." Joanna smiled. "I feel weird accepting the money now that Katie's gone. I mean, he's not my uncle, but the one time I sent it back, he showed up at the diner with even more money, plus balloons and a stuffed pink bear, and told me he'd do something similar anytime I refused his help."

Celeste smiled. "He sounds like a good guy to have in your corner."

"He definitely is." Joanna noticed the bits of napkin and blushed. "Geez. You'd think I'd know better than this, since I'm cleaning these messes up all day." She quickly swiped the pieces into the cup of her hand and shoved them into her apron. Several blonde hairs had pulled loose from Joanna's ponytail and she tucked them back in place. "I'm sorry. I feel like I'm kind of rambling here. You probably don't want all this information about my mom and Katie's family."

Celeste shook her head. "No. It's good. Who knows what's relevant, right? Tell me about the last day you saw Katie."

"It was an ordinary day." Joanna scratched at her elbow. "I shouldn't say that because obviously it wasn't ordinary, but at the time..." She hugged herself as if cold. "I woke up at six—that's my usual time—made a pot of coffee, showered, got ready for the breakfast shift here at the Sidewinder. Mostly I worked morning and lunch shifts because I wanted to be home with Katie after school.

"Katie woke up around six thirty. I remember her complaining her hair straightener wasn't getting hot. I asked her what she had going on that day and she said nothing extraordinary, a math quiz. She and her friend Liam planned to walk to Carol's for lunch. It's a little sandwich shop a few blocks from the school. After school, she had a shift at the little stone schoolhouse. It's the Graves visitor center and museum. It fits Katie's love of all things old and funky. She didn't have a car, so she walked there or Liam or I might give her a ride. Sometimes I picked her up, but that night she said she didn't need a ride and..." Joanna shook her head. "I didn't ask her why. If she was walking home, if someone else was driving her. I was already dressed, walking out the door, and I didn't ask. You never know what's going to matter later on. How those little unimportant questions mean everything." Unmasked misery settled over Joanna's features.

"I worked the morning shift, came home in the afternoon, changed and went to dinner and a movie with my boyfriend at the time, Cole. I knew Katie was working and wouldn't be home anyway and she always encouraged me to date—wanted to see me 'married with five kids,' is what she liked to say." Joanna smiled sadly. "I got home around eleven and she wasn't at the apartment. The schoolhouse closed at nine, but she was seventeen years old and she had a lot of freedom. I had rules, but I trusted Katie completely. I'd never worried about her staying out late with friends."

Joanna picked at the pink polish on her fingernails. Much of it had already flaked away, but she seemed intent on removing what remained.

"Anyway, I got home, ran a bath and went into the living room to grab my book. I was reading *Great Expectations*. I'd been suffering through it, trying to complete this 'fifty classic books everyone should read' list." Joanna's eyes flitted to the ceiling. "Katie teased me incessantly about that. 'Read what you want,' she kept saying. 'Leave those musty old classics for the librarians.' Which was funny because she'd read a lot of the classics, but only the stuff set in the sixties and seventies. Again, she was practically obsessed with that era. Anyway, I went to grab my book and there, on the corner of the white marble coffee table in our living room, was a spot of blood. Just one drop.

"I picked up my book, not thinking too much of it, and then... something in me went cold. I set the book back down, grabbed my cell phone, and called Katie. She didn't answer. I texted, nothing urgent right then, you know? I didn't want her to feel like I was checking up on her. She didn't respond. The bathtub was full, but I let it grow cold and I sat on the couch staring at the spot of blood. I still don't really understand why it scared me so much. Everything else in the apartment looked fine. No blood on the floor, nothing overturned, no signs at all that anything bad had happened. She could have gotten a bloody nose, cut her finger. Any number of things.

"After about an hour of no response, which was unusual for her, I called Liam. It was midnight by then and I worried he wouldn't answer, but he picked right up, said he didn't know where she was, but he'd try calling her and a few of their other friends. After another agonizing ten minutes, he called me back. No one knew where she was. He tried to reassure me she'd probably gone to hang out with another friend, someone he wasn't thinking of, but I heard something in his voice too, a bit of worry. So I called everyone I could think of. May, who ran the old schoolhouse, Katie's uncle, Randy, and a few of her other friends, and then after another half hour of no news, I called Liam back and he said, 'Let's go drive around and look for her.' So, we did. He picked me up since he knew all the popular spots. We drove to the schoolhouse first. It was locked up, lights off, no sign of her."

A single tear carved a path down Joanna's face. She swiped it away as if she didn't have time for it. "That's when this nightmare began. I didn't know it right then, but the night before had been my last good night's sleep, my last happy day. So, Liam and I drove and after the first hour or two we kind of stopped talking. It was like if we didn't say anything, didn't acknowledge the time passing and how scared we both were, maybe we'd suddenly find her or the phone would ring and everything would be fine."

"When did you report her missing?"

"The next morning at eight a.m. I tried to call in the middle of the night and they said, 'She's a teenager, she's probably out with friends. Call in the morning if she hasn't returned.' I was furious, but what could I do? Make them take the report? So, first thing the next morning, I walked into the police station and reported her missing, which… I don't know. It felt so anti-climactic. No one went out and started looking. Not the police, anyway. I did, and Floyd and Camile at the diner made some calls and got a big group to meet here at the Sidewinder in the afternoon and people went out and searched, but… no one found anything. It was like in those first days, I kept waiting for her to reappear. Every phone call I was sure would be her. Every time the bell over the door rang, I'd look up, expect to see her.

"The weekend after she disappeared, police did their first search. They walked the property around the schoolhouse and the forests on either side of the road back into town. They had a theory she might have gotten disoriented in the cold that night, wandered into the woods and succumbed to the elements, but…" Joanna shook her head. "I didn't think so because Randy, Liam and I walked that route the day after her disappearance in daylight and there were no tracks in the snow cutting off toward the woods. There was no sign of her at all."

Celeste's cell phone rang, and she looked down to see Jonathan's name. She hadn't told him she was driving to Graves. She ignored the call.

"This is a good start," Celeste said, "but I probably better get going. I have a two-hour drive back downstate."

"Yeah. Of course. In about fifteen minutes, the lunch rush will start, so this is a good time."

As if on cue, four women walked into the diner. They all greeted Joanna by name. "Jo, can you make muffins again for the book club?" a woman wearing a yellow parka asked.

"Absolutely. How many do you need?"

"Let's say two dozen. They're so good we can rarely stick to one each."

"Great. I'll drop them by the library?"

"You're the best."

"Oh, and cookies for the volunteers at hospice? We're doing a volunteer day next week," another woman, short and wearing a down coat that nearly hung to her ankles, said.

"I'd love to. Let me know what kind and when you need them."

"I need to take care of a few things at home," Celeste told Joanna. "But then I'll come here, rent a room for a few nights, maybe a week, and see what I can find out." Celeste shrugged on her coat and stepped into the bright, chilly afternoon.

"Wow. Really?" Joanna followed her onto the snowy sidewalk. "I'd hate for you to do all that. You can stay with me. The only other room is Katie's, but—"

Celeste shook her head. "It's not an issue. And I need my space. I work better that way."

Joanna's eyes welled with tears. "I don't even know what to say. I'm so grateful, Celeste."

"I'll see you soon," Celeste told her.

CELESTE CLIMBED into her driver's seat and sat behind the wheel, gazing at the street for several minutes. Joanna had returned to the diner and several more customers had hurried through the door.

Celeste tried to clear her mind. She searched for a thread of connection to Katie, but found her own inner voice, filled with self-doubt, talking to her instead. She didn't know what she'd expected. The phantom figure of Katie to appear and lead her to her body, to where she was being held captive, to where she'd run away to? Some absurd piece of her had believed if she came to Graves, that would be the nudge the spirit world needed to cough up its secrets.

Instead, Celeste felt thoroughly in over her head. She could still back out, tell Joanna she wasn't capable of helping after all. But even as the laundry list of excuses tumbled through her mind, she opened her phone and began searching for nearby hotels.

She was going to help find Katie and bring her home.

6

———

Joanna ladled soup into two bowls, set them on a tray and carried them to Jerome and Louis who rarely missed lunch at the Sidewinder. The lunch rush had hit with full force and though Joanna wanted nothing more than to scream for joy that Celeste had agreed to help her, work demanded her attention.

"Sausage potato, guys," she told them, sliding the bowls onto the table.

"I love bottomless bowl Tuesday," Louis announced.

"Looks good, Jo," Jerome said.

Louis leaned forward and inhaled. "Smells good too."

"How come you guys are in town?" Joanna asked. "I thought you migrated south for the winter."

Jerome nodded. "Heading to Clearwater next week after Katie's vigil. And after the burglary last year, we're trying to spend more time in the house. We have all the surveillance cameras now, but figured it's still good to have a physical presence at the house occasionally."

"Any news from police in the burglary?"

Louis rolled his eyes. "Graves P.D.? Yeah, right."

Jerome reached over and took Joanna's hand, and squeezed. "How about Katie? Anything?"

Joanna shook her head, tempted to tell them about Celeste, to yell it from the rooftops. "No updates from the police in months."

"Darn it," Jerome murmured.

"Don't give up hope," Louis added.

"Nope. That's all I've got," she said. "Enjoy your soup."

"How did it go?" Camile asked when Joanna walked into the kitchen to drop off a stack of dishes at the sink. Camile had her sleeves rolled to her elbows and was the only woman Joanna knew who could look perfectly natural washing dishes in high heels and a wool skirt.

"I told you I'd do those," Joanna said. "You're going to get your blouse all dirty before the meeting."

"Dirty, schmirty. Come on, spill your guts. What did that Celeste woman say?"

"She's going to help me." Joanna grinned.

Camile squealed and slapped her soapy hands together, sending a fluff of suds into the air.

Floyd turned from the enormous griddle where he was flipping burgers. "What are you two going on about?"

"That woman Jo told us about, Celeste, who has the online column, is going to help find Katie."

"Well, I'll be damned," Floyd said. "That's the best news we've had in days. And Jo, you got two orders coming into the window in T-minus thirty seconds."

Joanna grabbed the two plates, one thick with turkey, gravy and mashed potatoes and the other a cheeseburger and fries, and carried them across the restaurant to a couple near the window.

The bell over the door jingled and Katie's uncle Randy walked in carrying a bag of oranges.

"Hey, Randy. How are you?" Joanna asked, giving him a

half hug.

He handed her the oranges. "Flew in from Tampa. Brought you some oranges. How's it going around here? Any news?"

"There is, actually," she said. Before she could continue, a bustling group of middle-aged women clutching shopping bags, all talking animatedly, walked into the diner. "Let me take care of these ladies and I'll fill you in," she told him.

"You do your thing. I'm gonna grab that corner booth. I'll take a coffee when you get a sec. Jerome, Louis, how's it going?" Randy called to the two men.

"It's cold," Louis said.

"No kidding. I was just in St. Pete. Shouldn't you guys be down there sipping piña coladas on a beach?"

"Soon enough," Jerome said.

"That drafty old mansion's got to be a fortune to heat," Randy said as he slid into a booth.

"You have no idea," Louis agreed. "And don't even get me started on the dogs. They have to wear booties and sweaters to go out and piddle. If Jerome insists on keeping that house, he might have to leave me in Clearwater with the corgis and see to it himself."

"I'm not sure it's such a paradise down there right now," Jerome said, picking up a newspaper and waving it in the air. "There's an article about a serial killer in the *Tampa Bay Times*. Three girls in two years strangled."

Louis snatched the paper from Jerome's hand and tossed it onto the bench next to him. "No news talk at lunch. I told you not to bring that paper."

Jo, half listening to the exchange between Jerome and Louis, greeted the women who'd walked in, led them to a large table in the center of the diner and returned to the counter to grab their waters and sodas and Randy's coffee.

She slid the coffee before him and he smiled, pulling off his winter hat. "I need this. Took the red-eye last night and didn't sleep a wink, thanks to the gorilla sitting beside me who snored like a freight train."

"Why were you in Florida?" she asked, scanning her tables to see if anyone needed her.

"Business, the usual. Tell me the news."

"Well, there's a woman who's going to come stay in Graves for a few days and try to help me. She has an online advice column, and I reached out and she was here this morning."

Randy looked skeptical. "An online advice column? How is she going to help find Katie?"

The bell over the door jingled and a couple in matching red and white ski coats walked in. Joanna hurried over and seated them before returning to Randy.

"I'm not sure how exactly she's going to help, but... what other choices do I have? The detective on the case won't return my calls. I'm running out of options and... I don't know. I have a good feeling about her. I've been reading her column for years. She's very smart."

Randy sipped his coffee and nodded. "I keep thinking any day now one of us will pick up the phone and Katie will be on the other line."

AFTER JOANNA FINISHED HER SHIFT, she slipped out of her tennis shoes and into her heavy boots and coat. "See you guys tomorrow," she called to Floyd and Camile.

Randy stood and walked with her outside. "Walk you back to your apartment?"

"You don't have to do that. It's cold out."

He took a big breath in, stretched his arms wide. "Cold's good for ya. Haven't you ever watched anything about that Wim Hof guy who breaks a hole in the ice and sits in it for an hour a day or some crazy thing? He says it's good for the blood."

"Good for the blood, huh?"

"Oh, you know, circulation. It's supposed to have a bunch of health benefits. You should watch him sometime. Fascinating stuff."

Joanna nodded, but her mind had moved onto other things, primarily Celeste. She wanted so much to believe that this woman would somehow be the key to finding Katie. She knew it was likely a pipe dream. The woman herself had insisted Joanna have rock-bottom expectations and yet she felt hopeful for the first time in months.

When they reached the apartment building, Joanna stopped at her mailbox and pulled out the day's mail. "Ugh..." she muttered.

"What?" Randy looked over her shoulder.

"I'm still getting medical bills after my mom's death. They're never-ending."

"Here." Randy took out his wallet and handed her a hundred-dollar bill.

"No. Please. I'm not taking that."

"Come on. I roll around naked in money like this. Take it."

Joanna laughed. "That's called TMI."

"TM-what?"

"Too much information."

"Then take the money and I'll spare you further details." He stuck the hundred dollars into her stack of mail, which caused several pieces to shake loose and fall to the ground. Randy picked them up. "'Family Tree DNA,'" he said, reading the block letters on a mailer addressed to Katie.

Joanna tucked it back into the pile. "She gets all kinds of junk mail. That place, some makeup outlet that sends free samples every month—I kind of like those—and somehow, she ended up on a list that sends me pictures of shelter pets every week. It's seriously heartbreaking. If I didn't work seven days a week, I'd have adopted fifteen dogs and ten cats by now."

Randy chuckled as he followed her upstairs. "Considering your landlord is Raymond Perfect, the meanest old man in Graves, I would advise against that."

"Yeah. The last thing I need is an eviction notice on top of everything else." Joanna unlocked the door and dropped her mail on the table.

Randy opened her refrigerator. "Milk? That's all you've got to drink in this place?"

"Yep. And tap water. You're welcome to either." She kicked off her boots, hung up her coat and paused, staring into her dark living room. It didn't look different than it had when she left that morning and yet something felt off, some indiscernible change.

Scanning the furniture, the walls, the single hallway, she searched for the anomaly and found it. Her curtains, always shut, were slightly ajar, enough to peer down at Main Street.

Joanna thought back to the morning—the usual rush as she got dressed, scarfed down her cereal and threw on her coat and boots. Had she opened the curtains and looked out? She was certain she hadn't, and yet they were open. It was an absurd detail to get hung up on. Nothing else appeared amiss. Someone hadn't broken in simply to peer out her window. Still, she scanned the street below, half expecting to see someone looking back at her.

There was no one there.

7

As Celeste drove back to Grand Rapids, she thought about Joanna Ellis. The young woman had desperation in her eyes. Guilt squirmed in Celeste's belly as she imagined what the coming days would look like. How would she explain to Jonathan what she intended to do? How would she actually help find Katie?

Celeste's gaze drifted, landed on a little red-brick building with a dazzling black and purple sign. *Bloodline: Ink Tattoos by Marci.*

She slammed her foot on the brakes and twisted the wheel. The car behind her laid on the horn and she suspected the driver flipped her their middle finger, though she was already coasting into a parking spot, turning off the engine and climbing out.

Celeste didn't have a tattoo, had never even considered getting one until that moment. She pushed open the glass door and stepped in to the scents of ink and witch hazel, the sounds of country music pouring from the speakers. The wood floor gleamed. The red-painted walls were covered in framed images of tattooed bodies. A woman at the far end of the shop sat in one of two reclining black leather chairs. She stood, set a magazine on a table, and waved.

"Hi there. Welcome to Bloodline. What can I do for ya?" The woman was small, maybe five feet, with a black ponytail pulled high, which made her appear younger than she likely was. She wore a Minnie Mouse t-shirt paired with polka-dot leggings and earrings so long they brushed her shoulders. Tattoos covered both her arms.

Celeste glanced at the images on the walls. Tattoos of butterflies and serpents and the faces of celebrities. "I think I want a tattoo," she said.

The woman grinned and cocked her head. "You think, or you know? I'm not sure if anyone told you, but these little suckers"—she tapped her forearm—"are permanent. Have a seat, flip through some books. Personally, I love my ink and think bodies are meant to be decorated, but there are people who get a bug in their butt to get inked and regret it later. Part of not having those regrets is picking something that matters to you. Hear what I'm saying? If you tell me in ten minutes you want a rose tattooed on your boob, I'm gonna tell you to go home and think on it for a night or two."

Celeste nodded, sat down on a brown leather couch, and opened a binder of tattoos. She flipped the plastic pages, eyes skimming the drawings. In her mind, an image assembled. She rifled through her bag and found her notebook crammed with drawings of ravens and black feathers. She picked the best-looking one and sketched a single word beneath it: *Evolve.*

Celeste stood and walked to Marci. "I'd like something like this. The artistic version. Obviously, I failed art class."

Marci took the notebook, nodded, smiling. "A harbinger of death, or maybe birth. I've heard both versions of what the raven symbolizes. In any case, it's great. Where are we putting it?"

Celeste glanced toward the door. No one had appeared in

the parking lot. She unbuttoned her jeans and pulled them down to reveal the jagged scar that ran from her hip to midway down her outer thigh. "Here. On my thigh, not my hip."

"That's a wicked-looking scar."

"I was hit by a car last year."

"Damn. Okay. Well, let me grab ya a robe. You want to do this today? You're ready?"

"I'm ready."

"WHAT'S THIS?" Celeste asked, surprised, when she walked into the dining room at home.

The lights were dimmed. Candles burned in two tall crystal candle-holders she didn't even realize they owned. Jonathan had set the table. She smelled something cheesy and Italian.

"I made lasagna," he announced, took her bag from her shoulder and helped her out of her coat. He walked her things to the coat closet, then returned, untying his apron. "Here. Sit down. I thought I'd open a bottle of merlot to go with our dinner."

"Sounds lovely," she murmured, allowing him to press her into a chair.

She sat staring at the table covered in white linen. The candle flame flickered and bounced, cast dark shadows on the white cloth. She felt strange, slightly out-of-body, still buzzed from the pain of the tattoo, the ink flowing in her blood. Marci had said to expect as much. Celeste shivered without her coat on, sat for another moment entranced by the candle.

"I'm going to change into a sweater and flannel pants," she called, pushing back from the table. "I'm chilly."

"Okay." Jonathan appeared in the doorway with the pan of lasagna. "I need to grab a couple more things here and we'll be ready to eat."

He sat the lasagna on the table and Celeste recoiled at his hands. Both were dark red, as if smeared with blood.

"What?" he asked. "What's wrong?"

"Your hands. They're... Did you cut yourself?"

Jonathan frowned and turned his hands over, studied his palms. When he flipped them back to face Celeste, they were clean—no trace of red remained.

She opened her mouth, shook her head. "It must have been the candlelight casting... a shadow, maybe."

Celeste felt Jonathan's eyes on her back as she turned and hurried from the dining room.

AFTER DINNER, Jonathan led her upstairs. She eased onto the bed and he climbed in beside her. He slid his hand down her body, and Celeste winced when his fingers grazed the fresh tattoo still covered by a bandage. He felt the raised edge, and she opened her mouth to speak, explain, but he'd already pulled down the waistband of her sweatpants.

"What is this?" he asked, studying the white gauze as if she'd sprouted a tumor from her thigh.

"I got a tattoo today." She waited for his eyes to slide up to hers and when they did, she could see the shock and behind that anger.

"*You* got a tattoo?"

Something in his tone set her on edge, caused the ache in her body to deepen. She shuddered. "Yes, *I* did."

"Of what?" he demanded.

"A raven."

He blinked at her, lips parted, face pale. "Why would you do that? How could you do that without telling me?"

"It's my body, Jonathan. I don't think I need to consult you on everything I do with my own body."

"But… a tattoo? A trashy tattoo? My God, we used to roll our eyes at people who got tattoos. And now you're one of them."

Celeste stared at him, felt a spasm of rage in her guts at his comment, and yet… it didn't surprise her. She knew how Jonathan felt about tattoos, and he wasn't wrong that she'd once looked upon people with the same disdain. An odd superiority—about what, exactly? She didn't know now, could not fathom what had made her think such things. "I wanted one, so I got it. It's that simple."

"It's not that simple," Jonathan snapped, standing abruptly from the bed, his hard-on long gone. He snatched his robe from the back of the door and cinched it around his waist as if he'd suddenly found himself naked with a stranger. And Celeste knew that was likely exactly how he felt. She'd felt it herself more than once in his presence since the accident. "Who are you, Celeste? I feel like… I feel like I don't even know you anymore."

Celeste gazed at him, his hurt expression, and searched within herself for the woman he remembered. "I don't think you do, Jonathan. I don't even know this woman." She gestured at herself. "But this is me now. It is. I'm sorry, but—"

He turned and strode from the room before she could finish her sentence.

8

———

When Celeste woke the following morning, Jonathan had already left for work. He'd filled the kettle for tea and left her packet of oatmeal on the counter—the same breakfast she'd eaten for years. The gloopy oatmeal and bland tea sounded totally unappetizing. She brewed a pot of coffee, dark, and added honey and milk. She sat at the table that overlooked the backyard drenched in snow and watched a pair of scarlet cardinals hop from branch to branch on a small pine tree.

The tattoo pulsed beneath the bandage on her leg, a pleasant pain that focused her attention away from the deeper pain always throbbing from her left hip to her ankle.

After she drank her coffee, she searched for a pancake recipe. She'd made pancakes as a girl, often the one responsible for breakfast when her dad could be counted on to produce little more than a bowl of cereal.

Her phone rang and her brother's name, Adam, appeared on the screen.

"Good morning, little brother," she answered, pouring the last of the pancake batter into the sizzling pan.

"Good morning to you. I was afraid I'd missed you and maybe you went back to work this week."

"Nope. Still on leave."

"And how's that going?" Celeste could hear the concern in his voice buried beneath his forced cheeriness.

"It's going. I'm sure Dynamic Laboratories would like me to give them a return date, but..." She grabbed the spatula and flipped the pancake, smiling at its perfect golden color.

"But what? You're still in pain? Or is it... more of an emotional issue?"

"A little of both, I suspect."

"Did you call that therapist I sent you the email about?"

Celeste shifted the phone to her other ear and did heel slides—a necessary exercise, according to her physical therapist Lorenzo. She stopped at the glass doors and stared again into the wintry backyard. "No. I've been meaning to." But she'd been devoting her time to playing therapist through her advice column rather than seeking one out herself.

"Celeste, therapy can be really amazing. I've been seeing my therapist for years."

Celeste didn't ask how he felt that was going. They both knew he continued to deal with bouts of depression and crippling social anxiety.

"I'm going to call her. Soon..." Celeste trailed off as a vision of Adam's neighbor Henrietta materialized in her mind.

Celeste had met the woman several times during visits to Adam. Henrietta collected dog fur from all her neighbors and spun it into yarn. Twice she'd come over to Adam's house during Celeste's visits, once to deliver a pair of dog fur slippers and the second time a hat. Now Celeste saw Henrietta in an enormous field of wild flowers, two border collies walking beside her.

"How's Henrietta?" Celeste asked.

"Henrietta? I'd imagine she's fine. I haven't seen her much

lately—winter and all. What's going on with your leg? Improving?"

"Stronger every day."

Several dark birds, wings spread, glided into the backyard. They pecked relentlessly at the snow, and Celeste leaned toward the glass, trying to make sense of what they were eating. She stilled when she caught sight of several bright red splotches in the snow.

"What the—" A burning smell filled her nose and overhead the fire alarm began to wail. She whirled toward the stove to see black smoke billowing up from her forgotten pancake. "Shit. I've got to go."

"Celeste—"

Celeste dropped her phone and ran to the stove, yanked the pan off the burner and carried it across the room. She jerked open the glass door and stepped out in her slippers. The cold was sharp. The startled birds took flight, and Celeste tried to see what lay in the backyard, but smoke surging from the pan blocked her view. She set the pan on the snowy porch and walked to the rail and stared down.

It was a cardinal—likely one of the birds she'd been admiring. It lay sightless, head twisted to one side. What she'd thought was blood was the cardinal's bright red feathers.

WHEN JONATHAN ARRIVED HOME, Celeste sat at the kitchen table, her bag packed and on the floor beside her. She'd booked a room at Shanty Creek, an older ski resort less than ten miles from Graves.

He walked in and paused, eyes taking her and her suitcase in. "Are you going somewhere?" He'd already removed his coat and shoes and seemed vulnerable in his socked feet, his expression wary.

"I am, yes." Celeste had spent the better part of the afternoon imagining how she'd tell Jonathan she intended to go spend days, maybe weeks, up north searching for a missing seventeen-year-old she didn't know. In the end, she'd decided to lie. "You know I've been feeling off ever since the accident. I think I need a week or so to…" She spread her palms towards him. "Find myself."

"Find yourself?" He could not hide his disdain at the words. Celeste knew Jonathan hated the phrase 'find myself' nearly as much as the flippant saying 'it is what it is,' popular among the newly graduated twentysomethings at Dynamic Laboratories.

He walked to the cupboard and took out a glass, then grabbed the bottle of Scotch Celeste intended to take with her, twisted off the cap and poured. He sat across from her, body stiff, and crossed his legs. "Where might you go to find yourself? Is there a town somewhere where our lost selves run off to?"

She sighed. "I know you're upset and I understand why, but I need to do this for me. I do. I can't explain it beyond that."

"*Where* are you going?"

A part of her didn't want to tell him, wanted to offer another lie so that he couldn't track her down, but she opted now for the truth. He was her husband. He deserved that much. "Shanty Creek. It's a ski resort near Bellaire."

"You're going skiing?" He didn't even attempt to hide his incredulity.

"Of course not. Even before this"—she gestured at her leg—"I was a terrible skier. It's pretty, lots of woods and snow and fresh air."

He gestured at the backyard. "Lots of woods and snow and fresh air right outside, Celeste."

"The air is different up north." And though it wasn't about the air and they both knew it, it was true. Something happened when you passed a certain midpoint in Michigan. The air grew crisp, full of the scent of water and pine.

The explanation did little to soften his expression. "What about your doctor? And physical therapy? You can't up and leave—"

"I already called them both. My therapist emailed me exercises I can do on my own and I rescheduled my next doctor's visit for later this month."

"Celeste, you're still struggling to walk, to sleep. Do you really think it's safe to go up to some town where you don't know a single person? What if you fall?"

"Then I'll use my trusty little phone to call for help." She waved her cell phone. "Jonathan, I'm going to be fine. I'm not backpacking to an off-grid cabin in the forest. I am staying at a resort surrounded by people. Maybe part of the reason I need this is to establish a taste of independence again. For the last seven months I've needed so much help. I've almost forgotten what it's like to do it alone."

"But you don't have to do it alone."

"I want to. I need to."

"This is a mistake. I spoke with Mark Hansen today and he mentioned a great couples counselor he and Valorie saw years ago after she lost their first baby. Life-changing, he called her."

Guilt crept in. He was trying so hard and she owed it to him —to them—to do better. "When I get back, we'll go. Okay?"

He slumped lower in his chair, the fight draining out of him. "Fine. I can't stop you."

WHEN CELESTE ARRIVED IN GRAVES, she drove to the stone schoolhouse Katie had worked at the night of the disappearance. One car sat in the snowy parking lot. Celeste slowed, but didn't pull in. Beyond the trees, the sun had begun its descent.

Long shadows cast by the schoolhouse obscured the surrounding property. Though it was only a half mile outside of town, it felt isolated, unprotected.

As she passed through town, Celeste glimpsed Joanna through the lit windows of the Sidewinder. She almost pulled over, but the day had been long and she yearned for a glass of Scotch.

Her cell phone rang, and Adam's name appeared on the screen.

"Hey," she answered.

"Why'd you ask me about Henrietta?" he demanded.

"Huh?"

"This morning you asked about Henrietta. You've literally never done that."

Celeste said nothing. She already knew where the conversation was going.

"This afternoon there was an ambulance and cop car in her driveway. Her niece found her dead in the house. She's dead."

Henrietta filled Celeste's mind again and this time a sensation arrived as well—a sense of fullness in her chest, a sharp pain streaking down her left arm. "Heart attack," she murmured.

"How do you know that? Why did you ask me about her?"

"Lucky guess."

"It's not a lucky guess. You've met her three times. How could you guess that?"

As Celeste turned onto a country road that would take her to Bellaire, a figure ahead caught her attention. The girl stood in the shadow of the trees and Celeste braked, catching only a fleeting glimpse of long hair flowing out as the girl disappeared down a trail into the woods.

"Keep driving," Celeste murmured, but she'd already coasted to the shoulder of the road.

"What? What does that mean?" Adam asked.

"I've got to go, Adam. I'll call you later."

"No. Wait—"

She ended the call before he could say more.

It was Katie she'd seen vanishing into the woods. Katie had come to her once again, and she had to follow.

Celeste shoved open her door and groaned at the spasm of pain in her leg when she swung it out. Using her cane for support, she followed the trail, which, though dampened mostly by animal tracks, was heavy with snow.

Thick pines shielded her from the cutting wind. There was no sign of Katie ahead and the deeper she went into the dark trees, the heavier the silence became. Soon the only sound was the crunch of snow beneath her leather boots.

The trees split and she stepped into an opening. An old train track, thick drifts running down the embankment on either side, ran crosswise through the expanse. On the track sat an old rusted and graffitied train car. Through the open door, Celeste could see the black chasm inside the relic, bits of litter strewn along the wooden floor—pop bottles and candy wrappers.

Celeste searched the trees, but saw no sign of the apparition she'd followed into the forest.

She looked again at the train car and thought she could see something tucked in the far back, in the space where light could reach. Foreboding sending skitters of alarm up her spine, she stepped closer and braced one hand against the cold metal frame. Squinting, she tried to make sense of the movement and, before she could pull back, something plunged from the darkness and struck her in the face.

Celeste screamed and fell back, landing hard in the snow. The creature—a raven—flapped its wings frantically as it lit into the dusky gray sky. She watched it fly up and disappear over the trees.

For several seconds she didn't move, felt the cold damp

seeping through her jeans. With a huff, she struggled back to her feet and wiped snow from the seat of her pants. Her leg and hip pulsed with her heartbeat.

Celeste limped back down the trail and was nearly to her car when her right foot hit a patch of ice. Before she could even react, her leg slipped sideways and she plunged forward, landing on her hands and knees, her cane skidding away on the surface of the hard-packed snow.

Jonathan's words rang out in her head: *What if you fall?*

Celeste was not a big crier, but she felt tears creeping up. The emotion—the relentless vulnerability of her new life—made her angry and she wanted to scream.

Across the road a rusted Buick pulled into the ditch. A man climbed out and walked over. "Need a hand?" he asked. "I saw you go down. Icy as hell out here."

Face flushed, Celeste reached for his hand and tried not to groan when he pulled her to her feet and her entire left side howled in protest.

He looked older than her, though not by much. His eyes, likely once a pretty blue, had a jaundiced look. He wore a goatee that was patchy and his long hair, pulled into a ponytail, needed a wash.

"Thanks," she told him.

He walked over, picked up her cane, and handed it to her. Then his eyes trailed down to her leather boots. "Better get yourself some decent shoes." He raised one of his own boots, timeworn, with duct tape across the toe. "Had these for ten years. Ain't failed me yet."

"Yeah. Thanks again."

She watched him walk across the street, climb into his car and, with a wave, drive away.

Narrow, winding roads led to the Shanty Creek Resort and Ski Area. Steep tree-lined embankments bordered the narrow streets. Twice Celeste made a wrong turn and found her car struggling to navigate the icy driveways.

When she finally reached the building that held the condo she'd rented, she sighed, leaned her head back, and closed her eyes. Her left leg had gone numb and her hands ached from gripping the wheel.

The internal voice nagged her, demanded to know what she thought she was doing, repeated its insistence she call the whole thing off. She'd already fallen twice and hadn't even checked into her condo yet.

Celeste tuned it out.

After a few more deep breaths, she stepped from her car, grabbed her cane, and dragged her rolling duffel bag across the snowy parking lot to the double doors. Carpeted stairs led to the second floor. She typed in the code for the condo and opened the lockbox, retrieving the key.

Normally she would have sat her suitcase on the bed, unpacked and put away her clothes and toiletries, but now she rummaged for her Scotch and her painkillers. She swallowed two pain pills and then poured Scotch into a plastic cup and walked to a chair angled toward the sliding glass door that opened to her little balcony and looked out on the ski slope. It wasn't busy, but a handful of skiers, their bright parkas and snow pants like splatters of paint against the white hill, carved down the slopes.

9

The following day, Celeste slept late. She'd tossed the night before, strange dreams and constant pain keeping her awake until daylight trickled through the curtains.

It was nearly two in the afternoon when she parked her car in Graves. Celeste pulled her coat tighter and hurried to the door at the Sidewinder. She pushed inside, inhaled the smell of coffee and something hearty—chili, perhaps.

"You made it!" Joanna exclaimed. "Tanya comes on shift in ten minutes, then I'm done for the day." Joanna led her to a booth where a man sat flipping through a leather planner. "Celeste, this is Randy Mills, Katie's uncle. Randy, this is Celeste. She's the woman I told you about."

Randy slid from the booth and stood, offered Celeste his hand. He wore a collared sweater and jeans, his dark hair receding. Celeste pegged him for early to mid-forties.

"Hi, Celeste," he said. "I hear you're an advice columnist—"

"No. Not professionally anyway." Celeste shook her head. "I'm… a researcher hoping to put some of my skills to work in locating Katie."

"Oh. Okay." Randy looked vaguely confused, but gestured at the table. "Why don't you join me? I'll do anything I can to help. Jo knows that." He squeezed Joanna's shoulder, and she nodded.

"Sure." Celeste gritted her teeth and slid into the booth. She'd left her cane in the car, but already the ache had begun.

"Can I grab you a coffee or something else?" Joanna asked.

"Coffee would be great. The little machine in my room makes about a cup and a half, barely enough to get one eye peeled all the way open."

"That's a travesty," Randy said. "Fortunately, the Sidewinder has some killer joe, don't ya, Jo?"

Joanna rolled her eyes. "Watch out for those jokes, Celeste. If you laugh even once, he'll never stop telling them."

Celeste smiled. "Good tip."

"So how did you end up involved in all this?" Randy asked when Joanna walked away.

"It did begin with the advice column. It's something I started years ago as a bit of insomnia therapy."

"Insomnia therapy?"

"It gave me something to do on nights when I couldn't sleep."

He chuckled. "I usually opt for eating chips and watching true crime shows. You're clearly more ambitious than me."

"Here you go." Joanna slid a mug of coffee onto the table.

"Thank you," Celeste told Jo, who hurried away to check out a man standing at the register. Celeste ripped open a packet of sugar and added two creams to her coffee. She stirred it, took a sip and then took out her phone and opened the recording app, looking at Randy. "I'd love to hear your impression of Katie and if you have any thoughts on what might have happened to her. Do you mind if I record our conversation?"

Randy leaned back and folded his arms over his chest. "Not at all. Let's see... Katie is a good kid. I'm still not sure how my brother produced her. I've tried to help out when I can, you know? But I'm on the road quite a bit. I never missed a birthday," he said brightly. "Got her a vintage jean jacket from an antique store in Arizona for her seventeenth. She howled when she opened it. Seriously. Howled like a wolf."

"That's a really thoughtful gift."

He sipped his coffee. "I try. I mean, somebody's got to. God knows her dad will never step up and Jo does her best, but"—he nodded toward her bustling between the tables—"she's got her hands full keeping the lights on and rent paid."

"When was the last time you saw Katie?"

He rotated his coffee mug. "Well, I saw her that last day, briefly. Ran into her after school. She was downtown, getting ready to walk over to the schoolhouse for her shift. I offered her a ride, but she said no."

"Any idea why she said no?"

He shook his head. "Didn't even cross my mind to ask her. Katie did her own thing. She wasn't the kind of kid who told you every little thing about her life. Even Jo was in the dark with some of Katie's life."

"Like what?"

"Oh, I don't know. Her little friend Liam mentioned an on-again, off-again boyfriend, and Jo hadn't even known Katie was dating the boy—thought they were friends, maybe a little flirtation or whatever. But turns out they were... serious, or as serious as you get at seventeen. Anyone who's ever been that age knows it feels serious as life and death. I heard there was a rumor she took off because they broke up again and she was heartbroken, and in the early days I was apt to believe it. Like I said, she was a very independent girl. I thought she'd come blowin' back in on a Greyhound bus with some insane story about hitchhiking out to California. But then..." He spread his palms. "Here we are."

"Did she ever mention doing anything like that? Hitch-hiking out west?"

"Only in offhand ways. She idolized Janis Joplin and Jim Morrison and she thought their whole era was the best time in the history of the world. She used to say serial killers ruined it for everybody. They made hitching rides impossible."

The fine hairs on the back of Celeste's neck stood on end. "Serial killers?"

"Yeah, you know, Bundy and Kemper and all those psychos who preyed on lone girls hitchhiking. Anyway, I think she knew better than to hitchhike, but I've wondered if her head was a bit scrambled from the breakup, you know? Love can make us do some pretty stupid things."

"Have you told Jo that theory?"

The door to the diner opened and a woman wearing an outfit similar to Jo's—black slacks, white button-down shirt—walked in. She quickly clipped on a nametag that read 'Tanya' and tied an apron around her waist.

"Oh, sure," Randy said. "We've talked over the possibilities six ways to Sunday. I don't think there's a scenario we haven't turned over in our heads, but the problem is we don't have any real proof to support any of it. It's like she was walking down the road and a hole in the earth opened up and she fell in and it closed right up after. I mean, that's totally illogical, and yet in some way it feels as possible as anything else."

"Do you have any idea who'd want to hurt her?"

Randy slid his hands over his face, shook his head. "No. Katie wasn't a controversial girl. You know what I'm saying? She didn't rub people the wrong way. Everyone loved her."

His cell phone beeped and he read the message. "I've gotta jet. We have a shipment that arrived at the warehouse and apparently they can't get in. Jo has my number. Call or text if you have more questions."

"Thanks, Randy. Good to meet you."

A large man wearing a grease-stained apron lumbered out of the kitchen. "Randy, think you could get me some more of those griddle brushes?"

"I'm on it, Floyd. I'll call you later."

After Randy left, Floyd walked to Celeste and offered his hand. "I'm Floyd, owner of the Sidewinder and Jo's self-appointed godfather. I wanted to say thank you. She's gotten some of her zeal back since you agreed to help her find Katie."

"Of course. I'm happy to help and it's nice to meet you."

Joanna walked over, apron bundled in her hand. "I'm all set. We can go back to my apartment and talk there?" She gave Floyd a half hug. "See you tomorrow, old man."

Floyd clutched his chest and groaned. "Old man? You wound me." He laughed. "I'm kidding. Go on. Enjoy the rest of your afternoon."

Celeste took a last sip of her coffee, then stood and followed Joanna out the door.

"I live a couple of blocks away. I didn't drive," Joanna said, pointing down the road.

"You can ride with me."

"Are you sure?" Joanna brushed at her pants. "I smell like diner food."

"Positive. Come on."

Joanna slid into the passenger seat of Celeste's car and they made the short drive to her apartment building.

10

─────────

As they walked to the front door, Joanna frowned. "I'm sorry, there are stairs. This place is really old—no elevator."

"That's fine. I'm sure my physical therapist would say it's good for me."

Joanna fought the urge to offer Celeste her arm as they ascended. She suspected the woman found her injury a frustration and preferred not to be offered assistance. Joanna unlocked the door and glanced back at Celeste, embarrassed she hadn't taken the time to clean up that morning. Her counter was scattered with unopened mail, an empty mug, the dregs of her cereal.

"Come on in," Joanna said, hurrying to put the mug and bowl in the sink.

"Was someone just here?" Celeste asked.

Joanna shook her head, then followed Celeste's gaze to the tea kettle still sitting on the burner where she'd left it that morning after making tea. A thin line of steam rose from the spout. When Joanna held her hand near it, heat radiated off of the blue enamel, though the dial on the burner was set to off.

"That's weird," Joanna murmured. "I boiled water this morning, but that was hours ago."

Celeste braced a hand on a chair back, her face lined with pain.

"Here. Come sit down." Joanna led her to the living room. The tea kettle must have somehow stayed hot. It was the only logical explanation.

Celeste leaned heavily on her cane and Joanna wanted to help her, take her under one arm and support her to the couch, but she held back. Katie had once told Joanna there was such a thing as too helpful after Joanna had insisted on carrying an old man's groceries at the store, only to have him accuse her of treating him like a toddler.

"I could make a pot of coffee or—"

"Nothing for me. Thank you."

Joanna hurried to the window and opened the curtains wide, obliterating the murky interior.

Celeste scanned the apartment, and Joanna looked around self-consciously. She hadn't done a proper clean in months. Particles of dust floated in the sunlight streaming through the living room window. The blanket she'd used the night before sat crumpled on the couch.

"I'm sorry it's such a mess," Joanna murmured.

Celeste didn't respond. She stood very still and quiet. Her posture reminded Joanna of a hunting dog who'd gone on point, as if she sensed something Joanna could not.

Joanna wanted to ask if something was wrong, but again clamped her teeth shut. It was hard for her not to push. She wanted people to be comfortable. She wanted to make Celeste feel at home.

Celeste finally moved. A spasm of pain crossed her face as she stepped onto her injured leg. She walked into the living room and paused, looking down at the marble coffee table. Joanna's eyes drifted to the tabletop, her mind instantly jumping back nearly twelve months before to that single spot of blood.

"This is where you saw the blood?" Celeste asked, gesturing to the exact spot where the blood had been.

"Yes," Joanna confirmed, hurrying across the room and looking down at the table, half expecting a stain to remain, but of course there wasn't one. Joanna had cleaned the table many times since that first night.

"And the police never collected the blood?"

Joanna shook her head. "They didn't take Katie's disappearance seriously. It sat there for two days and finally I cleaned it. I couldn't stand to look at it anymore."

"That must have been really upsetting." Celeste pulled out her cell phone. "I'm going to turn on my voice recorder now and ask some questions. Sound good?"

"Of course, yes. Are you sure I can't get you some coffee or... something to eat? I could make you a sandwich or heat up some soup."

"Do you have anything hard? Scotch?"

Surprise lit Joanna's face, but she quickly wiped it away.

"I know that's a strange request, but it takes the edge off of this." Celeste touched her leg. "When it aches, it's hard to focus."

"Sure, yeah. Gosh. I get it. Umm..." Joanna stood and went to the kitchen rifling through cupboards before finally holding up a bottle. "Peppermint schnapps? It's left over from a Christmas party a couple of years ago. I've never really kept much alcohol in the apartment because of Katie, so..."

"That'd be great. Thanks."

"I can mix it with something."

"Nope. Toss it over a little ice and that's perfect."

Joanna opened the freezer door, balked at the empty ice cube trays. "I don't have ice. I'm sorry. This is embarrassing. I have those little ice cube trays, but I haven't made ice in ages."

"That's fine. No ice needed." Celeste sipped the schnapps and set her cell phone on the table between them. "Randy mentioned Katie might have had a breakup before she went missing."

Joanna's face flushed at the memory of learning Katie had been seeing someone. How had she been so oblivious? "I didn't know he was her boyfriend. I feel stupid now for not seeing it. Jesus, I was a teenage girl not that long ago, and yet I thought they were just friends."

"Why do you think she didn't tell you it was more than a friendship?"

Joanna stared at the corner of the table, wished the drop of blood wasn't seared in her memory. "Declan, that's his name. He has a reputation. Maybe that's not fair. His family has a reputation. The Boyds are difficult people. They're always fighting with someone. His dad, Warren, isn't even allowed in the diner because he's such a nightmare to wait on. He starts fights, complains about everything.

"They live outside of town and their neighbors are always complaining about the broken-down cars and junk Warren leaves all over the yard. Declan's older brother, Todd is a known troublemaker and drug user. He and some buddies got caught a couple of years ago breaking into some of the summer houses. Declan was implicated, but never got in trouble. I guess I always worried about the apple not falling far from the tree when it came to Declan. I tried not to dump that opinion on Katie, but I'm sure she picked up on it. And to tell you the truth, I worried about her tendency to be attracted to certain kinds of men. That's how my mom was. She was a loser magnet. I was afraid Katie might have that same... attraction. It's stupid to think that, but I worried about it."

"Did you talk to Declan after she went missing?"

"One time, and then you know what? His dad stormed into the diner and screamed in my face. Said 'don't be trying to pin

Katie taking off on my son,' and that 'she probably run off with some other boy she was seeing on the side.'"

"Wow. That's an extreme response."

"Warren is extreme."

"Tell me about the conversation you had with Declan."

"I caught up with him in the school parking lot. I was with Liam and we approached him as he was getting in his truck. I could tell right away he didn't like Liam. He sneered at him. I asked Declan about the last time he saw Katie. He claimed it was at school the last day she was seen, passed her in the halls, but they didn't talk. I asked if he had any clue where she'd gone, if she mentioned anything about leaving or about seeing someone that night.

"He said nope. And that was it. He got in his truck and peeled out, threw dirt up in our faces." Joanna worried at a thread that had come loose on the couch. If she continued picking at it she'd likely open a hole and make the old couch look even more run-down, but she couldn't help herself.

"I can understand why you didn't want her to date him. He sounds like a jerk."

"Exactly."

"Okay. So, we know she made it to the schoolhouse and worked her shift, right?"

"Yes."

"Who was the last person who saw her?"

"The last confirmed sighting was by Camile—Floyd's wife. She's on the board at the schoolhouse and she stopped in to pick up the mail. She said Katie was upstairs when she walked in, but came down and said hello. They chatted briefly. Camile was in a hurry because she had to get to the diner to meet Floyd. She said everything seemed normal. Katie told her the evening had been quiet, only a couple people stopped in, one sale of a book on Graves' history. Camile left and there hasn't been another sighting of Katie since."

"What time was that at?"

"Around seven."

"And the schoolhouse closed at what time?"

"Nine."

"And you know Katie closed that night? All the usual closing procedures were done?"

Joanna nodded. "The museum was locked, lights were off. Katie took the cash out and put it in the safe, not that there was much in there ever. Wanda, a volunteer there, opened the schoolhouse the next day, and noticed nothing unusual."

"Okay. And none of Katie's stuff was left behind?"

"No. Nothing."

"And Camile... she's someone you trust?"

"Oh, God, yes. Camile and Floyd have been like family to Katie and me. Truly. We've had holidays at their house. They don't have children. They treat me and Katie like surrogate daughters."

"Okay. Got it. So, Katie closed the museum at nine. It would have been full dark by that time, and cold, I'd imagine. But no one has come forward saying they picked her up, or she called for a ride?"

"No. And it wouldn't have been strange for her to walk back into town. She enjoyed walking, enjoyed being outside at night. Said that winter nights in Graves were some of her favorite times because everything was still and quiet."

"A seventeen-year-old girl who had no fear walking down an isolated country road in the winter at night?"

"I know. It's hard to believe, but it's true. That was Katie. She hated the feeling of being too connected, too available. And she was pretty fearless. The only thing I ever remember her being scared of was basements."

"Basements?"

"Yeah. The old Michigan kind. Our mom's house had one, and Katie insisted it was haunted. Damp stone walls and a floor made of dirt. She said it felt like a tomb down there. She got locked in there once as a toddler. I was at school. My mom had gotten drunk and passed out on the couch. I came home and heard this whimpering. Katie was crouched on the top step, had cried for hours, bloodied her fingers clawing at the door." Joanna's chest constricted at the memory. It still made her sick to think of the bolt secured in place. Someone had locked her in there, either their mother—drunk and sick of taking care of her—or Travis, also likely drunk or high. But the bolt hadn't locked itself. Joanna had never told Katie the door had been locked.

"That's disturbing."

"Yeah. But again, she was scared of virtually nothing else. Not walking alone at night, not strangers or spiders or heights. If someone grabbed her, she'd have fought. There was no disturbance at the schoolhouse, and like I said, Randy, Liam and I walked the road back into town. If someone pulled up and grabbed her, there should have been signs of that. Katie would have intentionally left stuff. I know it."

"So you think someone she knew took her?"

11

Joanna considered Graves. As a waitress at the Sidewinder, she knew practically everyone in town. So had Katie. "I can't imagine anyone who knew Katie wanting to hurt her."

"What about the police investigation? Are they in contact with you?"

Joanna sighed and stood. She grabbed the notebook from the kitchen counter and walked it to where Celeste sat. "I've called them six times in the last month and they haven't returned one of my calls. Not one."

"That's what all these dates are? Times you called?"

"The most recent calls, yes. They always tell me Detective Stark, he's the one working the case, is in a meeting or out."

"Was there ever a time when they were keeping you up to date? Staying in contact?"

"A little more in the beginning. We had Detective Marly then, but he ended up moving downstate with his wife a couple of months after Katie disappeared. He'd met Katie and wasn't as quick as some of the other people in town to say she ran off.

He came here to the apartment and looked around, called me when leads came in."

"What were those?"

"Umm…" Joanna took the notebook and flipped back toward the earliest pages. She'd started keeping notes in the book weeks after Katie disappeared. Camile had suggested it one day after Joanna had been furiously digging through her purse in search of a receipt she'd written a woman's name and number on after the lady mentioned seeing someone who looked like Katie. Joanna never had found the receipt and had broken down in the women's bathroom at the Sidewinder, locked in a stall, bawling, terrified she'd lost the one clue that might have led her to Katie. Camile had talked her down from the ledge, then driven her to a store so they could buy a notebook to keep all the future tips in.

"Random sightings mostly, none of which panned out." Joanna pointed to her hastily scrawled words.

Someone pounded on the door and Joanna jumped. "Just one second," she told Celeste.

Joanna rarely had visitors, other than an occasional drop-in from Randy or Camile. She pulled the door open to find her landlord Raymond in the hall. He stared at her from beady gray eyes sunken in his weathered face. His mouth was puckered in his signature scowl.

"Hi, Ray. Do you need something?"

He braced a hand on the doorframe and peered into her apartment.

"Are you looking for someone?" she asked.

"Yeah," he barked. "Whoever you had makin' that racket in here. Sounded like they had their music cranked so loud people in Bellaire could probably hear it."

Joanna frowned at him. "I worked at the diner all day. There wasn't anyone here."

His eyes narrowed on Celeste. "There's somebody in there now."

"She came in with me ten minutes ago."

"You tryin' to say I'm lying?" he demanded. "That music was so loud my entire ceiling was vibrating downstairs. I still have a headache. I come all the way up and pounded on this door and hollered and somebody turned that music down not five minutes later."

"I swear there was no one here."

He glared at her. "Think I'm hearing things, huh? Rents are goin' up all over the place and I'm still rentin' these apartments for peanuts and even then, I get taken advantage of. Can't even have a moment of peace."

"Ray, I'm really sorry. Truly, but the music had to have been coming from someplace else. I wasn't here and you know that... that Katie's been missing for nearly a year."

"Yeah, yeah." He offered her a dismissive wave. He walked away, grumbling, and Joanna swallowed the saliva that had pooled in her mouth.

She hated renting from Raymond. He was an unpleasant man who'd only gotten meaner as the years went on. Even Katie, who found a silver lining in everyone, had referred to him as Count Raymond, inspired by the similarly named Count Rugen, a character from *The Princess Bride* who delighted in the study and act of torture.

"Everything okay?" Celeste asked when Joanna returned to the living room.

Joanna nodded, though everything didn't feel okay. Her nerves pulsed beneath her skin and sweat coated the small of her back. It was not beneath Raymond to evict her. "My landlord said I had music playing too loud today, but I was at the diner all day. Maybe he's losing it."

"Does anyone else have a key or ever use your place? The tea kettle did seem like it had recently been used."

Joanna shook her head for longer than was necessary. "No. No one. Katie had a key, but no one else."

"You might want to think of getting your locks changed."

It took a moment for Joanna to understand the implication. "You think whoever took Katie is breaking into my apartment?"

Celeste's eyebrows pulled together. "To play music and make tea? Seems unlikely, but better safe than sorry."

Joanna thought of the sounds she'd heard in the previous nights, the curtains being moved, but she'd searched. There'd been no one in her apartment.

"Any other leads?" Celeste asked, gesturing at the notebook Joanna had left on the coffee table.

Joanna picked it up and flipped through the pages, notes scribbled throughout—messages about white pickup trucks, about Declan possibly having scratches on his face after Katie disappeared, about lights on at the schoolhouse at odd hours, about unconfirmed sightings.

Joanna found one and paused, remembering the phone call from Detective Marly, the way her heart had plummeted and her mouth had filled with spit as if she might vomit.

"A pair of jeans, panties and a sweater found in Mancelona. Possibly bloodstained." Joanna read her previous note. "They weren't hers. I was so sick on the drive to the police station, I nearly pulled over. I kept thinking 'the police found her clothes and they're bloody and slashed and the police will do a search and they'll find her body...'" Joanna pulled her eyes from the page, looked into Celeste's. "I knew the instant I saw them they weren't hers. The jeans were narrow, skinny jeans—another thing Katie wouldn't wear. It was a relief and also... I don't know, a disappointment, because it felt like maybe there was finally going to be an answer.

"I got back to the diner and Camile burst into tears when I told everyone they weren't hers. We all stood around crying and hugging and happy they weren't hers, but I had this very hollow feeling. We were no closer to the truth and Katie was still gone."

"No other leads?" Celeste asked.

Joanna could hear the disappointment in her voice. It was a feeling she knew well. "Crazy, right? How can that be it? Marly told me a few times there'd been other calls about sightings, but they'd ruled them out based on descriptions and stuff. But sometimes I got this sense that he leaned that way too, towards the possibility that she left. He'd say things like 'If somebody in Graves had hurt her, we'd have found her by now,' so... I don't know if that meant he thought someone outside of Graves had taken her or if he thought she left."

"Huh." Celeste thumbed through the notebook then leaned back. "Anything else going on in her life that you think could be relevant?"

Joanna stood and paced to the window and then back. She thought of the last night she'd been with Katie at the apartment. "There was one odd thing. The night before she went missing, she came home and seemed upset."

"Upset how?"

Joanna frowned. "I don't know exactly, but... I could tell she was trying to pretend everything was fine, but it wasn't. Her eyes were a little red-rimmed, like she'd been crying. I asked her what was wrong. I'd worked the evening shift at the diner, and she got home after me, probably around ten, and there was a moment where I thought she might tell me and then... she said she needed to take a shower. She always showered the night before school rather than in the morning. And afterwards she disappeared into her room, and we never talked about it. The next morning, like I said, we were both rushing around to get out the door."

"Did you ask her friends if anything had happened the night before?"

Joanna nodded. "No one knew. I thought she'd been going to hang out with Liam, but he said he'd ended up staying home to work on something for school. He didn't know why she'd been upset."

"And you never talked to anyone who confirmed where she'd been the night before?"

"No one."

"Huh. That's strange. And she came home after you, so she was definitely out somewhere that night?"

"Yes."

"But she didn't have a car, so she'd have had to walk or get a ride wherever she went."

Joanna nodded.

"How about her cell phone? Did the police ever track it?"

Joanna frowned. "She had it that night, but it was an old phone. It didn't have the 'find your phone' stuff there is now. It disappeared with her."

"How about phone records? Were you able to get those?"

"Yeah. Randy paid for her cell phone, but he showed me the call log for that night. She called Liam around five. He confirmed that, said they talked for about ten minutes, but then he got to Shanty Creek to ski and that was the last he spoke to her."

"And she didn't mention to Liam she was going anywhere after work?"

"No."

"How about any online connections, people she might have met through social media?"

"No. Like I said, Katie's old-school. Not only in the way she dresses and talks. She rarely carried her cell phone and refused to use social media. She insisted the internet had stolen people's ability to be present, to exist in the real world. Honestly, her objections to the internet obsession were a relief.

There was never any bullying on Facebook or whatever. She isn't one of those teenagers who sits across from you at dinner and stares down at her phone. She talks, makes eye contact, loves to chat up the waitress or waiter and ask people about their lives. She was always collecting people's stories."

"She sounds like a very special person."

"She is." Joanna almost said 'was,' felt the word tumbling around her brain, a steel bearing bashing away at her hope, at any belief that Katie could somehow still be alive.

"Okay. No phone. So, after Detective Marly moved, did you meet with the new detective or how did that hand-off go?"

Joanna released a harsh laugh. "No. I didn't even know Marly had moved and was no longer on the case. I'd called three or four times and not gotten a call back and finally I went into the station and the desk sergeant said, 'Marly's gone, moved a month ago. Detective Stark has the case now.' So, I demanded to see him, but the desk guy said he was busy and I said, 'Fine, I'll wait,' and I sat in the waiting area a solid hour before he finally came out and I could tell right away he was annoyed I was there.

"We went back to his office, and I asked if he wanted me to go over Katie's disappearance and he told me, no, he'd already looked through the file. So, then I asked if there were any updates. No updates. I asked if there'd ever been a follow-up interview with Declan and Stark said, 'Who's Declan?' He'd literally just told me he read the file, and he was asking me who Declan was?" Joanna could feel her face growing hot at the memory.

She'd been on edge that day. It had been the anniversary of their mother's death and all day she'd felt the constant swell of emotion—fear and despair and hopelessness. It had been gray and cold out and, in her mind, there'd been a running commentary about how she'd failed to protect Katie, how it was her fault, how even their mother with all her issues had managed to keep both her daughters alive.

"I yelled at him," Joanna admitted. "I yelled and cried and he looked at me like I was a nutcase. You know that look? Like a cross between sympathy and disgust. I stormed out of the office and, like I said, I've called six times in the last month with zero response. He won't talk to me now."

12

———

Celeste saw the fury on Joanna's face as she spoke. The police case in particular seemed to upset her.

"Do you mind if I look in Katie's bedroom?" Celeste asked.

Joanna blinked at her, as if surprised by the sudden shift in subject. "I've searched it top to bottom."

Celeste nodded. "I understand. It can help to have a fresh set of eyes look around. Someone with a different set of biases."

"Biases?"

"Yeah. Most people don't realize that if you handed a hundred people a photograph of a little kid on a swing, a hundred people would observe something different. Some of them would notice if the child was a girl or boy, some might pick up on the shadow of a person standing nearby, a dog in the background, how parched the grass looks. The details are endless. Our perception is so unique. That's one reason eyewitnesses are so unreliable. We see what we believe is there. We see based on a billion factors, from our biology to the way our mother held us as children."

"Meaning I might have missed something."

"You're very familiar with Katie's room and I'm not."

"Okay," Joanna murmured. "It's right over here."

Joanna stood and Celeste followed her down the hall. She stopped at a closed door on the right and took a breath as if gathering her courage. She shot Celeste a tight smile, then turned the knob and pushed the door open.

Celeste stepped into the doorway. The light was off, but sunlight cut through the blinds and cast a grid pattern on the dark carpet.

Joanna walked to a tall lamp with an amber shade hung with tassels. She turned it on and a warm glow lit the room. "If you want more light, there's a lamp on her desk and another one by her bed," Joanna said.

"This is good."

Joanna walked to Katie's bed and paused, staring down. "That's weird," she murmured.

"What?"

Joanna picked up a stuffed tie-dye bear. "I swear this was on her pillows. Never mind. I probably moved it."

Celeste let her eyes drift slowly over the twin bed covered in a bright flower-pattern bedspread. The flowers were big and cartoonish, seventies flower-power style.

A lava lamp sat on the bedside table. One wall contained an enormous Janis Joplin poster and a map of California. Another wall was covered in records, the ceiling obscured by more posters, including Jim Morrison, Blondie and Led Zeppelin.

Celeste listened and waited. She sensed something was in the room, some integral piece of the puzzle, but what and where?

"Katie didn't keep a diary?" Celeste asked.

Joanna shook her head. "No. I looked in case she had a secret one, but I never found anything."

"Is it okay if I touch some of her things?"

"By all means. I'll give you a few minutes alone."

Celeste closed her eyes, willed Katie to speak to her.

Nothing.

When she opened her eyes, she let them drift over Katie's things, searched for a pull, a nudge toward some space in the room. She didn't get one.

After a moment she walked in and let her fingers trail over Katie's bed, her desk. She picked up a framed photograph of Katie and Liam in roller skates, arms looped around each other's waists. She opened the closet and briefly touched several t-shirts before she knelt and scanned beneath the clothes. A few pairs of shoes, bags, shoeboxes.

Celeste sighed and stood. She'd hoped stepping into Katie's room would cause the girl's spirit to reveal something.

As she started toward the door, two words arose in Celeste's mind: *Scooby Doo*.

She turned back and searched for any item depicting the mystery-solving gang. She moved to the row of old metal lunch boxes on Katie's bookshelf and scanned each. No Scooby Doo.

Celeste found Joanna in the living room. She'd made her own glass of schnapps and sat perched on the edge of the couch, tapping both feet.

"Refill?" Joanna asked, leaning forward and lifting the bottle.

"I still have some left. Thank you." In truth, Celeste found the sickly sweet schnapps turned her stomach and she doubted she'd finish her glass. "Did Katie own anything connected to Scooby Doo?"

Joanna blinked at her "A pencil case."

"Can I see it?"

"Sure. Okay." Joanna looked puzzled, but she said nothing as she led Celeste back to Katie's room. Joanna opened the top drawer of Katie's desk to reveal a vintage metal pencil case with an image of Scooby and Shaggy in front of the Mystery Machine van.

Celeste took it out and flipped the lid. A jumble of jewelry sat inside, but Celeste was instantly drawn to a black lace choker with a white pearl flower in the center.

"Where did this come from?" Celeste picked up the choker.

Joanna took the necklace from Celeste's hand and shook her head. "I'm not sure. I don't remember ever seeing her wear it. Why are you interested in it?"

Celeste stared at the choker, couldn't shake the uneasy feeling that it was somehow connected to Katie's disappearance. "I can't give you an answer that will make sense. Do you mind if I take a picture of it?"

Joanna laid it out on Katie's desk. "I wish I could remember where it came from."

Celeste snapped a photo of the necklace with her phone.

Joanna reached into the case and took out a silver ID bracelet engraved with the words *Silver Girl*.

Celeste looked at it. "Silver Girl?"

"It was a nickname my mom gave her as a baby. Her hair was so blond it looked silver. Each year from the time she was five on, it got darker and darker, but we still called her 'silver girl.'"

Joanna returned the bracelet to the case and closed it. Celeste sensed she was struggling not to cry.

"How about her laptop?" Celeste pointed at it. "Did you search that?"

Joanna nodded. "Liam and I did after she disappeared. We didn't find anything, no emails about meeting someone, nothing like that."

"Did she use it often?"

"Not really. No. She wrote papers on it for school, mostly. It's old and half the time the internet wouldn't work. Usually if she needed to do internet stuff, she'd do it on a computer at school or at the Graves library."

"I'd like to meet Liam. Could we make that happen tomorrow?" Celeste asked.

"Absolutely. I'll text him right now."

"Perfect, and where can I find a cork board, that kind of thing?"

"A cork board?"

"Yeah. I always use them in the lab. Helps me organize my thoughts."

"The Graves hardware and grocery store has a bit of everything."

"Okay. Great. And the schoolhouse? If I stop by, will there be someone working who knew Katie?"

Joanna nodded. "Yes. May is there, and she oversees all the day-to-day operations. She'll happily talk to you and show you around."

CELESTE PULLED into the parking lot marked by a wooden sign that stated 'Graves Schoolhouse Museum.'

Only one other vehicle, a white Subaru, sat in the lot. Celeste climbed from her car and surveyed the fieldstone schoolhouse, stoic against the wintry landscape surrounding it. Tall narrow windows sat in time-worn frames. An odd sensation tickled the back of Celeste's neck as she stared at the schoolhouse. She swiped her hand beneath her hair as if expecting to come away with an insect, though she knew the tickle had occurred beneath her skin.

A monster oak tree stood off to one side, its branches skeletal. As she looked at it, a vision formed in her mind of a similar tree, massive, with a huge pulsing red root structure slithering beneath the soil.

From the oak, a raven cawed and took flight, passing over Celeste and disappearing into the dense pine forest.

When Celeste pushed open the schoolhouse door, it groaned, a distinctive sound, like a girl's terrified shriek.

"Don't mind the door," a woman called, waving Celeste forward. "It's old and cranky. Come in, come in." She stepped from a display of books and walked over. She was short and slim, wearing jeans and a Graves Badgers sweatshirt. Her gray hair was cut in a bob that framed her face. "Welcome to the stone schoolhouse, also known as the Graves Museum. I'm May. Would you like the guided tour? It's free."

"Actually, I wanted to ask you some questions about Katie Ellis."

May's hand went to her throat. "Katie? I... of course. I'd be happy to offer any assistance I can. Are you a private detective? I know Joanna was talking about hiring someone."

"No, but I am trying to help her figure out what happened to Katie." Above them, Celeste heard several creaks as if someone walked across the floor. "Is someone upstairs?"

May glanced up and shook her head. "This old schoolhouse rarely stops talking. The girls sometimes said it was haunted, and maybe it is in a way. I suspect any place old enough to witness the passage of a century has too many stories to tell to keep its mouth shut."

Celeste suspected May was right and they were not alone in the schoolhouse.

13

———

"Were you here the last night Katie was seen?" Celeste asked May, scanning the antique furniture and faded photographs arranged throughout the space.

May's mouth turned down. Her eyes grew misty. "I wish I had been. I was clear across the state, down in the Lansing area, visiting my sister, who had her hip replaced. She was doing fine, but bored out of her mind, so I'd gone down to keep her company for a few days. There are three other volunteers and two teens who worked part-time—Katie and Mara, both in high school—but Katie worked alone that night. Winter and all. It's as quiet as a graveyard here in January. Oh!" She paled and put a hand over her mouth. "I shouldn't have said that. That was a terrible thing to say."

"I understand how you meant it," Celeste assured her. "That was a usual thing then? Katie working alone?"

"Oh, yes. Only in summer during the weekends do we have two people here, one to explain some of the history and another to run our little gift shop. Even then one person could probably handle it, but now and again we'll get a big bus of tourists on some kind of wine outing over in Traverse City who make their way here to Graves. I know some locals get annoyed when the tourists roll through, but I appreciate the infusion of joy they bring. Gets us through these gray months."

"Do you remember the last time you saw Katie?"

"Most definitely. I talked with her and Jo on my way out of town to visit my sister. I stopped by the diner to get a big Styrofoam cup of coffee. Floyd, the owner of the Sidewinder, buys the good coffee, not the cheap stuff. Not that I'm against the cheap stuff." She chuckled and pointed to a coffee can on a cart near the door. "We don't get enough funding to buy Starbucks around here, but now and then I like to treat myself.

"I stopped into the diner and Jo was waiting tables and Katie was sitting in a booth working on some kind of school paper or something. I had a quick chat with them and told Katie I'd see her the following week." May's mouth pursed into a little bud. She shook her head slowly. "You never think twice about such things, do you? Not when people are young. When they get old or sick, we do a long goodbye, hugs and well-wishes and the works, but when someone is young, we take for granted we'll see them again in no time at all."

A phone near the cash register rang and May started towards it.

"I'm going to look around," Celeste told her.

May gave her a thumbs-up before picking up the phone. "Graves Schoolhouse Museum. This is May."

Celeste moved along one wall titled *Graves Through the Years*. Faded photographs hung in frames, spans of dates beneath, and for each decade a shelf displayed vintage items from that time period. The narrative went back to the mid-1800s when Graves was founded by a man named Howard Graves.

At the back of the first level stood a dark wooden staircase. A sign at the bottom stated *More History This Way* with an arrow pointing up the stairs. Celeste walked up, studying the sepia-toned photos that lined the wall.

She paused at the top of the stairs and frowned. Several mannequins dressed in the fashion of a bygone era stood posed near an old record player. One wore a sixties mod-style bright red and orange dress and had a wig of long flowing brown hair, parted in the middle, disturbingly similar to Katie.

As she moved around the room, she passed in front of an antique mirror. From the corner of her eye, she caught a glimpse of the sixties mannequin as it lifted its arm. Celeste spun around. The mannequin stood as it had been, unchanged, both arms near its sides.

AFTER SHE'D WALKED through the schoolhouse, Celeste returned to where May stood arranging pamphlets.

"May, you never noticed anything out of place after you came back from Lansing, right? Anything missing? Or stuff that had been disturbed, broken?"

"Not a thing," May said, "and believe me, Camile and I went through a complete inventory to make sure nothing had been stolen in case Katie's disappearance was a robbery gone wrong. I know this place like the back of my hand. It didn't look like even a book had been put back in the wrong place."

"Where's this lead?" Celeste asked, gesturing at a wooden door with an 'employees only' sign attached to the front.

"That's the root cellar. When the school was open, they had their own garden out back. The teachers and some kids tended it in the summer and they'd store all the canned fruits and veggies down there."

"Does anyone use it now?"

"Oh, no. No one except the spiders. I'm sure they're quite at home. We used to use it as storage, but it's so damp if you leave anything down there for a couple weeks or longer it gets mildewed."

"Is it locked other than this?" Celeste gestured at the small bolt attached to the outside of the door. A shudder ran through as she remembered the story Joanna had shared about a young Katie getting locked inside her mother's basement.

May reached past Celeste, pulled the lock aside, and turned the knob. The door swung open and a draft of cold, musty air wafted into their faces. A set of steep wooden steps descended into the darkness. It was so pitch black Celeste could not see where the steps ended.

"No need for additional locks. No one wants to go down there," May murmured.

***

CELESTE RETURNED to the condo with three large bulletin boards she'd picked up at the Graves Grocery and Hardware as well as a paper bag of Graves maps, post-it notes, pens and highlighters.

The struggle started when Celeste had to maneuver the corkboards into the condo at Shanty Creek. In the end she dropped three of them and had to backtrack to the staircase multiple times, once losing her cane and watching it tumble to the tiled lobby below, where it landed at the feet of a startled teenager wearing headphones. Fortunately, he ran the cane up to her and saved her yet another excruciating walk down the stairs.

Celeste swallowed a couple of pain pills and poured a glass of Scotch, then went to work attaching the bulletin boards to the wall with removable putty. She posted the maps first and placed red tacks in all the places Katie had visited on her last day. She tied string between the tacks, tracing her movements. Then she jotted down theories on post-it notes and put those on a separate board with space beneath to confirm or refute those theories. *Ran away, abducted, murdered.* She listed people who'd seen Katie the day she vanished, potential suspects, and weird bits of information she sensed were relevant such as the black and pearl choker.

IT WAS NEARLY two a.m. when Celeste limped into bed. Her left hip and leg were stiff and hot. She'd spent hours on the boards, listing every scenario of what might have happened to Katie and ordering the likelihood of each by probability. She didn't have enough information yet to reach any solid conclusions, but statistically, the most likely culprit was Declan Boyd. In the United States, nearly fifty percent of women murdered were killed by their intimate partner.

He'd been a somewhat secret boyfriend, and the relationship was volatile. Katie had known him and would have willingly gotten into his truck, which explained no signs of a struggle.

Celeste had done some digging online into the Boyd family. She'd found multiple legal notices regarding Warren Boyd, often him suing or being sued. She'd found one notice where Warren had been arrested for drunk and disorderly conduct, another where his son Todd had been arrested for burglarizing vacation properties. Declan clearly had been brought up in a dysfunctional family, which only further supported the likelihood that he'd hurt Katie.

Celeste settled back onto the pillows and pulled the covers up, grateful the bed came equipped with a heating blanket, which she turned on low, hoping that might soothe her sore body. Her stomach rumbled, and she tried to remember the last time she'd eaten—that morning, maybe.

When she closed her eyes, thoughts of Jonathan snuck in.

They'd spoken briefly hours before, and she'd offered a litany of untruths about what she'd been up to: reading, doing the physical therapy exercises, walking outside. He'd asked several times when she intended to come home and each time she'd changed the subject.

Thoughts of home made her left hip and leg itch. She reached down and felt the bandage from her tattoo. There was aftercare she'd neglected. Before her accident, she'd never neglected anything. She'd taken her vitamins every day, drunk sixty-four ounces of water, walked ten thousand steps. She'd cleaned the house, brushed the cat, never missed a day at work.

And now she was drifting to sleep in a stranger's bed, in an unfamiliar town, with details of the last night of a seventeen-year-old girl's life unraveling like spools of thread in her mind.

A SCREAM SPLIT THE NIGHT. Celeste jerked awake, sat up, and scrambled from her bed. The sudden weight on her leg sent a flaming poker into her brain and she gasped and braced both hands on the mattress.

For a moment she was disoriented, the shapes in the room unfamiliar, and then the memory registered. She was in the condo at Shanty Creek. Moonlight poured through a crack in the curtains and made the alien room less strange.

A second scream tore through the room, and Celeste recoiled. It had come from under her bed. Panting, pain causing her stomach to do loopy nauseous rolls, she bent and dropped to her knees, peering beneath the bed.

A girl's face, pale as the moonlight, eyes wide and full of terror, stared back at her.

"Help me," she whispered, one hand reaching forward. In the same instant, something—some*one*—jerked the girl from the opposite side of the bed as if they'd taken hold of both her legs and hauled her out.

Celeste cried out, reached for her hand, but it was gone, fading with the sound of her scream as she was dragged away into the darkness.

Celeste stared beneath the empty bed, seeing the loamy dark, traces of dust on the wood floor, nothing else. There was no thrashing girl on the other side, no pair of legs belonging to the person who'd pulled her out.

14

———

"I got an email from *Northern Michigan News*," Joanna said breathlessly as she walked into the diner. It wasn't quite six-thirty a.m. Camile and Floyd stood near the counter, talking and sipping coffee. Joanna slid two trays of muffins she'd baked the night before for the book club onto the counter. "They're going to send a reporter to cover the candle-light vigil."

They both looked up at the same time and Joanna saw something pinched in Camile's face. Floyd quickly hid his grim expression with a smile.

"What is it? What's wrong?" Joanna asked.

Camile glanced at Floyd, clearly didn't want to reveal what had them both so somber. "Most of the fliers we put up about the vigil have been torn down," Camile said.

Joanna blinked at her. "No. Why? Who would do that? Which ones got ripped down?"

"They're all gone from the telephone poles on the road near the schoolhouse. The ones downtown are mostly gone."

Joanna sat heavily in one of the chairs at the counter. "I don't get it. People loved Katie and we're trying so hard."

Through the speakers, Billie Holiday crooned *Gloomy Sunday*, lamenting the numberless shadows she lived with. Joanna felt her lip quivering, her eyes tearing up.

"Hold on now," Floyd said, rubbing her back and then pulling Camile closer when she too grew misty-eyed. "How many people see those fliers anyway? We put an ad in the *Graves Newspaper*. We've let everyone know to spread the word."

"How about social media?" Camile asked. "I'll post something to the Sidewinder page. And you should update the Come Home, Katie page."

Joanna nodded, swiped at her face. "Yeah. I haven't posted any updates in months."

"There. See," Floyd said. "Solutions. That's how we combat this kind of negativity. It was probably some little punks hell-bent on destruction and the fliers were their best choice to ruin something and not get caught."

"Or it was—" Camile started, but she quickly shut her mouth as two men ambled up to the door.

Joanna knew what Camile had been about to say. Maybe it was the person who'd hurt Katie, who'd taken her, doing their best to keep her story out of the public eye. It wasn't the first time someone had thwarted their efforts to bring attention to Katie's disappearance. One of their earlier searches had been called off by an anonymous person who'd called into a radio station advertising the search and told the DJ it had been cancelled. When Joanna had arrived at the schoolhouse, only five people had shown up, including Floyd, Camile, Randy and a few of Katie's school friends.

"Here come the Groovy Gramps," Floyd said. "I better get moving on the bacon."

The Groovy Gramps had acquired their name from Katie, who'd encountered them several mornings before school and noticed that one of them wore a cardigan with a peace sign sewn onto the pocket. The name had stuck and the group of seniors had eventually embraced it to the point where one of their wives had made them all matching tie-dye *Groovy Gramps* t-shirts for a cruise.

Joanna forced on a smile and opened the door for the men. "Good morning, Thad, Gene. How are ya?"

The two men, bundled in winter coats, one hobbling thanks to bad knees that he refused to get replaced, pushed into the diner.

"Not too shabby, Jo," Thad said, pulling off his fur-lined hat and heading for their usual table in the corner. "Though I woke up this morning and thought I'd been transported to the set of *Misery*. Snow piled to the windows and my wife standing over me like Annie Wilkes. Lucky for me she was just givin' me my daily pills."

Joanna laughed. "I don't think your wife would appreciate the comparison. How are you, Gene?"

"Be a hell of a lot better if I was in Florida," Gene grumbled, holding the backs of chairs as he followed Thad.

"The usual?" Joanna asked.

"Yep," Thad answered. "And how are you today, Jo? Any news on Kit Kat?"

Joanna's heart swelled at the nickname, which she rarely heard anymore. "No news, but we're holding a candlelight vigil at the stone schoolhouse on Saturday to try and get people talking again."

"We'll be there," Thad said.

"And are the rest of Groovy Gramps coming this morning?" She made her way to the counter and pulled out coffee mugs, trying to shift her focus to the men and away from thoughts about who would have been so cruel as to destroy the fliers about Katie's vigil.

"No Davis this morning," Thad said. "His wife called and he's down with some kind of sinus thing. Apparently, he was coughin' so bad last night she almost strangled him in his sleep."

Gene, still pulling off his gloves and scarf, grimaced. "Had my grandkids by last weekend and all three of them little snot factories. It's a miracle I'm not down with it myself, knock on wood." He rapped his knuckles on the table.

"Vinnie and Bart should be here anytime," Thad added.

"Speak of the devils," Gene said as a mustard-yellow sedan pulled into a spot in front of the diner.

Vinnie and Bart climbed from the car and hurried into the Sidewinder.

"Holy kamoly, it's cold out there!" Bart announced, rubbing his gloved hands together. "That coffee better be pipin' hot, Jo."

"Hot enough to melt those icicles hanging from your nose hairs," Thad called, taking a shaky sip of his own coffee.

"Brewed fresh," Joanna told him. "Short stacks and bacon for you both?"

"Yep, the usual," Bart said.

"Hold the bacon for me this morning," Vinnie said. "Had heartburn like a son of a bitch last night." He rubbed his sternum.

"I'll see your heartburn and raise you kidney stones," Gene said, scowling as he massaged his lower back. "And I gotta pass 'em too. Half thought about sending my car off a bridge on the way into town."

"What bridge?" Thad demanded. "Only bridge we got in this town runs over Hurdle Creek, which is about as deep as a teacup."

Camile grabbed Jo's elbow and steered her into the back. "Don't let this get you down. Okay, honey? The vigil is gonna be great."

"I bet my sister could get a good deal on candles," Floyd called above the bacon sizzling in one of the three frying pans he had on the stove. "She's ordering bulk stuff all the time for the flower shop and they deliver on Fridays, so let me know how many and I'll ask her to get them ordered."

"Candles," Joanna moaned. "I didn't even think of getting those. Leave it to me to put together a candlelight vigil and forget the candles."

"You've got a lot on your plate, honey," Camile said. "And we wouldn't have let you forget the candles."

"Thanks, Camile. I don't know what I'd do without you guys." The diner phone rang and Joanna hurried out to answer it. "Sidewinder. This is Jo. How can I help you?"

Silence.

Joanna looked at the caller I.D. Restricted number.

"Hello? Anyone there?" She waited, figured it was a call center that dialed numbers constantly and any minute some salesperson would click on, but then the faint sound of breath came over the line.

"Sidewinder," she said evenly, though her pulse had picked up. Someone was there listening.

For a moment she imagined Katie somewhere in the world, captive, picking up the phone, mouth duct-taped, and calling the diner.

Joanna clutched the phone tighter. "Katie?" she whispered.

She heard a click and the line went dead.

15

———

Celeste had drunk too much coffee. Her nerves jumped and skittered like water bugs on the surface of a pond.

After her encounter the night before, she'd been unable to fall back asleep. Instead, she'd gotten up and returned to work on Katie's case. She'd stared for most of the morning at the boards, searched for the spark of connection that would send her into the rabbit hole of research, but her mind refused to go there. It wanted to ruminate on the previous night's visit, on all the visits, on the apparitions and voices and shadowy figures that had entered her life when the doctors had brought her back from the dead.

Had it been Katie beneath the bed? This time giving her a glimpse into what had happened during her last night?

Espresso Mike's, the little coffee shop in Graves, had grown quiet. The busyness of the morning commute, which was little more than a trickle, had died nearly an hour before. Celeste had a list of people she wanted to talk to: Liam, Declan, the detective working Katie's case. Celeste had left a message with Detective Stark at the Graves police station to call her back, but she wouldn't hold her breath. Even the desk sergeant had been dismissive when she explained why she'd called.

"Do you have what you need?"

Celeste turned to see a coffee shop employee standing behind her. She had long blonde hair in a ponytail and unnerving pale blue eyes. Her nametag read 'Adrien.'

"I do. Thanks."

Adrien stared through the window, a yearning in her eyes as two teen girls holding hands walked by, their faces split with laughter.

"Have we met before, Adrien?" Celeste asked. A cold finger traced down her spine. *Pay attention,* it seemed to say, but she couldn't fathom what she was meant to pay attention to.

"I don't think so," Adrien murmured.

"What's your last name?"

"Collins," she said after a moment. "Enjoy your morning."

Celeste watched her walk behind the counter and disappear through a door into a back room.

WHEN CELESTE ARRIVED at the Sidewinder, she waited near the door as Joanna finished dropping off a tray of food to a family in a booth.

"Hi," Joanna said. "How's everything going? Did you talk to May?"

"I did. The schoolhouse was interesting." Celeste didn't add how uneasy she'd felt inside of it.

"She really loved that schoolhouse. Loves." Joanna shook her head, tearing up and then swiping in frustration at her eyes. "That's Liam." She pointed to a thin teenager with chin-length black hair parted on the side. He wore stylish black glasses and a black shirt buttoned high. He looked out of place against the other patrons, dressed in flannels and bulky sweaters. "He's expecting you."

"Perfect."

"Can I bring you something? Our special tonight is a hot roast beef sandwich. It's really good."

"How about a cup of water and a grilled cheese?"

"Sure. I'll have it over in a few minutes."

Celeste crossed the diner to where Liam sat scrolling through his phone. "Liam?"

He looked up and smiled, setting the cell face down. "Hi. You're Celeste?"

"I am. May I sit?"

"For sure." He glanced at her cane, which she wedged into the booth beside her. "Joanna said you got hit by a car. That's wack."

"It definitely wasn't my best day," Celeste told him.

"For real. It's really cool that you're helping find Katie. Jo has been giving off some serious depressed vibes. I even told my mom I thought we should try to get her to see a therapist. I've had a therapist since I was ten, but my mom felt like Jo might get offended."

"You've had a therapist since you were ten?"

"Yep. My parents got divorced. That's when it started, but Holly, my therapist, is like my lifeline. I run everything by her. Katie even came with me a few times. She's totally awesome."

"Why did Katie go with you? Were you and her ever... more than friends?"

Liam chuckled and brushed his long hair off his face. "No. Katie actually came to help me work out how I was going to come out."

"Come out?"

"Of the closet. I'm gay."

"Oh," Celeste said, warmth rushing into her face. "Okay, yeah. I understand. So Katie helped you work through that."

"Katie helped me with everything. She was like my unpaid everyday therapist." He laughed, but Celeste noticed his eyes swimming with tears. He reached forward and grabbed his pop, took a drink. "Sugar and caffeine," he said. "It's my 'don't cry' method. I don't know why, but it totally works."

Celeste smiled. "Did it go okay? Coming out?"

Liam fiddled with the straw in his plastic cup. "Mostly, yeah. My dad's still in denial. He moved up to Marquette a few years ago, so I rarely see him. Anytime I go, he points out every attractive girl at every place we visit, like if he finds one pretty enough, I suddenly won't be into guys anymore. It's fine though. I'm over it. Everybody in Graves knows at this point, but I don't exactly put it on display. I'm not rallying people to have a parade or anything. It's still pretty old-school around here, you know? We're definitely not in San Francisco, but another six months and I will be."

"You're moving to California?"

"Yep. I'm starting at San Francisco State next year. My cousin lives out there and I'm going to rent a room at her place. I'm sure it's going to be nuts. She's got like six room-mates, but I'm totally excited. I can't wait to get out of Graves. Except... well, for Katie. I feel wrong leaving without knowing, you know? And then there's this other part of me that tells myself maybe she's out there. Maybe she pursued that totally crazy dream of hitching a ride to California and living on a beach."

"Was that a dream she had?"

Liam took another drink, eyes again welling with tears. "Not gonna cry. See, I'm fine. 'Liam, you're fine,'" he told himself out loud. "Yeah, it was one of those dreams that she didn't actually intend to do. She would say it like... 'If it were fifty years ago and there were no weirdos, I'd love to hitch a ride in a converted school bus and head for California.' It wasn't a dream that existed in the here and now. You know? It was like dreaming of being alive during the roaring twenties so you could go to a speakeasy."

Celeste nodded. She got it. She'd had her own teenage dreams of travelling to some place where the grass was greener. For her it had been West Virginia, a place she'd lived until she was eight when her dad, a single father, had decided to relocate his two children to Michigan for work. Celeste had vague memories of childhood summers chasing shadows in the sun-drenched forest or finding bright pebbles in the cold mountain streams.

"Liam, do you mind if I record our conversation? I'm trying to keep track of all the information I'm getting about Katie, and my memory's atrocious and my handwriting's even worse, otherwise I'd take notes."

"Who will hear it?" he asked, face paling.

"No one but me. Really. It's just for me to start putting facts about Katie's life together."

"All right."

Celeste took out her cellphone and opened the recording app. "Did Katie know you were planning on San Francisco?" she asked.

"Not really. I mean, we hadn't started applying to colleges yet. We'd spitball places we'd love to go, but it was looking like she might end up in Florida because Jo's boyfriend had moved down there and wanted Jo and Katie to join him. Katie felt pretty conflicted about all that." Liam glanced at Jo, who was waiting on a table on the opposite side of the diner.

He dropped his voice. "She wanted to go for Jo's sake, you know? But that would have meant doing her senior year at a different school, which I can tell you she was not excited about. My mom told her she could live with us for the year and finish school here in Graves if she wanted to, and I think she was considering that, but she was worried Jo would feel pressured to stay, too. That's the way Jo is. Like, she took responsibility for Katie after their mom died and it became her whole life. If she left with her boyfriend and didn't take Katie, it would have eaten her up inside. So we spent a lot of time talking about that in the last weeks before Katie disappeared."

"Did Katie want to leave Graves? Did she have hopes of going to college somewhere else?"

"Oh, yeah. For sure. I mean, Graves is great for what it is. Everyone knows everyone. If your car battery dies, you can walk to any shop and ask for a jump. It's a decent town, but like I said, old-school. Even though Katie was into everything retro, she had that hippie way of seeing the world and that's not Graves. Graves is solidly blue-collar, conservative, you know? Work hard, play hard, go to church and die."

"And how about her sometimes-boyfriend, Declan? What can you tell me about him?"

Liam looked uncomfortable. "I do not know what she saw in him unless there's some truth to the idea that we're, like, attracted to our bad parent. You know? I read that somewhere once. That if one of your parents sucks, you'll likely search for that person as a mate to fill the void left by them. I seriously hope not—I do not want to end up with a guy like my dad." He shuddered.

"Anyway, Declan was like a younger Travis—Katie's dad. That whole 'F the world, I do it my way' mentality."

"That bad, huh?"

Liam's hair had again fallen across one eye and he fanned it back. "Maybe I'm biased," he admitted. "Warren Boyd is hard-core anti-gay. I'm pretty sure Declan and his brother Todd are too. Declan was into Katie, so he pretended to like me if I was around, but he didn't, not really. He's the kind of guy that if I encountered alone at night, I'd hide or run away from. He gives me that vibe, like he'd happily swerve to hit me if he saw me walking down the side of the road." Liam's eyes darted to her cane, and he covered his mouth. "Shit. Sorry. That was like totally not the right thing to say."

Celeste shook her head. "Don't worry about that. Do you think Declan could be violent?"

"Yeah. He and one of his buddies almost got expelled our sophomore year for kicking the crap out of some kid from another school after they lost a football game. What's crazy is the game wasn't even close. Graves got demolished, but still Declan and this kid, Steve, totally cornered a guy from the away team behind the stands and went apeshit on him. He lost a tooth and had to get stitches in his head."

"And they didn't get expelled?" Celeste asked, sick at the vision of the boy getting attacked. More reinforcement for the theory that Declan had hurt Katie.

"Nope. Declan and Steve said the kid started it, threw the first punch or whatever, which he might have once he got cornered by those two gorillas, but regardless of whoever started it, they went way too far. Declan's dad also stirred up a shitstorm at the mention of Declan getting expelled and, finally, they just suspended both kids for like two weeks."

"He got a slap on the wrist for putting a kid in the hospital?"

"Yeah."

"Was he ever violent with Katie?"

"I want to say no. We told each other almost everything, but... I've heard the stories about people who hide abuse and stuff, so I don't want to be naïve about it."

"Did you ever see any bruises?"

"No."

Liam's face darkened and for an instant, Katie sat beside him as if Celeste watched a movie screen and there was a sudden glitch, the girl appearing and disappearing in a split second. Celeste flinched and Liam looked around nervously.

"What is it?" he asked.

Celeste swallowed, pressed her trembling hands beneath her thighs on the leather seat. "Nothing. Sorry. Got a chill."

Liam blinked at her and nodded. "To answer your question, I do think it's possible Declan hurt Katie, but you didn't hear it from me. I've told Jo as much and I know she told the Graves police, but..." He fiddled with his straw. "People in this town try not to mess with the Boyds. I wouldn't be surprised if the police avoid them too."

"The Boyd family includes the dad, Warren, and two sons, Todd and Declan. Is there a mom around?"

"Rosie. Yeah. She's kind of reclusive. It's sad really. When we were kids, she volunteered at school, helped at holiday parties and events, and then at some point she stopped."

"She and Boyd are still married?"

"Oh, yeah. Though I doubt it's a happy home. I wouldn't be surprised if Warren beats her and the boys. They're all pretty screwed up around there."

"Okay. So, if you had to guess what happened to Katie, you'd be leaning toward what?"

Liam pushed his hands through his hair. He looked ill at ease. "I truly don't know. I wish I did. If I did, I'd say it, but..."

"I understand you don't know," Celeste said. "But you were her best friend. What's your gut telling you?"

His eyes darted around the restaurant as if he was worried someone might be eavesdropping. He leaned forward and dropped his voice. "Declan. Without a doubt."

16

———

"Why don't I get the impression that Jo suspects Declan of hurting Katie?" Celeste asked.

Liam glanced at Joanna. "She wants Katie to be alive. I do too, of course, but... it feels really unlikely."

"And you think he could have hurt her and kept his mouth shut?"

Liam stared off thoughtfully. "I get the sense Declan keeps a lot of secrets. Like I said, his family is screwed up, but you'll never hear him say that. His whole family hides what goes on at home."

"What makes you say that?"

Liam chewed the edge of his thumbnail. "Rumors around school mostly. And both his dad and brother have been arrested, but they strut around like they're untouchable."

"Do you have any idea where Katie was the night before she disappeared? Jo mentioned she came home that night acting upset."

Liam tugged on the collar of his shirt and shook his head. "No. I stayed home, had a school thing, so..."

"What were you guys supposed to do that night?"

"Um… God, I don't even remember now. Let's see, probably the usual—drive around, talk. We did that a lot, though in the summer we walked. Katie loves to walk."

"Why wouldn't you go to her apartment or your house to hang out and talk?"

"Oh, we did that too, but her place was small and like I mentioned, we were talking a lot about the whole Florida deal and she didn't want Jo to hear. I live with my mom and she kind of hovers, so if we want to talk alone, we drive."

"And you have no clue what she did that night?"

"No."

"All right." Celeste sighed, feeling as if she was going in circles, getting the same answers with no forward momentum. "Can you tell me about school? Was anything happening at school for Katie?"

"We only had a couple of classes together, P.E. and Chemistry. She was super into her yearbook project. That took up a lot of her time and I went with her for a couple of interviews. But in December our ski club season started, and I was gone a lot, either to Schuss or Boyne."

"Water and a grilled cheese," Joanna said, sliding the mug and plate from a tray in front of Celeste. "Everything going good here? Liam, do you need a refill?"

"No. I'm all set. Thanks, Jo."

"I'm good as well," Celeste said. "This looks great."

"Wave me over if you need anything," Joanna told them before heading to another table to drop off cups of water.

"Can you tell me more about Katie's yearbook project?" Celeste asked.

"She was interviewing people who'd been in Graves for a long time and had this idea of doing a little documentary of each decade from the fifties on. Originally it was supposed to be a couple-page spread in the yearbook, then it turned into a Graves history documentary and it continued to get bigger. She had a bunch of interviews and photos and all kinds of content."

"So she was meeting with a lot of people before she disappeared?"

"Yeah."

"Did she tell you about talking to anyone unusual?"

Liam shook his head.

"What's the yearbook teacher's name?"

"Mrs. Anderson. I saw her after school. She's usually at the school until five or so doing yearbook stuff. You could totally drop by and talk to her. Room 109."

Celeste scribbled down the information. "Great. I'll do that. What else can you tell me about Katie's life in the weeks and months before she disappeared?"

"She was working at the schoolhouse. You already know that. Her job and school took up a good chunk of her time. She'd been cramming for a chemistry test she dreaded—that was her worst subject—and doing the yearbook stuff. That was really it."

Across the restaurant, the door opened and Randy walked in. "Jo. Can you bring me a Dr. Pepper when you get a second?" he called out.

Joanna gave him a thumbs-up before grabbing a tray of drinks and carrying it to a trio of women at another table.

Randy walked to the booth where Celeste and Liam sat.

"Hey, Randy. How are you, man?" Liam asked, slapping Randy's raised hand.

"Living the dream, Liam." He set a gift bag on the table and pushed it toward Celeste. "This is for you."

She looked up, surprised. "For me? Why?"

He grinned and reached into the bag, pulling out a new coffee maker in its box. "Because you said you have one of those baby coffee pots in your condo and I died a little inside when I heard that. I don't advocate for much, but a good, large cup of coffee in the morning—we all need that. Especially if you're helping with our Katie." He reached inside the bag again. "And I even grabbed you a bag of my favorite coffee. The company names the blends after movies. Graveyard Shift is the best."

"Thank you. You didn't have to."

He waved the comment away. "Fill me in. Any developments?"

Liam slid from the booth. "You can take my seat. I have ski club tonight. I'll be up at Shanty, Celeste, so if you think of anything else, send me a text. I can always stop by or we can meet in the lodge."

"Thanks, Liam. I appreciate your talking to me. Have fun skiing." Celeste turned her attention to Randy. "Nothing groundbreaking yet, but I'm just getting started. I have my boards set up at the condo and I'm tackling interviews first. Heading to the high school after this."

"Are you? I haven't set foot in that place in ages." He chuckled. "The good ol' high school days. Can't say I miss 'em."

"You graduated from Graves High School?"

"Oh, yeah. Me and Travis both, though he graduated by the skin of his teeth."

Joanna stopped off and slid a pop in front of Randy and handed him a straw. "How's your day going, Randy?"

"Can't complain. How are you, Jo?"

"Running like a chicken with my head cut off as usual. But on a happy note, Northern Michigan News agreed to cover Katie's vigil." Joanna pulled a folded piece of paper from her apron and set it on the table.

Randy looked over the flier, then handed it to Celeste, who stared at the image of Katie. It was a picture she hadn't seen: Katie in a distressed-looking jean jacket and a pair of pink shorts with daisies on the pockets. She clutched a bouquet of black-eyed Susans in front of her.

"What a great picture," Celeste said.

"Isn't it?" Joanna murmured.

"That's the coat I bought her," Randy said, tapping the picture.

"Order up," Floyd bellowed from the kitchen.

"Duty calls," Joanna said. "Here. You can keep this, and here's one for you, Celeste." She handed another flier to Celeste before disappearing into the kitchen.

Randy shifted his attention back to Celeste. "You mentioned having your boards set up. What does that mean?"

Celeste fidgeted. She needed to move soon. Her hip toggled between numb and prickly. "Bulletin boards. That's how I've always worked, bulletin boards covered in sticky notes. I think of them like my mind map. Weird how when you pluck it out of your head and put it where you can see it, patterns emerge. Can I ask you a few questions about Travis? I'm trying to get a big picture of Katie's life."

"Sure. What do you want to know?"

"I guess start by telling me a little about him."

"Huh. Where to begin? Travis got the looks in our family." Randy chuckled. "Fat lotta good it did him. His lifestyle has stripped all that away. When we were young, he could have had any girl at school. Any one. You know who he picked? This sophomore named Trinity Belding. And no offense to Trinity, but she might have fallen off the ugly tree and hit a few branches. So why did he pick her? Because her dad was a drunk and Travis could go over and get wasted with Trinity. He never had an ambitious bone in his body. It was like he was born to get wasted."

"How did you end up so different?"

"We had a hard life, and we both wanted to make it easier. I did that by hustling, getting a good job, and ensuring I wouldn't spend the rest of my life in a trailer park. The way Travis escaped the hard life was by getting high and checking out of reality."

"You had a hard childhood? Can you tell me a little about that? What was your mother like?"

"A lot like Jo and Katie's mom. She did her best, but my dad left us when I was nine, Travis was seven. She married four more times after my dad. All of them were somehow worse than my dad, and believe me when I tell you he wasn't anyone special." Randy sighed. "He outlived her, though. My mom died five years ago, not long before Katie's, and my dad—the chronic smoker and drinker—is still livin' his best life."

"Is he?"

"Unlikely. More like he's living the same hell he's always lived. Last I heard, he was in some long-term motel downstate. Travis is better at keeping tabs on him. They talk now and then. They have a lot in common, those two."

"But you rose out of all of that? That's admirable."

"Thanks. I wish Travis could have, but... you never know, I guess. There's still time."

"How old are you and Travis, if you don't mind my asking?"

"I'm forty-three, Travis is forty-one."

"How did he handle Katie going missing?"

"Oh, he did what he always does—got so high he didn't remember his name for a week."

"And how did you handle it?"

Randy raised an eyebrow and smiled. "Same way I always handle things. Jumped into action. Helped organize the searches, printed fliers."

Celeste nibbled the edge of her sandwich. She'd barely eaten a quarter of it, but the pain in her leg made her stomach turn. She tried to think of what else she might need to know about Katie's absentee dad. "Is Travis dating anyone?"

Randy smirked. "Oh, sure. He's a regular Casanova. Despite his bad habits, the women flock to him like stink on shit. Never ceases to blow my mind how many women seem interested in Travis, warts and all."

"And how about you? Girlfriend? Wife?" She glanced at his hand—no wedding ring.

"Nope. Which is how I prefer it. I know you probably think that's unusual, but when you grow up around the kind of people I did, you learn to enjoy solitude. Life is unpredictable enough without the drama of other people. What about you, Celeste? I see a shadow where a ring used to be, but no ring."

Celeste rubbed her ring finger. The joints felt knobby, the spaces between too thin. "I'm married. My ring has been slipping off, so..." She twiddled the empty finger.

"How does your husband feel about you doing this?"

Celeste avoided looking at him. "Well, I didn't give him all the details. He'd have worried. Since the accident"—she patted her leg—"he worries."

"Joanna said you were hit by a car?"

"Yeah. I spent a month in the hospital."

Randy whistled. "Musta been in pretty awful shape."

"I was."

"And is that part of the impetus behind your coming here? You got a second chance at life, so now you're trying to pay it forward?"

Celeste pushed her sandwich around her plate, thought of seeing Katie the night she'd received Joanna's letter. "Something like that. Yeah." Celeste checked her phone. "I better get going so I can chat with the yearbook teacher before she goes home. Thanks for talking, Randy."

"Anything to help find Katie," he said. "Don't forget your coffee maker." He pushed the bag toward her.

"Thanks again."

Celeste feared the yearbook teacher would already have left for the day when she parked in the largely deserted lot at Graves High School.

She hurried from her car and through the entrance. To her right sat the main office, and she opened the door, but found no one inside. A map of the school hung from a wall next to a trophy case, and she paused, found 109, then started toward it.

As Celeste neared the room, she was relieved to discover the light still on inside. A woman stood at a back table, leafing through a stack of photos. She looked up at the sound of Celeste's shoes on the linoleum floor. "Hi there," she said.

"Are you Mrs. Anderson?"

"You found me."

"I was hoping to ask you a few questions about Katie Ellis."

"Katie Ellis?"

"Yeah. I'm helping her sister Joanna, and her friend Liam mentioned she was working on a big yearbook project last year."

"Sure, okay. I need to run out to my car and grab my pills. I forgot to stick them in my purse this morning and I need to take them every day at specific times. Thyroid issues. Do you mind if we walk and talk?"

"Not at all."

"And call me Linda. What was your name?"

"Celeste."

"And you have questions about Katie?"

"I'm helping Joanna find out what happened to her. Katie's friend Liam said Katie was working pretty hard on some stuff for the yearbook before she went missing—a throwback piece, trying to get photos and interviews with Graves residents."

Linda smiled sadly. "Yeah. She did a lot of interviews on video. I've never even watched them. I told her if she collected any more material, we'd need an entire book devoted to her section alone. We actually started talking about doing a supplement, but then... she didn't come back one day and..."

"Were you surprised when she went missing?"

Linda glanced at her as if the question were strange. "Of course. Yes. Katie was an A student, at least in my classes, which included a yearbook this year and Introduction to Film last year. She had a unique personality—a bit of rebellion, but a lot of heart, dedication and drive. Plus, losing her mom had forced her to step up. The cards were stacked against her, but she intended to do whatever it took to succeed. She hoped to get a scholarship. I shouldn't even say hoped—she told everyone she'd get one, she just had to set her sights on where and start making it happen. She never wanted to be a burden to Jo. I personally considered her disappearance highly unusual and frankly scary. I have a daughter in middle school. We only live a few blocks from the school, but I drop her off and pick her up now. I'm not risking it."

"You suspect someone kidnapped Katie?"

"Or killed her. I don't want to believe it. I want to tell myself our little town is immune from such evil, but no place is immune. The world is too big these days for any of us to believe it won't happen here. It happens everywhere. In some small town right now there's some kid or teenager going missing, getting abused or abducted or killed."

"What kinds of rumors are going around the school? Any theories talked about in the teachers' lounge? Or whispers among the students?"

Linda pushed open the double glass doors that led from the school and veered into the teachers' parking lot. She clicked the unlock button on her keys and stopped at a lime-green Toyota. From the glove box, she retrieved a bottle of prescription pills.

"There have been a few rumors," Linda said as they started back toward the school. "The primary one is she ran away. Katie was free-spirited. People who only saw the surface Katie would probably assume she'd be the type to run off, start a new life elsewhere."

"But you don't think so?"

"No."

Raised voices came from somewhere beside the school and Linda turned sharply and started toward them. Celeste hurried to follow, willing her left leg to keep up.

In a second parking lot labelled 'Student Parking,' Celeste saw the source of the voices. A tall boy with shaggy blond hair towered over a girl, a foot shorter than him at least. They stood near a compact red car and the boy appeared angry. He gripped one of the girl's arms tight and spoke with his face inches from hers.

"Declan, is there a problem?" Mrs. Anderson asked, her voice high.

The boy looked up, dropping the girl's arm and stepping away.

"Nope," he snapped. He glared at Linda Anderson, and then his eyes slid to Celeste before he turned and stomped away. He climbed into a rusted blue pickup truck and peeled from the parking lot.

Linda walked toward the girl. "Britny, are you okay?"

Celeste stayed back. The girl's eyes had filled with tears. Her lower lip quivered as she talked, but Celeste couldn't pick up on her words. The girl spoke with her teacher for several minutes before climbing into the little red car and driving away.

"Was that Declan Boyd?" Celeste asked, following her back into the school.

Linda glanced back, face grim, and nodded. "You've heard of him, then?"

"I heard he was dating Katie."

"Apparently, yes."

"Did you notice any changes in Declan in the days after Katie disappeared? Did he miss any school? Seem more withdrawn?"

Linda scrunched her forehead and shook her head slowly. "Honestly, I don't remember."

"Would you still have attendance records from last year? Could you check his attendance?"

"I'd have to find that specific book, and I'm not sure I'm allowed to give out that information. If the police requested it that'd be another story."

"I understand. You said Katie was taking a lot of videos. Did the police ever view any of it?"

Linda shook her head. "The police never spoke to me at all. I called once and told them I had these files of video interviews and they never called me back."

"Can I watch them?"

"I don't see why not. I planned to ask Jo if she wanted them, but life is so busy it got away from me."

They returned to Room 109 and Linda moved toward the back of the room. "Katie uploaded all her videos to a file on the computer back here. I'd offer to send the file, but video files are huge and, frankly, I doubt I could send it all." She looked at her watch. "I've got volleyball with the JV girls in about fifteen minutes. I'm the assistant coach and our regular coach is sick this week, so I need to leave, but I'd be happy to log you in and you can pick around in there. Each of the students had their own folder in the database labelled with their name, so it shouldn't be difficult."

Celeste stood next to Linda at the computer as she brought up the folder. "Here we go," Linda said, hovering the cursor over the name Katie Ellis. She clicked it and another window opened, this one filled with video files.

"There's a lot," Celeste murmured.

"There is. Like I said, we were talking about doing a supplemental publication because she'd gathered so many interviews, great material. I heard her talking about a little documentary too. It really bothers me now looking at all this work. A girl doesn't get up and walk out of her life when she's put this kind of work into something."

"I agree," Celeste said.

Linda started for the door. "I'd appreciate if you'd let me know if anything important comes up. I try not to think the worst about what might have happened, but..." Her mouth turned down.

"I'll let you know," Celeste said. "What time will they lock up?"

"With all the sports, there will be people going in and out of the school until eight. I'd plan to leave by then."

18

Celeste sat down at the computer and scrolled to the earliest videos and interviews recorded months before Katie vanished. They'd likely not be connected to her disappearance, but Celeste wanted a sense for what Katie was working on in the months leading up to her disappearance.

She clicked the first link and a video window spread across the screen. She hit play, adjusted the volume and waited for the image to load.

The camera was pointed at a wall of bushes. Celeste heard sounds of rustling, a giggle, and then the lens swung around and Katie's face filled the screen.

Long, flat brown hair, parted in the middle, hung over each of her shoulders. She wore a leather band stretched across her forehead, a style that harkened to a different time—a time of emerging women's rights and hope for a peaceful future. Celeste could see only the top of her t-shirt and the words *Me and Bobby McGee*, a Janis Joplin song.

"This is weird," Katie told the camera, sticking out her tongue and screwing up her eyes. "But what's weirder? Me videoing myself or me talking to myself about how weird it is?" She laughed then pursed her lips and cleared her throat. "Okay, here we go." She closed her eyes for a moment, her long black lashes brushing her skin. When she popped them back open, she'd gathered herself.

"Hey there, my fellow Graves High peers. Katie Ellis here. Today we're taking a walk down memory lane. I'm sure you're not surprised I've decided to spearhead this project, and though you may be currently yawning and rolling your eyes at the prospect of a Graves, Michigan, history lesson, I assure you this will be no History Channel exploration. I'm going to give you the dirt on Graves, so let's step back in time. We're starting today at Graves' graves—pun intended."

She pointed the camera at a metal sign attached to a stone wall that read 'Graves Cemetery.' Katie passed through the open iron gate into the rolling hills of the cemetery.

"Few of us at Graves High are unfamiliar with the resting place of our ancestors. I'd guess most of us have a grandma or grandpa here, maybe even some closer kin."

As Katie spoke, she videoed tombstones, and Celeste leaned closer as the camera seemed to falter on one tombstone. Celeste read the name: Naomi Ellis, Katie's mom.

Katie stopped at a tall faded tombstone, moss growing over the top. 'Howard Graves,' the name read. A layer of grime largely obscured the dates beneath.

"I know, I know," she said. "You're all groaning in your seats, right? Not more history on Howard Graves, but I'm not here to tell you how he came here in the late 1800s and helped get the railroad into town and then funded a post office and later a church. Bore me to tears, right? No. What we're here to talk about is what Howard Graves was into behind closed doors."

The camera moved closer to the tombstone and Katie's hand appeared on the screen. "Take a look right here," she said.

Celeste leaned forward and peered at the shape etched into the tombstone beneath Howard's name.

"This is a pentagram," Katie explained. "At the little stone schoolhouse, we have a whole wall of history about Howard Graves. And in a back room, we have a file cabinet full of the stuff that didn't make that wall. In those files, we have letters written to Howard about the 1800s spiritualist movement, which Howard was not simply a part of—he started it here in Graves. He held séances at his house. That big mansion out on Temple Road? Yep. The rumors that it's haunted may be true.

"Howard spent a lot of his time, especially in his later years, desperately trying to make contact, not with his deceased wife, but his deceased mistress, Gelda Fremont, who'd been murdered! Yes, Howard was not the goody-two-shoes Graves historians would have you believe. He had an affair with Gelda for nearly a decade, until she came to an untimely and brutal end one night while walking near the train tracks. And some people say she died right in the same spot that old train car sits, which I think we can all agree is disturbing considering some other Graves history."

There was some fumbling with the camera, and then Katie's face appeared. She held up a peace sign. "Peace, love and granola," she said.

The screen went dark.

In the hallway, several kids walked by talking and laughing. Celeste clicked play on the next video.

Katie stood in front of high, ornate-looking iron gates. In the background, a tall dust-colored mansion rose from the elaborately landscaped lawn.

"I have a treat for you all today. I managed to pull some strings and get a tour of Howard Graves' totally rad, and probably haunted, mansion. I mean, seriously. Imagine what people thought of this place when he built it. Today, this house is owned by Jerome Shaw and his partner Louis."

A moment later, a fifty-something man appeared at the gates and opened them. He wore dark slacks and a v-neck grey shirt. He was handsome, with silvery hair and green eyes.

"Katie," he said. "Wonderful to see you again. How are you?"

"I'm stellar, Jerome, and I'm already filming. Is that cool?"

"Sure, sure. Come on in. I put the dogs in the carriage house so you won't have to be subjected to their assault this time."

Katie laughed, but Celeste could not see her. She had focused the camera on the house that loomed larger as they walked towards it. "I'd hardly call anything corgis do an assault —more like love-bombing."

Jerome guffawed and slapped his hands together. "Love-bombing! Exactly." He took the wide front porch steps two at a time and turned to face the camera. "The house is made from sandstone block," he explained. "It's held up surprisingly well. Howard Graves was fascinated with Italian architecture and paid a pretty penny for a designer from Florence to come to America and help him design and build this house. It is truly a marvel."

Katie panned across the wide house, capturing a large turret and stained-glass windows. She followed him onto the porch, where a small ceramic skunk sat near the door.

"Aww," she said. "I like the skunk."

He winked, bent down and picked it up. "Hollow. We hide the spare key in this little guy. Oops." He put a hand over his mouth. "Better cut that out of the video."

"I will."

Jerome opened the door and Katie followed him inside.

"Original hardwood floors with inlay," Jerome described as the camera took in a long golden hallway with a wide staircase flanked by lion's head banisters. "Grand staircase. Off to the right, we have the formal living room. Obviously, the flat-screen TV isn't part of the original house, but many of the furnishings are. Howard Graves was quite compulsive and expected everything to remain immaculate, so when I bought this house, I discovered the carriage house stuffed with antiques, many from the time Howard himself lived here. Back here is the library. I know you were especially interested in this room, since this is where the séances took place."

The camera followed Jerome down the hall and into a room with stained-glass windows, an enormous marble fireplace and floor-to-ceiling bookshelves. Oil paintings hung from the walls, one depicting a vase of roses tilted, flowers spilling out, another a forest stream.

"Wowza," Katie breathed. "Look at all the books."

"Amazing, isn't it? And many of those are also antiques. Here, get a shot of this shelf right here."

Katie moved closer, and the video revealed a row of aged hardcover spines: *Letters on Demonology and Witchcraft* and *The True Fortune Teller*.

"Those are some creepy titles," she said. "And on the subject of creepy, have you ever had any strange experiences in the house?"

Jerome walked to the stained-glass windows. Colored light made his face glow red. "Oh, sure. Footsteps on that main staircase at night when I'm here alone. Bonnie, my older corgi, absolutely loves this room and in particular this chair right here"—he put his hand on a high-backed green velvet chair—"but my younger corgi, Clyde, hates this room. Won't set foot through the door, which of course is difficult for him because he loves to play shadow to Bonnie. She may come in here just to escape him, but I think she has a ghosty friend in here."

"A ghosty friend?"

"Certainly. I don't doubt this place is haunted, but I'm convinced the presence is a benevolent one. My partner, Louis, who has a bit of the sight, agrees. He told me once he walked into this room and a lovely woman in a long gray dress was

standing right there at that stained-glass window and then...
poof, she was gone."

"Really? Wow! That's bizarre. Who do you think it was?
Howard's wife?"

"Undoubtedly. There's a beautiful oil painting of her in the
garage and Louis is one hundred percent sure that's the woman
he saw."

"She died in childbirth," Katie said.

"Yes. I've been to the schoolhouse museum and read all the
history."

Katie panned to the stained-glass window and for an
instant, Celeste saw a reflection in the glass—a woman, not
Katie, staring back at her—but then the camera shifted and
took in the enormous bookshelf. The video slid left, capturing
several large paintings in gilded frames, an old-fashioned roll
desk open to reveal a quill pen and ink set, a stack of parch-
ment and a wax seal.

"Will you eventually live here full time or—?" Katie asked.

"Oh, God, no. Louis and I love this house, but it's as cold as
an icebox in the winter. We have to keep the heat on year-
round to preserve everything, but to actually live here around
the clock would be too much. We've grown far too accustomed
to our creature comforts, and during winter that comfort is our
house in Florida." He laughed.

They continued the tour, Jerome pointing out built-in cabi-
nets and original trim work.

"This might interest you." Jerome led Katie to the hall and
opened a utility closet. He picked up a plastic bucket on the
floor and took out a small rusted garden shovel that might once
have been red but was now a faded pink.

"A shovel?"

"It is indeed. A hand trowel, to be exact, but look here."

Katie sat the camera down and moved into the frame,
leaning close to examine the handle of the shovel.

"See there?" Jerome tapped his finger on the handle.

"Is it initials? B or an S and a K."

"Right you are. S.K. Have you heard of Sherry Kapolka?"

Katie's brow wrinkled. "The girl who was murdered in Graves like ten years ago?"

"Exactly. We didn't own the house back when Sherry died, but Louis got wind of a rumor she might have been here the day she was killed. Apparently, she'd been talking with the previous owners about doing some plant cuttings because Howard Graves had quite a green thumb and grew all sorts of interesting species of plants on the property. Someone reported seeing Sherry's car here the evening she went missing. And last summer when Louis was working out in the flower beds, he found this buried in the soil."

Katie listened riveted, eyes fixed on the shovel. "Did you call the police?"

"Oh, sure. And they said they'd send someone out to collect it." He shook his head. "Never have. Let me say, I wouldn't want to get murdered in this town because our P.D. is woefully indifferent. I've considered dropping it off myself, but I worry it will get tossed in a box somewhere and disappear forever. But Louis is after me to get rid of it."

"Why?" Katie seemed to struggle to take her eyes off the shovel and look back at Jerome's face.

"Originally, I put the shovel in a cabinet in the bathroom down the hall and the water turned on and off by itself. The door would open and shut. The incident that really spooked Louis was when he ran a hot bath, climbed in and the entire room turned as cold as ice in less than a minute. Frost on the interior windows and mirror, and his bathwater that had been scalding turned frigid."

"That is freaky. You think Sherry is haunting this house?"

Jerome returned the shovel to the bucket and tucked it back

into the closet. "I'm saying we found this shovel and the activity around here ramped up."

Katie appeared deep in thought as she disappeared behind the camera again. "Would you ever be open to trying to contact her? A séance or something?"

Jerome led Katie back out of the house. "Myself? No. But I wouldn't be opposed to someone else coming and trying to make contact."

After a few more minutes of house tour, Katie followed Jerome back to the driveway. "Thanks again, Jerome. See you on the flip side."

The video ended with a final panoramic shot of the house and a last glimpse of the stained-glass window. It was time-stamped in October, less than three months before Katie vanished.

19

Celeste watched video after video as Katie dished gossip about some of Graves' earliest inhabitants. She interviewed Graves' business owners, including Floyd from the Sidewinder, as well as the high school principal and a man who owned an apple orchard.

Celeste looked at the date of the next video, taken six weeks before Katie vanished. Katie's face appeared as she set up the camera and pointed it at a couch where an older woman sat. Katie hurried over and sat next to her. "Sorry this isn't more professional. I tried to get my friend Liam to be the cameraman, but he couldn't make it."

"That's fine. You said this is a school project?"

"Yes. I'm doing a bunch of interviews on Graves' history. I'll introduce you and we can jump right in."

"Sure."

Katie waved at the camera. "Katie Ellis here chatting with Donna Murden. You've owned the Sweet Freeze for years, right, Donna? It's such an iconic spot here in Graves with the best ice cream ever. The lemon poppyseed ice cream is off the hook."

The woman smiled, the lines in her face deepening, and

nodded, looking at the camera and then shifting her gaze back to Katie. "It's a popular flavor."

"I believe it," Katie said. "Can you give us a rundown of how the ice cream shop got started?"

"My mother opened the ice cream shop back in 1956. She was a typical fifties girl, stayed home and cared for her house and kids, but then my father had a massive heart attack. He survived, but it was clear he couldn't continue working like he had been and she needed an income. They sold his business and used the money to build the ice cream shop. I started working there when I was young, not even ten. I loved it. When my mom got too tired to keep it going, I took it over and, well, the rest is history."

"Will it stay in your family? Pass to your daughter?"

Donna smiled sadly. "Unlikely. My daughter Janie and her husband Brian moved to California a few years ago. They left after a tragedy and took Benjie, my grandson. I might well join them. Who knows how many good years have I left?"

"You'll sell the Sweet Freeze?"

"I might."

"The tragedy you referred to... that was the murder of Sherry Kapolka, your granddaughter?"

Donna blinked at Katie, then shot an uncomfortable glance at the camera. "I don't think we should talk about this for your high school project. It's not—"

"I can cut it out," Katie said. "But I am curious. Have they ever gotten close to a suspect or—"

"A suspect..." Donna shook her head slowly. "No. Not that we've ever been informed."

"Did Sherry's parents have any idea who might have hurt her?"

"No. She didn't have enemies. Sherry was the light of their lives, all our lives. My first grandchild. We adored her."

"Can you tell me about her? What she was like?"

Donna glanced again at the camera, mouth pursed, but Katie didn't offer to turn it off. She waited, hands still in her lap and Celeste suspected Katie was desperately trying to act casual about her questions when really she'd wanted to speak to Donna about Sherry all along.

Donna sighed and took off her glasses, revealing two little red marks where they'd rested on her nose. "Easy. That's how we always described her. She was an easy baby—never cried, never had the terrible twos or turned into one of those teenagers who thumbed their nose at you. She went with the flow of life. She loved nature. That was her element, you know? I remember one time Janie realized she'd gotten out of her playpen in the yard. She went wild looking for her. All the lakes and rivers around here, and they had a stream on their property. And sure enough, that's where she found Sherry, down at the bank of the stream, diaper soggy as she sat in the sand, water pooling between her pudgy legs. Scared the daylights out of Janie, but Sherry had that wandering personality.

"Sherry planted a beautiful garden and, in the winter, she filled Janie's house with potted plants. She wanted to open a flower shop here in Graves. She used to tell me she was going to save her money and build a flower shop connected to the Sweet Freeze. 'What could be better than ice cream and plants?' she said."

"I would have loved to go to a place like that, though to be honest, I can't keep a houseplant alive no matter how hard I try. I bought a little aloe plant last year, and it's all brown and shriveled."

"You and me both." Donna chuckled. "I can barely keep grass in my front yard, but that was Sherry. The reviver, Janie called her. She was always hauling plants home from friends to bring back from the dead. She was our light, and when she disappeared and then later when they found her..." The color seeped from Donna's face and she rested a hand on her chest. "Everything went dark." Donna's eyes drifted up to Katie, and she forced a smile. "I shouldn't be telling you all this. You wanted to talk about the Sweet Freeze."

"I don't mind, really. Maybe I could do a documentary on Sherry. You know? Try to bring some more awareness to her murder."

The lines near Donna's mouth deepened. "I don't think that's a good idea, Katie. How old are you?"

"Seventeen."

"Seventeen," Donna murmured. "So young. Sherry was nineteen. It would be reckless of me to encourage you to draw attention to her murder. It's unsolved. For all we know, the man who did it lives here in Graves. That's why Janie and Brian left. They couldn't go to the grocery store without wondering if they might be in the presence of the man who killed her. It drove them both mad."

"But not you?"

Donna pursed her lips. "I've lived here for my whole life. I can't imagine someone I know hurting our sweet Sherry. I believe someone from the outside came in and did what they did. It was only a few days after Labor Day weekend. Lots of tourists in town at that time of year."

"But... wasn't she found in the old train car? That's a local spot."

Celeste stared at the video. An old train car? She thought again of the train car she'd walked to her first night in Graves. What were the chances there were two such places in the small town?

"It is," Donna agreed. "But plenty of locals have shown that spot to visitors. And she wasn't killed there. There was another crime scene. They never found it, the police, but there was one."

Donna slid her glasses back on and changed the subject, returning to the history of the little ice cream shop. As Donna filled Katie in on the history of the Sweet Freeze, Celeste wrote the name 'Sherry Kapolka' and 'train car' in her notebook.

"I heard a rumor that Sherry might have been at the former Howard Graves mansion the evening she went missing," Katie said, rerouting the conversation to Sherry.

Donna's face sagged, and she shifted on the couch. Her eyes grew distant and when they refocused on Katie, her expression was troubled. "One tip came in that put Sherry's car in the driveway at the mansion, but it was weeks after she'd disappeared. She hadn't been found yet, so police went and looked around. They didn't find any evidence she'd been there."

Celeste watched Katie's expression, the shape of her mouth as if she desperately wanted to reveal something, and Celeste suspected it was the shovel Jerome and Louis had found. Before Katie could speak, Donna started again.

"I understand the urge to look into Sherry's case, but the man who murdered her is still out there," Donna said grimly.

The video ended abruptly, and the screen went dark. Celeste looked around. It was completely silent in the room and, beyond the doorway, the hall lights had been extinguished. She dug her cell phone from her purse to check the time and found the battery had died.

"Damn," she murmured, searching the computer screen and finding the clock in the lower right corner: nine p.m.

She scrolled back to the list of videos still available. She hated to leave without watching them, but she'd already stayed longer than Linda had advised. Still, she would not risk leaving them behind. It was possible an administrator at the school would tell Linda not to share the videos if she came back.

Celeste clicked a web browser and opened her Dropbox account. She uploaded each of the videos, including those she'd already watched, tapping her fingers impatiently.

When Celeste stood, a shock of pain lit through her left hip. She hadn't brought her cane in, and she braced both hands on the chair back and pumped her leg and wiggled her toes, trying to release the stiffness that had settled during the previous hours.

The long hall was dim and deserted, the only light a hazy red from an exit sign. She turned down the hall that led to the front doors. What if they were locked and she couldn't get out?

"They won't be," she whispered, but a sliver of fear had edged in, as if someone had dropped a single chip of ice down the back of her shirt. She shivered and tried to shrug off the uneasy sensation.

Donna's parting words hovered in her mind: *He's still out there...*

In front of her, a locker door swung open and slammed shut. Celeste froze. Another locker opened and slammed, and then another and another. She didn't move, every muscle grown taut as the formerly silent hall filled with the echoing bangs of locker doors.

A hush fell over the hall, and then another noise sounded behind her. Footsteps pounding toward her. Celeste gasped and spun around, threw her hands up to ward off an attack. She put too much weight on her left leg and felt it spasm. Her left knee buckled, and she veered sideways into the row of lockers.

No one advanced toward her. The hall stood empty.

She had to get out of the school. Pain and paranoia were a lethal combination, and she was suffering from both. Of course, it wasn't mere paranoia. The locker doors had opened and closed.

Something was in here with her.

Grinding her teeth against the pain rippling down her left side, Celeste hobbled quickly down the hall, sliding one hand along the lockers for support. As she passed the row of lockers that had opened and shut, she paused.

Number 64 had a printed photo taped to the front. *Have You Seen Katie Ellis?* Katie's face peered out from beneath the words and below that the facts of her disappearance. Someone had printed three letters in red marker in the lower corner of the paper: *R.I.P.*

20

———

Joanna spent the evening baking cookies for the hospice volunteers, as well as two more trays of muffins, mostly to procrastinate the things she needed to do, which included updating the Come Home, Katie Facebook page and assembling photos of her missing sister for the vigil.

Lemon raspberry muffin in hand, she walked to the table and flipped open her laptop—a hand-me-down from Floyd several years before that Joanna feared might soon stop turning on.

She logged into the Come Home, Katie Facebook page and posted an image of the vigil flier along with details. Two message notifications sat in her inbox. The first—spam— offered web design services. The second was from an account with no photo and the name Leslie Hilton.

I saw your page. I met Katie a month ago in northern California. She was backpacking through the redwoods. I'm positive it was her, though she now goes by the name Naomi. I thought you should know.

Naomi—their mother's name.

Hands shaking, Joanna clicked on Leslie Hilton's page.

There was no photo, no friends, no posts, no identifying information whatsoever. The only information stated that the profile had been created two days before the person had sent Joanna the private message, which had arrived three weeks ago.

She considered texting Liam or Randy or even Celeste. Instead, she closed out the window. It wasn't real. Whoever sent it knew Katie and knew her mother's name was Naomi. It was either a cruel prank—not the first she'd received—or intentionally misleading. If not, the sender would have had a real profile. They'd clearly created the account for one reason—to send Joanna the message.

Abandoning the muffin, her appetite gone, Joanna closed her computer and went to her bedroom. She pushed aside the clothes in her closet and bent down, retrieving a cardboard box. She carried it to the bed and sat beside it, peeling the tape off. A mound of photographs sat inside the box. There'd been a time when Joanna intended to organize them into albums or scrapbooks, but the hours always seemed to skitter away from her.

Katie had liked to remind her she did too much, took on too much, couldn't say no. But when Joanna tried to schedule lazy days, the looming emptiness drove her mad. She'd bake or clean or hover over Katie until she'd driven them both insane, at which point she'd go to the diner and wash dishes or visit the animal shelter and offer to walk the dogs.

She lifted the top layer of photos and fanned them across the bed, her guts instantly twisting at images of Katie as a toddler, her hair that shocking silver, short and curly then, her dimples like two crescent moons in her pudgy face. In one photo, she wore pink overalls with no shirt beneath. Her hands clutched an ice cream cone that had melted over her fingers and puddled on the hot-looking sidewalk beneath her. Katie didn't mind. Her eyes and smile were equally huge as she stared at the glob of multi-colored ice cream that remained on the sugar cone.

Joanna set it aside. She needed fifteen to twenty photos of Katie for the vigil.

As she picked up another photo, she spotted a single yellow and red polka-dot birthday candle on her bed, the tip singed. It must have somehow gotten dropped into the box of photos. Joanna set it aside and looked at the next picture—Katie and Joanna sat on the floor playing *Candy Land*. Katie looked around ten years old, Joanna sixteen or seventeen. On the floor beside Katie sat a tattered stuffed pink bunny. It had belonged to Joanna before she passed it down to Katie. One button eye dangled from its head by a piece of thread.

Joanna hadn't seen the bunny in years, but she knew it had made the trip to the apartment after their mom died because she remembered Katie, fourteen, lying on the couch with the bunny tucked under her arm while she watched a movie.

Joanna stood and walked to Katie's room, opened the door and turned on the lamp. She wanted to find the bunny and suspected the urge to locate it would not go away until she did. Under the bed seemed like the most likely location, but halfway across the room, she paused, eyes landing on Katie's bookshelf. A row of vintage lunch boxes lined the top shelf. They all faced out, but one, Joanna noticed, was angled. She'd looked at them too many times since Katie disappeared to talk herself into believing one hadn't been moved. Not only was the *Bewitched* metal lunch box angled, it had switched places with the Beatles lunch box. She stepped closer and stared at them.

"What is going on?" she murmured.

Joanna turned and considered the rest of the room, searched for any other evidence of an intruder. Nothing stood out.

She stepped to the window and peered through the blinds. The street below was dark, lit only by streetlamps. Streetlamps that had contained posters about Katie's vigil, many of which had been ripped down. Who had done it and why? She thought again of the stuffed pink bunny she'd been so desperate to find. Suddenly, she didn't care to find it. She needed to get out of the apartment. The little changes, shifts happening in Katie's room, were grating on her, sending her off-kilter. Was she changing things in the room and forgetting?

Joanna put on her boots and coat and left the apartment. She locked the door and headed for the parking lot.

Inside her car, ice cold and reluctant to start, she fought the tears that had become her constant companion. Usually, she only allowed them at night when lying alone in her bed. Now they slipped hot over her chilled face and dripped into the collar of her coat.

After a few tries, the old Ford came to life. Joanna cranked the heat, though the air blew icily from the vents as she pulled onto the road.

The schoolhouse was closed for the night, the windows dark, but Joanna pulled into the lot and parked. She stared at the building, something she'd done on so many of the nights since Katie vanished. Some piece of her sensed the building before her knew the truth. The field stones had witnessed what happened to Katie that night.

Had Declan walked in as her shift ended and coaxed her into his truck? Or had she started off down that remote stretch of road only to have a familiar face peer through a driver's window and offer her a ride?

She knew those weren't the only two possibilities. Though there'd been no signs of a struggle, a person with a weapon—a gun perhaps—might have forced her into a vehicle.

But Katie had once told Joanna she'd fight to the death before she'd be taken. Had those instincts to fight fled when a stranger flashed a gun in her face and demanded she get in his truck?

As Joanna stared at an upper window, a flash of movement caught her eye. She leaned forward in her seat and squinted, tried to understand what she was looking at, and with dawning horror realized it was a face. A pale face flanked by long straight hair.

"Katie..." Joanna shoved her car door open and leapt out. She ran to the front door and twisted the knob, though she'd known before she'd touched it it would be locked. "Katie!" she screamed and pounded both fists on the door.

She ran around the side of the schoolhouse, hit a patch of ice and went airborne. Joanna landed hard on her back, the impact sucking the breath from her lungs. Above her, the black sky dazzled with stars from the hit her head had taken when it smacked the icy ground.

The sound of a car turning into the schoolhouse lot split the night, and a fresh fear took hold of Joanna. Someone was there, perhaps the same someone who'd been at the schoolhouse a year before. Biting her lip against the shock of pain in the back of her head, she rolled onto her side and then her hands and knees. Maybe they hadn't seen her. She'd creep around the back or dart into the snowy woods.

As she stood and limped away, a voice called out.

"Joanna?"

She twisted around to see Randy climbing from his car.

"Oh, Jesus," she murmured, putting a hand on her thudding heart. "You scared me half to death."

"Me? I was driving by and saw you lying on the ground. I thought you were dead. What are you doing here?"

Joanna touched the back of her head, her hair damp—from snow, she hoped, and not blood. She pointed to the second story of the schoolhouse. "I saw Katie. I swear it. I saw her upstairs. Do you have your key?"

Randy frowned and looked at the schoolhouse. Joanna saw the reluctance in his eyes, but he sighed and fished his key from his pocket. She followed him to the front door. He unlocked it and she pushed past him.

"Katie?" she yelled, running through the length of the schoolhouse and taking the stairs two at a time to the second floor.

At the top of the stairs, she froze, staring at the girl at the window, long blonde-brown hair flowing down her back.

"Katie?" she whispered.

But as she moved closer, her eyes trailed down, and she took in the metal base where legs and feet should have been.

Randy arrived behind her at the top of the stairs. "It's a mannequin, Jo. They've been in here forever."

Joanna blinked at the back of the mannequin. She walked forward, spun it to see the face, and, yes, it was a mannequin with vacant painted-on blue eyes. The hope that had ballooned when she first looked up at the window dissolved and she sagged against the wall.

"It never use to be in front of that window," she murmured. "It was over there with those mannequins." She gestured at the other two mannequins in the corner.

"Someone must have moved it," he said. "Come on." He offered his hand. "Let's get out of here."

Joanna took his hand, and they walked side by side down the stairs. She knew he wanted to ask questions. The type that skirted around 'are you losing your mind?' He said nothing until they were outside at her car.

"You know who I ran into when I was in Florida?"

She looked back at the window again and frowned. The mannequin no longer resembled Katie. She couldn't imagine what had made her think so in the first place.

"Cole. I ran into Cole and he asked about you."

Joanna sighed and looked at Randy. "How is he then?"

"He's doing good. Down there making bank, but my point is he really wanted to know how you're doing, Jo."

"If he really cared, he'd have called me," she muttered.

"All I'm saying," Randy told her, opening her car door for her, "is this"—he gestured at the schoolhouse—"doesn't have to be your life."

Joanna stared at him. Randy didn't get it. He'd never even had a pet, let alone a baby sister he'd spent his life caring for.

"But it is my life," she murmured. She climbed into her car, waved goodbye, and drove away.

By the time she was back in her apartment, Joanna was dog tired, her face puffy and her nose clogged from all the tears she'd cried during her drive home.

As she closed the apartment door behind her, she paused at the sound of running water.

"Now what?" she muttered, kicking off her boots, hanging her coat on a chair back and walking to the bathroom. She pushed the door open.

Water flowed from the spout into the bathtub. It was nearly three-quarters full and, based on the steam in the room, hot.

Her hands shook as she twisted the knob to off. Though she knew she hadn't started the bath before she left, Joanna rewound the tape of those minutes leading up to walking out the door.

She sat there for several more minutes, the lip of the tub biting into her leg, the ache from falling at the schoolhouse vibrating up her back and head.

When she found the energy to stand, she walked on rubbery legs to her room and climbed into bed.

21

———

During the hours Celeste had sat in the Graves High School, the sky had dumped another few inches of white on the world. The trees were so heavy with it, their branches looked like the pallid arms of giants drooping toward the ground.

Celeste turned her car onto the maze of roads that led to the Shanty Creek condos. As she drove up an especially steep road, her car suddenly slowed, wheels spinning, but not getting traction.

"Come on," she murmured, turning her wheel, trying to catch the road edge, hoping there might be something for the tires to grip. There wasn't. The car spun, slipped sideways and rolled back down the hill.

As she sat, hands clutching the wheel, Celeste's stomach compressed into a tiny little ball. She'd let her phone die and now she was alone on a dark stretch of winding forest road with a car incapable of traversing the hills.

"Stay calm," she murmured. She'd turn the car around and drive back into Graves, stay at Joanna's for the night, or get a hotel room.

When the car stopped rolling, she backed onto the shoulder, but it was steeper than she realized and the rear tires slid. She pumped the brakes, but it was no use. The weight of the car on the icy embankment picked up speed, skidding backward and down.

For an instant she floated, reversing backwards into the drift on the side of the hill, then Celeste was jolted forward as the car came to an abrupt stop in the deep snow.

Panic edged in. She bit her lip, took a breath, and hit the gas pedal. Her wheels spun, snow shot up to the windows and the car sank lower in the drift.

"Oh, God…" she murmured.

Celeste was stranded on a forest road at night in a place she suspected somewhere not far away a murderer was preying upon teenage girls. For a moment, she thought of her house in Grand Rapids. Jonathan asleep in bed, Cash stretched out on the couch, the familiar sights and smells of home. She couldn't think about that. If she did, she'd curl into a ball and never leave the car.

She had two choices: stay with the car and try to flag someone down or walk.

Celeste grabbed her cane, slung her purse over her shoulder and struggled through the driver's door that would open only a few inches thanks to the waist-high snow piled against the car. It took several minutes to clear the embankment and by the time she reached the slick road, her leg and hip were howling. Resisting the desire to crawl back into the car, she started up the slippery road toward the condo.

The walk was excruciating. The cold had deepened. The wind howling in the trees blew gusts of icy snow into Celeste's face. It burrowed beneath the collar of her jacket, lodged in the tops of her boots. Her hip, leg and foot throbbed until each step became nausea-inducing.

Why hadn't she bought more suitable clothes for winter in

northern Michigan? What had she been thinking wearing leather boots and a suede coat? Her very first day, the man who'd helped her had told her to get decent boots and a coat. She'd completely ignored the suggestion.

She probably had half a mile to go and as her cane slipped repeatedly in the wet snow, Celeste feared she might not make it.

A vehicle turned onto the road. She looked back to see a large dark van barreling towards her. Panic streaked through her and for a few suspended seconds she was back in Grand Rapids, walking the stretch of undeveloped subdivision near her and Jonathan's home, the sound of an engine in her ears.

Celeste shook the memory away and stepped onto the shoulder. More snow filled her short leather boots. It soothed her left ankle, but stung her right and she knew after another ten minutes of walking with the ice in her boots her skin would grow raw.

The van pulled alongside her and stopped. The passenger window rolled down. It was dark inside, but she could see the driver was a large man with a knit hat and a bulky brown coat.

"Need a ride?"

Common sense told her to refuse, to say she was fine, to turn into the next driveway and wait until the van disappeared, but her body groaned to get in, choose warmth and a painless ride home. He'd have her back to the condo in two minutes. On her own, it'd take an hour, if she even made it.

"Umm... sure. I'm right up the road here at the ski resort condos." She pulled open the passenger door and the dome light flicked on, illuminating the van's interior. Between the two seats, paper bags of fast food, cigarette containers and other trash lay piled. Celeste had to kick more garbage aside in the passenger seat footwell.

The driver smiled at her, revealing a slightly crooked front tooth. His face was prickly with black hair and his nose had a weird bend as if it had been broken. Nothing in his appearance indicated he might be dangerous, but Celeste felt immediately uneasy as she settled into the van.

When Celeste closed the door, the light turned off, and she strained to stay close to the passenger side, ready to jump out if he tried anything. The mere thought of such a thing caused the throb in her leg to get louder.

"Ain't safe to be walkin' these roads at night. Almost hit ya myself."

"Yeah. My car got stuck at the bottom of the hill."

"Yer lucky I came along. More snow comin'. A little thing like you could get buried out here. Nobody'd find ya til the spring." He chuckled.

Celeste gripped her cane tighter and wished she'd opted to walk and take her chances with the ice and bitter cold.

"You injured?" he asked, pointing at the cane she clutched in her hand.

"No," Celeste blurted, not wanting to reveal any vulnerability. "I use it for the ice, so I don't slip."

His eyes bore into her for a moment, but she stared straight ahead through the windshield, wished he'd drive faster. The interior of the van stank of cigarette smoke and spoiled food. The man had the heat cranked, which had felt good when she first climbed in, but now, combined with the odors, made her stomach roll.

When he parked in front of her building, Celeste flung the passenger door open and practically fell onto the sidewalk. As she closed the door, she caught a glimpse into the back of the van where a shotgun lay amidst several toolboxes. She lurched away without even saying thanks. Blood thrummed in her ears and she almost fell twice, struggling into the building and up the stairs.

Celeste closed and locked her door and staggered to the

Scotch, not even bothering to pour it into a glass. She twisted off the top and drank it directly from the bottle.

Someone pounded on her door and she choked on the alcohol. It scorched her nose and throat. She coughed and grabbed a cup, filled it with water, and took a drink. The knock came again, louder.

Celeste limped to the door and peered through the fisheye lens. The man from the van stood outside. He'd followed her into the building. She held her breath, body going perfectly still.

22

———————

"You left your purse in my van!" the guy yelled, knocking a third time.

Celeste closed her eyes, inserted the side of her fist into her mouth, and bit down. She'd been so desperate to get out of his vehicle, she'd forgotten her purse.

Twisting the lock and clutching her cane, ready to raise it as a weapon, she opened the door.

He stared at her too long, didn't hold up her purse, and for a moment she thought he'd lied and she hadn't forgotten her purse. Then he smiled that creepy grin, eyes running the length of her. "Almost looked through it to see if you had any cash in there, but then remembered my mama taught me better than that."

"Thank you," she rasped, throat still tender from the Scotch. She reached for her purse, but he didn't let it go. Another shudder coursed down her spine.

"I didn't catch yer name," he told her, continuing to grip her bag, his eyes burrowing into her.

"Celeste," she said, trying to keep her voice even, not betray her fear.

"That's a real pretty name. I'm Warren. Warren Boyd. If you need help with yer car, call Neal's Auto in Graves. I'll come tow ya out. Give ya a real good deal." He winked and released her purse.

Celeste nearly fell back, remained upright, though her left leg trembled and threatened to buckle.

Warren's eyes moved to her leg, his head tilted slightly. He'd recognized her vulnerability. For a moment she saw a look cross over his face, there and gone. A predator who'd picked up the scent of injured prey.

"Thank you," she said, stepping quickly back into the room, slamming the door and locking it.

She stood, heart crashing against her breastbone, afraid to look through the peephole and discover him lurking outside, planning how to get in. When she finally peered through the door, the hall stood empty.

Celeste limped to the closet chair, sank down, and squeezed her purse against her stomach.

Warren Boyd, Declan's dad, had been the man who'd picked her up.

CELESTE FELL THROUGH DARKNESS. Black wings flapped against her face, feathers soft on her cheeks and lips. The feathers cleared and for a moment she stared at a group of birds— ravens, their dark bodies shimmering in the sweltering sun. She blinked at them and stepped forward. The birds took flight and the thing beneath them revealed itself, except it didn't. The flapping black feathers obscured it.

Celeste startled awake. She sat up, a post-it note stuck to her cheek. She'd fallen asleep at the little kitchen table, her laptop open before her. She'd spent hours after Warren had left answering questions in her Dear Celeste column. It soothed her, getting lost in someone else's problems.

THE NEXT MORNING, Celeste called a nearby tow place and paid by credit card to have her car pulled from the snowbank and dropped off at the condo.

After an hour test-driving trucks at dealerships in Traverse City, she picked out a black Toyota Tacoma. As the salesman drew up the paperwork to trade in her Accord and set up financing on the Tacoma, she called Jonathan.

"Hello." His voice sounded hesitant.

"Hi. How are you?"

"I'm fine. How are you?" There was a coolness between them, a distance.

"I'm pretty good, but you're going to see a chunk of money come out of our account today."

"And why is that?"

"Because I'm trading in the Accord and buying a pickup truck."

He said nothing for a moment and when he spoke, she could tell he was trying to suppress his disapproval. "A pickup truck? Why would you purchase a truck? Have you ever even driven a pickup truck?"

"I just did about twenty minutes ago. I need four-wheel drive up here."

"You're trading in your car for a truck because you're on a week-long vacation up north? Doesn't that seem a little rash?"

"No. I've thought about it and it's something I want to do."

"Fine." He sighed. "How's everything else going? How's your leg?"

"Things are good. My leg is fine. Sometimes it aches, but honestly, I've thought about it less up here. I think the change of scenery is helping me heal. Something about being in our house, on our road, seemed to be making it worse." It was a lie, of course. Her leg was as bad if not worse.

"Hmmm... that sounds like a psychological thing."

Cruz appeared, paperwork in hand.

"I've got to go," Celeste said. "I'll call you later."

Jonathan sighed. "Goodbye then."

FROM THE DEALERSHIP, Celeste drove to a backcountry store and bought high, waterproof winter boots and a heavy down jacket that fell to her knees, both recommended by the store employee, who also loaded her up with a hat, waterproof gloves and two packs of smart wool socks.

As she hobbled to her truck, huffing beneath the layers of her new clothing, Celeste's gaze landed on the store at the end of the shopping plaza. 'Divine Vision,' the sign read. The glass windows were covered by dark curtains, but an 'open' sign hung on the door.

Celeste shook her head, hoisted herself into the truck and started the ignition. For several minutes, she continued watching the shop. She'd never gone into a new age store, felt embarrassed at the prospect of going into one now. She inched from her parking space and drove across the lot, parking directly in front of the store. If she was going to go in, she wasn't breaking a sweat to get there.

The interior of the store was dim. Rows of glass shelves backlit by purple lights lined the room and held hunks of pink Himalayan salt and other stones and crystals. The sounds of drumming floated from the speakers and the space smelled strongly of some earthy, pungent incense that made Celeste instantly lightheaded.

A woman walked from behind a beaded curtain in the back

of the room. "Welcome. Are you here for the crystal reiki session?" The woman was small, maybe an inch over five feet, and wore a long plain black dress and a single beaded amber necklace.

"Umm… no. I was looking for some books, actually."

"Lovely. Our bookshelves are right back here." She gestured to a shelf lining the back wall. "Is there a particular book I can help you find?"

Celeste shook her head, didn't want to ask about medium or ghost books, felt silly for even being in the store.

"I'll leave you to it then. I'm setting up a room in the back for a healing session. Ring the bell when you're ready to check out." The woman disappeared behind the curtain.

Celeste made her way to the books, tempted to brace a steadying hand on the glass shelves as the incense and her throbbing leg made every step a chore, but afraid she'd send one of the glass shelves loaded with crystals crashing to the floor.

Celeste scanned the titles and selected two books, *Life after Life* by Raymond Moody and a book about talking to ghosts.

Next to the bookshelf hung a large bulletin board and Celeste's eyes caught on three letters in large block print at the top of one flier: 'NDE.'

She stepped closer and read.

Have you experienced an NDE/Near-Death Experience? If so, you're not alone.

Our group meets once a month at the Unitarian Universalist Church in Traverse City to talk about our NDEs and to assist each other with the challenges many of us have faced returning to the world.

Come share your story (or not) and hear the stories of others.

There was a website at the bottom of the page. Celeste took a photo with her phone and walked to the counter.

23

After Celeste returned to the condo, she texted Joanna.

Celeste: *Are you at the Sidewinder today?*

Ten minutes later a response popped onto her phone.

Joanna: *I'm here until two, working the breakfast and lunch shifts.*

Celeste: *Can we meet when you're done?*

Joanna: *Of course. I'm happy to come to you at Shanty Creek.*

Celeste set her glass down, moaned as she propped her leg on a stack of pillows. It throbbed dully despite the painkillers she'd swallowed a half hour before. She'd not been doing the physical therapy exercises Lorenzo had given her. Just the opposite—she'd been sitting for long stretches of time staring at her computer, walking without her cane, and skipping the baths and massages he had recommended.

Celeste opened her laptop and downloaded Katie's videos.

She hit play. The screen showed Katie walking to a small bistro-style table and sitting across from an older man who wore a fedora hat and a sweatshirt that said 'Groovy Gramp' in colorful letters.

"It's your cool cat, Katie Ellis, here from Graves High School talking to…"

"Thadeus Browning at your service. Thad to my friends, Pop-Pop to my grandkids."

"And you're a Graves lifer."

He chuckled. "All seventy-nine years I've been blessed with."

"And you were the one who found—"

"Hold on now," he cut in. "Let's do a little warm-up before we jump into the deep end, shall we? I like to wade in the shallows, get my feet wet. Graves used to be real special. And it still is for some of us, for parts of town, but the darkness has gotten in too. Sometimes I sit on my porch and look out at Graves and I can feel how something dark has started to get in. Course, it's not only here in Graves. This is a whole world problem, a human being problem." He rested a hand on his chest. "*Invasion of the Body Snatchers*. You seen that movie?"

Katie shook her head.

"You best watch it. Most of what I learned about how to deal with monsters came from films. My ma called me a movie buff. My dad liked to say if I kept watching so much television, I'd have a brain as rotted as those zombie films I liked to watch." He chuckled. "I think about that sometimes. How every generation is convinced the next will doom humanity."

"What do you mean when you say darkness has gotten into Graves?"

"You know what I mean. You've seen it with your own two eyes. Drugs, violence, hate. The murder of Sherry, the Graves Peeper, that family out on Decatur road whose house burned after some kind of meth explosion. It takes all kinds of forms. Mostly it dresses up as men doing terrible things to one another, sometimes as women too. I figure most of us here in Graves managed to turn the blind eye, as they say, not peer too closely at the dark mist floating in, but when Sherry

Kapolka got murdered right here in our own town, well, that woke us all right up. Sometimes I think that mist is a bit like the poppies in *Wizard of Oz*. You've seen that one haven't ya?" He didn't wait for Katie to answer. "That mist put everyone back to sleep just as quick as it could. Evil needs people to look the other way in order to do its work. It only needs a split second, but the sleepier people are the less they pay attention."

"You were the one who found Sherry's body?"

Thadeus scratched at his stubbly face, leaving finger marks in his soft jowls. "You ever have nightmares, Kit Kat?"

"Doesn't everyone?"

"Maybe. My wife never remembers her dreams, not even a hint, but I always have. I'll have dreams so real I confuse them with reality. If my parents were alive, I bet they'd say it's from all them scary movies. But I think dreams are something else, a message of some sort.

"I had one of those real-type nightmares a few weeks after Sherry came up missin'. In that nightmare, I was standing on the tracks that run through Graves and the train cars were whippin' by and suddenly Sherry Kapolka was staring at me through one of them windows."

He rubbed his face, broke off a piece of cookie and popped it in his mouth. "You tell Jo she's outdone herself with these gingersnaps." He pushed the plate toward Katie, but she shook her head. "Back to that nightmare. I struggled with it for about a week and then one afternoon, I leashed up my coonhound, Zippy, and I drove out to the old train station and I took her for a walk. To tell ya true, I didn't expect to find her out there, but Zippy started tuggin' me toward the old train car and she was scratchin' and barkin', wanted to get up inside of it, but I pulled her back, tied her off to a tree, and that's when... when the smell hit me."

Celeste's eyes flicked to Katie's face. The girl had gone pale.

She reached for a cookie and her fingers trembled slightly. She didn't eat it, but merely held it gripped in her hand.

"Probably shouldn't talk about, but... you don't forget and it's the smell that drew me to look in that train car. The door was closed and it took all my strength to yank it open. The *sound*." He made a face as if he could hear it all over again, brows knitted together, mouth trembling. "This ungodly screech, and you might not believe me, but it didn't sound like rusted hinges alone. It sounded like the shriek of a girl in pain. And then this monster swarm of flies came rushin' out of that train car." He blinked rapidly, touched his face again. "I'll never forget. I couldn't see real well, but... I could see enough."

"You saw Sherry?"

"I saw what was left of her. She'd been in there a month in the heat of summer." He took another cookie, broke it in half, shook his head sadly. "I've had a long life, seen a lot, but nothing like that. Nothing ever as horrible as that. Untied Zippy and we walked back to my truck and drove right to the police station. It's a miracle I walked out of there at all. Ended up in the emergency room the next day with my heart all out of whack. Bunch of arteries clogged up and the stress of that, of finding her that way. I wouldn't wish that on another living soul."

"Did you know Sherry?"

"I surely did. She used to bring plants into hospice two, three times a week. She was quite a green thumb. Always starting stuff from seed and growing it up then giving it away. Not your typical teenager, I can tell you that much. She'd sit with people, with the dying. She'd give them a plant and ask them to name it and then she'd write the plant's name on a little cardboard plaque so even when they were alone those folks could have somethin' to talk to. She'd tell the patients that this plant needs a lot of love to grow, so anytime you think of it, let yourself get all filled up with feelings of love and that will keep this plant healthy." He smiled sadly. "She made a lot of difference for those people. Her family were good people. I was sad her parents left, but I don't blame 'em one bit. I get the willies anytime I'm over by the train station, but I go there anyhow. I walk back to that train car thinkin' I'll find a clue they missed all those years ago. Spoken like a man who's watched too many movies. Course, these days the real clues can't be seen by the naked eye."

"Did you follow the police investigation at all?"

"Oh, sure. We all did. But I guess I had a special interest, having found her and having known her. I knew a couple of the policemen working her case and they were fit to be tied trying to get some kind of a decent lead. No one could understand how she went from buying a sandwich and a soda at the grocery to getting dumped in that train car. If she'd walked someone would have seen her, and why would she have walked? Had a perfectly good car right in the parking lot."

"Did the police ever release information about suspects? Persons of interest?"

"Nope. No names anyway, but the town was talkin'. Small towns always do."

"And who were they talking about?"

Something flickered in Thad's features, a reluctance, Celeste thought, to reveal his suspicions. "A few names of local boys came up."

"People Sherry went to school with?"

"Nope. Older. You turn off that camera and I'll give you some names."

Katie looked at the camera as if she'd forgotten it was there. "I'll cut it out. I promise. No names."

Thad ate part of a cookie, nodded. "A guy named Norm Little. He'd been spotted at the Graves Grocery that night stumblin' around drunker than a hoot owl. No alibi. Said he went home and blacked out. Police have hauled him in a few times over the years, but he's never cracked. If he did it, he don't remember. But last I heard they'd gotten some DNA off him, which didn't match what they found on Sherry."

"They found DNA on Sherry's body?"

"Yep, the kind that made 'em think whoever took Sherry did it for a sexual reason."

"She was raped?"

Thad appeared troubled by the question, but nodded. "Sherry's body was too degraded to say for certain."

"Who else did police look at?"

"Well, Warren Boyd for one."

"Warren? Declan and Todd's dad?"

"Yep. He's got a nasty temper and a couple of girls came forward and said he'd come on to them, made 'em feel uncomfortable."

"Did he have an alibi?"

"Now that I don't know."

"Anyone else?"

Thad's jaw tightened. He leaned back in his chair, crossed his arms over his chest and shook his head. "Nope. Nobody else I can remember."

Celeste suspected there'd been another name he held back.

"And they've never been able to match the DNA to her killer?" Katie asked.

"Not yet. But the clock's tickin' on that guy." Thad tapped his watch. "You seen that genetic genealogy stuff that's going on?"

"No."

"It's big stuff, groundbreaking for these old cases. They just caught a serial murderer out in California who killed a whole bunch of people decades ago."

"What is genetic genealogy?"

"I wish I could give you the technical, but this ol' brain is no longer up for the challenge. It's connected to those family DNA kits everybody's always doing. I've done one myself. That ain't quite true—my wife told me to spit in a little vial and she shipped it off in the mail and a few weeks later we found out I'm forty percent Scottish.

"Police can take some DNA of an unknown killer and put it into one of the family DNA sites and up pop some of their relatives. Then they build out a family tree and badda bing, badda boom, they've got their killer. It's revolutionary stuff. I sure hope I live to see it come to Graves and get some justice for Sherry."

"You believe the police here in Graves will use that at some point?"

"Every police station in the country will use it. When is the question."

"But in order for that to point to Sherry's killer, someone related to the killer must have submitted one of those tests."

"Therein lies the challenge, but I like to believe when the time comes the DNA is gonna be there."

After the video ended, Celeste grabbed a post-it note and wrote the name 'Thadeus Browning' and then added the words 'Graves Peeper,' 'Norm Little' and 'Warren Boyd.'

24

Celeste opened the door almost as soon as Joanna knocked.

"That was fast," Joanna exclaimed, holding up a Tupperware. "I brought cookies."

"Thanks. Come on in." Celeste turned and hobbled back into the room.

"Are you okay?" Joanna asked, following her inside and setting the cookies on the small kitchen counter.

Celeste dropped into a chair beneath a wall of bulletin boards. She pounded her fist on her left hip a few times and nodded. "Yeah. This thing is giving me grief today. I aggravated it last night when my car wouldn't make it up these damn hills and I had to get out and walk."

"Oh, my God. You walked back here? It practically snowed a foot last night. You should have called me."

"My phone died. And I didn't walk the whole way. A guy picked me up—a very creepy guy in a van."

"You got into a van with a man you didn't know?"

Celeste nodded. "Yeah, and honestly, I regretted it the second I was in there. And then I forgot my purse and he knocked on my condo door and about gave me a heart attack. He also introduced himself—Warren Boyd."

Joanna's heart skipped a beat. "Warren Boyd?"

"Yes. And let me say, he quickly moved to the top of my list of suspects. Every cell in my body was on edge around him."

Joanna clutched the fliers about Katie's vigil, eyes drifting to her photo. "You think Warren might have—?"

"I don't have much but my physical reaction to substantiate that, but he definitely spooked me."

Joanna shook her head and wished for the zillionth time she'd paid more attention to Katie and Declan's relationship. Maybe it would have mattered. She could have warned Katie away from him. "Why did Katie ever get involved with Declan? God! If we could go back in time and... and..."

"Yeah," Celeste murmured. "Do you want some coffee or—" Celeste started to stand, but Joanna jumped to her feet and waved her back down.

"No. No. You sit. I'll get us coffee and put a few cookies on a plate. Chocolate chip or oatmeal raisin?"

"Either's fine," Celeste told her.

Joanna's gaze drifted to the glass doors and the ski slope beyond. She felt a little bubble of sadness drift into her throat. She'd taken Katie to the ski hill a few times in years past. Neither of them knew how to ski and more than once they got tangled together in a heap at the base of the chairlift trying to get on. The last time they'd been with Cole and the sisters had been laughing so hard, unable to stand up, the lift operator had to stop the chairlift. It took Cole and the lift operator to get the girls back on their feet.

"I went to the high school yesterday and started watching Katie's interview videos. Have you seen them?" Celeste asked.

Joanna pulled her eyes from the glass doors. "For her year-book project? No. I mean..." Her face flushed. "I meant to go in there at some point and ask to see them, but... I was so busy it didn't seem important." Joanna opened the cupboards until she found coffee mugs. She filled two and looked in the mini fridge for cream. "Cream and sugar?" she asked Celeste.

"Yeah. Thanks."

Joanna carried the coffees and the container of cookies back to where Celeste sat. Her gaze stopped on the bulletin boards with a map of Graves marked by pushpins and thread and sticky notes listing names. She saw Declan, Warren and Todd Boyd all listed as possible suspects. When she spotted the theories, her breath caught: *abduction, murder...*

"I think you need to watch these. I've taken note of a few in particular, but I watched one where Katie was interviewing a man named Thadeus Browning."

"Thad?"

"Yeah. Do you know him?"

"Yes, really well. He's one of the Groovy Gramps. He's a regular at the Sidewinder."

"Did he ever tell you Katie interviewed him?"

Joanna frowned, tried to remember. "I don't know. He might have. She interviewed a bunch of the regulars, also Floyd and his wife, Camile."

"Well, she and Thad talked about a girl named Sherry Kapolka."

Joanna's eyes widened in surprise. "Sherry Kapolka?"

Celeste nodded. "Did you know her?"

"I knew of her. I was seventeen when she was killed, a junior. She'd been two years ahead of me at school. I remember seeing her in the halls. She graduated the year before she was killed, so I hadn't seen her in a while. After she disappeared, it was all anyone talked about. They'd found her car in the grocery store parking lot."

"Were you scared?"

"You know what's crazy? I wasn't scared. The rumor mill was on overtime, but I was so busy." Joanna thought back to that time. Life had been a combination of her mother's volatile relationship with Travis and Jo's own exhausting day-to-day life. Joanna had gone to school, come home and fixed dinner for Katie, then hurried off to the diner to wait tables. Rinse and repeat. She'd never gone out on dates. She'd rarely spent time with girlfriends. She hadn't even considered going to college because she knew she couldn't move away from Katie and leave her alone with their mother.

"The fear came when they found her body," Joanna murmured. "Or I guess... her remains. I remember being afraid after that."

"Did you know Thad found her body?"

Joanna shook her head, imagined Thad with his movie trivia and his heaping pancake breakfast and his laugh so loud the whole room took notice. "I never knew that."

"Katie did. She asked about it in the interview."

"But why? Why would she be asking about Sherry?"

"Katie was looking into Sherry's murder. I think it started with Katie's work on the yearbook piece. She was interviewing people, talking to business owners from different decades, visiting places where significant things happened. During her research she came upon the murder of Sherry and I think she got... hooked, for lack of a better word. I can see about halfway through the videos her focus shifts from Graves history to Sherry in particular."

"Really?" Joanna stood and paced back to the glass doors. She rubbed her arms, chilled. "I knew she'd been working on that project and I didn't even think to look through her videos. How could I be so dumb?"

"Your mind was elsewhere. Don't beat yourself up about it."

Joanna clasped opposite elbows, a memory swimming up. It had been Thanksgiving and she and Katie were rushing around the apartment getting food ready to take to Floyd and Camile's. Joanna had been bent over rifling through the refrigerator for a bottle of whipped cream to go with the pumpkin pie she'd made when Katie had asked the question.

"Do you remember Sherry Kapolka?" Katie had asked.

It had been such an odd question, and Joanna normally would have probed, pushed to understand why Katie was asking, but her mind was in multiple places. They had to stop and pick up bread rolls from the diner. And she still had to put on deodorant. She'd forgotten after she'd taken a shower.

"Umm... who?"

"Sherry Kapolka. The girl who got murdered in Graves."

Joanna had looked up to see Katie near the door. She was tying her rust-colored scarf around her neck, pulling her long hair free.

"Jesus. Sherry Kapolka? I remember her. Sure, but I didn't know her. Not really. I saw her at school. It was tragic, so sad, especially for her family, but let's not go there right now... Can you cover the pumpkin pie with tin foil? I have to put on deodorant."

And that had been it. Joanna had hurried to the bathroom and forgotten all about the conversation.

"She asked me about her," Joanna breathed, eyes lifting to Celeste's. "About six weeks before she went missing, she asked me. I was so distracted. It was Thanksgiving and..." Joanna shook her head. "But... what does that mean? Do you think the person who killed Sherry found out Katie was looking and..." She didn't finish the sentence, couldn't truly wrap her mind around the possibility. Sherry's murder had been unsolved, and it hadn't been for lack of an investigation. For the year after Sherry's murder, people in Graves had talked of little else, but then without updates, the hysteria had faded and the case had apparently gone cold. Katie couldn't have possibly discovered the killer who had eluded the police.

"Let's not make any assumptions. Her asking questions doesn't prove her disappearance is connected to Sherry's murder."

"But it's one hell of a coincidence."

"I agree."

Joanna shuddered, thought back to those weird days in Graves after they'd found Sherry's body. For the rest of the summer and into the fall, it was a ghost town. The streets, usually a regular thoroughfare for teens walking and riding bikes, had become deserted. Everyone was scared, the mothers most of all. Except not Joanna and Katie's mother, not really. Naomi Ellis had been desperate to hang onto Travis. That summer had been one of the worst. Between them the walls shook from their screaming or their lovemaking, all of it burrowing into Joanna's skull like a family of termites.

"This might be a long shot, but did you ever hear any rumors about Warren Boyd being connected to Sherry's murder?" Celeste asked.

25

"Warren Boyd," Joanna murmured. She'd never liked Warren Boyd, but a killer? "No. Not that I remember."

"Thad mentioned a couple possible suspects during his interview with Katie," Celeste explained.

"And Warren Boyd was one of them?"

"Yes, and a guy named Norm Little."

"Norm Little died three months ago."

"He did?"

Joanna nodded. "His sister comes into the Sidewinder. He had liver cancer. He'd been a heavy drinker."

"That was the link to Sherry," Celeste said. "Thad mentioned Norm was in the grocery store parking lot the night Sherry disappeared. He was drunk and didn't have an alibi."

"And Warren was the other suspect."

"Yes."

"I feel bad for his wife, Rosie. She graduated with my mom."

"Liam mentioned Rosie became reclusive at some point,

stopped helping at the school and whatnot. Any idea when that happened?"

Joanna licked her lips, frowned again, thinking back to that period of time. She knew Rosie peripherally, but a particular incident stuck out in her mind. She'd been at the diner when Rosie had come in with her two boys, who'd been young then, Declan maybe seven and Todd ten. The three of them had ordered ice cream sundaes and when Joanna checked in on them, the boys had devoured theirs, but Rosie's sat untouched, melted, the cherry floating in the milky vanilla ice cream. Rosie had appeared glassy-eyed, far away. Todd had snapped his fingers in her face to get her attention. She'd barely said a word, paid and the three of them had left.

"Yeah," Joanna murmured. "I do remember something strange. Rosie came in with the boys the summer Sherry was killed. I don't think they'd found her body yet. She was really out of it. I'd never seen her look like that. I remember at the time thinking she must be scared like everyone else. It was that summer she started to seem different. Before, I'd run into her in town and then..." Joanna shook her head. "She kind of withdrew from the world. Do you think... she might have known Warren was involved?"

Celeste held up a hand. "It's possible. Again, we can't make that leap, but let's say hypothetically Katie started looking into Sherry's murder and found something out. Maybe she even talked to Declan about it and he let something slip to his dad. Or maybe she somehow linked Warren to Sherry's murder, and Declan told his dad what Katie had found out. These are theories only. Right now, I have no evidence at all to back them up, but... theories are a jumping-off point. The goal now is to prove or disprove it."

"And how do we do that?"

"We need to find out if Warren had an alibi for the time Sherry went missing and for the time Katie went missing."

"How can we find that out though? We can't exactly ask him. I mean we can, but I promise you it won't go well."

"No, and if he was involved, it would be a very dangerous thing to do. There's one person in his life who'd know that, assuming she remembers."

"Rosie," Joanna murmured.

"Exactly."

"Okay. I'll approach her. I can use her friendship with my mom as my way in, tell her I'd like to know what my mom was like in high school."

"Perfect. And when you ask her, try to be subtle. You don't want her going straight to Warren and telling him you asked those questions."

"Yeah. Okay."

"I haven't watched all the videos, but I've downloaded them and I can forward them to you. There are a lot of videos, more than twenty."

"Twenty," Joanna echoed, chest tightening. Her sister had taken twenty videos in the months before she vanished and Joanna had never even bothered to ask about them.

Joanna's gaze drifted past Celeste and landed on a diamond ring with a gold band sitting on the side table. It looked like a wedding ring. "Are you married, Celeste?" Joanna nodded at the ring.

Celeste glanced at the ring. "Yes. Jonathan. We've been married for eight years. My ring keeps slipping off, so I've stopped wearing it."

Joanna was surprised Celeste hadn't mentioned him. Then again, they'd spent little time discussing Celeste's life other than the first day when she'd admitted to having been in the hit-and-run. "Do you have kids?"

"No kids."

"And your husband doesn't mind you coming up here and getting involved in all this? He must be an understanding guy."

Celeste set her pen down and looked up at Joanna, her expression unreadable. "He doesn't know. I told him I was going up north to get away, to get my head on straight. Things have been different since the accident, so it wasn't a completely bizarre thing to do."

Joanna blushed, embarrassed she'd asked and sensing Celeste did not care to talk about her personal life.

"How about you, Jo? Boyfriend? Anyone special in your life?"

Jo's shoulders slumped a little lower as she thought of Cole. "Not in a while. I had a boyfriend, Cole. That ended not long after Katie went missing, which made everything more terrible."

"Why did it end?"

"He wanted to leave Graves. His brother lived in Florida and made really good money in construction. His brother had been asking Cole for years to come move down and suddenly there was a job opening. He wanted me to go, but... well, I would never have left Katie. She and I had actually talked about it though, about going down for a few visits and seeing what we thought. She was graduating the next year and we could have moved to Florida, started over. She could have finished her senior year down there. It always felt like a bit of wishful thinking, but Cole got us excited about the idea. It was cold here in northern Michigan and he was telling us how Florida was seventy and sunny and full of palm trees."

It was agony now for Joanna to remember those nights sitting around her kitchen table, the three of them eating dinner, Jo's feet aching from hours at the diner. She'd been imagining waking up and picking a mango off the tree in the backyard, drinking fresh-squeezed orange juice, swimming in December.

"And he left after Katie vanished?"

"He came back a few times. During the first two months he

called a lot, checked in. We pretended it was going to be a long-distance thing, but then... I didn't have the energy. Every bit of me that wasn't working to pay bills was searching for Katie. And I guess I resented him too. I didn't realize it at the time. He accused me of it, of resenting him for getting a life. That was the last time we talked. I screamed at him. I was so angry and hurt and... also not surprised. You know?

"Some part of me always expected him to abandon me because that's what people do. The minute things get hard, they walk out. My dad did it, Katie's dad. Even my mom, in a way. She raised us, but she was also absent, always putting her boyfriends first, either trying to find one or trying to keep one. I vowed to never do that to Katie. If we'd gone to Florida, she would have been the decider. I would never have left her. But now..." Joanna's mouth turned down. "I think, *What if we had decided to go? Would that have changed everything?* No matter what, we were finishing out her junior year here in Graves, but maybe if she knew we were moving, she'd have been home that night, packing or planning or something. Something other than what put her in the path of... whoever or whatever."

"And what would you have done if you'd all gone to Florida?" Celeste asked. "Stuck with restaurant work or—"

"I always wanted to be a nurse. I got sick when I was young and ended up in the hospital for two weeks and I had the most amazing nurse, Freida. When I look back now, I think she filled the void where my mom should have been. In those days, my mom was working two jobs and in every spare moment she was at the bar or on dates. She was desperately trying to find a boyfriend, or I guess a future husband, which... I don't know. She's gone now and I try to see things from her perspective—single, broke, with a young daughter who was sick a lot."

"Why were you sick so often?"

"Well, it was partially our lifestyle. Our house was freezing in the winter. We had a propane tank and my mom never had money to fill it, so we'd go weeks without heat and then the pipes would freeze and we wouldn't have running water."

"But she worked two jobs?"

Joanna nodded. "Yeah, but it was never enough. When she met Travis, she thought she'd found the answer to her prayers, but I knew right away he was bad news. I was only eight but I remember the first night he came over he brought a case of beer and drank the whole thing, all of it, by himself. I sat at the table eating animal crackers watching him open can after can with my mom batting her eyelashes at him and laughing too loud at his jokes. Ugh." Joanna rubbed the hollows beneath her eyes. "I tried to tell her that he seemed... not okay, that she shouldn't see him again, but what did I know? And really, I was eight. How could I, a child, have more sense about men than she did? He moved in, she got pregnant. He shifted from beer to liquor to a variety of hard drugs. He was also a lot younger than my mom. When they met, she was in her mid-thirties and he was like twenty-three. Even as a little kid I knew he'd never stick around and yet somehow my mom didn't see it."

"Have you considered nursing school now?"

Joanna shrugged. "Maybe after everything with Katie is resolved."

"What if it never gets resolved?"

Joanna frowned. "I can't think like that."

"Still," Celeste went on, "you could do classes online. Or start taking a couple community college classes."

"Graves doesn't have a community college."

"Maybe you want to eventually leave Graves."

Joanna shook her head, couldn't stomach the thought of leaving Graves—not only because of Katie, though she was the primary reason. "Graves is all I've ever known. Floyd and Camile are like family, all my regulars at the diner. I've never even left the state and I've rarely left Graves other than a few trips to Traverse City and one time I went to Detroit for a Tigers game with my mom, Travis and Katie when Katie was like two. That's it."

"There's a much bigger world out there."

"So I've heard." She thought again of those fights on the phone with Cole after he'd left. He'd started with trying to talk her into going down, insisted they could still search for Katie from afar, said Florida was a whole new world compared to Graves. It had done little more than seal the end of their relationship. He'd moved on without her.

Joanna stood and refilled her coffee. When she walked the pot to Celeste, she shook her head.

"How about the Graves Peeper?" Celeste asked. "Ever heard of him?"

"The Graves Peeper? No. Who was he?"

"Someone Thad mentioned. He was talking about bad things that had happened in Graves."

"It doesn't ring a bell," Joanna said.

Celeste sat forward, a little gasp escaping as she shifted her left leg. Joanna stood to help her, but she waved her away. "No. I'm okay. But I do have somewhere to be in an hour and, considering I move tortoise speeds these days, I need to go get changed. Do you think you could talk to Rosie today? Last night when Warren dropped me off, he said I could call Neal's Auto for a tow, so he must be working today."

Joanna abhorred the thought of talking to Rosie Boyd, but she nodded. "Yeah. I'll go over there. Maybe I'll stop home and grab some muffins."

"Try to sweeten her up?"

"Yeah. If such a thing is possible."

26

———

After Joanna left, Celeste hurried into the shower. As she sudsed her hair and body, she thought of Warren Boyd. Had he been the person behind Sherry's murder and Katie's disappearance and, if he had, how could they prove it?

Something creaked in the bathroom and she froze, straining to hear the sound over the running water. It got louder and through the curtain she saw the door to the bathroom swing open. The silhouette of a person—a man—stood in the bathroom doorway.

Celeste yanked the shower handle off and snatched her towel from the hook, wrapping it quickly around her chest and searching the shower for a weapon. There was nothing. She grabbed a shampoo bottle and pressed her back against the slippery wall, bracing herself for an attack.

It didn't come and as she stared at the dark rectangle of the open bathroom door through the sheer curtain, she could no longer discern a human-shaped form standing there.

Her heart thumping madly in her ears, she reached forward and pulled the curtain aside.

No one stood in the hall beyond the bathroom.

Still, someone had opened the bathroom door. Celeste stepped gingerly from the shower and listened. She thought again of Warren Boyd. Had the man returned and broken into the condo? Was he in that moment standing behind her bedroom door waiting for her?

She'd left her cell phone in the living room. Biting her cheek, trying to not make a single noise, she opened the cupboard beneath the sink and found an aerosol can of hair spray. It wasn't much, but if she could spray it into the man's eyes, it might buy her enough time to get out of the apartment.

She crept from the room, stopping every few feet, tense for even the slightest sound—a release of breath, a creak in the floorboards.

Nothing.

She went to the living room first, slipped out of her towel and shrugged on her heavy coat. She picked up her phone and dialed 911, but didn't hit send. In the kitchen she grabbed a small, but sharp paring knife.

As she moved down the hall to her bedroom, she tried to open herself to that other sense that had followed her after her near-death experience. Surely that sixth sense would warn her if danger lurked only feet away.

No alarm bells rang in her head, no disembodied voices whispered to run.

When she opened the door to her bedroom, it looked unchanged. She moved cautiously through the space, peering behind the door, opening the closet and then finally pausing near the bed, not close enough that someone beneath could reach and grab her. She remembered her terrible vision nights before, the screaming girl reaching for her as some phantom monster dragged her out the other side and vanished.

Celeste knelt and peered under the bed. There was no one there.

For several minutes she sat on the floor, willing her heart to slow, her shaking hands to still.

When she'd gotten control of her body once more, Celeste hurried into jeans and a black sweater. The thought of sitting in a room with a group of strangers sharing one of the most peculiar, yet powerful moments of her life made her stomach churn, all made more unpleasant by the adrenaline bath she'd spent the previous several minutes steeped in.

She wanted nothing more than to pour another drink, settle back onto the couch and spend the rest of the afternoon scouring the internet for information about Sherry Kapolka. Instead, she forced herself to drink a glass of water, eat half of one of Joanna's cookies, and take two painkillers before walking to her new truck.

CELESTE PARKED outside the brick building, which, according to the sign, housed the Unitarian Universalist church. She grabbed her purse and stepped out. For a moment, she considered leaving her cane behind, but her femur and hip bone seemed to be grinding beneath her skin, in a constant feud with one another.

Through the double glass doors, she found a sign that pointed to a large room.

The room held a long table covered by a blue cloth. Someone had arranged platters of cookies and a pumper pot of coffee with Styrofoam cups. A circle of chairs occupied the center of the room and the whole thing looked uncomfortably like an AA meeting. Not that Celeste had ever been to one, but she'd watched enough television to get the gist.

"Hi! Welcome." A small woman with black hair, silver at the roots, hurried over. She wore a sticker with her name, Brenda, stuck high on the chest of her green blazer.

"Hi," Celeste said. "This is the place for the NDE meeting?"

"It is. I'm putting refreshments out now. I figured I had a few minutes before everyone would start arriving."

"I like to be early," Celeste admitted. And she did. At times it had felt like an inconvenience. She'd frittered away hours of her life sitting in parking lots waiting for classes to begin, stores to open, people to arrive. Since the accident, time had become more fluid, harder to keep track of, and if she planned to arrive early, she usually made it on time.

"A good quality to have," the woman said. "I'm Brenda. Here, let me grab you a name tag." Brenda left and returned with a roll of stickers stating, 'Hi! My name is...' "What was your name, honey?" Brenda asked.

"Celeste."

"Oooh, that's a pretty name. How do you spell that?"

Celeste spelled her name while Brenda wrote it in black permanent marker before peeling off the sticker and handing it to her.

"Celeste, help yourself to a coffee, a cookie. Can I help you get something?" Her eyes shifted down to Celeste's cane.

"No. I can manage. Thanks. Should other people be coming soon?"

Brenda nodded and looked at her watch. "Anytime now. We hold the meeting once a month, so the turnout is hit or miss. This time of year with the weather, you never know, but there will be a few of us, I'm sure."

"Did you have an, um... an NDE?"

Brenda nodded and smiled. "I did. Twelve years ago. I had an allergic reaction to the anesthesia during gallbladder surgery. Changed my whole life. I saw my deceased parents, my dog Gina who'd died the year before. I realized that there's nothing more important in this life than loving. That's it. So simple, isn't it?"

Celeste nodded, saw the flurry of black wings flapping, so

many birds, ravens, and then she'd been enveloped. Never had she experienced such comfort, peace. But then she'd come back to her body and into the harsh world and she still hadn't made sense of it all.

A man wearing a heavy gray coat, a flannel scarf, and fuzzy earmuffs walked into the room. "Brrr!" he announced, rubbing his hands together. "Been in Michigan for twenty years and I still can't get used to the winter."

"Hi, Stan. This is Celeste. Celeste, Stan," Brenda said.

"Hi," Celeste told him. She poured a cup of coffee and carried it to the circle of chairs, watching as Stan shrugged off his layers and consumed nearly the entire coat rack with his winter wear.

After a moment, two more people walked in. A mother and daughter, Celeste thought. The daughter looked to be in her early teens and she eyed Celeste curiously. Her mother appeared nervous as she introduced herself as Nina and her daughter as Ellie. Ellie grabbed three chocolate chip cookies and walked to the chair next to Celeste, plopping down, her eyes going immediately to Celeste's cane.

"Did that happen when you died?" Ellie asked.

Celeste stared at her and then, after a moment, nodded. "Yes."

Ellie took a bite of a cookie, bobbed her head as if she approved of the taste. "I got lucky. The doctors told my parents they'd have to amputate my arm." She pulled up the sleeve of her hooded sweatshirt to reveal a long shiny scar. "But they ended up saving it. I'm right-handed, so that would have totally sucked."

Nina appeared, a cup of coffee in her hand, and sat next to her daughter. Her eyes too drifted to Celeste's cane, but she quickly looked away as if it were impolite.

"Did you introduce yourself, Ellie?" her mom asked.

"I'm Ellie," the girl said, brushing a lock of dark hair off her forehead.

"I'm Celeste," Celeste told them.

After a few minutes, another person walked in, a middle-aged woman wearing a gray tracksuit. She greeted Stan and Brenda as if she knew them well.

Once everyone was seated, Brenda began.

"It's ten after, so I think it's safe to get started. I'm Brenda, and I began leading these monthly meetings nearly a decade ago. After I died on the operating table and had a near-death experience, I returned to the world different. But when I tried to understand my experience, to share my experience, I discovered a void. My family and friends didn't get it. Some of them were curious—they listened and asked questions—but many of them found my story of leaving this world unnerving. After a few months, they didn't want to hear about it anymore.

"That's when my hunt for others began, and it didn't take long to discover there are many of us. There are NDEers who have written books, who speak all over the world. Many of us are compelled to take this wisdom and share it. At the very least, we long for someone else who understands, and thus, the meetings were born. Originally, we met in my living room, but my cats all went haywire with a group of strangers tromping about, so five years ago we moved here. In that time, I have met hundreds of people who've had near-death experiences. This is a safe place for you, for me, for all of us to share. If you don't want to share today, that's fine too. I like to open the floor up to whoever wants to start and if no one volunteers, I'll begin by sharing my story."

Ellie stood, face flushing crimson. She looked at her mother as she spoke. "Umm... so like last year, I, uh... was in a car accident with my best friend. She actually... umm..." Ellie blinked at her mother, eyes watering. "She didn't make it." Tears streamed down her face and she opened and closed her mouth as if trying to go on, but was unable to speak.

"You don't have to share," Nina told her.

Ellie shook her head. "No. I want to." She wiped her face and looked at the floor. "We ran a stop sign. Jessica was driving. I don't remember the collision. I remember looking to the left and seeing headlights right there, so close, and I think we both screamed and then..." She looked up, searched the group, landed on Celeste as if she were someone safe to stare at. "And then I was suddenly in this river. It was so warm and..." She smiled. "Happy. This joy surrounded me and this light, and Jessica was in the river. And we were both smiling and laughing and I realized this was like... a river of unconditional love.

"Jessica walked away across the river and I could see all these people on the other side. They were full of light, really shiny and beautiful, and I wanted to go there too, so I started to follow her, but then suddenly there was this woman beside me and she was so warm and loving and even though she wasn't opening her mouth, I could hear her thoughts and she was thinking that I had to go back, that it wasn't my time.

"I felt very sad then, so sad watching Jessica as she slipped into all those people and all that love. And then this woman led me the other way, but we weren't walking. One moment we were moving toward the opposite bank of the river and the next we were in the hospital and I was above my body and that woman was still with me and my mom was there." Ellie looked at her mom, who smiled, cheeks wet with tears.

"After I woke up, I was confused, but also... I wanted so bad to tell everyone what had happened, where I'd been, and so I did. I told everyone, and the doctors seemed... I don't know, like I was babbling, you know? The way a teacher looks at you at school sometimes, like they're only half listening because you're talking nonsense. Anyway, I told my mom, and she cried and told me that Jessica had died, but I already knew. My mom brought a notebook to the hospital, and I told her the story and she wrote it all down. I think she was afraid I'd forget it, but I knew I'd never forget. It was the most real thing I've ever experienced. Like it makes this world seem like virtual reality or something, you know?"

Celeste noticed the others in the circle bobbing their heads in agreement, and she too understood Ellie's description. What had happened during her near-death experience had felt more real than any moment she'd ever experienced in her life on earth.

27

The Boyds lived in a modular home that had once been white and now appeared yellowish with dark spots, dirt or mold. Sheets hung in the windows rather than curtains.

When Joanna walked up the rickety wooden stairs to the front porch, a black and white cat darted from between the steps. Joanna gasped, dropped the paper bag of muffins she'd picked up at home and grabbed for the rail, nearly losing her footing and plunging sideways off the steps. Two muffins spilled from the bag onto the icy porch. Heart thrumming in her ears, she scooped the bag up, pausing at a single blue birthday candle sticking up from the snow.

"Weird," she murmured, brushing snow from the bottom of the paper bag. She'd packed six of the muffins and the remaining four appeared mostly undamaged.

When Joanna opened the screen door, it drooped and swung away from the frame, connected only by the top hinge. The rusted creak made her skin crawl. She took a breath and knocked, praying Rosie was home and that Todd and Declan were not. Declan might have stayed home sick from school.

Joanna didn't have a clue what Todd did, but she hoped he worked.

No one came to the door, but a dog barked inside. Like the windows, a sheet obscured the glass and Joanna couldn't see into the house.

Joanna shifted from foot to foot, glancing back at her car, willing herself to stay put. She wanted to flee, not only from Rosie's house, but from everything, from the last year of her life. If only she'd gone to Florida with Cole, insisted she and Katie move when he did. Screw finishing her schooling in Graves. Katie could have graduated learning to surf, spending her afternoons on the beach.

The door jerked open and Joanna jumped, nearly dropped the bag of muffins a second time.

Rosie Boyd looked up at her through watery eyes. She wore pink sweatpants and a gray t-shirt with a neckline stretched wide as if someone had yanked it. Her hair, which Joanna remembered had been a golden brown years before, had mostly turned gray. A small wiry-haired dog barked and tried repeatedly to lunge between Rosie's legs at Joanna.

"Tater, shut up and get back," Rosie shouted. "Jesus Christ, I swear to God you're gonna live in that pen out back full-time if you keep this barkin' up. Hold on." Rosie grabbed the dog and dragged him out of the room.

Joanna stared into the space she'd disappeared from. To her right stood the living room, murky and thick with leftover cigarette smoke. The sound of a television drifted from that direction. To her left was the kitchen, a small dingy area with dishes piled high in the sink. Most of the walls were bare or marred with jagged holes, as if someone had punched them. An odd painting—old with an ornate frame—hung on the opposite wall. It depicted a vase of roses that had fallen over and spilled across a wooden table.

Rosie reappeared, hitching up her pants and grumbling

under her breath about the dog. She saw Joanna's eyes on the painting. "My son got that for me. Roses and all."

"That was nice of him. I'm sorry to come over unannounced," Joanna said, holding up the paper bag. "I made you some muffins."

Rosie's eyes shifted from the bag to Joanna's face. "Who are you?" she demanded.

Joanna looked at her, surprised. She'd known Rosie most of her life. They'd seen each other around town, at school, at the diner. "I'm Joanna Ellis. Naomi Ellis's daughter."

Rosie blinked at her, lifted a hand to tuck her hair behind her ear. "Naomi's daughter," she said. "Huh. Okay. Hardly recognized ya all grown up."

"Yeah. It's been a while." Joanna didn't know how long it'd been since she'd seen Rosie, but the woman had seen her since she'd grown up. "Do you have some time to talk? I was missing my mom this week, and I knew you were friends in high school. I'd love to hear a little about what she was like when you were young."

Rosie scratched beneath her right eye, which was slightly discolored, as if in the previous weeks it had been bruised. "When we were young," she murmured, as if trying to imagine how such a time had ever existed at all. "I guess that'd be fine. Come on in."

Joanna walked in behind Rosie, who sank onto one of two threadbare couches that faced a large flat-screen TV. One corner of the image was a spiderweb of squiggles, as if someone had previously punched or thrown something at the screen.

"Seen this?" Rosie gestured at the TV. "They go into people's houses and clean 'em up, organize 'em."

"No. I haven't seen it," Joanna said, sitting on the couch diagonal to Rosie.

"Wish they'd come to my house and do it. Course Warren and the boys would destroy it in an hour, so what's the point?"

"Is Todd still living here?" Joanna asked.

Rosie's eyes stayed planted on the television and Joanna wasn't sure she'd heard her. Finally, when the show broke for a commercial, Rosie swiveled to face Joanna and nodded. "Most of the time. Got a girl he sees up in Gaylord, so he stays there now and again. I keep thinkin' if he moves out maybe I'll turn his room into a sewin' room. You know? I used to do that, sew and mend people's clothes. I could do that still, I bet. Don't have a sewin' machine no more, sold it a couple years back, but I still got needle and thread."

"That seems like a good idea," Joanna agreed, though she knew from the look in Rosie's eyes that it was a far-off and highly unlikely possibility. "Can you tell me a little about my mom when you were young? You graduated the same year, right?"

Rosie leaned back and buried her hands in her sweatshirt. From another room, the dog started barking again. "Tater! Shut up!" she yelled. "God, that dog drives me batty. Declan wanted that dog, but you know who takes care of it? Me."

Joanna thought of Katie, who'd also wanted a dog and a kitten and at one point a bird. Joanna had promised her someday they'd move into a house and then they'd get a pet, whatever Katie wanted. The day had never come.

"We graduated together," Rosie confirmed. "Cut from the same cloth, me and your mom. Boy-crazy. Course, I'd already landed Warren by then." She snorted. "Really thought I'd caught a lucky break. Shoulda listened to my daddy, who said Warren wasn't worth the cost of the makeup I put on to go on a date with him. I look back on us girls and I'm grateful I never had a daughter. Girls get all the heartache, all the abuse. It all lands on the girls."

"Have you and Warren been having problems?"

Rosie stood up, cringed, and rubbed her lower back. "I need

a smoke." She grabbed a packet off a coffee table and shook one out, offering the pack to Joanna.

"No, thank you."

Rosie propped a cigarette on her lip and lit it before settling back onto the couch. "Warren and I ain't ever had anything but problems. But I made my bed and I lie in it. Nobody else would want me now. As useful as a flat tire, that's what he calls me."

"That's cruel."

"Well, he ain't nice. You know his type. Your mama went for the same ones. Buck, that was her guy in high school. She'd practically wet her pants, she'd get so excited to see him. Then he started screwin' Kimmy Henderson behind your ma's back. They got in a catfight, your ma and Kimmy, in the parking lot of Graves Grocery." Rosie chuckled. "We all were there, Buck leaning against his pickup like he was God's gift—sick bastard —Warren and the other guys rootin' the girls on. It was terrible. There's somethin' so wrong about seeing two girls punchin' and clawin' at each other. Your ma's lip was split. She had a big scratch on her forehead from Kimmy's Lee press-on nails. That was the end of Buck, and then... let's see. What was your daddy's name? Tommy?"

"Tony," Joanna corrected.

"Yeah. That's right. He was from down by Detroit, an outsider. She loved that. Course, then he turned out to have a wanderin' eye like Buck did."

"Does Warren have a wandering eye?" Joanna asked, hoping she could steer the conversation to Warren without arousing Rosie's suspicion.

Rosie took a drag on her cigarette, blew the smoke straight up. "He had one in high school and he has one today. Not that I care anymore. If it keeps him away from me, so be it."

"I heard a weird rumor... umm... Was he suspected in the murder of Sherry Kapolka?" It was not the gentle approach she'd intended, but the words suddenly rolled out and hung in the smoky air between them.

"Who?" Rosie asked, but the question lacked conviction. Rosie knew exactly who Joanna was talking about.

"The girl who was found murdered here in Graves ten years ago. Her grandma Linda owns the Sweet Freeze."

Rosie glowered at the TV where the show had come back on. "That guy's as queer as a three-dollar bill," she said, gesturing at the screen. "Ain't ever seen a man do all that tidying. Little cubbies with labels on 'em. Who does he think he's foolin'?"

Joanna shifted the focus. "Rosie… do you have any idea what happened to my sister?"

Rosie sat up straighter, dropped her cigarette in a pop can and stared for a moment at the rose painting. "Your sister? The one Declan went out with?"

"Yes. Katie."

"Course I don't," she snapped.

"Was Warren home that night? The night Katie went missing?"

Rosie's eyes had taken on a faraway quality. "Home with me, I'm sure. Like I told the police."

"That's what you told the police?"

"Uh-huh. Yep, all three of 'em home, probably playing board games and eating spaghetti. The Boyds—one little happy family." She released a strangled laugh and then the laughter grew strangled. Rosie put her hands over her face and cried, rocking back and forth.

Joanna stood and moved next to her, putting a hand on her middle back and rubbing little circles. She'd done it to Katie to soothe her when she'd been sick to her stomach. Rosie's spine poked through her sweatshirt. She smelled vaguely sour and something rattled in her throat as she wept. Rosie did not sound well. Joanna's heart hurt for the woman. Her life had unraveled in much the same way as Joanna's mother's life. What teenage girl in love ever had the foresight to imagine how wrong it might all go?

And she thought of Katie falling for a guy like Declan Boyd. Had that been her fatal mistake?

"Please, Rosie. If you have any idea what happened to my sister..."

Rosie pulled on her hair. Several strands broke free and Joanna watched them drift to the floor.

Rosie shook her head slowly. "I don't. I swear I don't. I wasn't home that night."

"Can I ask where you were?"

"At Denny's."

"Denny's? The restaurant?"

Rosie pulled more hair free, and Joanna had to tuck her hands beneath her legs to keep from reaching over and trapping Rosie's hands in her own.

"Denny Dixon's," Rosie murmured.

Joanna stared at Rosie, trying to make sense of the revelation. Denny Dixon was Graves' requisite drug dealer. Joanna had driven to his run-down trailer multiple times in her teen years to report back to her mother about whether Travis's car was parked outside. It nearly always was. "Why were you there?"

"Why do you think I was there?" Rosie grabbed the sleeve of her sweatshirt and yanked it up to reveal a line of small scars crowded along the shriveled skin of her forearm.

"You were using heroin?"

Rosie sagged back against the couch, took a deep pull on her cigarette. "Yep. And picked up some Hepatitis C too, so you can believe me when I tell you I know a bit about what your mother went through. Poor thing. I visited her once before she passed. She was pretty far gone though, didn't recognize me."

"When did you start using?" Joanna thought back to that long-ago day in the diner when Rosie had brought in her sons.

Rosie lit another cigarette. "God only knows. It's not as if I celebrate the anniversary every year."

"I remember you coming into the diner with Todd and Declan. It was the summer Sherry Kapolka disappeared. Do you remember Sherry?" Joanna tried again.

Rosie nodded grimly. "Not easy to forget her."

"Was Warren ever questioned regarding her death?"

"Warren…" she murmured. "Sure, he was. Most of the men in Graves were, and Warren had been at the bar that night, so a'course they wanted to talk to all those men. Figured one of 'em got drunk and grabbed Sherry for a good time, took things too far."

"Was he ever unaccounted for that night?"

"You think he'd tell me? He said he went to the bar and crashed out in his truck til morning. That's all I know."

"Okay. And what about Katie? Is it possible that Warren—?"

Before she could finish her question, the door crashed open and Warren walked in red-faced. "This goddamn bologna is spoiled. Probably gonna be pukin' my guts out." He flung a paper bag at Rosie. It hit her in the face and fell to the floor.

Warren's gaze shifted from Rosie to Joanna. He went rigid, a vein in his head bulging and purple.

28

A s Stan stood to share his near-death experience, Celeste watched another man slip into the room. He looked around Celeste's age, mid- to late thirties, with dark hair that brushed his ears and a dark goatee. He wore jeans and a long-sleeved shirt with the words 'Elder Creek Nursery' on the front. He mouthed 'sorry' at Stan and took a seat near Brenda, who whispered something in his ear.

Stan described suffering a massive heart attack-a widow maker-and hovering above his body in the hospital before his consciousness was whisked away to another dimension, where he'd seen his father, who'd died when he was only fifteen. He described how another entity—an angel, he called it—showed him a review of his past as if he watched it on a movie screen. He felt the emotions of every living being he'd ever encountered, how he'd made some of them feel pain and others feel love. There was no judgment in this place, no sadness, no shame.

"After I woke," Stan continued, "I was different. I remembered every moment. I remembered that experience more vividly than the birth of my children, than my wedding day. I knew my life would never be the same, but I didn't know how much would change. I told my wife about what happened and she..." He scratched his jaw, eyes troubled. "She stopped me, said, 'I don't want to hear this.' My wife was Catholic, a very devout Catholic, and she'd always accepted my lack of faith, I guess you'd call it. I only went to church with her on holidays.

"But after I died, I saw everything differently. I knew God existed, but it wasn't a Catholic God, a God who sits in judgment, who punishes. She didn't want to hear about my new beliefs. She went so far as to talk to her priest and he told her near-death experiences were a trick of the Devil. She pulled away from me. And maybe I pulled away from her. Like I said, I was different, a different man.

"I'd worked in banking my whole life. I quit." He laughed. "Just walked in and handed in my resignation letter, and I didn't blink an eye because I knew that was the wrong path for me. I started painting even though I'd never painted a day in my life. I became a driver for the elderly. That's what I do now. I pick up senior citizens from assisted living facilities and I take them grocery shopping, to their doctors' appointments. I took a seventy-five percent pay cut. Truly. I now earn a quarter of what I made as a banker and I have never been happier, more fulfilled. My wife and I got divorced one year after my NDE. She was against divorce, completely, but she was even more against the man I'd become. She could not tolerate me in her life after I changed."

Celeste thought of Jonathan. Of the way their marriage had become increasingly strained in the months since she died and came back, the way he looked at her as if she were a stranger.

WHEN THE MEETING ENDED, Celeste stood and made her way to the refreshments. She filled a cup of water and waited to speak with Brenda, who was bidding farewell to several people.

"I'm sorry if I missed your story today," the man who'd walked in late said. He grabbed a cookie from the table.

"I didn't share it."

"And why is that?"

Celeste shrugged, tried to ease off her cane a bit.

"Sharing it helps."

"With what?"

"Integration, bringing it into the physical world. Making it part of this life."

"Hmm... Maybe next time."

"If you're not ready to do it in group, consider contacting me directly." He took a card from his wallet and handed it to her.

"'Memento mori.'" Celeste read the words in simple black font on the front of the card. She turned it over and read the words 'memento vivere.' At the bottom of the card was his name, Harris Mayne, and a phone number. "What does it mean?"

"'Remember you must die' and 'remember you must live.' No truer words once you've crossed over. Think about calling me, day or night. The beginning is the hardest. It helps to have community." He nodded at her and walked from the room.

Brenda strolled over to her. "Thank you so much for joining us today, Celeste. I do hope you'll be back. I always post the meeting date and time on the website. My email is there as well and you can message me anytime."

"Thank you. Before I go, I do have one question. Do you have any... uh... abilities since your NDE?"

"Abilities?"

Celeste pushed a hand through her hair, wished she could stop the warmth from flooding her face. "Psychic abilities?"

"Ah, I see. I personally do not, not in the way I've heard some people do. Harris, for instance"—she gestured toward the door the man had left through—"bit of a mind reader since he came back. I also met a woman who's a medium now, and a good one—told me all about my mother, who passed when I was fifteen. A part of me wishes I'd come back with some of those gifts, but then I think back to the days when I died and returned and how hard it was to be here in the world, how people looked at me like I was nuttier than pesto. Probably a good thing I wasn't speaking to their dead relatives. Is that something you've experienced since your near-death?"

Celeste fiddled with her cane. "I think so. It's hard to know sometimes."

"Well, if you want some advice, Harris is the man to speak to. He does a lot of work with people who've had NDEs and, like I said, he has some gifts of his own."

"I might do that," Celeste said. "Thanks again for the meeting."

WHEN CELESTE CLIMBED into her truck, she saw a missed call and text from Jonathan.

Jonathan: *I tried to call. I'd like an update on how you're doing. Please call me.*

Celeste bit her cheek, hovered with her finger over his name. She wanted to hit send, wanted to share with Jonathan the stories of others who'd experienced what she had. *See!* she'd say. *I'm not crazy!* But she couldn't bring herself to do it.

There was a deep loneliness at the edge of her world, a desire for the connection she and Jonathan had once shared, but... she didn't think there was a bridge long enough to cross that chasm. If she called him and shared the stories, it would only confirm his fears that she'd lost her mind.

She texted him instead.

Celeste: *Can't talk now. All is well. I'll call later.*

29

Joanna stood quickly. Rosie bent down and shakily grabbed the sack lunch.

"What are you doing here?" Warren demanded. Though he lobbed the question at Joanna, his eyes, furious, moved to Rosie.

"She... uh... she, umm..." Rosie stammered, squeezing the paper bag so hard it popped.

"I came to talk to her about my mom," Joanna blurted. "Katie's vigil is coming up, and I was looking through old photographs and I saw one with Rosie here." Joanna put a trembling hand on Rosie's arm. "So I brought over some muffins and asked her to tell me stories about my mom."

He glared at them. In the small house, the ceilings suddenly too low, he loomed huge. Joanna had never noticed how large he really was, how easily he could stride across the room and smash their heads together.

When he moved, she flinched, but instead of advancing on them, he turned, jerked open the refrigerator and took out a can of beer. He walked to the door he'd just come in and paused. "If I get sick from the bologna, there'll be hell to pay," he told Rosie.

Joanna watched him stomp out, waited until he'd disappeared around the back of the house. Was he going to one of his sheds to get a hammer to return and beat them both to death? The options were many and terrifying.

Joanna turned to Rosie, tried to quell her shuddering voice. "I better go, but, umm, Rosie, are you safe here with him?"

Rosie, eyes cloudy, stared at her as if Joanna weren't there at all. She still clutched the bag in her hand and it had squished to the point Joanna could smell the rancid meat inside.

"Rosie?" Joanna touched the woman's shoulder, and she winced.

"Huh?" Rosie's eyes cleared.

"Are you safe here?"

Rosie's hand drifted up to her eye. She turned, picked up her cigarettes, and disappeared down the hall. A moment later, a door closed.

Joanna stared after her, but understood there'd be no parting goodbye. She hurried out to her car and drove away.

WHEN JOANNA GOT HOME, her apartment, usually cool, was blazing hot. She checked the thermostat, mouth falling open when she read the temperature—eighty-five degrees.

"What the hell?" she muttered, turning it down to sixty-five. She walked to the radiator and recoiled at the heat coming off the cast iron.

Hopefully, whatever malfunction had caused the thermostat to go bananas hadn't happened in the morning. She hated to imagine her heat bill otherwise.

She had a million things to do to prepare for Katie's vigil on Saturday, but the encounter with Warren had thrown her off-kilter. Pulling off her coat and sweater in the sweltering room, she fished her cell phone from her pocket and called Celeste.

"How'd it go?" Celeste answered.

Joanna walked to the window and balanced the phone on her shoulder as she pushed it open. "Not great. Rosie is like a wounded animal and she doesn't have a clue where Warren was the night Katie disappeared because she was out at Denny Dixon's trailer getting high."

"Getting high?"

"Yeah. On heroin."

"Did you know she used drugs?"

"Nope. And the highlight of my visit was when Warren came slamming through the door and hurled his lunch in her face."

"That's terrifying. I'd imagine it's too late to say we should have thought through the plan a tad longer. How did you get out of there?"

"After my life flashed before my eyes, he grabbed a beer and left and Rosie went back to her bedroom. I haven't reversed out of a driveway so fast in my life. Then I came home to my apartment scorching like the Sahara Desert."

"What does that mean?"

"Somehow my thermostat jumped up to eighty-five degrees. I need to get out of here. There are a couple restaurants at Shanty Creek. Do you want to meet?"

"I can do that."

JOANNA WALKED into the restaurant and bar and stopped at the bulletin board inside the door. She took a flier about Katie's vigil from her bag and tacked it on the corkboard.

"Sit wherever you like," the bartender called.

"Thanks," Joanna told him, sliding into a table near the

door to reduce the distance Celeste would have to maneuver with her cane.

When she walked in, Joanna waved and Celeste hobbled over, easing into a chair.

"How are your leg and hip doing? Any better?"

Celeste smiled grimly. "Every day."

Joanna didn't press, though she suspected Celeste was not telling her the whole truth.

The waiter, a young guy with spiky black hair, stopped at their table. Joanna ordered a cherry Coke, Celeste a Scotch on the rocks.

"And some fries, please?" Joanna asked. "I'm starving. You'd think I'd be sick of French fries. I've been eating them at the diner for a decade and yet..." She shrugged. "They're my comfort food."

Celeste took a notebook from her bag. "You said Rosie claimed Warren was at a bar the night Sherry disappeared, then he slept in his truck."

"Right."

"How about a bartender? The owner of the bar? A regular we could get in contact with?"

Joanna crossed her legs and considered the bars in Graves. There were really only two. One was the Rusty Spicket, a few miles out of town and popular with locals, and the other was Tipsy Tim's, which Joanna didn't think had been open yet during the time Sherry died.

"It's possible," Joanna said. "He'd have likely been at the Rusty Spicket. Dwayne Williams owns that place and has forever."

Someone pounded on the window near the table and Joanna looked up to see Randy standing outside. She smiled and waved. As he walked toward the door, she saw another man trailing behind him.

"Oh, no," she muttered.

"What?" Celeste asked, lifting her eyes to the window.

Joanna dropped her voice. "It's Katie's dad, Travis."

"Good evening, ladies," Randy said, pulling out a chair at their table.

"Jo-Jo. Hey," Travis said.

She dragged her eyes up to meet his. He'd aged since the last time she'd seen him months before, but looked less bedraggled than that day when he'd shown up at the diner high on something and demanding to see Naomi, Joanna's dead mother.

When Floyd had attempted to escort him out, he'd grown belligerent, throwing punches and shrieking like a caged animal. They'd finally called the police and watched through the diner window as two cops wrangled him into the backseat.

Now his eyes, usually bloodshot, were surprisingly clear. Stubble covered his chin, but his hair had been cut recently. He wore jeans and a t-shirt. He was a far cry from the man Joanna's mother had fallen in love with. The former Travis, despite his bad habits, had been good-looking, muscled, even charming. But the drugs had quickly stripped all of that away, revealing the troubled man beneath the facade.

"When did you come back into town?" Joanna asked, not bothering to hide her contempt. She knew better than to play nice with Travis. He preyed on sympathy to get money for drugs, places to crash, anything he could weasel out of somebody who took pity on him.

"Well, that's not a very nice welcome for your stepdad."

"You're not her stepdad," Randy said.

Travis held out his hands, palms up, fingertips stained by years of chewing tobacco. "I'm clean. Just got my thirty-day coin. See?" He held up the sobriety token. "Randy's been nice enough to let me crash at his place for a few weeks. I've already started the job hunt. Floyd's not hiring, is he?"

Joanna stared at Travis, speechless. Randy elbowed him.

"He's kidding. You're kidding, right?"

Travis appeared confused. "No. I could help in the kitchen. I had that job when I was sixteen. Remember that, Randy? I worked at Vinnie's Hot Dog Truck. It was hotter than a sauna in there. Worst summer of my life, but all the free hot dogs I could eat."

"This is Celeste. Celeste, Travis," Joanna said through gritted teeth. "And no, Floyd isn't hiring."

Travis winked at Celeste. "We meet again," he said.

30

Joanna stared back and forth between them. "You already met?"

"I rescued this damsel in distress on a patch of ice by the railroad trail."

"Thanks again for that," Celeste murmured.

"Why were you by the railroad trail?" Randy asked.

"I thought I saw a... umm... a dog. I wanted to make sure it didn't get hit," Celeste explained.

Joanna saw Celeste's eye twitch as she answered and wondered if the story was a lie.

"Randy and I looked up your column, Dear Celeste."

"Oh, really?" Celeste's cheeks grew pink.

"Yeah. You talked that lady out of disowning her son for stealing money for drugs, said that addiction is a disease. Good stuff, and you had all kinds of science in there to back it up."

"Travis, stop making everyone uncomfortable," Randy said.

"What?" he demanded. "What did I say?"

Randy rolled his eyes. The server returned and dropped off their drinks

"Can I get an old-fashioned?" Randy asked.

"And for you?" The server looked at Travis.

"Umm…" Travis scratched a scar on the table. Joanna sensed his struggle already beginning as he stared up at the chalkboard sign, filled with cocktails and craft beer choices. "A cup of, umm…"

"Coffee," Randy finished for him. "With cream."

"Gotcha," the server said, turning and walking away.

"What are you ladies chatting about tonight?" Randy asked.

"The Boyds," Joanna said. "I stopped by to talk with Rosie today and Warren showed up. It was not a pleasant experience."

"Why would you visit Rosie?" Randy asked.

"I know Rosie," Travis murmured.

"I bet you do," Joanna said.

Randy looked between Travis and Joanna. "What does that mean? Don't tell me you're screwing Warren Boyd's wife. Do you have a death wish?"

"Screwin' her?" Travis guffawed. "You seen Rosie Boyd lately? Gag me."

Joanna eyed Travis, wondering if he had any clue how his own looks had deteriorated during his decades of drug abuse.

"Then how do you know her?"

"They both spent a lot of time at Denny Dixon's trailer," Joanna answered.

Randy whistled. "No shit? Rosie's a tweaker? Huh. I guess that explains why I never see her around town anymore."

"Do you guys know anything about the murder of Sherry Kapolka?" Celeste asked. She'd finished her drink and when the server arrived with Randy's and Travis's, she ordered another.

"Sure," Randy said. "It was big news when it happened."

"I knew Sherry," Travis said, taking a sip of his coffee, but eyeing Randy's glass.

"You did?" Joanna asked him. "How? She was like ten years younger than you."

Travis shrugged. "Saw her around sometimes."

"Why are you asking?" Randy asked. "Do you think it's connected to Katie?"

Travis winced at the mention of Katie. He wrapped both his hands around his mug and stared into his milky coffee.

Joanna watched him. She'd never suspected Travis of hurting Katie, but she'd noticed from the beginning his reluctance to talk about her disappearance. "I read the few articles I could find about Sherry online. She went missing in the summer, found a month later in that old train car in Graves. Do you guys remember anything about her murder? Hearing rumors about who might have been involved? I didn't read anything about a boyfriend—"

"Nah. She was single," Travis interrupted.

"How would you know that?" Joanna demanded.

Travis added more cream to his coffee, took a sip and scowled. "Has coffee always tasted this bad?"

"I doubt you've tasted anything in a decade," Randy said.

"How did you know Sherry was single?" Joanna asked again.

Travis blinked at her as if he'd forgotten he said the words to begin with. "Not sure. I remember hearin' it around."

"I read she spent the day at the beach here in Bellaire and was last spotted at the grocery store in Graves," Celeste said.

"Yep," Randy agreed. "The grocery store was papered with fliers and her mom Janie set up a table outside in the evenings for weeks. She asked every person who walked in if they'd seen Sherry. I got so I started drivin' to Kalkaska for groceries. I understand why she did it, but man, it was hard to see her there cryin' night after night."

"I remember that," Joanna murmured, a memory swimming up. She'd been with her mom and they'd started toward the store when her mother had seen Janie Kapolka and gone as white as a sheet. Joanna had sensed that Janie's naked grief made her mother uncomfortable.

"Did you ever hear talk about suspects?" Celeste asked.

"Specifically, if Warren Boyd was involved?" Joanna asked, knowing Celeste was skirting around the question.

Randy finished his drink. Travis stared at the empty glass and picked at the skin on his lower lip.

"I heard something like that," Randy confirmed. "He and a few guys had been out at the Rusty Spicket that night, so I think they all got looked at."

"Warren's a hothead, beats the shit out of Rosie," Travis said. "I've seen some shiners on her that looked like she went a few rounds with Mike Tyson."

"Do you think he could be involved?" Celeste asked, pen poised above her notebook.

"Wouldn't put it past him," Travis said.

"I also read an article that possibly put Sherry's car in the driveway of the Graves mansion the night she went missing. Apparently, the owner had told her she could do some plant cuttings because there were some unique species in the landscaping there. Did you guys ever hear that?"

Randy shook his head. "The prevailing theory was she walked out of the grocery store and met up with a friend, a guy maybe, and he had ill intentions."

"I heard about the mansion thing," Travis said, rotating his coffee mug.

"Warren Boyd used to do some handyman work at the mansion back in the day, maybe around that time," Randy added. "Before he got started working at the auto shop, he did handyman stuff for years."

The door opened, a gust of snow swirling around three teenagers layered in snowboard gear. "Dude, you were shredding out there," a tall boy dressed in mismatched snowboard clothes said.

The kid he'd spoken to stripped off his goggles and black face mask. Joanna stared at him and then nudged Celeste with her foot under the table. It was Declan Boyd. Celeste turned and stared at him. Soon, Randy and Travis followed suit.

"It was all right," Declan muttered. "This hill sucks balls, but we don't exactly have Colorado mountains to drive to."

"As if you could afford a lift ticket in Colorado," the third boy sneered. He was shorter than the other two and wore an expensive-looking neon orange and black jacket and matching snow pants.

"Fuck off, Taylor. If I had Daddy's money, I could buy all the lift tickets I wanted. Too bad you can't use that money to buy any skillz."

The first boy howled. "Burned!"

"Whatever," Taylor snapped. "You're no Shaun White."

"Declan. Check this out." The tall boy tapped a finger on the flier Celeste had hung up.

Declan snatched it off and crumpled it up.

Travis was out of his seat before Joanna could speak. He closed the gap between him and Declan in seconds and grabbed hold of Declan's faded green jacket. Declan's eyes went wide. His friends both stumbled back.

Randy leapt from his chair and strode across the room, ripped Travis away, shoved Declan out of reach.

"You little motherfucker," Travis shrieked, grabbing at the paper in Declan's hand. Declan opened his fist and dropped it.

"Get out. All of you," the bartender growled, coming from behind the counter. "Get out of here."

Declan said nothing. He turned and darted from the restaurant, his friends on his heels.

Randy started to push Travis out the door, but the

bartender put a hand on his arm. "I meant the kids, Randy. You know you're always welcome here."

"Yeah. Thanks. We probably better get going, though." Randy walked over and dropped twenty dollars on the table. "Sorry, Jo, Celeste," he told them.

Stunned, Joanna shook her head. She turned to Celeste, who looked pale, shaken.

"Why don't we go up to my condo," Celeste murmured.

"Yeah."

31

Celeste walked straight to her little kitchenette and poured a glass of Scotch. Her leg ached, but she wanted the alcohol for her nerves. There'd been a moment when she'd seen Declan with his face covered in blood, his eyes swollen nearly shut, holding one of his teeth in his open palm.

The vision had passed by the time the bartender tossed Declan and his friends from the restaurant, but there'd been a terrible moment where she expected it to come to pass right there in front of them.

"Would you like one?" she asked Joanna.

Joanna, who appeared equally frazzled, nodded. "I think I do. Thanks."

Celeste took down a second glass, added ice and walked the glass to Joanna. "Did you ever wonder if Travis could be involved in Katie's disappearance?"

Joanna pulled out her ponytail and massaged her scalp, closing her eyes. "No. I never even considered it, but he was weird down there tonight, wasn't he? And the way he went after Declan..." She shook her head. "I've never seen him like that, but why would he hurt Katie? What would the motive be?"

"Drugs? Money? Maybe he encountered her that night and he needed a fix—flipped out when she turned him down."

Joanna scratched her head. "The police talked to him at some point. The detective told me Travis was out of town that night."

"Did you ever ask him yourself?"

Joanna shook her head. "I couldn't... be around him. He was using at a whole other level when she went missing and, honestly, I was drowning. I was either searching for Katie or I was working."

"How about life insurance money? Was there any of that on Katie?"

Joanna shook her head. "God, no. She was seventeen. Who puts life insurance on a seventeen-year-old?"

"People do it," Celeste murmured, thinking of a Dear Celeste letter she'd gotten in the previous year when a newly married woman discovered her husband had taken out large insurance policies on her and his three stepkids.

"The thing with Travis is he could never have covered up the crime if he hurt Katie. He's never in his right mind. If he'd hurt her—"

"What if he had help? Maybe a drug friend."

"But even then, are two guys either high or desperate to get high going to successfully kidnap a girl and then... cover up whatever they did? Make sure she's never found?"

Celeste wrote his name down on a post-it note, added it to the bulletin board with her list of suspects. "The reason police look first at the inner circle is because most crimes are committed by someone people know. They're leaning on probabilities, which makes sense to me. In the lab, probabilities rule. Based on what we just witnessed, I think we need to consider him."

Joanna took a drink and coughed. "Ugh. This stuff burns."

Celeste smiled. "That's part of why I like it."

"Someone ripped down all the fliers Floyd, Camile and I hung up downtown. I guess I know who it was now. I mean, that points to Declan. Doesn't it? Why else would he tear them down?"

Celeste looked at the board, at Declan's name. Statistically, he was the most likely killer. The problem Celeste had with Declan was the sense that Katie's disappearance was connected to Sherry Kapolka's death, a murder that had happened when Declan would have been seven or eight years old.

A knock on the door startled Celeste from her thoughts.

"I'll get it," Joanna said. She opened the door and Celeste saw Travis standing in the hallway.

"Hey. Uh, hi. Is it okay if I come in really quick?" He peeked past Joanna, who'd turned back to Celeste, her face filled with dread.

Celeste braced a hand on the arm of her chair and stood. Joanna opened the door wider, but didn't move so he could step inside.

"I asked Randy to bring me back so I could apologize. I'm sorry. Okay? Jo, Celeste? I was out of line down there even though that little shit deserved it. I shouldn't have—you know —in front of you ladies. And I'm sorry. Being sober..." He held out his palms. "It's harder than I figured it'd be. Guess that's why I never did it before." He chuckled, eyes moving between Joanna and Celeste.

"You're forgiven, Travis," Joanna said. "Is that it?"

His eyes flickered past her, landed on Celeste's boards. She wanted to give Joanna a signal—*block his view!*—but Joanna didn't realize he was reading the list of suspects and had likely landed on his own name.

"Sure. Okay," he mumbled. "Good to see you again," he told

Celeste. He cast a final glance at the board before he turned back and disappeared down the hall.

Joanna closed the door.

"He saw his name up there," Celeste said.

Joanna froze, put both hands to her mouth. "Shit. What do I do? Call Randy and tell him we don't really think Travis is a suspect?"

"Would it help?"

Joanna rubbed her eyes. "Probably not. I better go home. The vigil's the day after tomorrow and I still have so much to do."

"Probably a good idea," Celeste agreed, glad Joanna had suggested it. Celeste was ready for time alone. Between the NDE meeting and the encounter between Travis and Declan, she felt drained, ready to close her door to the world.

"I wanted to ask you quick," Celeste said. "I saw an article about a burglary at the Graves mansion in January of last year."

"Yeah," Joanna said. "Jerome told me all about it. The thieves stole a bunch of antiques. They don't know when exactly it happened because they rarely visit the house in the winter. Jerome and Louis stopped in for a weekend at the end of January, otherwise they might not have realized they'd been robbed until the spring."

"And it's still unsolved?"

Joanna nodded. "Why?"

"I'm not sure. The scientist in me wonders about the statistical likelihood of two major events happening in such a small town in the same month—especially in winter, when the town shrinks."

Joanna leaned against the wall, cupped a hand over her mouth to muffle a yawn. Celeste, too, felt as if she were running on empty. She hadn't had a decent night's sleep in months, not since the accident. She'd almost forgotten what it felt like.

"I'm not making the connection."

"Neither am I. Not yet anyway. Go home. Get some rest. I'll talk to you tomorrow."

As she had nearly every night since coming to Graves, Celeste stayed up into the early morning hours. After researching Sherry Kapolka, she read half the book on mediumship, and then answered five Dear Celeste letters.

She settled beneath the layers of comforters, the heating blanket and the Scotch rocking her down. Her body sank into the mattress, her mind into the liminal space, not awake, not yet dreaming.

Blood thrummed its usual steady throb into her hip and leg, always giving more attention to the damaged parts of her. She slipped further down, bits fluttering behind her eyelids— memories of the day and then memories from further back, memories thrumming in that left leg, the sudden sound of a machine too close, stones grinding under tires, the crack of something.

Me, Celeste thought distantly. *The crack of me.*

Celeste plummeted, body spasming in that half sleep, falling, then suddenly aware of the firm bed, the heat of the blankets, and a distant sound—voices.

She twitched beneath the covers, fumbled her arm—heavy —to the dial on the heating blanket, switched it off.

Voices again, closer now, steps away, in the next room.

Her mouth felt cottony, her body dropping like a lead weight toward sleep as her mind clawed back to consciousness. Celeste forced her eyes open, blinked into the darkness.

The voices again, more distinct. A teenage girl pleading...

"I won't tell, I swear."

Celeste sat bolt upright in bed, the thickness in her mind washed away in an instant.

A man spoke, too low for Celeste to make out words. The girl began to cry—she was negotiating with the man, begging.

Celeste stood from the bed, gasped at the jolt of lightning that streaked through her hip. Steeling herself against the pins and needles piercing her left foot, she clutched her cane, both for support and for a weapon. She hobbled from the room, sure that the girl and the man struggled in her living room.

She moved into the dark space, searched the shapes of her furniture, then gripped her cane harder and reached for the light switch. The fixture turned on, washed away the shadows. No one stood in the condo. It was dead silent.

Had the voices come from a nearby apartment? No. No, because the one next to hers was vacant. The opposite side held a man who rarely visited. She'd not once since moving in heard the voices of other tenants.

The voices had emerged from her living room. She was sure of it in the same way she was sure she'd seen Katie that night on the snowy path behind her house. And she was also sure she'd heard the girl's voice before. It belonged to Adrien Collins, the barista from the coffee shop in Graves.

Celeste thought again of the sense that she was straddling two worlds. She had died and been brought back and had somehow carried the dead with her.

Her rational mind refuted the theory, rolled her eyes, castigated her. But as Celeste limped to her kitchen to fill a glass with Scotch she caught the faint traces of a smell, two smells, a sweet fruit-scented perfume and the dank bitterness of cigarette smoke. It drifted in through a single breath, one inhale, and in the next breath she detected no trace of either scent.

"Except Adrien isn't dead," she murmured.

She considered Brenda's admission that Harris had come back with psychic abilities. It was after three a.m.—far too late to call him—and yet she fished his card from her purse and stared at it.

"No," she muttered, shoving the card back into her purse.

Calling at three in the morning was a surefire way to let someone know you'd lost it.

32

———

I
t was after nine a.m. when Celeste walked into Espresso Mike's. Three people stood in line, waiting to order. Celeste scanned the faces of the two boys working. No Adrien.

She waited in line and ordered a cappuccino to go. "Is Adrien working today?" she asked.

The boy who'd taken her order, nametag Seth, looked at her quizzically. "Adrien? I don't know who that is. Are you sure she works here?"

"Yeah. She was in here a few days ago."

Seth turned to his co-worker, busy preparing Celeste's cappuccino. "Do we have an Adrien who works here?"

The second boy shook his head. "Nope. It's us, Jenny and Felicity, unless Mike hired someone else."

"Mike's the owner," Seth explained. "I've never heard of an Adrien, but Mike comes in on Sundays, so you could check in with him then."

"All right. Thanks," Celeste murmured, thinking again of the girl who'd spoken to her. She'd acted like an employee, had on an Espresso Mike's shirt and everything, though Celeste realized the boys' shirts were different. Adrien's had been a stiff-looking polo with 'Espresso Mike's' sewn into the right chest. The guys before her wore t-shirts, 'Espresso Mike's' stamped above a dancing coffee bean.

She took her drink and returned to her car, sitting for several minutes and watching the coffee shop. She half expected to see the girl through the window, discover the three employees were playing some kind of prank. The girl never appeared and, after Celeste finished her cappuccino, she drove away.

CELESTE PARKED at the road edge near the trail that led to the abandoned train car. She hadn't gotten the hang of walking in the snow in her new heavy boots. Though her feet stayed warm and dry, the weight of the boots tugged on her left ankle and hip with each step.

When she reached the train car, the most recent snow had mostly obscured the train tracks, though they showed in patches. There were footprints around the car, though not many. Celeste spotted several cigarette butts on the top of the snow and wondered who'd walked out there and smoked them. Had they known what had been previously discovered in the train car?

Celeste swiped the snow off the floor of the train car and sat in the opening, resting her cane beside her. She twisted around and looked into the gloomy interior. Only feet away from where she sat, Sherry's body had been disposed of. How long had she lain in the claustrophobic space, the heavy door obliterating the light? The mere thought of it made Celeste's skin crawl, and she stood and limped away, watching the dark opening as if some beast lingered inside—had been about to pull her in.

Something brushed against her leg and she screamed, eyes

taking in a flurry of movement beneath her. A midsize black dog with a caramel-colored snout and floppy black ears sniffed her boots.

"Don't worry. She doesn't bite," a man called.

Celeste turned to see an old man bundled in a heavy Carhartt jacket, knee-high boots and a fur-lined hat hobbling towards her. He too held a cane and as Celeste stared at him, she realized she was looking at the man from the video interview with Katie, Thad Browning.

His eyes shifted to her cane, and he smiled, holding up his own cane, then made a face when he nearly tipped over. "I was about to say we got something in common, but I best not be liftin' this thing up or you'll have to dig me out of the snow."

Celeste leaned down and scratched behind the dog's ears. "I've been pretty close to a few face-falls myself," she admitted.

"I rarely see anyone out here," he said. "Come here, Boomer. Give the lady a break." He fished a treat from his pocket and the dog bounced over and ate it before running off to sniff a row of pine trees.

"You're Thad, right?"

His eyes went wide, and he looked down as if he expected his name to be sewn into his jacket. "My memory ain't what it used to be, but I'm sure I'd remember if we'd met."

"We haven't. I'm in town helping Joanna Ellis find Katie, and I watched the interview you did with her."

"Oh, golly. Well, I'm glad to hear it. Jo could use all the help she can get. Poor thing. She's as raggedy as Little Orphan Annie lately with no Daddy Warbucks to rescue her. You saw the interview, huh? I wondered what happened to those videos Katie took."

"They were still at the school. Jo hadn't had a chance to watch them. Would you be up for answering a few questions?" Celeste asked.

"I don't see why not. Must be somebody wanted us to meet,

because here we both are. Probably need to have a seat, though." He moved to the train car and sat in the opening she'd vacated minutes before.

"In the video, you mentioned someone named the Graves Peeper. Can you tell me more about him?"

"The Graves Peeper?" He pulled off his gloves and massaged his knuckles. "You know what's crazy? We joked about him in the beginning. A dirty old man peeking in windows or a teenager who hadn't sprouted hair on their balls. It seemed harmless. But then the rapes started."

"Rapes? Here in Graves?"

"One in Graves. One in Bellaire. One in Mancelona."

"And when did this happen?"

"Fourteen, fifteen years ago."

"I searched online for the Graves Peeper and didn't find anything."

"Well, you wouldn't. That was a name a few of us locals tossed around."

"And you believe the Peeping Tom turned into a rapist?"

"Yep. I know it. My closest friend in them days was Gordie Crenshaw and his son, Luke, was the detective on those peeper cases. Gordie was a retired state trooper himself, so Luke ran everything by Gordie. Luke also worked the rape here in Graves and helped with the one in Bellaire, because that was a Graves girl. Two of the girls who saw the Peeping Tom got a pretty good look at his mask—a camouflage knit thing with eye holes and a mouth hole. Same type of mask reported by the girls who got raped."

"Did they ever catch him?"

"Nope. Three rapes and he fell off the radar, but Gordie and I suspected he went quiet because he nearly killed the third girl and figured the heat would be on him."

"What did he do to her?"

Thad rubbed his jaw. "He strangled her, left her for dead."

"Oh, my God."

"Yeah. It was bad for her, real bad. They didn't release the names of the victims, but I knew her because she lived down the block from me—Adrien."

"Wait," Celeste broke in. "Adrien Collins?"

Thad raised both eyebrows. "You knew her? A sad, sad story. She wasn't the same after... the incident. I used to talk to her mom and the poor woman was going plumb crazy trying to get help for Adrien, who'd started havin' a lot of mental problems after she was attacked. Nightmares and panic attacks. She slept on the floor in her mother's room. Stopped showering. He attacked her when she was in the shower—that's how come she didn't hear him break into her apartment—so then she was terrified of the shower bein' on. Eighteen years old, shoulda been headin' off to college, startin' her life, and instead she moved back in with her parents, became a prisoner of one horrible night. In the end, she couldn't take it and... took a bunch of pills and went to sleep."

Celeste stared at him. "She killed herself?" She thought again of the pretty girl with the ice-blue eyes, the girl she swore she'd heard in her condo in the dead of night pleading for her life. "Are you sure?"

Thad looked annoyed at the question. "It's not something you forget. I went to her funeral. She looked so peaceful, angelic, but every person in that church knew it was plain wrong to be sending off a young girl whose whole life was waitin' for her."

Maybe it had been a different girl in the coffee shop, another Adrien Collins—a completely random coincidence. "Adrien was assaulted here in Graves?"

Thad shook his head. "She was attacked in Bellaire. She was livin' in an apartment at the ski resort. She worked here at the coffee shop in Graves during the week and as a ski instructor at the resort on the weekends."

"She worked at the coffee shop? Espresso Mike's?" Celeste's mouth had gone dry.

"Yep, and taught skiing at Shanty Creek on the weekends. That's where she lived."

Adrien Collins had lived at the same place Celeste had moved into days before.

"Did police ever connect the Graves Peeper to Sherry's murder?"

Thad looked thoughtful. "Hmm... Probably should've, huh? I never even thought about it myself. But when Sherry got killed, that peeper turned rapist had gone quiet. It had been years. It feels like a stretch to connect the two."

"Does it? Graves is a small town and we're talking about a sexual predator."

"You're not wrong about that," he agreed.

"Did you hold back a suspect name in your interview with Katie? You named Norm Little and Warren Boyd. Was there someone else you were reluctant to disclose?"

Thad lifted his cane and cracked it on the side of the train car. "Boomer. Git away from there. Come on."

Celeste looked to where the dog was furiously digging a hole near a tree. She seemed not to have heard her owner's reprimand.

"She's wily, that dog. My last coonhound, Zippy, obeyed every command, but Boomer must be deaf in both ears. Katie told me she was gonna cut that part out of the video, the namin' part."

"I'd imagine she never got around to it," Celeste said.

A pained look crossed Thad's face, and he nodded. "I was holdin' back when I talked to Katie and the reason is simple. The other person police were lookin' at for Sherry's murder was Travis Mills."

"Katie's dad? What made the detectives suspect Travis?"

"Coupla things. People saw Travis talkin' to Sherry at the

beach the day she went missing. He was partying up there with some of his buddies. No business talkin' to her at all. Travis was thirty or so, had a little daughter, Katie, and was livin' with Jo's mom. But he never had loyalty to anyone. Drugs'll do that to a person. I lost a brother to drugs when I was a young man. He was a stranger to me by the time he died. You seen that movie *Trainspotting*?"

Celeste shook her head.

"You want a glimpse into the sordid mind of a drug addict, that's the one to watch. There's a scene where this group of druggies realizes their baby is dead in the crib. That scene gave me nightmares for weeks. That's what happens to a person who gets sucked into that black hole. Even their most precious gift —their own child—becomes collateral damage.

"Anyhow, Travis told police he'd been gone all night, crashed with those buddies at their cabin when Sherry went missin'. But a guy workin' the gas station not a mile up the road from Graves Grocery put Travis in town at that fuel station, buying a fifth of vodka around midnight."

"And police believe Sherry vanished from the Graves Grocery parking lot?"

"Oh, sure. Any knucklehead with half a brain could surmise that. Her car was there with her sandwich and a pop still in the bag. And it seemed obvious someone she knew pulled up because no one heard a scream, saw a commotion."

"What if someone with a gun forced her into their car?"

Thad squirmed. "This ain't a La-Z-Boy, that's for sure. Good golly, Miss Molly, I gotta stand up. Hold on now." He gripped the doorframe of the train car with one hand and steadied his hand on his cane, struggling to his feet. He bent his legs a few times and rubbed his backside. "It's possible someone got her that way. Course, that opens up the whole world for who mighta done it."

"But police suspected someone local?"

"Yeah. On account of no struggle and this." He patted his hand on the side of the train car. "Someone passin' through isn't likely to bring her to a place like this. Isn't likely to even know it exists."

"Why do you think the killer left her here? There are woods everywhere. Why not conceal her?"

"Sick in the head. Wasn't enough to kill her. He wanted someone to find her and he probably figured it'd be kids because that's the types who come out here usually."

"I read an article that mentioned a sighting of Sherry's car at the former Howard Graves mansion."

"Yeah." Thad bobbed his head. "I remember hearin' that, but nobody ever confirmed it."

"Do you have any... theories?"

Thad looked thoughtful. "If I had to bet money on one of the three suspects police looked at a decade ago? My wager would be on Warren Boyd."

33

Celeste parked at a little building divided into parts—a convenience store on one end and a taco shop on the other. She'd wanted to drive straight back to the condo after talking with Thad, but she was out of Scotch.

She should have gone to the Graves Grocery and bought real food. Instead, she opted for a bag of pretzels and a box of granola bars. At the counter, she pointed to the shelves of liquor. "A fifth of Johnnie Walker Scotch, please."

The door near the taco counter on the opposite side of the store opened and Celeste glanced over as Declan Boyd walked in. She paid and shuffled back into the shelves to watch him.

The girl at the taco counter smiled. "Hi, Declan."

"Pepsi," he told her.

Celeste hadn't gotten a great look at Declan when she'd seen him in the parking lot at Graves High, but she studied him now. He was a good-looking kid, tall and broad, though some of that might have been a trick of his bulky winter coat. He had shaggy blond hair, a strong jaw, full lips. She struggled to find the resemblance between him and his father, Warren.

"We're totally out of Pepsi. How about diet?" the girl behind the counter asked. She leaned forward so her meager cleavage showed in the deep cut of her blue sweater. Her eyes were locked on Declan, and Celeste could feel her desperation to please him. She felt something else too—some presence near the girl, a grandfather, she thought, warning her away from the young man with the scar near his temple that looked disturbingly to Celeste like a cigarette burn.

"Diet?" Declan snapped. "I'd rather drink piss. Just get me a Mountain Dew."

The girl dipped behind a tall soda fountain machine and reappeared a moment later with a large Styrofoam cup, a straw sticking out. "It's on me," she told Declan, offering him a flirty smile as he took the cup.

He didn't even thank her. He turned and walked out the door. Celeste hurried out the convenience store side and watched Declan as he strode across the lot to his pickup.

"Declan!" she called, walking toward him, forcing her left leg to stop wobbling.

He turned and glared at her. "Yeah?"

"I wondered if you had a few minutes to talk. I'm trying to help the Ellis family locate Katie."

He sneered. 'The Ellis family? You mean Jo and that psycho who tried to knock me out? Who's he trying to kid? As if he ever gave a shit about Katie."

"Can you tell me anything at all about the last day Katie was seen? Please. I need two minutes."

He opened the driver's side door, and she expected him to get in and drive away. He turned back, his eyes mean. Now Celeste saw the resemblance between Warren and his son.

"She left, all right? What do you want me to say? She thought she was better than me and she thought she was better than this town."

"You believe she ran away?"

"She was seventeen. It ain't a crime to leave. People do it all the time."

"But to leave and not tell her sister…"

He stared at her as if she didn't get it, would never get it. "She never coulda told Joanna. The only way to escape a place like Graves is to disappear."

BACK AT THE CONDO, Celeste stared at her boards and the names there: Warren, Declan, Travis.

Declan had seemed full of emotion, primarily anger. Was he telling the truth? Did he truly believe Katie had taken off, convinced it'd be easier on her sister if she disappeared than to tell her she wanted her independence, her own life?

Her phone rang and Jonathan's name appeared on the screen. She let it ring, not wanting him to realize she'd ignored his call. She'd talked to him only a couple of times since leaving. The previous day he'd accused her of running away, of refusing to deal with her situation, their situation. She'd pretended she had a massage scheduled and ended the call.

The truth was Jonathan wasn't wrong and she knew it. She'd driven away from her former life and put on the persona of Dear Celeste, and Dear Celeste didn't have a husband, a job, a three-bedroom house and a cat. She was wholly immersed in the dilemmas of others—in this case, Joanna.

Glass of Scotch in hand, she opened her laptop and typed in 'Adrien Collins, Graves, Michigan.' No news articles populated, but an obituary did. Celeste's eyes locked onto the photo of the girl who she'd seen days before in the coffee shop at Espresso Mike's. The girl who'd been dead for years. Pale blue eyes, close-set, a smile that revealed two rows of straight white teeth. Dark blonde hair pinned back by two sparkly barrettes.

She wore a necklace, a black lace choker with a pearl in the center.

Celeste rubbed her eyes, opened them. The choker remained around the girl's neck. It was not a vision, a figment of her imagination.

The obituary described Adrien's love of skiing in the winter and playing softball in the spring. She'd been accepted to Michigan Tech, but would never make the journey north, where she hoped to become an engineer. She was survived by her parents and two siblings.

Celeste stared at the obituary and searched for a sense of her. Was she trapped between the land of the living and the dead? Why had she appeared to Celeste, so real?

Celeste copied the link to the obituary and emailed it to Joanna with a message. *This is Adrien Collins. She committed suicide after being assaulted by a rapist thirteen years ago. Look at her picture, at what she's wearing around her neck.*

The choker wasn't irrefutable proof the man who'd attacked Adrien had abducted Katie. What if Katie had somehow purchased an identical necklace?

Even as she tried to explain it away, Celeste knew she'd been shown the choker in Katie's room for a reason and the reason stared back at her from Adrien's obituary. It had belonged to this girl, and the man who'd stolen it from her had later given it to Katie Ellis.

All the threads traced back to Celeste's newfound psychic ability and yet the otherworldly messages did little to shed light on the very real issue of Katie's disappearance.

Celeste typed in a new search: 'psychic mediums.'

She scanned the articles and opened one on a forum titled: 'I'm a medium. Ask me anything.'

The first poster had written: *Any person who claims they are a medium is a vile, repulsive human being who exploits vulnerable people searching for closure regarding a loved one. You don't see dead people. You are a fake, a phony, and you should be ashamed of yourself. Fuck you telling lies for your own gain.*

Celeste frowned and read further down. A few people had posted questions, but many, like the first response, had only cruel comments insisting the creator of the post was a liar and a fraud and should be imprisoned for their abuse of people who were suffering.

She read the posts until her eyelids drooped. The hatred people lobbed at those claiming psychic or medium abilities exhausted and scared her.

The nightmare took her almost as soon as she nodded off.

Celeste climbed into the old train car. It stank of decay and flies buzzed around her head. Suddenly the door slammed behind her, obliterating the light. She flailed in the dark compartment, spun around and tried to open the door. It wouldn't budge. It was stifling hot in the train car, suffocating, and the smell... Oh, God, the smell.

Beneath her something wet and sticky seeped into her shoes, and each time she lifted her foot, her shoe released a grotesque squelching sound.

Slippery hands with sharp fingernails grabbed at her and the voices of girls pleaded: "Help us, help us, help us." The putrid smell grew worse.

Flies landed on Celeste's arms and face, crept up her nose, burrowed in her ears. She swatted them away, pushed back at the girls.

Outside the train car she heard the crunching of twigs and knew the man lurked there, a predator stalking her, inhaling her fear, reveling in it.

Still, she screamed and pounded on the door. She couldn't suck in a breath. Flies filled her nose, poured into her mouth.

The door jerked open and she fell forward.

Celeste jolted awake and her arm struck the empty glass of Scotch resting on the arm of the chair she'd dozed off in. It clattered to the carpet.

For a moment she was still there, trapped in the train car full of dead girls, flies crawling into her eyes. Her heart hammered and her breath chugged in quick gasps. As she stared at the room, focused on the unremarkable painting of the mallard ducks on the opposite wall, her panic slowly subsided.

Shaky, she stood and made her way to the kitchen. She drank a glass of water, took two pain pills and leaned heavily against the counter, watching skiers on the hill outside. It was after eight p.m.

Overriding the voice in her head insisting she not, Celeste dug the card for Harris Mayne out of her purse, took out her cell phone and called him.

"This is Harris."

Celeste held the phone to her ear and suddenly didn't know what to say, wished she hadn't called him.

"Hello?" he said.

She opened her mouth.

"Celeste?"

Her eyes widened. "How did you know it was me?"

"It happens sometimes. I'm not always right."

"But what happens?"

"I saw your face in my mind."

"And that started happening after—"

"My NDE. Yes."

"Oh. Okay, well, yes. Obviously, it's me. I wondered if we could talk, if I could tell you my... story."

"Yes. When would you like to meet?"

"I know it's kind of late, but... tonight?"

"Sure. I'll come to you."

34

I t took an hour for Harris to reach her condo and Celeste nearly phoned him twice to call the whole thing off. The thought of confessing the psychic stuff to another person out loud caused her to grow hot and itchy. It felt like crossing a line—admitting not only was it real, but she needed help to manage it. Except in the modern world, there were no psychic therapists. Or maybe there were, and she'd merely lived in such a tiny, scientifically minded community she'd never learned of their existence.

The waiting at least gave her the nervous energy to do the heel slides she'd neglected since leaving Grand Rapids. Afterwards she took a quick shower, pausing to stare at the tattoo of the raven on her thigh. The redness was gone. She smoothed her fingers along the word 'evolve.' Was that what she was doing?

When he knocked on the door, Celeste hurriedly pulled on terrycloth pants and a t-shirt. She opened the door, her heart working overtime.

"Hi," she said.

Harris stood in the hall. Snowflakes caught in his facial hair.

"Come on in," she said.

He walked into the condo and sat down. "Do you live here?"

"No. In Grand Rapids. I'm up here helping someone. That's part of the problem, I guess."

"And what is the problem, exactly?"

Celeste limped to a chair opposite him and half fell into it. "Sorry. This leg and hip give me a lot of trouble."

"I can see that. Don't apologize. It took me a year and a half to physically recover from my near-death. And 'recover' isn't quite the right word. The body is forever different. We can't exactly recover who or what we were before."

"A year and a half," Celeste murmured. The thought of another year of limping around, of waiting for mobility to return, made her want to scream.

"Don't dwell on all that right now. Let's start with your near-death. Tell me about it."

Celeste reached for the glass of Scotch she'd poured before Harris arrived, took a sip. "Do you want one? It's Scotch."

"No. Thank you."

"I'm not sure where to begin."

"Start the day of the accident and tell me everything you remember about being on this side and the other side."

"It's going to sound crazy."

"I can assure you it won't. I've been there, remember? And I've been listening to stories of NDEs for eight years. I've heard a lot of them."

"Okay." Celeste looked toward the window. It was dark, but the ski slope was lit for night skiing. "Here's what I remember. It was an ordinary Sunday morning. I got up around six, joined Jonathan, my husband, for coffee. We each read our papers, mine the *Grand Rapids Press*, his the *Wall Street Journal*. Then I put on my tennis shoes and walked out the door like I'd done a thousand other times. It was around seven and our neighborhood is very quiet at that time. I rarely even see lights on in other houses, let alone anyone else on the road.

"I was thinking about this pharmaceutical we'd been developing at the lab to curb impulsive behavior. Walking always helped with those sorts of breakthroughs. I was about a half mile from our house in this stretch that's woods on one side and a series of undeveloped lots on the other side. I was immersed in my own thoughts and heard an engine, and I sidestepped, but not much, because again, there was no one else on the road. I assumed they'd drive around me.

"And then… wham. I don't… remember pain, only a massive impact, and I was thrown out of my body. Birds suddenly surrounded me, or black feathers, raven feathers, as if I were standing in the center of a cyclone among the most beautiful benevolent ravens. When the birds cleared, I was looking down at my body. I'd been hit and my leg was tucked beneath me at this impossible angle. I'd been thrown right out of my tennis shoes. I don't know how long I lay there, but people started arriving and I watched my husband running down the road.

"I remember moving upward so fast and then I was in this darkness, this infinite darkness, which might sound scary, but it wasn't. It was the most beautiful, warm, easy darkness. And I understood something had happened, but I didn't realize I was dead. I felt… no attachment to what had been happening before. A very loving feminine presence accompanied me. She felt like… like my mother."

"Is your mother no longer living?"

Celeste frowned, shook her head slowly. "I don't actually know. She abandoned my family when I was three. My brother was one. She walked out on us. We never heard from her again. But… she was there. So that must mean she's dead, right?"

"Possibly. But beyond this life, our ideas of 'mother' and 'father' aren't quite the same. At least that was my impression."

"When I woke, Jonathan told me I'd been in a coma for ten days. I found out I'd suffered a traumatic brain injury, shattered my hip and leg, broken several ribs and had internal bleeding. Again, I don't remember any pain. None. Not before, but after..." Her fingers trailed to her hip to the tattoo that now ran alongside her scar. "The pain was excruciating. It's gotten better, but not all the way. It's like everything changed. My body, my brain, my consciousness.

"Before the accident I didn't believe in God, period. I wasn't atheist. I didn't have a religion or belief system at all. I leaned toward something very bleak, the light snuffing out and eternal darkness taking over, if there was anything to even take over. Mostly, I thought consciousness ended with the brain, but now I know it doesn't. This life, this world, feels so much less real than before the accident and yet being back here makes me question everything.

"I tried to talk about it in the first hours in the hospital, but my husband"—Celeste folded her arms across her chest—"looked at me like I'd suffered brain damage. And in his defense, I did suffer brain damage, but not the kind that caused me to hallucinate what had happened. He demanded the doctors run more brain scans. Even after I was discharged, I tried once to tell him and he... stared at me like he was terrified. Terrified that I'd been irrevocably changed, damaged. And I was irrevocably changed, but... not for the worse. I don't think, anyway.

"Except for the other stuff I came back with... the, um..." Celeste chewed her lip. "The psychic stuff and the ghosts."

"You're seeing ghosts?"

"Among other things."

"Okay. I understand why you're feeling overwhelmed by all that."

"Do you ever see spirits?"

Harris shook his head. "No. I saw spirits on the other side, but that's different. Tell me about it."

Celeste pushed her hands through her hair and closed her eyes, self-conscious at the prospect of baring it all to a complete stranger. "It started as soon as I woke up in the hospital. There are a lot of spirits in there—unsurprising, right? They'd come into my room and disappear. Sometimes they're people, sometimes a voice or an image or an object pops into my head.

"And now I'm here trying to help this woman Joanna find her little sister who vanished a year ago. Before I committed to helping her, I saw her sister, Katie. She came to me and... I'm afraid she's dead. I'm at a loss as to what to do with the things I'm seeing. It's not black and white. I've spent my whole life as a logical thinker, a left-brain-type person, and now..." She shook her head. "I'm falling apart. I'm having terrible dreams and honestly, I don't know what's dream and what's reality."

"It's not unusual to struggle after a near-death experience. In fact, it's quite common even without the extra perceptions. A lot of NDEers I've met talk about how having this amazing experience—this knowledge that we all have a purpose, that our spirits go on—should have made them immune to depression, anxiety, despair. Instead, a lot of them were bombarded with those feelings when they returned to life. They struggled with living in a world so full of pain, so divided. Heap on the strain that happens when they tell their loved ones they saw their dead relatives, spoke with God, and life gets awfully difficult. I struggled when I came back. I was severely injured. I'd been in a car accident. My wife and daughter both died."

Celeste stared at him. "I'm sorry," she said, embarrassed she'd been rambling on and hadn't even asked about his experience.

"Don't," he told her.

"Don't what?"

"Feel ashamed you didn't ask me to share. I'm here to help you. Returning to life here on earth is difficult. I considered killing myself. I knew my wife and daughter were on the other side. I knew if I stayed here, the road ahead would be terrible. My career might be over. I'm a detective and if I never recovered full mobility, that was gone. I'd be returning to a house crammed with the remnants of a life that I loved, a life that I took for granted. A house filled with my wife's stuff, her clothes and perfume, my daughter's toys, her baby dolls." Tears filled his eyes, and he took a couple of deep breaths. "But I also understood I came back for a reason. And so I took it a minute at a time until I could tolerate being here again.

"Once I integrated the experience and made it through the first few years of coming to terms with the new reality, I realized it made me better as a detective. I can foresee when I walk into a room if a perp has a gun and if he's intending to use it or if he's simply scared. I can sense the intention, the energy of people and that makes me better able to handle them and to help them. I'm also not afraid of death anymore. I look forward to it, in fact."

"I'm not sure if I'm afraid of death," Celeste admitted. "I think what I'm mostly afraid of is not being able to go back to my former life. I never wanted some extraordinary experience. I was pretty happy with my comfortable, mundane life and now... I've been shoved out of it. I can't get back in."

"Do you want back in?"

Celeste took another drink, pressed the cool cup against her head. "I don't think so."

"My advice? No radical changes during year one. Your body is healing. Let that happen first. Like I said, one minute at a time. You're up north searching for a missing girl and in your life before you were...?"

"A pharmaceutical scientist."

"That's a leap."

"Tell me about it."

"The detective in me is curious about your boards here." Harris stood and walked to the bulletin boards. "This is her case?"

"Yeah. Do you get, umm… any impressions from it?"

He smiled. "As in psychic impressions?"

"Or just detective ones."

"I have a friend you should talk to."

"Who?"

"Her name is Eliza. I met her about two years after my NDE. She had a near-death experience and came back able to see spirits. It's her full-time job these days."

"You work with her? On cases?"

"Sometimes, yeah. I reach out to her, ask if she can pick up anything from a victim. It's not foolproof—sometimes our signals get a bit mixed up—but often it points me in the right direction. She works with a lot of cops, though they won't tell you that. She also works with a lot of people who share the gift. She helps them work with it so it's not so all-consuming. Are you up for meeting her?"

"Sure. Why not? I'm doing all kinds of unusual things these days."

35

Joanna opened the email from Celeste and clicked a link that took her to an obituary for a young woman named Adrien Collins. She zoomed in on the photograph and froze. The choker Celeste had seen in Katie's pencil case encircled the girl's neck.

Hands shaking, she picked up the phone and dialed Celeste, but got her voicemail. "I saw the obituary. What does this mean? Please call me."

When five minutes passed without a return call, Joanna went into Katie's room and opened the pencil case. She picked up the choker and desperately searched her memory for Katie having worn it. However impossible it seemed, Joanna wondered if Adrien's family had donated it and Katie had bought it at a thrift store. Nearly everything Katie owned was vintage or secondhand. Except the choker was not Katie's style. She found it hard to believe her sister would ever have purchased it.

Joanna took a picture of the choker with her cellphone and texted it to Liam. *Do you know where Katie got this necklace?*

Liam responded almost immediately. *Never seen it. Why?*

Joanna considered how to respond and ended with: *I'll explain later.*

Choker in her hand, Joanna grabbed her keys and left the apartment.

She drove to the Graves cemetery, the choker burning a hole in her pocket, and parked. She cut across the Graves family headstones and a tall, faded angel carved from limestone, the name long since eroded by the elements. As she crested the hill that led to her mother's grave, she froze.

Someone else knelt at her mother's headstone.

Joanna quickly ducked behind a tree and watched. After a moment, the man stood. It was Travis.

He'd left a single red rose on top of the headstone and his face looked streaked and blotchy, as if he'd been crying. She watched him carve a path across the cemetery to another headstone and pause there for several minutes. Again, he left behind a single red rose.

She'd never known Travis to visit her mother's grave. Was it sobriety bringing him to the graveyard or guilt?

After he'd driven away, Joanna walked to her mother's tombstone. The red rose made her uneasy, and after staring at it for several seconds she moved it behind the grave so she didn't have to look at it.

"Hi, Mom," she murmured, bending down and swiping the snow off the base of the stone with her gloved hand.

In life, Joanna had never had deep talks with her mom. She hadn't run to her for advice or for solace when life got too hard. The truth was that when Joanna had left home, life got easier. She had only herself to worry about, to care for. No more Travis rampaging through the house slamming cupboards and doors because he had to go to work and the only thing he really wanted to do was get high. No more mood swings from her mother, chipper one minute and blackly depressed the next. Even Katie, for all Joanna loved her, had been a whirlwind of energy, of activity. In her mother's house, Joanna had felt as if she lived in a hurricane, trapped in the center, helpless against the chaos around her.

When her mother had received her cancer diagnosis, Joanna had moved back home. It had made her physically ill, but Joanna had done what was right. She'd stepped up and taken care of her mother and Katie. Travis was long gone by then.

"What do I do, Mom?" She turned her face to the sky, the gray cloud cover.

When Joanna returned her car, she noticed a missed call from Celeste and dialed her back.

"Hi. I've got an appointment in a couple minutes," Celeste said. "But we need to track down who gave Katie that necklace."

"Here's the thing. What if Katie bought it from a second-hand store?"

Celeste was quiet for a moment. "It's possible, but let's rule out the alternatives and see if we can find out who gave it to her."

"I asked Liam and he didn't know."

"Keep asking. I'll see you at the schoolhouse in a few hours."

"Okay. Yeah."

Joanna drove to Randy's house to pick up his projector and blow-up screen to display a slideshow of Katie's photos. He came outside when she arrived.

"I could have brought this tonight," he said.

"I know, but I'm nervous and trying to stay busy today. I told Floyd I'd work the breakfast shift at the diner this morning and he refused. Apparently he's forgotten that idle time does little more than leave me chewing my nails to stubs."

"Why are you nervous?"

"What if no one shows up?"

"Not gonna happen. Half the town'll be there."

"I hope so. I baked enough cookies to feed all of northern Michigan." Joanna noticed Travis's car wasn't in the driveway. "No Travis?"

"Nope. Supposedly at a job interview."

"Well, here's hoping it sticks this time."

"Yeah. I'm not convinced, but time will tell."

"I saw him at the cemetery this morning. He was putting red roses on my mom's grave and your mom's."

Randy shook his head and sighed. "That's part of the problem with sober Travis. He's a dewy-eyed toddler when he's not high. He cries about everything. I regretted letting him stay here on night one when I woke up to find him watching *Saving Private Ryan* and bawling like a baby. It's like he wants to feel miserable. Probably looking for an excuse to relapse."

Joanna sighed, wished Travis's wellbeing didn't matter to her. Mostly it didn't, but growing up watching her mother love him, watching her mother's desperation for him to be the man she needed, knowing how a decent father could change Katie's life, had forced her to care. So even with her mother gone and Katie missing for a year, some piece of her hoped Travis would turn his life around.

Randy loaded the projector and screen into her trunk. Before she left, Joanna grabbed the choker from the car and held it out. "Ever seen this?"

He picked it up. "What is it?"

"A necklace I found in Katie's room." She thought of Celeste adding Travis's name to the suspect list, the mention of him as possibly connected to Sherry's murder. "I wondered if Travis gave it to her at some point."

"Doubtful. Has he ever given her anything? You want me to keep it and ask him?"

She shook her head. If Travis had given the choker to her and had originally stolen it during the brutal assault of another young woman, she didn't want him to know they'd made the link. "See you at the vigil."

"I'll be there."

As she drove to the diner, Joanna considered whether Travis could have killed Sherry and gotten away with it. She thought so—not because Travis was a clever psychopath who'd managed to commit the perfect murder, but because he'd done all sorts of stupid things and floated under the radar of police. Had he come onto Sherry the night she disappeared and, in a drug-fueled rage, killed her then hid her body in the train car and benefited from the sweltering summer and passage of time?

It was possible. But that didn't prove he'd hurt Katie. Even if she had suspected Travis of being involved in Sherry's murder, Joanna could not imagine him hurting her. But what if he'd shoved her and she'd hit her head?

"No more," Joanna murmured, shaking the thoughts loose.

The vigil was only hours away and she needed to focus.

36

Celeste parked in front of the old-style house converted into offices on the outskirts of Traverse City. She walked through the front door, following Harris' directions to the second floor, and stopped at a partially opened door labelled 'Psychic Medium Eliza Kent.'

"Eliza?" Celeste asked, poking her head inside.

"And you're Celeste. Harris told me to expect you. Come on in."

Celeste shook Eliza's hand. Other than fingers covered in rings with interesting-looking stones, Eliza didn't look the way Celeste envisioned a psychic medium. She wore a gray turtleneck and black pleated slacks. Her hair was short and curly and dark. A pair of reading glasses hung from a simple silver chain around her neck.

"Have a seat," Eliza said, gesturing at the chair opposite her.

Celeste sat and crossed her legs.

Eliza's office was inviting, with soft earth-colored armchairs. A large Aztec area rug covered most of the wood floor. From a shelf in the corner of the room a salt lamp glowed.

"Harris tells me you had an NDE?"

"Yes. Last summer."

"And you came back with some extra gifts?"

"It seems that way."

Eliza smiled. "It's a lot in the beginning. Harris said you're getting a lot of input and also having some nightmares?"

"All of the above. I've already had trouble sleeping since the accident and now the visions and nightmares are making it practically impossible."

Eliza stood and walked to her bookshelf. "The good news is there's an off switch. You don't have to see and hear and feel it all. And it's not complicated. Think about when you take a book to a coffee shop and read. There's conversations happening, coffee grinding, horns honking on the street. You can tune in and hear all that noise, or you can read your book and be transported to an entirely different realm." She picked up a book and carried it over. "You have to start applying that same tuning out and turning off to spirits and to energy. Discernment comes first. Begin to notice what's coming from spirits and what's part of this reality. Once you can sense those variations, you ignore or refuse to interact with spirits when it's disruptive. A voice wakes you in the night, a spirit at the foot of your bed— 'I'm sleeping now. Go away.'"

Eliza pressed the book into her hands. "This is yours now. A friend of mine wrote it—a talented medium who came into the world with her abilities and they wreaked havoc on her young life. She developed a lot of rituals, practices, to protect herself from unwanted contact."

"Thank you. I'll read it," Celeste murmured. "And what about using it? I'm helping this woman find her missing sister and I'm getting visions of... spirits, of objects. I feel like Katie, the one who's missing, is trying to show me what happened."

Eliza looked at her sympathetically. "Unfortunately, it doesn't always work like that. Believe me, I know. I had my near-death experience when I was forty-five, fifteen years ago.

When I came back, I had these psychic perceptions and I knew why. I'd died and been brought back with these abilities—to find my long-lost brother, who'd been abducted from our yard when he was five and I was nine.

"I started having vision after vision of this forest path called Broomhead Trail. I could see the sign posted at the trailhead. I searched and searched. It wasn't online. No one had ever heard of it. Then one day I was driving to this older gentleman's house to do a psychic reading—this was a few years after my NDE— and wouldn't you know, I lost service about five minutes from his house, so I was trying to get there by memory of what I'd seen on the GPS map, and of course I took a so-called wrong turn—the universe loves to disguise mistakes as clues—and not a half mile down that road was this old, faded, bullet-riddled sign: 'Broomhead Trail.'" Eliza pulled up her sleeve and held out her forearm. "Goosebumps from head to toe.

"I couldn't call anyone because I had no service, and I couldn't drive away. I was sure if I did, I'd never find it again. Like it would have disappeared on me. So I parked in the ditch. If there'd ever been a parking area, it was long gone. I followed what was left of the trail—overgrown with weeds to my knees, but still there—and I turned on my timer so I knew how long I was walking for. Turned out to be forty minutes. Forty minutes! At least I'd worn sensible shoes that morning or that walk would have left me with blisters the size of hot-air balloons. Let's just say I lost the client I'd been going to read for, but this little voice urged me on.

"I was walking and this chill came over me. I looked up and a couple yards off the path there was this mound. Not real big, but noticeable from the land around. I'd found his grave. I didn't dig, didn't want to do anything to disturb the scene. I ran ninety miles an hour back to my car and drove with my cell in one hand waiting for the signal and the instant it connected I called the cold case detective who had Simon's case. Thank heavens he took pity on me and came out, brought a shovel and another detective with a video camera."

"And they found Simon?" Celeste asked, sliding to the edge of her seat.

Eliza sighed. "No, but there was a body there, all right. A young man who'd been murdered by his wife and her lover. Hodge was his name. He'd been in the military, came home on leave and they killed him. The wife told the army he'd gone AWOL. The craziest part, Celeste? I started seeing that place a month before they killed him."

Celeste's eyes went wide. "But how? How is that even possible?"

"Yeah, exactly. Try explaining that to the cops. They thought I was crazier than a soup sandwich before that happened. Anyway, that's when I realized this gift doesn't work the way we want it to. Even when we convince ourselves of one thing, it's liable to smack you upside the head and remind you of who's really in control and it sure as heck isn't you."

"Did you ever find Simon?"

Eliza's face fell. She shook her head. "He's still missing, but he visits me and he sends me Petoskey stones." She gestured at the windowsill lined with Petoskeys. "Simon was quite the rockhound."

Celeste stared at the row of stones. "How does he send you Petoskey stones?"

Eliza's eyes sparkled. She stood and walked to the ledge and picked one up. "This one he stuck in my shoe." She laughed. "But usually, he's less obvious than that. He puts them in my path or maybe he nudges me toward their path. It's hard to nail down the mechanics of spirit as I'm sure you're aware. I've found these stones in mall parking lots, the footwell of my car, and even once on an airplane. That's how many of our departed loved ones reach us, through signs, little reminders they're nearby. They're easy to miss especially when we've spent most of our lives in the land of logic-denying the magic and mystery of this extraordinary life.

"Part of why I so desperately wanted to find Simon was for my mother, who never recovered after he was taken. I saw him on the other side and I came back and told her. Maybe that's the real reason I had the NDE, not to develop some psychic gift that would lead me to his earthly remains, but to bring peace to my mother. She's with him now and so is my father as of a year ago.

"That's an important part in all this. What comes through might never give people the answers they're searching for, but it might bring them a reprieve from their grief if you can show them the end of this life is not the end of life and that their loved ones are always here. They are always with us. Always. We struggle with the idea of that in these human bodies. Our brains, as magnificent as they are, can't comprehend what's beyond this life. Katie might be coming to you, not to help solve the mystery of her death, but to help her sister heal and move on with her life."

Celeste sagged back in her chair. It was a noble purpose, as worthy as anything else, and yet Celeste felt sick at the thought of never knowing—of Joanna never knowing. "How do you understand it? The gift, as you call it?"

"I don't try to. This gift, the visions, the voices, the dreams are a practice of listening and relinquishing control—having faith in the guidance that's coming through even when it makes no sense to my logical brain. I was a very pragmatic person before my stroke. I worked as an accountant."

"I was a scientist," Celeste said.

Eliza nodded. "So you get it. And yet as a scientist you're on the frontier. You can look under a microscope and constantly see that things are not how they appear to the naked eye. I once read that a single drop of blood contains more than a million cells."

"Approximately five million."

"Exactly. And there was a time in history when humans, despite their big brains and developed cultures, would have laughed in the face of a person who said such a thing. Now it's common knowledge. What I'm getting at is the world tells us what we're supposed to believe and expects us to filter out evidence to the contrary. I say 'phooey' to that. Anytime I question what I'm receiving, I go back to my experience of crossing over. On that side, I understood that everything here has meaning. This brain might not get it, but my soul"—Eliza put a hand over her heart—"knows the truth."

Celeste smiled. Eliza's words comforted her in a way that nothing had since her near-death. "And this is your job now? Working as a medium?"

"This is it. I help part-time in an animal shelter, which is a palate cleanser after all the time spent in the energy of spirit. It gets exhausting. Think long and hard about embarking on this journey, Celeste. Mediums receive a lot of hate. It's how people react to things they don't understand or any ideas that challenge their belief system."

"I'm not going to become a medium," Celeste said quickly. "I'm a scientist and I'll go back to that job after I help Joanna. This is a one-off thing."

"Okay," Eliza said, though her expression was skeptical. "I have a reading in about twenty minutes, but before you go, do you want me to see if I can pick up anything about Katie?"

"That'd be great. Do you need a picture or—"

"Sure. Let's try that."

Celeste opened her phone, found photos of Katie she'd saved online and handed it over.

Eliza closed her eyes and began to breathe deeply. She said nothing for several minutes. "Hmm... okay. I'm not getting Katie, but I'm getting someone connected to her. An N name. I think it's Mom. She's showing me music, lots of albums, the Bee

Gees, the Doors and a, uh... I'm feeling some guilt from her, regret about not being better for her daughters.

"I do sense Katie has crossed, though again, she's not coming through. There's a tree coming in, very deep roots. I am also seeing... a hole, an opening, almost like a doorway that leads into the ground." Eliza opened her eyes. "Did any of that land for you?"

Celeste nodded though the details did little to shed light on Katie's whereabouts. "Katie's mom's name was Naomi and Katie loved sixties and seventies music. I've also been a seeing a tree with roots."

Someone knocked on the door.

Eliza glanced at the clock. "They're early," she said. "I hope this has helped, Celeste."

"It has, truly. I do wonder what to make of the hole in the ground. Do you think Katie is buried?"

Eliza scrunched her face, shook her head slowly. "I honestly can't say. I wish I could give you more than that. There's nothing straightforward about what comes through. Is anything I said relevant to Katie's disappearance? Maybe. You won't know til you know."

37

––––––

Celeste drove to the schoolhouse and parked. She climbed from her car and walked to the towering oak tree, but this time the vision of the red roots didn't emerge. She circled it once and wondered if the tree was connected to Katie's disappearance.

"Here for the vigil already?" May asked when Celeste walked into the schoolhouse. "Goodness. How time gets away from me."

Celeste gazed around the old schoolhouse, felt again the heaviness, the sense of something hovering nearby. "I'm early," Celeste said. "But I wanted to spend some time here. Is that okay?"

May grinned. "It certainly is. And I don't blame you one bit. I've always felt at home in this place. Maybe it's all this old stuff reminding me of better days, simpler days."

Celeste did not feel at home in the schoolhouse. She felt uneasy. "I think I'll go upstairs if that's okay."

"Go right ahead."

Celeste made her way up the creaky wooden steps, jarred again by the mannequin with the long brown hair, which was now in front of one window, as if gazing out. Slowly, she moved through the schoolhouse, searching for the tendril of knowing, some nudge that pointed her toward what had happened to Katie the night she vanished.

When no stroke of insight occurred, Celeste returned to the first floor. "May, do you know who moved the mannequin upstairs in front of the window? The one with the long brown hair?"

May closed her book and shook her head. "I'm not sure. Maybe Wanda. She's been here a few days this week. Either that or the mannequin walked over there on her own." May made a mock-scared face. "I sure hope not."

Celeste forced a smile, but didn't find the idea funny. It gave her the creeps. "Is there a person or group who owns the museum?"

"It's part of a trust and there's a board that manages it."

"Who's on the board?"

"There's six of us. I'm the only one who regularly works here in the museum, but the board consists of myself, Camile and Floyd Harper, Darcy Pruit—she's a teacher at Graves High—Randy Mills and Fiona Boyd. We all have our area of focus. I'm in charge of daily operations."

"Fiona Boyd? Is she related to Warren Boyd?"

May pursed her lips. "Yes. Fiona is Warren's sister."

"And who has keys or access to the museum?"

"Everyone on the board, plus Henry and Loretta Lewis. They do the cleaning. And any staff who close or open the museum."

"And after hours, does anyone check on the place?"

"Oh, no. I mean, we've never had issues with theft or anything. Our treasures aren't exactly valuable. They're nostalgic, memorable, but no one is selling one of these"—she tapped her finger on faded Graves postcards—"for any sum of money that would make them worth stealing."

Celeste's eyes landed on the cellar door. "All right. Do you mind if I look in the cellar?"

May wrinkled her nose. "I don't mind, but are you sure you want to? It's pretty nasty down there."

"I'd like to take a quick peek around. Is there a light?"

"Yes. Unfortunately, it's one of those old hanging bulbs at the bottom of the stairs."

"I can find it. Thank you." Celeste slid the deadbolt aside and opened the door. A rush of icy air and a rank odor surrounded her.

As she moved down the stairs, her footfalls swallowed by the black void below, gooseflesh raced up her spine and down her arms. She'd had a fear of confined spaces since childhood—one of those impossible-to-pinpoint phobias that had caused her to loathe elevators, airplanes and tunnels of any sort. Now, as she descended into the ground, the weight of the old stone schoolhouse above her and the dense rock and dirt surrounding her made Celeste want to turn and rush back toward the light. The sense of being swallowed so consumed her, she barely noticed the throb in her leg with each step.

"I'm fine," she muttered, irritated with the panic trying to get a grip on her.

At the bottom of the stairs, Celeste reached toward the cobwebbed ceiling, grimaced at the soft tangle of silky web that ensnared her fingers. Something skittered across the back of her hand and she gasped and ripped her arm away.

"Just do it," she commanded, darting her hand back up and yanking the rusted chain.

A single dim bulb crackled to life. The bulb illuminated a dank, musty cellar with stone walls and a dirt and stone floor. Beyond the bulb's meager glow, black shadows crowded in. Old wooden crates, stained and damp-looking, sat piled against the wall.

She thought of Eliza's advice on connecting to spirits and

how she'd arranged her office with specific music, crystals, and candles to open to the other side. Celeste had none of those things and frankly wouldn't know what to do with them if she did.

Something lingered nearby, made her feel as if she were being watched, though no one else could have been down there. The few shelves would be impossible to hide behind. The someone watching her no longer had a body.

As she walked the perimeter of the cellar, Celeste glimpsed a corner of white plastic poking from a wall of bricks. Celeste gripped the plastic edge between her thumb and forefinger and wiggled. The object was tucked in tight, but moved slightly, making it clear the bricks were merely stacked rather than cemented in place. She crammed her fingers under the brick above it and shimmied it until it pulled loose, causing bricks above it to shift and settle. For a moment, Celeste feared the entire wall would collapse. It didn't.

She stared at the item she'd pulled free. It was a cell phone, the screen cracked and dark.

Celeste made her way back to the steps and paused beneath the hanging bulb. She tried to turn the phone on, but nothing happened. It was broken or had a dead battery.

The hanging bulb flickered, released a fizzing sound, and popped. The room went black. Fear cascaded over Celeste's body. She dropped the phone in her purse and stretched her arms, feeling for the stairs. When she reached them, the door at the top slammed closed.

The old childhood fear swooped down and ensnared her. Celeste couldn't move. The black was dizzying, and she suddenly wasn't sure which direction the stairs were.

Breath rasping, hip and leg suddenly on fire, Celeste lowered to the ground and groped along the floor toward the stairs. Dirt and pebbles and dead bugs rolled beneath her palms. She crawled forward, rapid-fire blinked, but it did nothing to bring the room into focus. When her hand landed on the lowermost wooden step, she cried out in relief. Slow, careful, she crawled to the top of the stairs.

Celeste stood and twisted the knob, tried to push the door open, but it didn't budge. More terror—the kind that might make her go mad if it lived in her brain for even another second —swallowed her.

"May! May, are you there? Help me!" Celeste shouted. Her whole body had gone cold and the heaviness behind crawled toward her like a poisonous mist.

The knob wiggled. "Oh, goodness. I'm so sorry. The wind must have blown the door closed, and the knob is stuck. Hold on."

For an instant Celeste was somewhere else, hot blinding sun and a gathering of ravens and the ravens suddenly flew all at once as if she'd startled them. Black iridescent wings flapped and hit her in the face and then she was being closed in, shut inside some tiny compartment, the light becoming a sliver and then there was no light at all.

Celeste teetered on the top step, felt herself losing touch with the ground beneath her. Her sense of up and down scrambled. She'd fall back and down the stairs, hit the stone floor behind her, and whatever waited would surround her, suffocate her.

Suddenly, the door inches from her nose pulled open and May, seeing her sway, took hold of her arm and pulled her forward into the schoolhouse.

38

Joanna followed Floyd and Camile's truck into the schoolhouse parking lot. Floyd wedged a box of candles under one arm and opened the door to the schoolhouse and Joanna, carrying a box of paper plates and napkins, a coffee tucked beneath her chin, walked in.

Joanna smiled, sliding the box onto a table. "I saw your truck outside. You didn't have to come so early," she told Celeste.

Celeste brushed her hair away from her face, which Joanna noticed looked pale and clammy.

"Are you feeling okay?" Joanna asked after sipping her coffee.

Celeste opened her mouth, but before she could speak, Floyd appeared. Celeste blanched and stood quickly. "Floyd, your ear is bleeding!" Celeste's eyes practically bulged in her head as she pointed at Floyd.

Floyd stopped, startled, and looked to Joanna, who stared at the side of Floyd's head, the same side Celeste was staring at in horror. There was nothing there.

"Celeste, where? I don't see any blood." Joanna circled

around Floyd. He'd set the box down quickly and was carefully working his fingers around both of his ears.

Celeste looked at Joanna, then back at Floyd, and shook her head slowly. She touched her temple. "I'm sorry. I must have… I guess I'm seeing things."

"Are you sure you're feeling all right? You look pale."

"Yeah," Celeste murmured. "I'm fine. I just need to go out to my truck and take a pain pill. I'll be back to help in a couple of minutes."

"Okay. But really, Celeste, if your leg is bothering you, you can relax. Camile brought sandwiches and chili. I baked a backseat full of cookies and muffins. There's coffee and tea."

"I'm okay. Really. Thank you."

Joanna watched Celeste walk outside. She turned to Floyd, who also stared after Celeste.

"Huh," he said. "That was odd."

"Yeah," she agreed.

Floyd opened the door for Camile, who walked in with a large crockpot of chili.

"We have two long tables outside," Floyd said. "When people park and walk up, we'll give them a flier with Katie's information and a candle."

"How are we lighting the candles?" Camile asked, plugging the crockpot cord into an outlet.

"Oh, no," Joanna groaned. "I meant to buy a bunch of matches. I'll text Randy and see if he can get some."

"Tell him to get lights," Floyd said. "The campfire kind."

Joanna turned to Camile. "Does this look okay? I changed three times. I want to make a good impression, you know. So the reporters take Katie's disappearance seriously." Joanna looked down at the dark slacks and pine-green blouse she'd put on. She'd also worn a pair of her mother's pearl earrings. It was the most dressed up she'd been in months.

"You look lovely," Camile assured her. "Perfect."

"Okay." Joanna sighed and wrung her hands. She didn't know what she'd been thinking drinking more coffee. She was already terribly jittery and could feel sweat beginning to form beneath her arms.

May, who'd been on the phone, walked over. "That was the principal at Graves Elementary. She set up school visits for three grades next month."

"That's great," Camile said.

May frowned and looked at the bench where Celeste had been sitting. "Did Celeste leave?"

"No. She went out to her truck. She'll be right back," Joanna explained.

"Oh, good. I was worried we scared her away. She went to look around in the cellar and the door blew closed and I couldn't get it open. She looked ready to run out of here screaming when I finally got it open."

"It blew closed?" Joanna murmured. "And she was locked down there?"

"Only for about a minute, but I'm sure that was long enough."

Floyd stared at the door. "How did it blow shut? Was there a window open in the schoolhouse?"

May shook her head.

"Then how did a draft blow it closed?"

"I was clear on the other side of the room and suddenly it slammed and she started pounding on the door and yelling. I surely didn't close it."

"Of course you didn't." Joanna patted May's arm. "Weird though, and creepy. No wonder she looked sick when we came in."

"Camile," May said. "What happened to that big rug that was rolled up in the storage room? That old ratty thing that used to be upstairs. I thought we'd lay it by the door, since so many people will be tromping around in their snow boots, but I couldn't find it."

Camile looked puzzled. "I'm not sure. I forgot all about that thing. We had that dumpster here over the summer. Someone probably threw it out."

"The *Graves News* is here," Floyd announced, pointing through the window.

A surge of fear and hope streaked through Joanna when she leaned over and saw the reporter and cameraman piling from the news van. Finally, people were paying attention. Between what Celeste was uncovering, and the attention brought by the vigil, Katie might finally get found.

"They're early," Joanna said, swallowing the tremor in her voice. "But that's fine. I'm going to get the baked goods and—"

Floyd put a hand on her shoulder. "I'll get the cookies. You go meet the reporter and give them the details of Katie's disappearance. You want them to have all the facts. It's good they're early. You have their undivided attention. Go on."

By SEVEN P.M. the schoolhouse parking lot was packed with cars and more lined the snowy embankments on either side of the road. People milled around the schoolhouse, eating from paper cups of chili and talking about Katie.

At seven-thirty, Floyd ushered everyone outside, where Liam, Randy and Travis walked amongst the group lighting candles.

Joanna stepped onto the little podium Floyd and Randy had erected in front of the schoolhouse. She'd talked to dozens of people that night, stared into the over-bright camera lights and told Katie's story repeatedly. Now she gazed out at a crowd of people—the Graves community—many of them holding candles that flickered in the darkness. Her chest filled and tears tried to swim into her eyes. She blinked them away.

"I want to extend my deepest gratitude to you all for coming tonight," Joanna said. "Katie was last seen here one year ago today. We know she closed the museum at nine o'clock and from that moment on, her whereabouts are unknown. That day Katie was wearing her corduroy coat, a long-sleeved Jim Morrison t-shirt and bell-bottom jeans. We suspect, but don't know, that she walked back into town and it's possible someone picked her up during that time.

"Katie loved candles. She burned them all the time. Even as a little girl, her favorite part of her birthday was the candles on her cake. She cried when she had to blow them out." Joanna smiled sadly, a hollowness in her stomach at the memory. "As I look out and see your flames, I feel hope that Katie's flame still burns, that amidst the darkness of the world and perhaps even the darkness that she encountered that night, a flame of hope lives on. I ask that you all take these candles home tonight, relight them and put them in your window as a reminder to everyone in Graves that Katie is still out there and that we are still looking."

As Joanna scanned the crowd, she saw Cole, her ex-boyfriend, standing next to several other Graves locals. Their eyes met, and he smiled.

Joanna swallowed and continued, "Floyd and Camile, who many of you know from the Sidewinder, have generously offered a five-thousand-dollar reward to anyone who provides a tip that leads to the recovery of Katie—living or..." Her voice broke and Floyd stepped in, put an arm around her.

"Any information that helps us locate Katie is what we're looking for," Floyd boomed. "Please don't hold back. There's a Facebook page and the police have a tip line. Even if you called something in a year ago, there's a new detective on the case and sometimes information falls through the cracks."

Joanna stood in the crook of Floyd's arm. He smelled of

aftershave and the distinctive spices he used on the burgers at the diner.

As Floyd talked, someone in the crowd gasped and pointed. Joanna turned. Flames leapt in an upstairs window of the schoolhouse.

THE FIRE, apparently started when someone left a lit vigil candle on the windowsill, burned only a single curtain.

"If that mannequin had been an inch closer," a man said, gesturing at the mannequin that resembled Katie, "she'd have gone up like that in those old-timey clothes." He snapped his fingers. "Nothing was flame-retardant back when they were making those."

After several people had extinguished the fire, Floyd said a few more words, and the vigil came to an end.

Joanna talked with three reporters who promised to feature articles on Katie's case. "Front page," the guy from *Up North News* told her. She was light on her feet when she went into the schoolhouse to start packing everything up.

"Did anyone see who put that candle upstairs?" Floyd asked, frowning. The schoolhouse still stank of burned fabric.

"Probably someone thinking it was a good deed and then didn't come forward because they nearly burned the place down," Camile said.

"I didn't see anyone," Joanna admitted, "though my mind was elsewhere."

Celeste stood at a table helping Camile box up paper plates and cups.

"You really don't have to stay and help clean up," Joanna said as Celeste bent down and grabbed a bag of trash, forehead creased with discomfort.

"I want to. Really."

"You've already helped me so much, Celeste, and I wonder if..." She looked at Celeste's cane. "If maybe you're overdoing it."

Celeste shook her head. "This is what I'm meant to do right now. Okay? Trust me." Celeste pointed through the window at a man in the parking area talking to Randy. "Is that the guy who owns the Graves mansion?"

"Yeah. Jerome Shaw."

"Katie interviewed him before she disappeared. I'm going to go chat with him."

***

Joanna rode a wave of euphoria as she parked behind her building, partially fueled by exhaustion and adrenaline, but mostly her exultation arose from the vigil. All the Graves residents had been standing there, candles lighting the dark, and as she'd driven home, she'd seen many of those candles in people's windows.

Newspaper reporters would be releasing front-page articles about Katie's vanishing! And even Cole had shown up. Had he come all the way from Florida to attend Katie's vigil? Joanna had hoped to talk to him, but by that time the interviews were over, he'd been gone.

Joanna skipped up the stairs and froze. The door to her apartment stood ajar.

39

No sounds emerged from within and she thought of Katie's door opening or closing of its own free will. But this door had been locked. She never left without locking it first, so if it had managed to open on its own, it had also slid the lock aside first. She looked behind her down the carpeted stairway, musty from the wet of melted snow and heat blasting from the old vents. There were still a few people out there on Main Street. She should turn back and get help.

Instead, she took another step closer to her door and then another, straining forward, listening. She nudged the door open with her fingertips, but stayed back, watched it swing in and stared at the floor, undulating. For a moment she thought her vision had blurred and then she realized the linoleum floor was underwater.

"Oh, my God..." she murmured, stepping all the way in.

A sound came from further in the apartment and her landlord, Raymond, stomped into the kitchen from the bathroom. He held an armful of Joanna's bath towels and he looked furious. He glared at her before dropping the towels onto the floor and kicking them around to soak up the water. Joanna looked at the kitchen sink, full to overflowing.

"You left your sink on. You plugged the drain and left your sink." He shook his head, the towels doing little to absorb the water.

"But I didn't. I swear." Joanna thought back to the afternoon. She'd rushed home, changed her clothes several times, grabbed the trays of cookies and muffins and left. She hadn't even used the sink. "I swear to you, Ray, I was at a vigil tonight for Katie. I never even turned the sink on. someone's been breaking in here. It has to be that. Stuff has been moved and—"

He put a hand up to silence her, stalked by. "This is your responsibility, and you can forget about getting your security deposit back. I think it's time for you to start looking for a new place."

"But Ray, I didn't do this."

He snorted and thundered out, his footfalls heavy as he stomped down the stairs.

Joanna stared at the floor and then the sink and back to the floor. Her mind, which minutes before had been an effervescent bubble of hope, zinged a million miles a second. Had she turned on the faucet, maybe intended to rinse a few dishes and then, distracted by thoughts of the vigil, left without turning it off?

"No," she muttered.

Someone had been breaking in. They'd been moving stuff. They wanted Joanna to think she'd done it—to think she was losing her mind.

***

Joanna didn't know if Cole was staying at his mother's house while he was in town, but she drove there anyway. She pounded on the door, her body a tangle of nerves, tears in her eyes.

When Cole opened the door, Joanna threw herself into his arms and sobbed. He nearly staggered, but held her.

"Whoa, Jo-Jo. Just breathe. What's going on?"

She didn't speak, cried into his faded Florida Gators t-shirt that smelled of him—oak moss and his familiar sweat. His arms, strong, his chest, hard, all of it wrapped around her and she'd not even known how desperately she missed folding into him and feeling his sturdiness.

When the weeping slowed, he dried her cheeks and smiled down at her. "That was a good cry. Are you okay? Did something happen at the vigil?"

Joanna wiped her nose on the sleeve of her coat, not the most attractive maneuver, but better than standing with snot running down her face. "No... umm..." She saw the apartment again, the floor drowning in an inch of water, Ray's face filled with accusation. "When I got home tonight, my apartment was flooded."

"Shit. Did a pipe break?"

She shook her head. "The sink was left on, but Cole, I didn't do it. I swear I didn't, but Ray says I did and he's going to evict me."

Cole scowled. "Ray's an asshole. Who did it, then? Was someone else there?"

Joanna shook her head, knew her next words were the unbelievable ones. "Stuff like that's been happening. I came home the other night and my bathtub was full. Things have been moved in Katie's room. Someone must be fucking with me. I wonder... is it the person who took Katie? Are they trying to make me feel insane?"

"By filling up your bathtub? Overflowing your sink? Maybe there's a plumbing issue. This sounds like a Ray problem to me. I know he thinks it's totally acceptable to be a slumlord, but he can't evict you because his plumbing needs updating. That's on him."

Joanna doubted the issue was plumbing, but she didn't say it because right then she wanted an easy, logical explanation that didn't involve a psycho sneaking into her apartment.

Behind Cole, a woman walked into view, pretty with shiny black hair that brushed her shoulders. She wore pajamas, a matching pink t-shirt and shorts covered in little palm trees. Her shirt protruded out at her belly. She was pregnant.

"Cole? Is everything all right?" the woman asked.

Joanna stared too long at the woman, at the bump beneath her t-shirt, and then up at her questioning brown eyes. When Joanna shifted her attention to Cole, she saw the misery in his face.

"Jo." He stepped aside, waved the woman forward. "This is Maggie, my girlfriend."

Joanna blinked at her, painted on a smile, though it felt clown-like, hideous. She was aware of how bedraggled she looked compared to this woman, glowing from her pregnancy, fresh-faced and filled with hope for the future.

Joanna took a step back, that horrible smile still cracking her face. She needed to say something, a polite hello, congratulations. She nearly tripped on the top step.

Cole moved forward as if to catch her, but she twisted away and ran to her car. "Joanna, wait," he called.

But she didn't wait. She climbed in, prayed the engine would turn over and sped away.

40

"This house is really beautiful," Celeste said, following Jerome inside the former Howard Graves mansion. "Are you sure it's not too late? I don't want to wake your partner."

"No such luck," a man called from the living room. Celeste looked in to see him stretched on a couch, a pile of tissues on the table beside him and two corgis curled between his legs. "This sinus infection has me awake all hours of the night," he said.

"Celeste, this is my partner, Louis. Louis, this is Celeste."

Louis squinted at her. "I let you go to one event alone and you bring home a woman?"

Jerome laughed. "Celeste is helping Joanna find Katie. She wanted to chat, so here we are. I told her we're night owls and you know how much I love to show this place off... so why not? Celeste, can I get you a glass of wine?"

"That'd be great," Celeste said. She'd been daydreaming about a glass of Scotch all through the vigil. Wine would have to suffice until she got back to the condo. The terror of her cellar ordeal had largely faded, but she was running on empty.

"How'd the vigil go?" Louis asked Celeste while Jerome disappeared to the kitchen for the wine.

"Really good. Joanna looked happy and there was a pretty big turnout, including several newspeople, so that might bring somebody out of the woodwork."

"I sure hope so," Louis said. "I met Katie a few times at the diner. Super kid. She loved to pick my brain about all the bands I saw in the seventies. Not often I get to wax on about seeing Pink Floyd at the Spectrum in Philadelphia, summer of 1975, back when I still had hair."

"You're gorgeous with or without hair," Jerome said, handing Celeste her wine.

"And that's why I love you," Louis murmured, closing his eyes.

"We're going to chat in the library," Jerome told him. "You try to doze for a bit."

"Yes, Captain."

Celeste followed Jerome down the hall to the library. She thought of Katie's video and the brief face of a woman in the stained-glass window. Jerome turned on a lamp and the shadows were washed away.

"I love this room," Jerome said. "It's by far my favorite in the house."

"I saw it during your interview with Katie. It's lovely."

"Have a seat. These are original chairs." He rested a hand on the back of one of two wingback chairs with velvet cushions. "I had them restored because the upholstery had gotten rather mildewed."

Celeste sat, eyes drifting to the bookcase that contained the eerie titles Katie had zoomed in on during her interview.

"This might be a long shot," Celeste started, "but I've been wondering if Katie's disappearance might be connected to the murder of Sherry Kapolka. In the video, you mentioned having found a shovel that might have been Sherry's."

Jerome's mouth turned down. "You suspect whoever killed Sherry also hurt Katie?"

"It's a theory I'm considering."

"Huh." Jerome leaned back, brushed the creases out of his pants. "That happened a long time ago, but gosh, I hope my talking to Katie about that trowel didn't somehow lead to her looking into Sherry's death."

Celeste didn't tell him she suspected it was. "Do you still have the trowel?"

"I do."

"Can I see it?"

He looked surprised. "Just a moment." He walked into the hall and returned a minute later, handing her the faded shovel.

Celeste held it in her hand, tried to open to Sherry. She heard the sound click-clacking down the hall. One of the corgis appeared in the doorway and stared at her. He barked once and walked away.

A barrage of images filled her mind, almost too fast to make sense of.

Scooping ice cream into a sugar cone, the smile of Sherry's mother as she brushed hair off Sherry's forehead and kissed it, the cool water as she plunged forward into a lake, Sherry's hand clutching a handful of some bushy green plant, and finally a car, a large convertible car—white with a tan roof—parked near a tall iron gate.

Celeste blinked and rotated the trowel, searched for more, but the images had stopped, though the car remained fixed in her mind. The car had been parked at the gate in front of the Graves mansion. "Do you know if the previous owner of this house had a white convertible?"

Jerome shook his head. "I couldn't tell you. I never met him. Everything went through our agent. Did you see something? Do you have the sight? Louis does, only a touch according to him, but I'm sure it's more than that."

"I sometimes get impressions," Celeste admitted, hoping he wouldn't push for more details.

"Is the shovel Sherry's?"

Celeste nodded slowly. "I think it is, yes." She didn't think it was—she knew it—but she flashed again on Eliza's words to be careful about sharing her visions.

"And you think a white convertible is connected to her murder?"

Celeste rubbed her eyes, yawned. "I honestly don't know." She stood slowly, holding onto the chair back for support. "I better head out. I'm fading fast."

"Before you go, I have something I'd like to show you." Jerome disappeared for several minutes. When he returned, he held a beautiful cane with a black wood shaft topped by a curved brass raven. "It's a Victorian walking stick," he explained. "I found it a few years back in the carriage house. One dealer who examined it told me this was called Odin's Crow." He tapped the bird. "But it has an extra-special feature." Jerome wiggled the bird, and it detached from the wood base. As he pulled it away, he revealed a steel blade. "How nifty is that? It's called a sword blade, though it's more like a dagger. Apparently, they used to be relatively common."

Celeste stared at the cane, unable to steal her eyes from the curved black raven and the metallic blade glinting in the light. "Would you be willing to sell it?"

He grinned. "I'll do one better." He handed it to her. "You can have it. And let me tell you a little secret—Louis told me a few weeks ago that I was going to meet someone this cane was meant for and when I met them, I would know. And here you are."

Celeste held the cane. It seemed alive in her hands. "Thank you," she whispered.

"The look on your face makes it all worth it. And thank you

for helping Joanna. She's like the town's daughter. Katie, too. And we all want to know the truth."

CELESTE BOLTED UPRIGHT in bed and stared into the dark room. She squinted toward the fuzzy shape of the dresser and the small chair beside it.

Something had dragged her from sleep. The hairs on her arms and the back of her neck stood on end. She strained, listening, but heard nothing.

Her mouth was dry, sour-tasting. The warmth of the bed lulled her, but she needed a drink of water, would never fall back asleep with her tongue sticking like sandpaper to the roof of her mouth.

She stood, groaned as her leg came back to life and searched for her cane in the darkness. Clutching it in her hand, she left the bedroom and made her way to the kitchen, filled a glass with tepid water and slurped it down.

The cold hit her then, a sharp breeze across her bare legs. She lifted her eyes to the sliding glass door that led to the balcony. It stood open and beyond it, barely illuminated by moonlight, was the silhouette of a man. He stood perfectly still and facing her, she thought, watching her watching him.

41

Every cell in her brain shrieked at her to run, but her body couldn't so much as flinch. She stood frozen in place. And then he moved, his hand darting to the sliding door to shove it open the rest of the way.

Celeste shrieked, lunged backwards, slammed her hip into the corner of the counter. Balance teetering, she righted herself and twisted around. For a split second she thought of running to her room, locking her door, calling the police, but she couldn't get there without crossing his path. She turned instead toward the exterior door, pulled the deadlock back and lurched into the hallway, scrambling, nearly falling again as she struggled away from the man who'd definitely have now made it into the condo and would be right on her heels.

Pain reverberated through her left side, but she ignored it. She couldn't treat her left leg gingerly now, couldn't think forward to the potential future pain. If she paused for even a moment, he would be on her and there'd be no future to contemplate.

Rather than turn left and run down the stairs, risking losing her balance or him shoving her from behind, she turned right, fled down the hall and up the stairs to the next floor, clutching the banister, holding her breath to make as little noise as possible.

At the third floor, she met another long hall, two doors leading into condos, their residents—if there were any—likely dead asleep. Halfway down the halls stood a maintenance door and an entry into a lit vending area and arcade. A pinball machine cast a trajectory of dazzling lights across the gray carpet. Celeste limped into the room and to the far back where several video game arcade machines, labeled 'out of order,' sat along one wall. She wriggled herself behind one of the machines and held very still when footsteps moved through the hall outside the room. She could not see the man, but heard his footfalls enter the arcade, the sound of him moving amongst the games. If he found her now, she was as good as dead.

She closed her eyes and waited.

***

CELESTE SAT on the edge of her couch. One policeman sat opposite her taking notes. The other stood on the balcony, cold air sweeping through the condo as he examined the door.

After nearly an hour wedged behind the out-of-order Pac-Man machine, Celeste had wriggled out, praying the man wasn't hiding in the hall waiting for her. He hadn't been and, rather than return to her condo to call the police, Celeste had knocked on doors until another resident opened theirs and allowed her to use their cell phone to report the break-in.

Only when the officers arrived had Celeste returned to her condo, the door still standing ajar. They'd walked in ahead of her, asked her to wait in the hall while they did a sweep of the interior. When they'd double-checked no one lurked inside, they'd asked her to come in and describe what happened.

"So you woke up because you heard a sound?" the younger officer, his chin dotted with acne, asked.

"Yes. But then I didn't hear anything else, so I came out to get a drink and that's when I felt the draft." She gestured at the door.

"And the balcony door was open?"

"Yes, and there was a man standing on the balcony."

"And he attacked you?" the officer asked.

Celeste shook her head. "He chased me. Had he caught me... I don't know what he intended to do. I ran up to the third floor and hid in the arcade."

"And he followed you?"

"Yes. He walked into the arcade and then he left."

"Did he have a weapon?"

"I didn't get a good look at him—only his silhouette on the balcony."

"How do you know it was a man?"

"I can't say for certain, but he looked like a man," she explained. He'd also felt like a man, but she didn't add that detail.

"No sign that he forced this door," the second officer said, walking inside. He slid the door open and closed several times, locked it, tried to pull it open. It didn't budge. "Could you have left it unlocked?"

"No. I've barely opened that door since I've come here and, when I have, I've locked it. I'm sure of it." And she was, because she was investigating the disappearance of a girl and too many disturbing stories had emerged—stories about a rapist who'd gotten away, a murderer still at large.

"But he didn't steal anything?" the officer across from her asked.

"It doesn't seem that way. No."

The second officer paused near her kitchenette. He picked up a mostly empty bottle of Scotch, next to another, entirely empty, bottle of Scotch. "Were you drinking last night?"

Celeste gaped at him. "I had *a* drink before I went to bed."

"You weren't drunk then?"

"I'm not sure how that's relevant to a man climbing onto my balcony and breaking in, but no. I wasn't drunk."

"Just covering our bases." The second officer shot his partner a look.

The officer across from her stood and closed his notepad. "We'll get the report in our system, and if we find anything out, we'll give you a call."

"And if he comes back?" she demanded.

"I'd start by making sure everything's locked good."

After the police left, Celeste wedged a chair beneath the door handle and stuck a broomstick in the crease of the sliding door to ensure no one could force it open. She poured a glass of Scotch and stared into the amber liquid, saw again the judgment in the eyes of the officer who'd asked if she'd been drinking.

As she carried it to the couch, she paused, eyes caught on her boards. They were undisturbed, except beneath the list of suspects, the two colored pieces of paper with the names Declan and Warren Boyd were gone.

42

"Here." Floyd handed Joanna a small box with the words 'Minicam Pro' on the outside.

"What is it?" she asked.

She'd spent the previous night in Floyd and Camile's guest bedroom. They'd graciously invited her in when she'd shown up puffy-eyed and exhausted. That morning she'd woken up at six to find Floyd making waffles and Camile brewing coffee.

Joanna had filled them in on the previous night's events, beginning with returning home to find her kitchen flooded to discovering Cole had moved on with his life. She'd also told them about the strange occurrences—the steaming teakettle, the items moved in Katie's room, the parted curtains and full bathtub.

"It's a camera," Floyd said. "Small enough to be concealed. We'll put it in your apartment. I bought a bunch of these last year after somebody broke into our pole barn. I put one out there and a couple around our house. I ordered extra. Whoever turned on your water is clearly messing with you. They might have far worse intentions."

Joanna rubbed her eyes. She'd barely slept the night before, rewinding again and again the vision of Maggie—Cole's new girlfriend. It made little sense to her how after a year apart, she felt heartbroken all over again.

"What if I did it? Turned the water on? Moved stuff around in Katie's room?" she murmured.

"Then you'll catch yourself," he said. "I put two at the schoolhouse last week."

"You did?" Joanna tried to remember seeing a camera during the vigil.

"I hid them. I thought it might be a good idea to have footage of the vigil. They say people who commit crimes like to revisit the scene, especially if there's a lot of publicity or whatever."

"Have you watched it?" Joanna thought of the night before, how buoyant she'd felt, finally getting some interest in Katie's disappearance. What if whoever had taken Katie had been in the crowd? Eating the cookies Joanna had baked, holding a candle in Katie's honor.

"Not all of it. But I did want to show you something." Floyd took out his phone and scrolled to an app. He opened it and clicked the previous day's date. A long list of time stamps filled the screen. "You can click on a time. The camera picks up movement. That's when it records. Obviously, it recorded most of yesterday."

As Joanna watched, the schoolhouse interior filled the screen. Celeste walked into view and slid the deadbolt back on the door leading into the cellar. She disappeared into the darkness and minutes ticked by.

For a moment the image grew fuzzy, indistinct, as if a shadow had obscured the view. The hairs on the back of Joanna's neck prickled. The screen cleared and the cellar door suddenly slammed shut.

Joanna jumped. Within seconds, May was at the door

wiggling the knob and reassuring Celeste. The audio quality was poor, but Joanna could hear enough of the exchange to know Celeste had been yelling for help and May was trying to get the door open. It seemed to be stuck and then, as May pulled, it burst open and Celeste practically fell out, her face a mask of terror.

"She looks so scared," Joanna said.

"Yeah. What I found odd was how the door, totally unprovoked, slammed shut. Nothing else in the room moved. I watched the video three times. See right there?" He pointed to the edge of a table where a stack of papers sat. "If there'd been a breeze strong enough to blow the door, it should have moved those papers."

"What do you think it was, then?" Joanna asked, frowning at the screen as May led Celeste to a bench where she half-collapsed.

"That I don't know, but you saw how the screen went blurry. It gave me the willies when I watched it."

Joanna nodded, brushed a hand against the back of her neck. "Yeah. It's strange, but—" Before she finished, her cell phone rang. Celeste's name appeared on the screen.

"Take your call," Floyd said. "I need to get ready to head to the diner."

"Hello?" Joanna answered.

"Hi," Celeste said. "Are you working this morning?"

"I am. I stayed at Floyd and Camile's last night. We're all heading that way in a few minutes. Is everything okay?" Joanna heard a strain in Celeste's voice.

"No. Someone broke into my condo last night."

"What?" Joanna stood and paced away from the kitchen, gripping the phone hard to the side of her head.

"He climbed onto my balcony. Luckily I woke up and saw him coming in and managed to escape. I hid on the third floor until he left."

"Oh, my God. Are you all right? Did you see him? Do you have any idea who it was?"

"I'm okay. And I didn't see him. It was dark, but I told the police he didn't take anything, and he didn't, not really. But I realized Declan and Warren Boyd's names are gone from my boards."

"They're gone?"

"Yeah. The post-its are gone. I searched everywhere, thought maybe they'd gotten blown off. They didn't. I think he took them."

"Why would he do that? Do you think that means... that one of them broke in last night? That they're behind Katie's disappearance?"

"I don't know, but... obviously we can't ignore the significance of that. At the same time, it's so obvious it belongs on one of those 'stupidest criminals ever' shows."

"Have you called the police and told them?"

"No. I'll give it the day and see if they show up first. Maybe they flew off, got stuck to my socks and ended up in the hamper."

"Both names?"

"Not likely, I know."

Joanna thought again of her apartment, the water left running, the curtains parted, the sense of being watched. "Someone broke into my apartment yesterday and turned on the water in my sink. It overflowed all over my floor."

"They broke in to overflow the sink?"

"Yeah, it sounds mental."

"It is mental, but that doesn't mean it's not real. I've read about a few serial killers who mess with people's heads—leave uneaten food on the counter, steal trivial things like the batteries from remotes."

"Serial killer?" Joanna braced a hand on the wall and closed her eyes.

"I'm not saying that's what's happening, but if Sherry and Katie's disappearances were connected, that does imply a repeat killer."

When Joanna opened her eyes, a framed photograph hung before her. It was Katie, Joanna, Floyd and Camile dressed in Halloween costumes—the Beatles, at Katie's insistence—standing beneath the big red awning at the Sidewinder. Joanna took a few steps and sank onto the couch, shaking her head, refusing to link the face of her beautiful sister with the term 'serial killer.'

Celeste, as if sensing her distress, softened her tone. "I might be wrong, but it might be time to get the locks changed."

The couch was the type you could fall into, snuggle deep and disappear, and Joanna wanted to do that, but she forced herself to her feet and blocked out any thought except the one that included Katie coming home. "Ray is going to evict me, so why bother?"

"He's going to evict you? But someone broke in. Did you call the police?"

"No, I didn't, because... well, I didn't want them to think I was crazy. The door hadn't been forced and all the person did was leave the water on. What police officer is going to buy that story?"

"One who understands power and manipulation. One who can connect the dots. I don't think it's a coincidence someone broke into both of our places the same night you held Katie's vigil."

"None of the Boyds were at the vigil," Joanna murmured.

"I'm serious about getting your locks changed, Joanna. I get the sense that we're getting close to the truth. We might be setting him off."

Him.

"Floyd gave me a hidden camera. What if I wait to change the locks and try to catch who's breaking in during the act?"

Celeste said nothing for a moment. "I don't think that's safe. I understand why you'd want to, but—hold on. Someone is knocking at my door. I'll come into the diner after I take a shower, okay?"

"Okay. Good. Maybe we can regroup and talk through some things. I'll be done after the lunch shift. And check who's at the door before you open it."

"I will," Celeste assured her.

Joanna slipped her phone in her pocket, pulled her hair into a ponytail and got ready to go to the diner.

43

Celeste moved toward her door as the person outside knocked a second time. She thought of the man from her balcony and grabbed her cane, ready to shake the dagger free if necessary. She peered through the peephole and then pulled the chair from beneath the doorknob, unbolted the door and opened it to Jonathan, who stood in the hall.

"Jonathan! What are you doing here?" She stepped into the hall and hugged him. His body was stiff beneath her arms, but the mere sight of him made the terror of the previous hours less harrowing.

"I came to surprise you," he said, though he didn't smile. When she stepped back, his disapproval was plain. "You're not eating. You look like you've lost ten pounds."

Celeste's hand drifted to her shirt. She pulled it out slightly, a half unconscious bid to hide her spindly ribs.

His eyes followed the movement and lingered an extra beat on her body, frown deepening. "What is *that*?"

She looked down. Such was the repulsion on his face, she

expected to see a rat circling around her feet. She realized he was looking at her cane. "What does it look like? It's a cane."

Without an invitation, he brushed past her into the condo. Celeste turned and bit her lip. The space was a mess. One empty Scotch bottle on the counter, a second three-quarters gone. Dishes piled in the little sink. Her clothes strewn over chair backs.

Though what Jonathan had focused on was not the mess, but the bulletin boards. He moved toward them slowly, reading her post-its, her theories, staring first at Katie's missing poster, then the flier for her vigil. His expression made her want to crawl beneath a blanket and hide, a child whose parent had caught them sneaking candy into their bedroom. "What is this?" he demanded.

Celeste blinked at the boards, tried to view things through Jonathan's eyes. "It's the reason I came up here, to help a woman search for her missing sister."

He stared at her as if he didn't know her at all, as if in the days she'd been gone she'd morphed into something unrecognizable. He bent over, picked up a bottle of her prescription painkillers and shook it. The bottle was empty.

"Celeste, it's time to go home." He moved without waiting for her response, gathering the papers and notebooks and pushing them haphazardly into her laptop backpack. He disappeared down the hall and she heard the zipper on her suitcase, the sound of him stuffing clothes inside.

Her mind reeled. She should yell at him, demand he leave. Who did he think he was, coming to the condo and forcing her, an adult woman, to abandon what she'd spent days working on, just as they were so close...

"You have to bring me back," she said when he walked out with her suitcase.

He stared at her. "Fine. I'll bring you back, but right now, we're going home." His eyes moved past her and his body stiffened.

Celeste turned and saw her wedding ring on the table by the couch. "It's been falling off," she said.

"Sure. I'm getting your stuff."

Celeste didn't have the energy to fight him and some piece of her wanted him to make her leave. The night before, a masked man had entered her condo. She'd come so close to... what, being murdered? She thought so, and what would happen that night if the man came back again?

Celeste followed Jonathan from the condo, leaning heavily on her cane because her left leg and hip hurt so badly from her scramble to the third floor the night before she could hardly tolerate it.

Jonathan loaded her bags into the trunk and opened the passenger door for her. She slid into the seat, her mind a blur of thoughts all obscured by a weariness so deep her organs were tired. Maybe it was best simply to leave, return to her former, safe, familiar life. What had she been thinking, getting involved in the disappearance of a teenager she'd never known? Potentially putting herself and Joanna in grave danger?

As Jonathan drove from the parking lot, Celeste spoke. "I need to stop at the Sidewinder first. It's a diner in Graves."

"I hardly think—"

"Jonathan. I have to stop. Turn right up here."

JONATHAN PARKED at the curb and Celeste struggled to get out of the car and through the snowbank on the passenger side. She righted herself and was halfway to the door when she realized Jonathan was following her inside.

He beat her there and pulled the door open. She walked

into the bustling restaurant that smelled of bacon and was loud with the sounds of chatter.

Joanna stood at a table, tray balanced on one hand as she slid mugs of coffee to the four women. She spotted Celeste and walked over. "Hi. It's getting busy, but you could sit at the counter. Are you hungry?"

"I need to go home for a few days," Celeste said, forcing a smile she didn't feel. "But I'll be back. Soon. Okay?"

"Is everything all right, Celeste?" Joanna asked, her eyes shifting to Jonathan, who stood near the door, stony-faced.

"Yeah. I'm okay. This is my husband, Jonathan."

He walked over and extended his hand, eyes boring into Joanna as if she were Celeste's adolescent friend who'd talked her into underage drinking or sneaking out. Embarrassed, Celeste looked away.

"Nice to meet you," Joanna murmured, shaking his hand quickly.

Floyd came out of the kitchen and walked toward them. "Celeste, Joanna told me what happened last night."

Joanna broke in quickly, exchanging a look with Celeste. "Celeste has to go back to Grand Rapids for a few days. This is her husband, Jonathan."

"Pleasure to meet you, Jon," Floyd said. "Celeste has been a godsend to us around here. Really making some headway in the case."

"Jonathan," Jonathan replied coolly, his eyes sliding to Celeste. "Glad to hear your trip's been productive."

Celeste swallowed the thickness in her throat. "I'll see you guys soon," she told Joanna and Floyd.

Jonathan put his hand on the small of her back and guided her toward the door. Celeste glanced back and caught the uncertainty on Floyd's face, the concern on Joanna's.

THE WARMTH and lull of the car, coupled with too many restless nights, drew Celeste into a deep, troubled sleep. She dreamed of a masked man standing in the doorway of her bedroom at the condo. When she woke with a cry, Jonathan was behind the wheel. He reached a hand to her arm and patted it.

"We're almost there," he murmured.

"Home?" she asked, struggling to get her seat upright. She pulled her bottle of water from the passenger side holder and took a drink, swishing it around in her mouth before swallowing. She wanted a couple of pain pills, but they were trapped inside her bag in the trunk.

"To the hospital. I called Dr. Caswell, and he squeezed you in for an appointment."

"Dr. Caswell? Why?"

Jonathan pinned on a tight smile. "Because you've clearly had a tough week and I think it's a good idea to get everything checked out."

CELESTE SAT ALONE in the examination room. She'd stripped out of her clothes and put on a paper gown, open in the back. Her leg and hip throbbed.

When her doctor arrived, his dark eyebrows pulled together as he surveyed her and then glanced at the chart the nurse had left in the door. "How are you feeling, Celeste?" He pressed a stethoscope against her chest.

She recoiled from the cold metal and the paper beneath her crinkled. "I feel fine."

"Big deep breath," he said. "And let it go." He moved away, wrote something on her chart. "Jonathan is anxious about you. He wanted me to suggest a couple of nights here at the hospital. We can run some tests, make sure everything is in tiptop shape."

"Jonathan wants to commit me?"

"Not commit, no. This isn't a psychiatric facility. We admit, not commit. He wants to give you a break. Help you get back on your feet. Celeste, you've lost fifteen pounds since we last saw you and you were already thin. You're barely able to walk. It's clear to me that something is wrong—"

"No. Absolutely not. I'm not staying overnight. If you want to do some blood work, I'll go to the lab on my way out."

The doctor pursed his lips, wrote something else down. "Well, as you know, you're an adult and the choice is yours. But I think blood work is a good idea, and I'd also advise a visit to your surgeon, have him take a look at the leg and hip, and a visit to your psychiatrist."

"Are you refilling my pain prescription? I'm getting low?"

He sighed, flipped a page on the chart. "Technically, you're not due for a refill for another week."

"I'm still in a lot of pain, Dr. Caswell. Constant pain."

"Are you doing your exercises?"

She turned away, looked at the poster hanging above the sink. It was a quote by Rumi: *The wound is the place where the light enters you.*

"No," she said, still staring at the poster. "I'm not."

"I see." Dr. Caswell tapped his pencil on his clipboard. "Let's do this then. You go home and have a week of self-care, do your exercises, maybe talk to a nutritionist about a diet that can help you put on a little weight, and next week, I'll see you again right back here and we'll fill your prescription."

44

Floyd accompanied Joanna home after the lunch rush ended. Together they used towels to soak up the remaining water. Joanna did her best not to cry throughout the entire process.

When they finished, Floyd helped her set up the hidden camera. They placed it in a fake plant on a table in the living room and angled it at her front door. Then Floyd installed the app on her phone and showed her how to access the videos.

"It has a motion sensor. When it detects movement, you'll get an alert on our phone. Open the app and voilà, real-time footage. It's great unless you have chickens like we do, which means the god-awful thing pings twenty-four seven at the barn, but I must admit I rather delight in watching those little fools running around."

"Thanks, Floyd." Joanna walked him back downstairs and hugged him goodbye. "I don't know what I'd do without you and Camile."

He tweaked her nose. "We love you, Joanna, and Katie too. There's going to come a point when it's not hard, this life stuff. I promise."

She watched him walk away down the sidewalk.

As she turned back to her apartment, someone called her name. She turned to see Cole walking toward her. Joanna was tempted to run back upstairs to her apartment and hide, but he'd already seen her and the scene the night before was enough embarrassment.

"Hey," he said.

"Hey."

Face tan, hair streaked blond by the Florida sun, he looked good. "Jo, I'm so sorry about last night."

She patted at her hair, wished she'd opted for a shower at Floyd's that morning. "It's okay, Cole. I shouldn't have assumed..." That he'd waited for her, that he was still single, that he'd flown to Michigan for the vigil in hopes of winning her back.

"Don't. This is on me, completely. I don't know what I was thinking about, going to Katie's vigil."

Her eyes narrowed at him. "You practically lived with us for a while there. It's okay to have gone to the vigil for Katie. It didn't have to be about us and obviously it wasn't. You're going to be a dad. Congratulations."

He rocked on his feet, stuffed his hands in his pockets, did the sheepish smile that Joanna remembered from the very first day they'd met and he'd crashed into her at the Sidewinder as she was carrying a tray with four plates of pancakes and syrup. "Wild, right?" he asked.

It physically hurt to look at him, to see that smile, to remember all the good times when she'd had Katie and Cole and her world wasn't a never-ending dark night.

"It is," she said, but her voice cracked and she began to cry. "Good to see you." She turned and hurried away, not into her apartment, but down the alley behind the building to her car. She needed to drive, put some distance between herself and Graves.

When she pulled from the parking lot, she passed Cole, but couldn't look at him. She turned the opposite direction on the road.

As she drove through downtown, Joanna stopped at a red light. A group of girls around Katie's age stood on the corner, laughing. They walked across the street, arms linked, their cheeks pink from the cold. As they hurried into Espresso Mike's, Joanna's stomach shrank into a tiny, painful pit. She squeezed the wheel tighter and closed her eyes against the immediate wave of helplessness.

She might never find Katie, might never know what happened to her baby sister.

JOANNA DROVE until nearly eleven at night. She'd never been an aimless driver, hated to waste the gas, but for the first time she understood why some people found it soothing. She'd listened to hours of music, a pastime she'd abandoned after Katie vanished because it was too hard to hear any of Katie's songs or any ballad about heartache or loss. Tonight, she'd found a current hits station that played upbeat dance songs and though she'd cried a few times, she'd mostly slipped into a mindless lull, listening to songs and watching the snowy road unroll before her.

When she parked behind her building, she sat for several minutes, reluctant to go inside. Even after Katie'd disappeared, she'd always felt safe in her apartment, but that was quickly disintegrating. She checked the camera app, but there'd been no notifications.

Joanna stepped from her car and started toward the building. Behind her, near the dumpster, something clattered. She turned around, searched the darkness, but couldn't see anything. It was likely a raccoon. They'd had them before.

Still, she picked up her pace, watching every patch of darkness.

She came to the corner of the building, turned toward her door, and froze when she spotted the man coming around the other side. He wore a bulky black coat, a black knit mask, and black leather gloves.

He was walking toward her, moving quickly. Joanna turned and sprinted back down the alley, listening for his footfalls but unable to hear anything over her feet crunching through the snow. She bypassed her car and ducked behind the dumpster.

Her whole body had broken out in a sweat. She felt the dampness beneath the waistband of her jeans, between her shoulder blades. Her heart pounded a relentless surge of blood into her ears and head.

A single thought whistled through her head. *Serial killer.* Celeste believed a serial killer might be behind Katie's disappearance, Sherry Kapolka's murder.

Hunched down, sick with fear, Joanna waited for the man to step around the dumpster. Minutes passed, and she heard it, a rustling inches away. She recoiled as something crashed to the ground in front of her.

A pizza box lay in the snow, a raccoon perched on the edge of the dumpster watching her from two glowing yellow eyes.

"It's a raccoon," she murmured.

Still, she searched for the man, half expected to discover him waiting for her to reveal her hiding spot. He wasn't there, hadn't followed her. Joanna's paranoia had gotten the best of her. For all she knew, he was a local at the Sidewinder and she'd just fled from him in terror.

Joanna's cell rang, and she jumped. "This night's gonna be the end of me," she said, digging the phone out of her purse.

"Hi, Camile," she answered.

"Jo..." Camile's voice broke.

"What's wrong?"

"It's Floyd." Her voice was thick, strangled with emotion.

Joanna's stomach plummeted. "What's wrong with Floyd? Did he have a—?" She didn't say 'heart attack,' but she thought it. The year before, Floyd's doctor had put him on a whole series of medications for heart issues.

"No. He... he fell down the stairs at the schoolhouse. He... he's in a coma, Jo. They don't know if he's going to make it."

"No..." Joanna moaned. "What hospital are you at?"

"Traverse City."

"I'm coming there now."

45

———

Celeste looked at the alarm clock beside the bed. She'd slept for twelve hours. Sensitive to the ache in her hip and leg, she moved slowly, putting on her robe and slippers before making her way downstairs.

She'd assumed Jonathan had left for work, but then heard his voice drifting from the study. "The truth is," Jonathan said, "I sometimes wonder if it was an accident or if she stepped in front of the car. She'd been kind of low in the days before, frustrated with something at the lab. I don't even know anymore."

Cash appeared at her feet, rubbed his sleek fur along her shins and released a loud meow.

"I better get going," Jonathan said. "I'll talk to you later."

Celeste's body trembled, her fists at her side. How could he be saying such a thing? Lying, implying she'd tried to commit suicide? "You said I tried to kill myself," she blurted the moment he walked into the hall.

His face paled, eyes went wide. "You're awake."

"Yes, I'm fucking awake, and I just overheard you tell someone I intentionally stepped in front of that car, that I tried to commit suicide."

He shook his head. "That's not what I said. I said I wondered, and... well, I did, Celeste. Okay? You hadn't been yourself before the accident. You surely haven't been yourself since the accident. I—" He wrung his hands, pushed his fingers through his short hair. "I'm struggling here. I'm searching for something that makes sense, something that explains what happened to my wife."

"I told you what happened," she hissed. "I told you in the hospital and you didn't want to hear it."

He nearly rolled his eyes. She saw the movement, but he caught himself. "The dying thing? Come on, Celeste. You're a scientist. There's been research done on this. It's a physiological reaction, the brain's response to oxygen deprivation. Not to mention all the drugs they were pumping into you."

"I flatlined in the operating room. I was clinically dead."

"And were quickly revived."

"You were wearing one slipper," Celeste said. "You came running down the road to where I'd been hit and you lost one of your slippers in the ditch. You were standing over me wearing one slipper."

He stared at her, mouth half-open. "What are you trying to say?"

"How could I know that? How could my brain, while I was unconscious, have hallucinated floating away from my body and looking down and seeing you standing there in one slipper?"

"The woman who called it in must have told you—"

"You were with me when I talked to Doris. She didn't mention it. I didn't ask her about that."

"Well, then... I don't know. I must have mentioned it."

She released an angry laugh. "You're so blind, Jonathan. It's not your fault. Truly. It's not. Before the accident I was too, but now—"

"Now what? You're the Messiah? You're all-knowing? Listen

to yourself! You sound like a crazy person. And not only that, you look like a crazy person. You're as skinny as a weed. You're obviously drinking too much. You went through a month's supply of painkillers in less than two weeks. You are not okay!"

Tears blurred Celeste's eyes. She wanted to scream at him, to rush forward and beat her fists against his chest. Instead, she turned, limped back upstairs and climbed into bed.

As THEY ATE DINNER, Celeste did her best to keep the conversation going, despite struggling to look Jonathan in the eyes. She had not forgiven him for what he'd said on the phone that morning, but she knew arguing about it was futile.

"I scheduled Lorenzo to come over tomorrow for your exercises," Jonathan said.

"Thanks," Celeste murmured, taking a bite of the beef stroganoff he'd made.

Jonathan rarely cooked, but when he did, he followed every step of the recipe to a t. The stroganoff was delicious, the wine he'd paired it with perfectly complementary. Celeste tried to feel grateful for her husband, for the care he'd taken with their dinner. Mostly, she felt a simmering rage beneath the surface of her skin. The food was delicious, but she nearly gagged on every bite.

"Mark Hansen is at the lab this week. He'd love to see you. Maybe you want to come to work tomorrow or the next day? For a few hours. Try to get back into your routine."

Celeste chewed, swallowed, and took a sip of wine. She would have preferred Scotch, longed to be back in the condo staring at her bulletin boards, fitting the pieces together. They'd been getting closer. That was why the man had attacked. She imagined him again, tried to draw on some detail she'd logged, but forgotten in her flight. He did not become clear, but each time she thought of him the vision of the tree, red roots sinking into the earth, popped into her mind.

"Did you hear me, Celeste?" Jonathan asked.

She looked up. "No. I'm sorry. What did you say?"

"I asked if you wanted to come into work with me tomorrow? I could drive you home at lunch. A half day. You can see Mark and check out what we're working on."

Celeste shook her head, drained her glass of wine. "No. I'm not ready."

Jonathan pursed his lips, but said nothing. He turned his attention to his plate, jabbed a noodle, and shoved it into his mouth.

***

Celeste waited until Jonathan's breath had grown slow and deep. She slid from the bed, careful to make little noise as she crept from the bedroom and eased the door shut behind her.

On the first floor, she carried her purse to the couch, rifling through until she found the cell phone from the schoolhouse cellar. She'd meant to show it to Joanna, ask her if she recognized it, but the terror of being locked in the cellar had wiped it from her mind. She'd only remembered it during dinner when she noticed Jonathan's cell resting on the windowsill.

She took it out and turned it over. It might be totally irrelevant. It didn't have a distinctive case, but on the back was a single, partially peeled-away sticker with two words remaining: 'Kozmic Blues.'

The phone was older than Celeste's and her charging cord didn't match. She walked to the study and opened drawers until she found the plastic bag of old cords, searching for one that would fit. She found it, returned to the living room, and plugged it in. While she waited for it to charge, unsure if it would, she turned her own cell phone on and read the texts she'd received since leaving Graves. She'd gotten one from Joanna.

Hey, checking in. Is everything okay?

It was nearly two a.m. Celeste didn't want to text Joanna and risk waking her.

She opened a web browser and typed the words from the sticker on the back of the phone. The first hit was an album by Janis Joplin: *I Got Dem Ol' Kozmic Blues Again, Mama!*

Celeste's mouth went dry as she blinked at the album name and then stared at the phone. It was Katie's phone. It had to be. Who else would have marked their phone with a Janis Joplin album sticker? But how had it ended up crushed between two bricks in a cellar wall at the schoolhouse?

She picked up the phone and pressed the button to turn it on. Nothing. The screen remained dark, the spiderwebbed glass caked with dirt. Had the person who attacked Katie hidden it? Or had Katie herself crammed it between the bricks? She thought of Declan's claim that Katie had run away. What if she had staged the whole thing, set up some ride, and left her cell phone at the last place she'd been to ensure no one could track her?

No. Every fiber of Celeste's being believed Katie Ellis remained in Graves.

Celeste bit her lip and again tried to turn on the phone, but the screen remained blank.

Frustrated, she stood and walked to the kitchen, searched the cupboards, but found no Scotch, which meant Jonathan had either hidden it or thrown it away because when she'd left for Graves there'd been two bottles in the cupboard. In the recesses of the freezer she found a bottle of vodka. She poured a shot and sipped it, staring through the glass doors at the dark back porch.

No footprints in the snow beckoned her toward the dark forest, but Katie appeared beside her in the glass. Celeste stared at her, mouth open, ice trickling down her spine. Katie stared at Celeste through cloudy eyes. She held up her hand, palm out, and Celeste saw the network of blood vessels and arteries all branching toward her wrist like the roots of a tree.

Something beeped from the opposite room and Celeste jumped. When she returned her gaze to the glass, Katie was gone.

Celeste walked into the living room and stared at the broken phone, face up on the couch, the screen lit. It beeped again and again, a flood of messages that had come in over the previous months populating.

Hands shaking, Celeste picked up the phone. She clicked the text messages—so many, too many to read them all. Messages from Joanna, Liam, Declan, Floyd, Randy, Travis and many more—people whose names she didn't recognize.

She opened Declan's messages, scrolled down. The last one he'd sent had been two months before.

If you're out there somewhere, please send me a message. I swear I'll never contact you again. I just want to know if you're alive.

The phone had only saved the messages from the previous four months, which meant it likely automatically deleted them after a certain passage of time.

"Damn it," she muttered. The key to Katie's disappearance might well have been in those texts. She sighed and opened Katie's pictures.

In the days before Katie went missing, she had taken a few photos. One of her and Liam outside Graves High School, Katie's face tilted up to catching a falling snowflake on her tongue; another of Joanna at the diner, hair loose from its pony-tail, as she stood at the counter laughing. Celeste studied Joanna, the stiffness gone from her shoulders, her face soft, happy. The photo had captured the Joanna who'd existed before Katie vanished and, like Celeste's own former self, was never coming back.

Celeste opened a video file dated the day before Katie vanished. Celeste clicked it and the little loading wheel appeared on the screen. Seconds passed, a minute, and she feared the video would not load at all.

Then finally it did. Celeste enlarged the screen and turned the volume high.

The camera wobbled as someone propped it up. Though the room was dark, candles flickered from bases on the wood floor and in the center sat a Ouija board. "Come on, guys. Sit." Katie spoke and then moved into frame, taking a place behind the Ouija board. A moment later Liam appeared and sat to her left. Declan moved into the frame and took the place to her right.

Liam stared at the Ouija board as if afraid of what they were about to do, but Declan looked everywhere else, scanning the room. After a moment of studying the dark shapes Celeste understood where the teenagers were at: Jerome and Louis's house, the mansion that had once belonged to Howard Graves. In the background, Celeste could see the lower half of the stained-glass window.

Declan shifted and his knee bumped a candle. Katie let out a little shriek. "Be careful," she hissed. "Leave no trace, remember? I don't want Jerome to know we were here."

"Then he shouldn't have told you where he keeps the spare key," Declan retorted.

"All right," she murmured, closing her eyes and taking a deep breath. When she opened them, her eyes flicked to Declan. "Hey." Katie nudged him. "Pay attention. We really have to focus for this to work."

He looked at her. "Katie, this isn't going to work, okay? But fine. Look. Undivided attention on the board."

Katie looked at Liam. "You ready?"

Liam's face paled. "Not really, but... I guess."

"Okay." Katie took a grimy-looking shard of glass.

"What the fuck is that?" Declan demanded. Liam stared at the glass like it might come to life and attack him.

"It's a piece of glass from the train car," Katie said. "I needed something connected to her."

"Jesus," Liam whimpered.

"Chill out, Liam," she said. "Concentrate. Both of you." Katie closed her eyes, lifted the glass high for a moment and then waved it over the board. "Sherry Kapolka, if you're here, please speak to us through the board."

She set the glass aside and put her fingertips on the plastic planchette. "Come on," she said, looking from Declan, attention elsewhere, to Liam, who hurriedly put his fingers on the planchette.

"Sherry," Katie murmured again. "If you're here, send us a message."

The three teenagers didn't speak. Nothing moved in the video but flickering candles and the shadows they cast.

"Sherry. If you're here—"

The planchette moved. Liam pulled his hands back. Katie's eyes went big, flames from the candles flickering in her green irises. Declan stared at the board uncertainly.

46

———

Camile had clearly been crying for hours. Her eyes were red-rimmed and bloodshot. She sat on the edge of the chair next to Floyd's bed clutching his hand. When Joanna walked in, the tears started again and Camile stood, rushing into her arms. "Oh, Jo. What will we do? What will we do if he doesn't wake up?"

Joanna shook her head, couldn't even attempt to answer such a question. She stared at Floyd, at his bruised, bandaged head, at the I.V running from his arm. His skin was an unnatural gray. She shifted her eyes to the floor and cried.

———

"WHY WAS HE AT THE SCHOOLHOUSE?" Joanna asked after she'd settled at a table with Camile in the hospital cafeteria. Joanna had bought them each a cup of coffee, but neither of them took a drink.

Camile dabbed at her eyes then blew her nose on a napkin. She shook her head. "I don't know why. It was the strangest thing. I was in bed reading and all of a sudden I heard the door downstairs open and slam shut and Floyd's car started up and he left."

"And he went to the schoolhouse?" Joanna murmured.

"Yeah. And thank God he had his cell phone when he fell. He called me. I could barely understand him, but he said 'schoolhouse, ambulance' and that was it."

"He hung up?"

"No. He must have passed out. I was scared. I called the police on my way to the schoolhouse and I went in and found him at the bottom of the stairs. He had blood coming out of his ear, his nose. It was all over the floor. I thought…" She couldn't finish the sentence.

"Out of his ear?" Joanna asked, gooseflesh prickling her arms as she remembered Celeste at the vigil insisting Floyd was bleeding from his ear.

"Yes. I must have gone into shock. I don't even remember the paramedics taking him out."

"He just got up and ran out of the house?"

Camile nodded.

"Was there anything weird at the schoolhouse? Why do you think he did that?"

Camile shook her head. "I genuinely do not have a clue. Maybe he left something during the vigil the other night and went back to get it, but I don't understand why he didn't come upstairs and tell me unless—maybe he assumed I'd fallen asleep and didn't want to wake me."

Joanna thought of the camera he'd helped her install in her apartment, the same ones he had at the schoolhouse. "Do you have his phone?"

Camile paled and brushed her hair off her face. "No. I couldn't find it. I looked at the schoolhouse, but it wasn't there so then I thought maybe a paramedic picked it up, but they both said they didn't see a cell phone. It makes no sense."

"The fall down the stairs was definitely an accident?" Joanna asked.

Camile stared at her as if she didn't understand the question. "How do you mean?"

"There weren't any signs of a struggle at the schoolhouse, any signs he had an altercation with someone?"

Camile shook her head several times. "I didn't go upstairs, but... it was after eleven at night. The schoolhouse was closed."

Joanna nodded and dropped the line of questioning, aware that Camile was growing agitated at the mere mention of it not having been an accident.

WHEN JOANNA ASKED Camile for the key to the schoolhouse to search for Floyd's phone, Camile handed it over without a question. Joanna left Camile dozing in the chair next to Floyd's bed.

When she arrived at the schoolhouse, the dark sky was clear and shone with a thousand stars. The air was so cold her lungs ached.

Joanna unlocked the door and pushed it open. The weight of what had happened only hours before permeated the space. She flipped on lights and locked the door behind her, trying not to think of the cascade of disturbing events that had pervaded the previous days.

When she reached the back of the room and saw the pool of congealed blood at the base of the stairs, her stomach flipped. She stepped over it and moved up the staircase slowly. Halfway up she saw another splotch of blood and then several more. At the top of the stairs, she saw a spray of blood on the wall above the banister.

Nothing about the scene supported a fall down the stairs.

47

"Celeste?"

Celeste jumped and dropped the phone, looked up to see Jonathan in the living room doorway. She put a hand on her chest. "I didn't hear you come down."

The phone lay face-up, the video continuing to play. Celeste bent forward, grabbed it and pressed stop.

Jonathan's eyes narrowed on the phone. "Whose phone is that?" he asked.

"It's... Joanna's," she lied. "An old one she asked me to check out."

"For what?"

"For... I don't know. She couldn't get it to work. I told her I'd try."

"Seems you were successful."

Celeste nodded.

"Dr. Caswell said you're suffering from exhaustion. You need to sleep, Celeste."

"I did for a bit, or I tried." She sighed and looked at the ceiling. "What do you want me to say? Am I supposed to apologize to you for having insomnia?"

"No. You were supposed to take the sleeping pills your doctor prescribed today."

Celeste thought of the pills still sitting in her purse. She'd been vaguely furious the doctor agreed to prescribe sleeping pills but refused pain medicine, as if one might work without the other. "I don't want to feel out of it."

"You need the rest."

"Fine." She stood and walked into the kitchen, pulled the pills from her purse and shook one into her hand. Jonathan followed her, watched from the doorway as she popped the pill in her mouth and took a drink of water. "Happy?"

"I'm not the enemy, Celeste."

"I know that."

"Can we go back to bed?"

Celeste nodded. She followed him upstairs. "I have to use the bathroom." She slipped inside, closed the door and spit the pill into the toilet. She flushed and watched it disappear down the drain.

When she climbed into bed next to Jonathan, he reached for her, his hands hesitant and then more sure as he groped beneath her shirt.

"Is this okay?" he murmured.

"Yes," she whispered as his hands grew more urgent, desperate.

Celeste tried not to flinch at his touch. It felt good, the softness of his fingers, the warmth of him, and yet... the image in her mind, the one swinging like a pendulum, was the man on her balcony, the shadowy figure, and thoughts of the girls who'd been attacked in Graves by a man who stole through the windows and sexually assaulted them. She'd never been violated in that way, and shame coursed through her as she thought of that man as Jonathan kissed her, as if Jonathan had ever been anything but loving to her.

She kissed him back, pressed against him, and forced her body to comply.

———

THE NEXT MORNING, Celeste found Jonathan at the kitchen table drinking coffee and reading the newspaper. "Good morning," she told him, stopping to kiss him on her way to the coffeepot.

He stood and followed her, stood behind her and wrapped his arms around her waist. "I've missed you," he said into the top of her head.

She turned and kissed him again, longer.

"You sit," he murmured. "I'll get your coffee."

She walked to the table and eased into a chair. Jonathan filled a mug and sat in front of her.

"Cream and honey?" she asked.

"Oh, yeah. I keep forgetting, you're not taking it black anymore." He set skim milk and the honey canister on the table. Celeste spooned honey in and added milk, thinking about how to pose the question rolling in her mind.

"Maybe after you come home from work today, you could take me back up north." She watched him as she said the words, saw his jaw tighten.

"It's not a great day. I might not make it out of there as early as I'd like."

"You said you'd drive me back, Jonathan."

"Goddamn it, Celeste." He slammed the side of his fist on the table. Coffee sloshed across the surface. "You've been home for two days. I'm absolutely buried at work, buried, and the only thing you can think of is running back up north to root around in the woods for details on some girl who disappeared who you don't even know."

Celeste took a napkin from the holder and wiped up the

spilled coffee. "I understand you're busy, but I didn't ask you to come up there and get me."

He stood up so fast his chair wobbled and nearly tipped over. Without a word, he stormed from the room. Several minutes later, she heard his car door slam and the sound of him driving away.

CELESTE ALMOST CALLED him and apologized, but the truth was, she didn't feel sorry. She felt angry. He had shown up unannounced, forced her to come back and leave her vehicle, and now he'd left for work with her trapped in their home with no means of escape.

She walked into the living room. Katie's phone no longer sat on the arm of the couch. Had Jonathan taken it? Anger mounted. She walked into the room and looked under the pillows, then beneath the couch. Nothing. She marched to the kitchen, fished her cell from her purse, ready to call him, demand to know what he'd done with it, when she spotted Katie's phone on the edge of the counter. She hadn't put it there. Had he looked through it?

It didn't matter. She picked up, opened the video she'd been watching the night before, and hit play.

Again she watched Katie, Liam and Declan gathered around the Ouija board. It moved ever so slightly and then something banged elsewhere in the house. Liam started. Katie's eyes shifted away from the camera and a strange look crossed Declan's face.

"What was that?" Liam whispered.

A moment later, voices drifted in.

"Declan? You in here? Where are you?"

Katie's mouth fell open. She turned and gaped at Declan. "Is that Todd? Did you tell Todd we were coming here?"

"Holy shit," a male off-camera voice said. "This place is stocked. We're going to make a killing. Fuckin' A. Declan, dude, where are you?"

Declan looked at Katie. "We need the money," he muttered. "Okay? Jerome won't miss it. I told you about my mom."

Katie grabbed his arm, fingernails digging into his wrist. "You told him to come here to steal?" she shrilled. "How could you do this?"

Declan almost looked sad, as if he knew the choice would be the end of them, but then he shook her off, stood and disappeared from the image.

Liam looked scared, eyes saucers in his face. "What do we do?" he asked.

Katie turned to look at him, eyes filled with tears. She reached forward and turned off the camera.

Celeste stared at the dark screen. The night before Katie had vanished, she'd been at the former Graves mansion where Declan and his brother Todd and someone else had robbed the house. She thought back to her conversation with Liam. He had been there? Why had he said nothing?

She tried to call Joanna but got her voicemail.

"Hey. It's Celeste. Sorry I didn't respond to your texts. I found Katie's phone at the schoolhouse and there's something on it I think is important. Call me as soon as you can."

After she hung up, she dialed Megan, who answered on the first ring.

"Hi, my friend, who hasn't called me back in a week."

"I'm sorry, and I promise I'll explain, but Megan, I need a huge favor."

"YOU'VE BEEN UP in some backwoods town for a week investigating the disappearance of a seventeen-year-old? Why didn't you tell me any of this?" Megan demanded as she merged onto the highway going north.

"I don't know. Maybe for the same reason I didn't tell Jonathan, because it doesn't make sense. I'm supposed to have some logical explanation for why I'm doing it. I'm supposed to have some proof that I can actually make a difference, that this matters, but... I don't. I have a..." Celeste touched her chest, saw those fluttering dark wings and then light. "An impulse. An unignorable urge to do this."

Megan glanced at her, her face sad. "Why do you feel you'd need to explain yourself to me? I'm not Jonathan. No offense to the man, I love him dearly, but we've always been able to talk to each other honestly. I mean, you're the person I confess things I'm reluctant to tell my own diary. I have to admit I feel hurt you didn't think you could tell me."

"I'm sorry. I should have told you."

"How did you get involved with this to begin with?"

Celeste gazed out the window, tense at the thought of how Jonathan would feel when he returned and found her gone. She'd left him a note, but it would do little to mollify him. "It started with the Dear Celeste column."

Megan looked at her. "The Dear Celeste column?"

"It's an advice column. I started it right before Jonathan and I got married."

Meghan's mouth fell open. "Wait. You've had an advice column for eight years and you never told me?"

"It's not... It wasn't a big deal. Sometimes at night if I couldn't sleep, I'd answer questions. That's it. I never even thought about it during the daylight hours. That's the truth. Before the accident, anyway, but then after..."

"Then after what? What changed?"

Celeste pressed her thumb into the crease between her hip and leg, tried to massage away the ache too deep for her to reach. "Everything was different, is different. And when I returned to the column, I couldn't stop thinking about it. It seemed so much more important than the rest of my previous life, my job at the lab, always chasing the next level of success."

"And how does that connect to the missing girl?"

"Her sister wrote to me and asked for help."

"And you said you'd help her?"

Celeste nodded, notebook open on her lap, pen scratching the page.

"What are you drawing?"

Celeste shook her head. "Something I keep... seeing in my head."

"From birds to trees, huh? Maybe you're meant to be a park ranger in your future life."

Celeste rubbed her leg. "Doubtful with this bum leg."

"Looks like a family tree," Megan said. "My sister-in-law did one last year through one of those genealogy places. She had them all framed and gave us each one for Christmas."

"A family tree." Celeste considered the image, roots red like blood.

48

———

As Joanna drove back into downtown Graves, her cell phone rang. "Celeste, hi. I'm sorry. I saw you called earlier, but things have been crazy."

"Jo, I found Katie's phone."

Joanna left off the gas. "You what?"

"I found her phone at the schoolhouse in the cellar. I forgot about it and then I got home. It was dead, but I plugged it in and it's Katie's phone."

Joanna gripped the wheel harder. "Did you look at it? What's on it? Where are you?"

"My friend dropped me at the condo about ten minutes ago. There's a video on the phone Katie took the night before she went missing. She was at the Graves mansion with Declan and Liam. They had a Ouija board and were trying to contact Sherry Kapolka. Declan's brother showed up. I think the Boyds robbed Jerome's house and they might have killed Katie so she wouldn't tell."

Joanna blinked through the windshield—she couldn't speak, couldn't breathe. Behind her, a man driving a car honked at her and she turned the wheel and pulled to the side of the road. Her whole body had gone cold. Her mind tried to get a grip, focus on what Celeste was telling her. The door to the bookstore opened and Liam walked out.

"You said Liam was there?" Joanna murmured.

She felt sick watching him, thought back to those first days. Liam had been with her every step of the way. He'd driven as they searched for Katie. He'd told Joanna a hundred times to not panic, she'd come home. He'd known that the night before she vanished she'd witnessed her boyfriend and his brother commit a robbery. He'd been there and said nothing.

"Can you send me the video?" Joanna asked.

"Yes. I'll send it now."

"Okay. I'm looking at Liam. I'll call you back."

Joanna jumped out of her car and stepped into the path as Liam hurried toward her, head down against the wind, the cords of his earbuds dangling from his knit cap. His gaze lifted and he caught sight of her, paused and smiled.

Joanna did not return his smile. "Do you have a minute to talk?"

His smile fell away.

Joanna opened the passenger door for him and he slid into her car. Joanna climbed into the driver's seat. Her phone pinged and her stomach clenched when Katie's name appeared on the screen. She knew Celeste had sent the message from Katie's phone, but still it took her breath away to see that name on the screen after a year.

"Is everything okay?" he asked, glancing at her, then quickly staring at his knees.

She opened the video on her phone, held it out and clicked play.

Liam physically recoiled from the image as it played. Joanna grew still. She watched her baby sister, glowing in the firelight, her skin soft and pale and her hair perfectly straight. God, she was beautiful. Had been beautiful. That was the truth, wasn't it? Not was. Katie *had been* beautiful.

In the car beside Joanna, Liam released a whimper. She looked at his face. Tears streamed from his eyes.

Joanna too cried as she watched her sister's face, the eagerness there, her fingers on the planchette as she encouraged the two people beside her, her best friend and her boyfriend, people she trusted, to do the same.

As the video played, Todd's voice echoed from elsewhere in the house. Declan walked from the room and the despair in Katie's eyes made Joanna nearly double over in pain.

Liam cried harder, released little gasps as he rocked back and forth in his seat.

Joanna said nothing. She waited, watched him, resisted her natural inclination to rub his back, to tell him it was okay. It wasn't okay.

He wiped at his face, still didn't look at her. "I wanted to tell you. I swear. I wanted so bad to tell you, but..."

"But what?"

"I went to Declan first. I called him the night Katie hadn't come home. He said to stop freaking out, she was probably fine. He swore he didn't know where she was, said he was home with Todd—they were playing video games. He swore it, Jo. He swore he hadn't hurt her."

"And that was it? You took his word for it? Why would you cover for him?"

"I told him I was going to tell. I was going to the police. And the next night, his dad ran me off the road on my way back from Shanty Creek. He dragged me out of the car, told me I was a faggot and he'd... he'd kill me and hide my body where no one would ever find me."

Joanna stared at him, remembered back to the first week after Katie had vanished. She'd come up behind Liam in the store, touched his shoulder and he'd screamed. They'd laughed about it, but he'd been off. She'd thought it was Katie being gone. They were all on edge. "Warren Boyd threatened to kill you?"

Liam swiped his face. "And that wasn't the end. Todd did too. And they snuck some of the stuff they'd stolen from the Graves mansion into my backpack and into my car. Todd told me they'd deny everything, say I was part of the robbery. It's never stopped."

"They're still threatening you?"

He nodded. "My, umm… my dog disappeared."

Joanna's heart sank. "Bertie?"

More tears poured down his face. "I know it was them. I know… um…" He hiccupped. "Bertie disappeared in the fall and I came out to my car after working on the homecoming parade one night at school and her collar was tucked under my windshield wiper blade."

Joanna's shoulders slumped forward. "They've been torturing you. Liam, you should have told me. We should have gone to the police."

"I know. I do. I'm sorry. I was afraid and… I let Katie down and I let you down."

"You need to go home and tell your mom what's been going on. Tell her everything. I have to post a sign at the Sidewinder and take care of a couple things for Camile. Tomorrow we're going to the police, okay?"

He ran his sleeve across his face. "Okay. You're right. It's time." He opened the door and paused, his eyes red. "I'm sorry, Joanna."

"I know, Liam. It's okay."

Joanna climbed from her car and walked to the man standing in front of the Sidewinder, hands cupped around his eyes as he peered into the dark restaurant. "I'm sorry," she told him. "The diner is closed. The owner had an accident and—"

He turned to her. "You're Joanna Ellis."

"Yes."

"I saw you on the news the other night. You were talkin' about your sister who went missing."

"Okay." Joanna tried not to look as impatient as she felt.

"After I saw ya, I was talkin' to a friend of mine who works at the high school and he mentioned your sister was seeing Declan Boyd when she went missin'."

"She was. Yes."

He shoved his hands in his pockets and shot a quick glance down the street. "I have a cabin out by the Boyds' for hunting, mostly. I come up a few times a year in the winter to let my dogs run. It's tucked back in the woods, but if I look south, I'm staring right into Warren Boyd's backyard. Yard maybe ain't the right word unless we're talkin' about a junkyard, but don't even get me started on that.

"Right around the time your girl went missin' I was up at my cabin. I remember the date because it was my son's birthday —January eighteenth—and we'd come up a few days ahead to go to some snowmobile party in Gaylord. Anyway, I was out pretty late one night getting wood for the wood burner when I noticed some activity over at the Boyds'. Three of 'em were out behind the house and one of 'em had a flashlight, helpin' the others, who were carryin' something out to an old shed they have on the property."

A chill settled over Joanna.

"Whatever they were carrying musta been kind of heavy because it took two of 'em. I know Warren was there because I heard him cussin' at some point. Again, I couldn't tell what he was goin' on about. He had this whisper-yell going, which again makes me think it was the boys out there with him because he don't blink an eye at reaming out those two. Whatever they had, they put in one of the sheds. And ever since that night, there's been a big padlock on that shed. I didn't know about your sister back then. I live down by Flint and the first I got wind of your sister missing was on the Up North News after your vigil."

Joanna had said nothing as the man spoke, and when his expression grew concerned, she realized she'd begun to cry. Hot tears rolled over her cheeks.

"Oh, gosh," he said, pulling off his hat and twisting it in his hands. "I didn't mean to upset you. I'm awful sorry I didn't realize sooner, and it might not have a thing to do with your sister. Okay, now. So umm... What can I do? How can I help?"

Joanna tilted her face to the sky. The story he'd told was playing out in her head. A black winter's night, Warren, Declan and Todd carrying something heavy—carrying Katie—out to the shed to hide her body.

Something in her was breaking, snapping to pieces and jabbing her in all the places it hurt—in her heart—over and over until she might crumple right there on the sidewalk and die.

As if sensing her impending collapse, the man stuffed his hat on his head and wrapped a steadying arm around her waist. "Don't pass out on me. Okay, hon? You don't want to fall and crack your head open on this icy cold sidewalk. I can tell you that for sure." He led her to a bench and quickly wiped the snow away, pulled off his jacket, and laid it out. She sat down hard, her teeth chattering.

"Maybe I should call someone," he said, more to himself than her, looking up and down the street as if the answer might materialize. "An ambulance? Do you need to go to the hospital?"

The tears had slowed, but the explosion in her chest continued to ripple out. Every inch of her body hurt with the realization of what he'd told her.

Finally, she opened her mouth and through cold, dry lips, she whispered, "No."

He didn't look convinced, but after a moment sat beside her.

"I feel lousy about this, about not telling ya sooner, but like I said, I never had a clue Declan Boyd's girlfriend went missin' around then. Whatever you need me to do, say the word. I can go to the police station right now."

Joanna swallowed and shook her head. "Not right now, but soon. Umm... can you give me your phone number?" She took out her cell phone, amazed she was opening her contacts, typing his number in, that some part of her brain continued to work despite discovering that Katie's corpse had likely been in a shed on the Boyds' property for the last year.

49

Joanna parked at Celeste's condo and nearly slipped in the parking lot, sprinting to the building.

The instant Celeste opened the door, Joanna rushed in and blurted out what the man had told her. "He saw the Boyds carrying something heavy to their shed in the middle of the night. And they've been threatening Liam since Katie disappeared. He thinks they killed his dog! We have to go to the shed. He said it's been padlocked since that night." Joanna paced the length of the room, wringing her hands.

"But you said the guy doesn't live there year-round. Whatever they put in there—and you don't know it's Katie—could have been moved months ago."

"I have to know. I'm going to the Boyds' and I'm looking, because if I go to the police they might drag their feet and if Katie is still in the shed, she won't be by the time the police get warrants, assuming they ever do."

Celeste unscrewed the top on a bottle of Scotch and poured a glass. "Okay," she said. "Let's figure out a plan."

JOANNA DIRECTED Celeste to Randy's house. Celeste waited in the truck while Joanna rushed up to Randy's house, knocking loudly.

Randy opened the door. "Jo. Hey." Randy hugged her. "I heard about Floyd. How's he doing?"

"Oh. Umm… I haven't talked to Camile since this morning. He's in a coma and actually"—she dropped her voice—"I don't think he fell."

Randy looked puzzled. "But wasn't he at the bottom of the stairs at the schoolhouse?"

"Yeah, but there was blood at the top. I think someone hit him and that's why he fell."

"Holy shit."

"Is Travis here?"

He stepped back, held the door open. "Unfortunately, yes. He's"—Randy made air quotes—"'job hunting' on my couch. Please tell me that's not why you want to see Travis. You don't think he—?"

Joanna frowned. She hadn't thought about that, but the truth was everything she'd learned in the previous hours pointed squarely at the Boyds. "No. That's not it. I need some of his information for something I'm filling out for Katie," she lied.

"Oh, all right."

"It's nice you're letting him stay here."

"Yeah, well, it's temporary and I've locked up anything he could pawn, so hopefully I won't regret it." Randy led her down the hall to the living room.

"Hi, Travis," she told him.

Travis lounged on the couch, legs stretched out with his socked feet on the coffee table. Randy narrowed his eyes at Travis' feet and he quickly moved them to the floor.

"Oops," he said. "Sorry, Randy. I forgot."

"Try to remember," Randy said sharply. "I've got a business

call in a few minutes. I'll be in my office if you need anything, Jo."

Joanna walked into the living room and perched on the edge of a brown leather chair. Randy's house was immaculate, and she saw Travis sat on a blanket, as if Randy insisted he put a layer between himself and the furniture. She lowered her voice. "I need a favor."

A startled expression crossed Travis's face. She couldn't remember a time—ever—when she'd asked Travis for anything.

"I need you to ask Denny Dixon to call Rosie Boyd to his trailer."

Travis's mouth dropped open. He reached into his pocket and pulled something out, his sobriety coin. She was asking the man who'd been a drug addict nearly his entire adult life to talk to his drug dealer, the type of behavior that could easily lead to a relapse.

"I know this is a big ask."

"Why?" He stared at the coin, flipping it again and again between his fingers.

"Because I believe the Boyds killed Katie and I think I can prove it, but I need a half hour alone at their house."

"You think what?" His voice was loud, and Joanna put a finger to her lips.

"Shh... I don't want Randy to hear us." Joanna trusted Randy, but she knew he'd never condone her trespassing on the Boyds' property. He was a rule-follower and would insist she go to the police and not put herself in danger.

"Warren Boyd will shoot you on sight if he catches you in his house."

"I don't intend to go in his house, but I need access to his property. Can you do it? Ask Denny to reach out to Rosie."

"I don't talk to Denny no more. I can't, Jo. Okay? I can't

because if I do… if I do…" He stood and paced away from the couch, licked his chapped lips.

The mere mention of his drug dealer had him desperate for a fix. She saw it in his eyes, in the twitch of his hands as he walked. A feverish sheen broke out on his forehead. She should take it back, but she didn't. "I need you to do this for Katie, Travis."

I need you to do this to make up for all the things you didn't do, for all the ways you failed her, my mom, me. You owe her this much.

He tapped his fingers against his leg, bit his lip, nodded as if agreeing with the voice in his own head. "Okay. Yeah. Sure. I'll do it."

"Today. Right now. You can use my phone."

He stared at her, his eyes slightly cloudy. "Maybe take me there, huh? You could drop me off. I'd drive myself, but the Buick's leaking oil. I've got a pan under it in the driveway. Randy keeps threatening to have it towed."

"I will not drive you there because you don't need to go there. You need to make this phone call and then go tell Randy you're on the verge of a relapse so he can help keep you sober."

Anger flashed in Travis's eyes, but she stared him down, refused to shrink from the belligerence she knew he could launch into at any moment. He stared back at her, hands fisted at his sides. "It's not that simple. What if Denny has nothing for her or what if Rosie doesn't have any money?"

"Even better," Joanna said. "It'll take at least thirty minutes for her to drive there and back. That should give me enough time."

Travis walked to a side table and picked up a bag of M&Ms. He poured a few into his hand, chomped them quickly and refilled his palm twice more, not talking, staring toward the window.

"Travis, you won't use this as an excuse to get high. You're going to call Denny and ask him to invite Rosie to his trailer, and then you're going to tell Randy to get you to a meeting. For Katie."

He blinked at her, swallowed the candy, and then took his coin out again. "For Katie," he whispered.

"You can do this, Travis. I know you can. I need you to do it right now." She handed him her cell phone.

"Pull in the driveway," Joanna told Celeste. "It's fine. We saw Rosie leave. Everyone's gone."

"This is insane," Celeste murmured, but she did as Joanna asked and pulled her truck into the Boyds' driveway.

"Wish me luck." Joanna opened the door.

"If I honk, run like hell. I'll pick you up down the road."

"I will."

Joanna bypassed the house and hurried into the large back-yard scattered with old rusted cars on blocks. Multiple ramshackle outbuildings dotted the property, and she veered to the first. It had an aluminum roof and sides. The door was little more than a piece of plywood leaning against the metal eave. It couldn't have been the one. The second was a wooden struc-ture, and the door was flimsy. When she pushed it in, it swung open. The interior was stuffed from floor to ceiling with rusted car parts, tools and half-empty cans of motor oil.

When she approached the third shed, the most stable-looking out of the three, she slowed, eyes drawn to the heavy padlock attached to the door. She'd never get it open.

A single small window peered out from the side of the shed, the grime so thick on the glass she could see nothing when she peered in. Using the sleeve of her coat, she scrubbed it away, but a dirty rag on the inside blocked her view.

Joanna turned and searched the snowy ground, found what she needed, a large metal pole. She picked it, returned to the shed and slammed it against the window. The glass fractured and fell inside.

She plucked the remaining shards from the frame and then dragged a tire and then a second one beneath the window, stacking them. She climbed up, braced her hands on the frame, and stuck one leg through the window.

If Celeste honked, Joanna would never have time to get out of the shed if one of the Boyds came home. But she couldn't consider that scenario. The clock was ticking. They didn't know where Todd was or how long Rosie would be gone.

50

Celeste stared at the Boyds' house. The roof sagged above the dull gray exterior. A black and white cat slinked into the driveway and stopped, staring at Celeste. In the side yard an old rusted swing set stood, half buried in snow, one broken swing swaying by its chain.

Stomach a roiling ball of nerves, Celeste wondered when her common sense had abandoned her. Never in her former life would she have done what she was doing now—driven to the house of a known hothead who'd likely committed murder so she could be the getaway driver for a woman who'd be as helpless as Celeste if any of the Boyd men came home and discovered them.

Joanna had disappeared into the backyard ten minutes before and twice Celeste had nearly beeped the horn when a vehicle passed on the country road behind her. She held her hand poised above the wheel now, ready to slam the horn if someone pulled in.

She could see Jonathan's face in her mind, hear the harsh words he'd spew at her if he had any clue what she was doing. He hadn't yet called, didn't realize she'd fled back up north, but he'd know soon enough when he got home and found the note she'd left on their kitchen table.

"He's coming."

Celeste jumped at the girl's voice, spoken from the backseat. Her eyes lifted to the rear view mirror. There was no one there, nothing, but she knew Katie was warning her.

Instead of honking, Celeste reversed out of the driveway so fast her truck slid sideways. She righted it and drove onto the side of the road. Clenching her jaw against the shards of glass gyrating beneath her hip, she popped the hood and struggled from her car.

THOUGH SHE DIDN'T RECOGNIZE the man who parked in front of her on the road, his pickup releasing plumes of black smoke into the frigid winter air, she knew he was Todd Boyd. He shared features with both his father and Declan.

As Todd vacillated between leering at her and picking around under the hood of her truck, Celeste pretended to accidentally lay on the horn. Todd jumped and then laughed. "That's one way to get a man excited," he called.

Celeste called out, "Sorry," but mostly she watched the Boyd property, releasing a relieved breath when minutes later Joanna darted across the snowy yard and into the woods.

After Todd tried for the third time to coax Celeste into his driveway, where he promised his mechanic dad would happily look at her truck that evening, she feigned surprise when it started right up. His last attempt was to ask for her number, which she declined to give him. She drove away slowly, waiting until she was sure he'd parked and gone into his house before she pulled near the area of trees Joanna had run into.

As Joanna ran to the truck, Celeste saw red drops falling from her hand and splattering the snow. Blood.

Joanna leapt into the passenger seat and froze as Warren Boyd passed in his truck, his gaze locking on them both.

"He saw us," Joanna shrilled.

Celeste slammed on the gas, the truck fishtailed, and they sped away. "You're bleeding."

Joanna looked down, apparently surprised to discover blood dripping from her hand. She pulled off her scarf and wrapped it around her palm.

"What did you find?" Celeste asked, almost afraid to know.

Joanna looked pale, her whole body trembling. "She wasn't in there."

Celeste sagged back against her seat, a mixture of disappointment and relief rushing through her. Joanna needed closure, but it made Celeste sick to imagine her finding Katie's body crammed in a shed full of junk.

"But it was full of Jerome's antiques. Full. Everything stolen in that robbery is in the Boyds' shed."

"Okay. That's it then. The police will go after them for that. They'll get search warrants. We'll show them the video of Katie and Declan and… they'll take it seriously. They'll get a forensics team out there."

"What if the police won't listen to us? They have to go right now! Warren saw us. The second he sees that broken window he'll start moving stuff."

"I have a friend who might help us." Celeste pawed in her purse, found her cell phone, and called Harris Mayne.

———

HARRIS, it turned out, knew Detective Stark and when they arrived at the Graves police department, Stark was more than willing to hear them out. After they'd finished showing him the video and Joanna confirmed she'd seen the antiques in the Boyds' shed, he dispatched a team. In the meantime, Stark also took statements from the witness who'd seen the Boyds in the middle of the night shortly after Katie disappeared, as well as Liam, who even offered text messages to prove they'd been threatening him.

It was dusk when Graves police surrounded the Boyds' home. Joanna, Celeste and Harris had parked in the driveway of the neighbor who'd given Joanna the tip about the Boyds' shed. When they arrived at his house, he'd offered them binoculars so they could watch the arrests.

One by one, Warren, Todd and Declan were all taken from the house in handcuffs.

"Do you see Declan and Todd?" Joanna murmured.

Celeste stared at the two young men, their faces bloodied and swollen. She suspected their dad had beaten them both for allowing someone to get wind of the robbery. She thought back to her vision of Declan in the restaurant by her condo and, though he might well have murdered Katie or assisted in her disposal, Celeste felt bad for the teenager whose troubled life was about to get much worse.

Celeste turned to Harris, whose face was drawn as he watched the scene unfold. "Thank you for meeting us at the station tonight. We were really afraid they might not listen otherwise."

"Most police want to do the right thing, even the ones who sometimes seem like they don't. Not all of them, but most. I'm happy to help."

IT WAS dark when Celeste returned to the condo. Jonathan had been calling for the previous two hours and though she hadn't picked up, she'd texted that she'd call him in the morning. She didn't have the energy for the fight that was coming.

As she dug through her purse for her pain pills, she realized she'd forgotten to give Joanna Katie's phone. She turned it on and scrolled to Katie's photos, careful not to cut her finger on the broken screen.

In a separate album titled 'Yearbook,' she found several more videos and photos. Celeste opened the first video.

The camera captured a bleak-looking room with pocked linoleum floors and a scarred wooden table with a man sitting behind it. Katie took a chair angled toward him so she was in profile.

She turned and smiled at the camera. "Katie Ellis here, talking with Graves detective Patrick Marly."

"You're Naomi Ellis's girl?" he asked.

"One of them, yes."

"I know Jo from the diner and I knew your mom way back in the day when the world was young. I'm really sorry she passed."

"Thank you. Did you and my mom go to school together?"

"We sure did. I was a couple of years ahead of her, but I remember her well. The desk sergeant said you're doing a school project on the history of Graves?"

"Yes."

"Well, I can point you to some real old-timers who are pushing eighty, ninety years in Graves if you'd like."

"I wondered if we could talk specifically about the murder of Sherry Kapolka. You worked her case, right?"

51

———

The detective's face darkened, and he shifted back in his seat as if trying to put distance between himself and Katie. "I'm still working her case. It's an open investigation."

"Have there been any leads?"

He folded his hands on the table and his lips thinned into a line. "There's a lot of Graves history that's far more pleasant. Did you know Graves produced our very own *Jeopardy!* winner? It's true. Lawrence Dean. He worked at the hardware and grocery, of all places. Went on *Jeopardy!* and won. I can tell you every TV in Graves was tuned to *Jeopardy!* that night and we had a big celebration when he came back home. Course, then he took his winnings and moved out of Graves. Or," he started quickly before Katie could interrupt, "did you know Peter Hampton grew a world record pumpkin in 1992? That thing was the size of a pony. I kid you not."

"Those are great stories, really, but... well, I think talking about Sherry's case could help you solve it."

He looked skeptical. "Talking about any cold case usually leads to one place, and that's the gossip mill. I can tell you right now, we don't have the manpower in Graves to spend six months chasing down every crazy lead that gets phoned in when these cases suddenly come back into the public consciousness. What solves a case like Sherry's is a DNA match. Some day that perpetrator is gonna get himself arrested and on that day, CODIS will link him to Sherry's murder and the case will get solved."

"When he kills someone else then? That's what you're waiting for?"

The detective shifted, cleared his throat. "No. That is not what we're waiting for, but we can't make a match if he's not in the system."

"Have you taken DNA from suspects?"

"I can't give you that kind of information. As I mentioned—"

"It's an ongoing investigation, yeah. But if you have suspects, why wouldn't you collect DNA?"

"Technically, you need a warrant to collect someone's DNA."

"Technically, but can't you grab it out of people's garbage or if they drop a cigarette butt?"

He chuckled. "You've got your mother's spirit. She was a tenacious little thing too. Course, later in her life, she spent her energy trying to keep your dad out of jail."

Katie said nothing, but something crossed her features, a tremor of hurt.

"We talked to your dad, you know? Back when Sherry Kapolka went missing. Somebody put him in the area of the grocery store that night. Did you know that?"

Katie stared at the detective, clearly shocked by the revelation. "But it couldn't have been him. He's been arrested. You have his DNA."

"He's never been arrested for a felony. That's what allows us to take DNA samples."

"Did anything else connect him to the murder?"

The detective crossed his arms over his chest. "He was seen talking to her at the Bellaire Beach that day and his alibi didn't check out."

"That's not enough to get a warrant for his DNA?"

"Nope. It's not."

"What about genetic genealogy? Have you tried that to solve her case?"

"Come again?"

"Genetic genealogy. Police all over the country are using it. There's a huge public database of DNA that people send in from family ancestry tests. Genealogists can link the killer's DNA to distant relatives if they're in the database and eventually track them down that way."

Marly scratched his head, glanced at his watch. "Almost lunch time. Sorry to cut you off short, but I'm meeting the missus and she doesn't respond kindly if I'm late." He stood and stretched.

"But wait. Genetic genealogy would be a way to connect the DNA from Sherry's case to her killer. Isn't that worth being late for lunch?"

Marly offered her a placating smile. "I admire your spunk, truly, but we don't have a person on staff who does such things and we don't have the funding for it. I can't even imagine what kind of money we'd need to hire one of those fancy genealogy people. Sherry's killer will get caught. Okay? Sooner or later, he'll mess up, get arrested and boom. We've got him."

When the video ended, Celeste stared at the dark screen. The detective who'd worked Katie's disappearance had spoken with her about Sherry's murder. Had he ever told Joanna?

Celeste opened the next video.

Katie's face blocked the screen as she set up the camera. She walked backwards and sat on her bed. Her long hair was tucked beneath a tie-dye bandana and she wore a jean jacket and orange bell-bottom pants.

"Look what came today." She smiled and held up a package. "Oh, no. I sound like one of those crazy people on YouTube who do unboxing videos right now. Well, I am excited, though it feels weird to say that, because the point of this is to get my DNA into the public database in the hopes of catching Sherry Kapolka's killer.

"Do I want it to be my dad? No. Obviously not, and maybe this will have been a colossal waste of time, and I'll end up deleting all these videos, but I'm giving it a shot. Who knows, maybe I'm going to be a documentarian instead of a fashion designer. It might be an easier gig than trying to revive bell-bottoms and vests with tassels.

"Anyway, this kit is pretty far out. Basically, I spit in this little tube"—she held it up—"and send it off to this ancestry company. Eventually I'll find out some groovy stuff like where I hail from—hopefully Haight-Ashbury. I'm kidding. The results don't get that specific. But once I get my profile back, I can upload my DNA profile, which apparently is just a big string of numbers, to this database called GED Match and that platform is open to the public, which means police can use it to make connections to DNA in their system.

"Does my completing this profile mean Sherry's killer's going to get caught? Probably not. But hey, if all of us did this, every cold case murder with DNA would be solved." She snapped her fingers. "Like that. So why not?"

She stood and walked toward the camera. "I'll be back with an update when these results come back. Until then, later days."

The video ended.

Celeste turned to her boards, where Travis's name remained beneath the list of suspects. Katie had suspected her dad. Would she have confronted him? Was it possible they were wrong about the Boyds and Travis had killed his daughter to silence her?

Celeste returned to the photos Katie had placed in the 'Yearbook' album, many of which appeared to be old black and white or sepia-toned images she'd scanned from somewhere. Antiquated images of the Graves High School, the Sidewinder and the schoolhouse filled the album.

As she scrolled, Celeste paused on a black and white photo. In the background stood the stone schoolhouse in its younger days. Three girls wearing plain white frocks, each holding an armful of vegetables, stood next to open double doors set at a diagonal against the back of the schoolhouse. They led into an external stairway that fed into the cellar.

A chill ran through Celeste as she thought of the position of the brick wall where she'd found Katie's phone. It seemed to line up with where those outer stairs fed into the schoolhouse.

52

After the Boyds' arrest, Joanna had returned to the hospital to check on Floyd, which gave Camile a chance to run home and take a shower and put on a change of clothes.

Though his eyes were closed, and his breathing managed by a ventilator, Joanna filled Floyd in on all that had occurred in the previous hours. She held his hand and hoped that news of the Boyds' arrest would somehow reach him and bring him some peace. She suspected Warren had been the one who'd attacked him, but still hadn't puzzled out why Warren had been at the schoolhouse, unless, like the Graves mansion, it was another burglary underway.

An alarm beeped on her phone and she looked down to see a notification from the camera app Floyd had installed.

Movement detected.

She clicked the message, and the app opened, showing live footage of the interior of her apartment. The camera showed the front door, half of the kitchen and part of the living room. A man was in her apartment.

Joanna clenched the phone tighter and tried to make out

any distinguishing features. He wore a dark hooded sweatshirt and a full-knit face mask. He moved quickly, closed the door behind him, removing the key from the lock and sticking it in his pocket before he disappeared into the hallway.

How did he have a key? Unless he had Katie's key, and her abductor was at that moment in Joanna's apartment.

The man had not reappeared, but suddenly the blue light on one burner on the stove lit up. Joanna squinted at the image. The flame went out and relit. The light above the oven flicked on-off and back on. Minutes passed, and the man reappeared. He opened the door and Joanna stared at the back of his sweatshirt, the logo of a golden skull wearing a crown—the crown partially peeled away.

"Travis," she whispered.

Travis had been the one breaking into her apartment. For what? Drug money? She put tips in her bureau every night. They'd never been touched.

Joanna squeezed Floyd's hand. "I have to go, Floyd." She leaned over, kissed his cheek and ran from the hospital.

SNOW PUMMELED the windshield as she drove from the hospital in Traverse City back to Graves. She tried to call Randy, but didn't get him and hoped he'd be home where they could confront Travis together.

When she arrived at Randy's house, only Travis's Buick sat in the driveway. She parked behind it and considered whether to go inside. After several minutes of debate, she threw her door open, ran through the falling snow, and banged on the front door.

No answer.

Using the sides of both her fists, she knocked again, but again no one appeared. Maybe Travis was gone with Randy, but how could that be? She'd seen Travis in her house only thirty minutes before.

With a shaky breath, Joanna twisted the knob. The door opened and swung in.

From somewhere in the house, she heard loud metallic thunks. Tension humming through her body, she walked down the hall, following the disturbing sound. The noise grew louder, reverberated through the floor and walls.

Her eyes fixed on the only lit room, Randy's study. The door stood open.

Suddenly the clanging stopped, and she heard something else, the shuffling of papers. Joanna walked to the open doorway, peered inside.

Travis looked deranged. Sweat coated his face, his hair stood on end. An axe lay on the floor at his feet and Randy's safe, the top ripped open, stood before him on the ground. Travis clutched a package in his hand.

"Travis," Joanna said.

He jumped and spun towards her. She flinched, but his eyes, rather than full of anger, appeared confused, frightened.

"Are you trying to find money?" she asked.

Of course he was, and that was why he'd been at her apartment. She'd planted the seed by telling him to call Denny Dixon. He was on the verge of a relapse and it was all her fault.

He blinked at her and then held out the little box in his hand. She walked over, took it and studied the label, aware of the axe within arm's reach if Travis decided he was willing to kill her for a fix.

The box was addressed to Family Ancestry DNA in Connecticut. The return name and address was Katie Ellis, Joanna's apartment listed beneath.

It had never been mailed.

"I don't understand," she murmured, tearing the box open. Inside sat a small plastic vial filled with a clear liquid. Katie had been about to send out a DNA test, but how had it ended up in Randy's safe?

She moved closer to Travis, and he flinched. She stared into the crater he'd formed with the axe. An assortment of random, seemingly valueless items lay inside. A pair of plastic heart-shaped sunglasses, a woman's pink and white striped sandal, several pieces of costume jewelry. A dozen newspaper clippings at least.

Joanna drew them out, flipped through, scanning several of the headlines: *Second Girl Found Slain in Pinellas County, Florida, This Year; Nineteen-Year-Old Disappears During Bike Ride; Who Killed Sherry Kapolka?; Sexual Assault Reported by Graves Teen.* The newspapers-from news outlets in Florida and northern Michigan-spanned from weeks before to fifteen years in the past. As she shuffled the pages, two squares of yellow paper floated free and landed on the floor. Joanna peered down at the post-it notes-the names written in black ink, Warren and Declan Boyd in Celeste's careful handwriting.

Palms sweating, she dropped the newspapers and peered into the safe again. Her eye caught on a cell phone tucked in a corner. She picked it up, recognized it instantly by the case—a photo menagerie of jazz legends.

"This is Floyd's," she whispered.

Travis's face had gone slack, his eyes blank. Joanna struggled to accept what it all meant.

For a moment, she considered reaching into the safe with both hands, digging everything out, fanning it across the floor, but the tick of a clock over Randy's desk snagged her attention. He could return at any moment and find her there in the study.

Joanna reached into the black metal box a final time, pushed things aside and, resting in the bottom, she saw the beaded peace sign that had hung from Katie's keys. Joanna picked it up, held it in her trembling hand.

Travis released a strangled cry, clapped his hands over his ears, and shook his head from side to side.

"I have to go," Joanna murmured, the rush of blood in her ears drowning out Travis's whimpers. She turned and started out and then paused in the doorway. "Travis. Can I take you somewhere?"

He stared at her, hands still clapped on his head, eyes bulging.

She knew the look. He'd plummeted off the edge. She'd never get him into the car. As she drove away from Randy's house, she called the police and asked to speak to Detective Stark.

53

Celeste drove into what a meteorologist would describe as whiteout conditions, the visibility reduced to a foot or two beyond her front bumper. Past that, the world was a blur of white.

She imagined what Jonathan would say, what he'd already said. 'You're reckless. It's as if you don't value your life at all.'

The schoolhouse stood dark and empty when she pulled in and parked. Celeste bundled her coat around her, drew up her hood and stepped into the blowing snow.

Cane in hand, she hunched forward and walked around the back of the schoolhouse, searching for the double doors that led into the root cellar. Everything was buried in snow and she pushed her cane along the back edge until it struck something hard.

She scooped snow away until she discovered the double doors were gone, replaced by a large heavy piece of metal bolted to the stone base that had once been part of the stairway. Still, she sensed Katie's remains were likely hidden in that ancient stairwell.

Now was the time to call the police. As she walked to the

front of the schoolhouse, a light flickered on and off upstairs. For a moment it illuminated the long-haired mannequin who so resembled Katie.

Celeste walked to the front door. Locked. She started back toward her car. She'd get her cell phone, call the police, and then call Joanna.

Halfway across the parking lot, headlights swept over her and a car pulled in, parked next to her truck. Randy climbed out and, shielding his eyes from the snow, jogged over. "Holy snow!" he yelled. "Are you okay? What are you doing here?"

Celeste used one hand to zip her coat higher, leaning on her cane for support. "Don't you have a key, Randy? Can we go inside?"

He looked at the schoolhouse and nodded.

Celeste followed him to the door and when he unlocked it and pushed it open, a gust of snow followed them inside. The wind blew a stack of fliers left over from Katie's vigil across the room and one landed at their feet. Katie stared up at them.

"You shouldn't be out in this weather," Randy said. "It's only going to get worse."

Celeste brushed snow off her coat. "I know, but I wanted to check something out."

"What?" Randy asked, pulling off his hat and scarf.

Celeste eyed the cellar door. "Do you know when the external stairway got closed off?"

He stared at her. "The external stairway? How do you even know about that?"

"Katie had a picture of it on her phone."

He looked at her strangely. "On her phone? We never found Katie's phone."

"I found it," Celeste said. "In the cellar here at the schoolhouse."

"Wow. That's..." He shook his head. "What does that mean?"

"What I'm afraid it means is that Katie is in that old stairwell."

His mouth fell open, and he gazed at the cellar door. "No. How?"

"I don't know. It had to be someone who knew that brick wall down there was only stacked. When did the stairway get closed off?"

He scratched his chin, frowned. "Ten, fifteen years ago."

"Who did it?"

"I'm not sure."

"Maybe we should go down and... and check."

He looked sick at the prospect, but nodded slowly.

"I could be wrong," she said, thinking again of Eliza's advice: 'You don't know until you know.' "And I'd hate to call police out here and get everyone upset, especially with Floyd in the hospital."

"Okay," he murmured. "Probably safer being here than on the roads right now, but it's going to get a lot more uncomfortable in this schoolhouse if we find something."

"I left my cell phone in my car. Do you have yours or a flashlight?"

"Yeah, but there's a light down there."

"It blew the last time I was here."

"Oh. All right. Let's get this over with, then." Randy walked to the door, unbolted it, and pulled it open.

Celeste followed, but as she neared the open door, her eye caught on a series of framed newspaper articles hanging on the wall. One in the center stated: *Graves Schoolhouse Museum Welcomes Randy Mills to the Board of Trustees.*

Beneath it was a photo and in it a white convertible with a tan roof. The man standing beside the car, one foot propped on the bumper, was Randy Mills.

54

Joanna drove into downtown Graves. The snow pummeled the windshield, the world beyond obscured, like flying through space. There were no other cars on the road.

As she passed the schoolhouse, she saw Celeste's truck and, beside it, Randy's BMW. Her stomach plummeted, and she hit the brake. The car slid, refused to stop on the icy road. Joanna twisted the wheel, a surge of panic flooding her as she fought to regain control. The car skidded and smashed into a snowbank, causing Joanna's head to snap forward, her teeth to clack together.

She stared through the falling snow at the schoolhouse, pulse pounding, the wind shrieking around her car. Randy didn't know what she'd discovered, but when he got home and saw Travis had busted open his safe, he'd realize the truth was out.

Joanna called Detective Stark again. Surprisingly, he did not sound annoyed at the repeat call. "I'm at the schoolhouse and Randy is here and so is Celeste. I'm afraid he's going to hurt her. I'm going inside."

"Do not go inside. We will dispatch officers immediately. Do not go inside—"

"Please hurry." She hung up and tucked the phone into her pocket. The Graves police station was on the opposite side of town and the blizzard would slow down whoever came, but if she didn't go and Randy killed Celeste, Joanna would never recover.

In all likelihood, everything was fine. Randy was in the dark on what Joanna had discovered. She just had to play it cool until police arrived.

When she walked into the schoolhouse, the door to the cellar stood open. Within seconds Randy appeared in the doorway, sweat on his upper lip, his breath shallow.

"Hey," he said, surprised. "I thought I heard somebody up here."

Joanna painted on a smile. "I saw your car and Celeste's truck and stopped. Is she here?" Joanna looked toward the cellar doorway, strained to hear any sound from below.

He shook his head, ran a black-gloved hand through his hair. "No. It's the strangest thing. That's why I stopped. I saw her truck, but then I came inside." He shrugged. "She's nowhere to be found. I'm gonna lock up and head out before this storm gets worse."

"With her truck here?"

"Maybe she parked it and her husband picked her up again because of the storm. Who knows, right?" He chuckled.

"I stopped by your house and Travis was in rough shape, really bad. You should head home before he walks out of there with your flat-screen TV." Joanna continued listening, but heard nothing from the basement. She shoved her hands in the pockets of her coat to hide their shaking.

"Is he? Probably a good idea. Go ahead." He gestured at the door. "I'll lock up after you."

Joanna searched for an excuse, a reason to stay. "Oh, yeah.

Actually I told Camile I'd look for Floyd's phone if I had time to stop over here, so…"

He stared at her. "I'll help you."

Joanna swallowed and tried to keep the smile on her face, though it had turned waxy and she suspected it looked more like a grimace. Randy stepped toward her and she flinched, but he merely plucked a pine needle from her hair, a stowaway from her earlier dash through the woods flanking the Boyds' property.

"Why don't you start upstairs and I'll check down?" she suggested.

"Sure." His voice had gone flat and there was an unhinged expression in his eyes.

As they walked toward the back of the schoolhouse, Joanna's every nerve on fire, she thought of ways to stall him to give the police time to arrive. She feigned looking for Floyd's phone, peering behind a tall antique milk can, 'Graves Dairy' stamped on the side. As she bent over, something dropped from her coat pocket and hit the wood floor with a thud.

Floyd's phone lay on the ground between them.

55

Celeste woke in a black so deep she almost thought she'd died again. But that black—that beautiful velvet darkness, empty yet simultaneously filled with the most exquisite peace—was not this black. This black was cold and damp and penetrated the viscera of her body.

The edges of rough stone steps dug into her back, hips, and legs. Pain came in waves, causing her stomach to roll turbulently, her head to pulse.

Though air was abundant, she struggled to breathe, to open her lungs. Blinking rapidly, fighting the panic coursing through her blood like poison, she tried to push herself upright with her hands, only to discover they were completely numb and bound behind her back, trapped beneath her.

Her last moments of consciousness were grainy, but she remembered locking on that photo of Randy next to the convertible and in the next instant his hands grabbing the front of her coat. He'd shoved her through the cellar doorway and pushed her down the stairs. A brief memory of her arms flailing, her cane spinning loose from her hand and falling into nothing was the last thing she recalled.

He'd walled her into the old stone stairway. But she wasn't dead. Something warm oozed beneath her hairline at the base of her skull and she could smell it was blood—her blood—but she was alive.

Somehow, that knowledge didn't bring her relief. The terror closed in, her breath gusting in tiny ragged bursts, as if she breathed through a pinhole that continued shrinking.

A gargoyle seemed to be perched atop her chest, pressing down, squeezing the breath out of her, slobbering its dank musty breath into her face. And there were things crowded in there with her, dark, shadowy things that could not be seen, only felt. They circled around her, inhaled her fear, crept closer.

Not everything that comes through is from the light.

Her body began to shake, her teeth chattering so hard she bit her tongue, tasted pennies.

What if Randy never came back? Celeste would rather he kill her than leave her in there.

"Help me," she whispered. "Please, help me."

Shhh...

The voice continued in her mind, soft, soothing, a woman singing a song like a lullaby about ice cream castles and Ferris wheels. Somehow she knew the voice and knew the song and yet no memory emerged to accompany it.

Celeste stopped fighting. She relaxed, let her eyes close, though the darkness remained the same, and listened to the song sung in her head by a woman she didn't know, but sensed had once been her mother.

Her breath slowed and the pain melted away. And soon she wasn't in her body anymore. She'd left it, left the schoolhouse and slipped seamless into the stream of energy and light. She drifted in the night sky and into the cosmos and she remembered her body was merely the shell and she wouldn't miss it when it was gone. She'd hardly remember it at all.

When Celeste came to, the dark seemed less oppressive and the fear, though not gone, had dampened to a manageable level.

Her wrists stung as she grated them against the twine, twisting and wiggling her hands. On and on it went until suddenly the twine grew looser. She pulled her wrists apart and slipped one hand free, almost crying out. When her arms broke free, she nearly wept.

Leaning heavily on the stone wall, she stood and groped for the brick wall, nearly collapsing when she felt the opening. He hadn't bricked her in. The bottom half of the wall was in place, but above it, the bricks were gone. Why had he left it open? Surely, he'd be coming back to finish the job.

Find me.

Katie's voice, so clear it was as if it had emerged directly into her ear.

Through the opening in the brick wall, Celeste could detect the faintest trickle of light from upstairs. She knew at any moment, Randy could come back.

Celeste wanted more than anything to climb out of that stairway and escape. Instead, she turned back. Hands in front of her, Celeste felt along the stone stairway, gritty. She clenched her teeth against the pain as she groped up the stairs, hands feeling along the hard clammy surface.

Her hand brushed against something coarse, scratchy, the back of a carpet or rug. She moved her hands down the length of it. It was rolled up, wrapped around something—someone.

Celeste paused. A sob filled her throat.

She'd found Katie.

56

Joanna didn't look at Randy. She ran, sprinting toward the back of the schoolhouse, though she knew the only exit was in the opposite direction. She darted behind a long, chest-high dresser and spun to face Randy, who stood on the opposite side. His pupils were enormous, nearly blocking out the blue in his eyes. A half smile played on his lips. She didn't recognize the man in front of her.

"How could you do it? To Katie? To Floyd?" she stuttered, wondering how long it had been since she'd called Stark.

"This hardly seems like a good time for twenty questions, Jo."

"If you tell me…" She listened for sirens in the distance, heard only the howling of the wind outside. "I won't run. If Katie's gone, what do I have to live for?"

"Promise?" he asked, eyes twinkling. The delight in his face terrified her even more than what she realized he held in his hand—an open hunting knife.

"I promise," she lied.

He relaxed, not as if he expected her not to run—Joanna thought he wanted her to run—but because he believed he had all the time in the world. Outside snow was piling to the windows. The roads were empty. "She was going to put me in prison. I can't live the rest of my life in a cage."

"So you murdered your seventeen-year-old niece."

Randy looked annoyed. "She forced my hand. I told her to drop the whole DNA thing, for her dad's sake. Clearly it wasn't her dad I was worried about, but still. Who did she think she was? That's a violation of my human rights. I've never been arrested. The police do not have my DNA and she had no right, none, to give it to them, but that's exactly what she'd have been doing, lining me up for a lifetime in prison."

"Because you're a murderer, a serial killer."

His eyes narrowed at her, but he didn't respond.

"It was you breaking into my apartment, dressing in Travis's sweatshirt in case someone saw you. Why?" she demanded.

Randy frowned. "I had the key. I'd hardly calling it breaking in. I couldn't help myself. I'd got this idea in my head Katie had left something else—something more than the DNA kit, which I took that first night and accidentally left that drop of blood behind. Silly Randy." He chuckled, tapping the blade of the knife against his temple. "Musta cut myself when... well, you know... and didn't even realize it. Anyway, every couple weeks I'd get a thought in my head that there was something else in the apartment, something Katie had left behind that might implicate me. Turned into a bit of a compulsion. Too bad I didn't find that necklace." He rolled his eyes. "Forgot all about that damn thing."

"You gave her the choker?"

"Yeah. Stupid of me, but it was right after your mom died and I didn't want to show up empty handed. Grabbed that choker out of my safe, wrapped it up and gave it to her." His eyes widened. "How did you get into my safe?"

She ignored the question. "When you broke into my apartment you turned on the faucets, opened the curtains. Why? To fuck with me?"

He looked perplexed. "I never did that."

"You moved stuff around in Katie's room?"

He raised an eyebrow. "You might be losin' it, Jo. I was careful to put everything exactly where it had been. I'm a neat freak. You know that."

"Did Katie know you murdered Sherry?"

"Well, I didn't tell her that, but... I'm sure she put two and two together in the end."

Joanna's mouth had gone dry. Her mind searched for ways buy more time. "Where's Celeste? Did you... did you kill Celeste?"

He blinked at her. "Celeste is with Katie now."

Something in Joanna broke and for a second her knees nearly buckled. Randy recognized the weakness and bolted around the dresser. He almost had her. His fingers caught her coat, but she shrugged out of it and broke free, raced for the stairs. She took them two at a time, him hot on her heels. When she reached the top, the mannequin with the long brown hair stood nearly blocking her way. She dodged it, but Randy hit it full force, lost his balance and plunged to the floor. The knife skittered away and before he could jump back to his feet, Joanna circled back and sprinted down the stairs.

She was nearly at the front door when he caught her a second time, one hand knotted in the back of her shirt. He jerked her off her feet, shoved her to the ground and put his knee in her back.

"Fucking bitch," he muttered.

Joanna struggled, kicked her legs, but he wrenched her arms behind her.

"I've wanted this, Joanna," Randy said his breath hot in her ear. "I want you to know, years ago, when Travis was getting busy with your mom and I saw you for the first time, I started dreaming about the day I'd do this to you."

Joanna's skin crawled and she screamed and tried to buck him off of her. It did no good. He outweighed her by fifty pounds at least.

The police would be there at any moment, if she could hold him off a bit longer. And yet she still didn't hear the sirens.

From the open doorway at the top of the cellar stairs, something moved. Joanna stared as Celeste, face bloody, jaw clenched, limped into view. She held her cane and lifted it and put it down gently so as not to alert Randy.

Joanna struggled harder, screamed, did her best to block out the sound of Celeste creeping toward them.

Randy laughed and yanked her head back by her hair. "Yes! Scream. No one can hear you. I love when they scream!"

Eyes locked on Joanna's, Celeste pulled a raven-handled dagger from the top of her cane. Randy heard her. But it was too late. Celeste stabbed the dagger hard into his shoulder. It ripped through skin and muscle and buried in the bone. She tried to pull it free, but Randy screamed and dove at her, knocked her off her feet.

He wrapped his hands around Celeste's throat and bashed her head into the floor. Joanna grabbed hold of his jacket, tried to yank him off her. He turned and punched her hard in the stomach. She gasped and doubled over, fell to her knees.

The door to the schoolhouse burst open and Detective Stark and another man, guns raised, ran inside.

57

———————

Celeste lay shivering in the hospital bed. On the opposite side of the room, a young woman, her face drooping from the stroke that had taken her life, stared at Celeste until the door opened and a nurse walked in, scattering the dead girl into nothingness.

"How are you feeling?" the nurse asked.

"Cold," Celeste admitted.

"I can help with that." Joanna peeked into the room. She held up a checkered fleece blanket.

"Are you up for a visitor?" The nurse eyed Joanna warily.

"Yes. Thank you."

Joanna walked in and spread the blanket over Celeste. She'd been crying, but was putting on a brave face for Celeste. "Has the doctor visited?" she asked.

"Yes. A concussion. Some pretty bad bruising on my bad leg and hip, but that's it. Nothing's broken, so that's a relief."

"Yeah." Joanna sat and took her hand. "I'm so sorry, Celeste. He could have killed you."

"We stopped him," Celeste said. "It was worth it."

"There are other girls," Joanna said. "I found newspaper

articles at his house. There have been murders in Florida, probably other places."

Celeste stared at the ceiling, grateful for the pain medicine keeping all the sharp edges a little fuzzy. "I never even put his name on a post-it note," Celeste murmured.

Joanna sat in the chair beside her, eyes welling with tears. "I loved him, trusted him. Katie loved and trusted him. I never... not even for a second." Her voice broke.

Celeste thought of all the visions, the visitors. Why hadn't there even been a warning? Why hadn't she gotten a feeling something was wrong with Randy? She'd looked at everyone but him. "He fooled everyone, Jo. And the truth is you shouldn't have had to wonder about him. He was family, after all."

The door swung open and Jonathan burst in, face flushed, eyes panicky. He rushed toward Celeste, slowing when he saw the bruises on her face, the bandage on her head. A groan slipped from his mouth and he reached for her hand.

Joanna stood. "I'll give you guys some time," she murmured.

Celeste watched her go, knew the night ahead would be long and dark for Joanna Ellis.

Joanna lingered at the gravesite long after everyone had left. The mound of dark soil stood stark against the sparkling snow.

"You finally get Mom all to yourself," she murmured, remembering how Katie, as a little girl, had demanded to know why Joanna had gotten their mom alone for so many years and she always had to share her.

Most of the Graves community had come out to pay their respects. When the service ended, the line of cars, tie-dye flags hooked to their windows, had driven away, the procession headed for the Sidewinder.

Floyd, though awake and doing better every day, was still in the hospital. Camile had organized the post-funeral gathering and Joanna would go there soon, but first she wanted time alone to say goodbye.

Except now that the moment had come, she couldn't find the words. "How do I possibly say goodbye to you?" she whispered, holding the ragged pink bunny they'd each loved as children so tight her hands ached. She had intended to put it in

Katie's casket, but at the last minute couldn't bear to part with it.

Joanna knelt, rested her hand on the cold dirt and did her best to forget her sister was lying beneath it. She tilted her face to the sky, felt the cold winter sunlight. "Fly high, silver girl," she murmured.

When Joanna walked to her car, she paused and stared at the ground. Inches away from her tire lay a pink and white striped birthday candle.

***

TWO MONTHS HAD PASSED since Katie's funeral, a seeming lifetime, and though Joanna and Celeste had regularly talked on the phone, they'd not seen each other in weeks.

"You didn't have to drive all the way up here," Joanna told Celeste when she arrived at the Sidewinder. "I would have come to you for a change."

Celeste smiled and slid into the booth across from Joanna, scanning the Sidewinder that was packed, every table full—largely because Floyd and Camile had put it on the market and soon the diner would be no more. "I couldn't pass up one more visit to the Sidewinder."

Joanna gazed around the diner, heart heavy. "Yeah. I think I'll miss this place most of all."

"Arizona, huh?"

Joanna pulled her sleeves down over her hands. "Crazy, right? I've never even been out of Michigan and now I'm moving clear across the country. But I'll have Camile and Floyd and there are a bunch of nursing schools in Phoenix, which is exciting and scary. I'm going to be that old, jaded former waitress in class with a bunch of eighteen-year-olds."

"You are anything but old and jaded. I think what you're doing is very brave. You deserve it, Jo. It's going to be amazing."

Joanna fiddled with the handle on her cup of coffee. "I'm sure you're right," she said with forced courage. "The house Camile and Floyd have been renting down there for years comes with a mother-in-law suite, so I'll have my own space. We'll all three be flying back for Randy's trial, but the prosecutor thinks we're looking at minimum of a year until the trial starts. They want to build the case to include Sherry's murder and possibly the murders in Florida. They have the DNA match now to Sherry, plus DNA under Katie's fingernails." Her stomach hurt when she thought of that, of Katie fighting for her life with one of the only people in the world she'd trusted. "No DNA in the Florida cases though. Apparently, he was getting better at covering his tracks."

"No confession though?"

"No. Other than what he said to me in the schoolhouse, which is hearsay. He stopped talking the minute they arrested him, but Travis confessed to helping him move Sherry's car into the Graves Grocery parking lot the night she was murdered, so they have a witness, plus DNA. It's a solid case and they're still hoping he'll make a deal and save everyone from going to trial, but"—she shook her head—"he won't. He'd sooner die than admit to his crimes. The couple of interviews I've watched of him, he's playing the victim, saying police planted evidence, pointing the finger at Warren Boyd. It'll be a circus. I'm sorry you're going to be caught up in it, too."

Celeste waved the comment away. "I'm happy to testify if it puts Randy away for good. What's happening with the Boyd case?"

"Warren and Todd are still in jail. Apparently, some women's group helped Rosie raise money to get Declan out on bond."

"Maybe this will help Declan get his life on track. Nothing like a good scare to force you to evolve."

"I hope so," Joanna said. "Katie clearly saw something

special in him. I'd like to believe there's a chance he'll one day see it too."

"How's Floyd?" Celeste asked.

"Pretty good. Still in pain. He's come in a few times to cook, but he gets worn out after an hour or so. No memory of the night at the schoolhouse. Fortunately, the video evidence is on his phone—not the push down the stairs, but Randy entering the schoolhouse and then later Floyd arriving and shortly after Randy running out. It's been nice staying with them, helping take care of him, sitting on the couch and watching movies in the evening, not feeling so alone for a change. I can't imagine going through this without them."

"They're good people," Celeste agreed.

"What's next for you, Celeste?"

Celeste gazed at the window. The snow had mostly melted and the first spring buds had appeared on the trees. "I've officially turned in my resignation at Dynamic Laboratories. Jonathan and I have started marriage counseling and"—she shrugged—"I don't know what's next. Which is new for me, so it's fun, but like you said, a little scary."

After they ate lunch and talked more of the future trial against Randy, Joanna walked Celeste to her truck.

"Before you go," Celeste said, "I'd like to tell you something."

Joanna stared at the woman, at the seeming war in her eyes, about what she needed to say. "It's okay," Joanna told her. "What is it? You can tell me."

"Ever since my accident, I've been able to see spirits—hear them, feel them. The night I read your email, Katie came to me. She wanted me to help you."

A bubble of grief, of desperation for it to be true, floated up and lodged in Joanna's throat.

"She's not gone, Jo. Even now, she's here, just not the way

she was. It was Katie moving stuff in your apartment, turning on the water, cranking up the heat. She tried to warn you when Randy snuck in."

Joanna thought of the video of Randy entering her apartment. He'd been nowhere near the kitchen, but a burner and a light had turned on.

"Why can't I see her? Why isn't she coming to me?" Joanna's lips trembled.

Celeste smiled sadly. "I'm not sure why we can't all perceive spirits. It would be so much easier if we could."

"Can you... feel her now? Is she telling you anything?"

Celeste closed her eyes and took a couple of deep breaths. When she opened them, she stared at Joanna curiously. "I met a woman who told me our loved ones who have died give us signs to let us know they're nearby. I don't know what it means exactly, but Katie is showing me birthday candles."

CELESTE SAT at the kitchen table, sun streaming through the glass doors. Her brother had just left after spending the weekend with her and Jonathan and the house felt empty without him.

Cash circled around her legs and purred. She pulled him into her lap and, after scratching under his chin for a while, she opened her laptop.

She saw an email from Harris.

Celeste,

Great to hear from you and overjoyed you're recovering from your harrowing ordeal. I've been following the case against Randy Mills on the news. It's a pretty hot topic up here. Eliza and I are coming to Grand Rapids in late April for an NDE conference. We'd love for you to join us.

Keep in touch,

Harris

Celeste glanced through the dozen-plus Dear Celeste questions she intended to answer and an online registration to fill out for a genetic genealogy course she'd signed up for.

Another email titled *Case Update* sat in her inbox. She clicked it.

This is Detective Bowman at the Grand Rapids Police Department. Forensic examination of the shattered pieces of the vehicle found at the scene of your hit-and-run accident have been confirmed to be part of a Jeep Cherokee with a color described by the manufacturer as 'winter chill pearl coat.' It's a silver color.

I'm reaching out to give you this update and see if you are aware of anyone in your neighborhood who currently drives or previously drove a vehicle of this make and color. Or perhaps a work colleague or someone in your social circle. Please call or email at your earliest convenience.

LEANING ON HER CANE, Celeste knocked on the door of the blue and white house she'd passed the morning she was hit. The owner, Doris Macintosh, had witnessed the accident and called the police.

Doris opened the door and smiled. "If it isn't my miracle neighbor. How are you, Celeste?"

"I'm doing better every day." Not an entirely true statement, considering the attack in Graves. Still, Celeste had hope that one day she'd be fully recovered, though she'd grown rather attached to her cane and wasn't sure if she could part with it when the day came. "Do you have a few minutes to talk?"

"You betcha. Come on in. I've got a pot of mulled cider that's ready to drink. Would you like a cup?"

"It sounds delicious, but I better not." Celeste hadn't weaned herself off the Scotch, but wasn't allowing herself any alcohol before five. "Doris, did you recognize the car that hit me that day? Had you ever seen it in the neighborhood?"

Doris shook her head. "No. It was an SUV of some sort, a silvery blue type color. I didn't recognize it."

"I received an email from the police. They said it was a winter chill pearl Jeep Cherokee. I don't know anyone with that kind of vehicle either."

"Winter chill pearl, huh? That's a fancy name for silver."

"Yeah," Celeste murmured. She'd never seen the vehicle that hit her and though she'd performed an online search of the color and model of the SUV after she read the email from police, it jarred no memories loose.

A little dog trotted into the room and Doris scooped her up. "This is Lizzie. We might even call her your guardian angel. The morning you were hit, Lizzie hopped right up on the back of the couch in front of my picture window and started howling like her butt was on fire. Mind you, that's not Lizzie. I can count on one hand how many times she's barked at folks walking by. It's not her nature. I walked over to see what all the fuss was about and saw you out walking, which was no big show. I'd seen you pass by plenty of other mornings. I sat Lizzie on the floor and she popped right back up there like a jack-in-the-box. And when I looked, that car was coming down the road too fast for this neighborhood."

Celeste stared through the window, imagined her former self out there, two strong legs as she speed-walked, lost in her thoughts. "Doris, Jonathan mentioned I might have stepped in front of the car on purpose. Did you see anything like that?" Her neck grew hot as she asked the question, but it had been bothering her ever since Jonathan had uttered the words.

Doris's mouth fell open. "I most certainly did not. You

stepped out of the way and that SUV, rather than moving to the opposite side of the road, swerved and went straight for you. And I told the police as much, too. It wasn't an accident. It was attempted murder."

ALSO BY J.R. ERICKSON

Dear Celeste Novels

Troubled Spirits:

Where paranormal fiction and true crime meet.

The Northern Michigan Asylum Series:

Ghost stories inspired by a real former asylum.

You can find all my novels and join my reader team to find out about new releases, book giveaways, and more at www.jrericksonauthor.com

ACKNOWLEDGMENTS

Many thanks to the people who made this book possible. Thank you to Team Miblart for the beautiful cover. Thank you to RJ Locksley for copy editing *Come Home, Katie*. Many thanks to Will St. John for beta reading the original manuscript, and to Emily H., Saundra W., Travis P., Rhonda R., and Robin W. for finding those final pesky typos that slip in. Thank you to Sherry Kapolka for offering up her name as a character in this novel. Thank you to my amazing Advanced Reader Team. Lastly, and most of all, thank you to my family and friends for always supporting and encouraging me on this journey.

ABOUT THE AUTHOR

J.R. Erickson, also known as Jacki Riegle, is an indie author who writes ghost stories. She is the author of the Troubled Spirits Series, which blends true crime with paranormal murder mysteries. Her Northern Michigan Asylum Series are stand-alone paranormal novels inspired by a real former asylum in Traverse City.

These days, Jacki passes the time in the Traverse City area with her excavator husband, her wild little boy, and her three kitties.

To find out more about J.R. Erickson, visit her website at www.jrericksonauthor.com.

9 781959 125082